THE DISAPPEARING MAN

Center Point
Large Print

Also by Doug Peterson and available from Center Point Large Print:

The Puzzle People

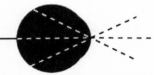

**This Large Print Book carries the
Seal of Approval of N.A.V.H.**

THE
DISAPPEARING MAN

BASED ON A TRUE STORY

DOUG
PETERSON

CENTER POINT LARGE PRINT
THORNDIKE, MAINE

This Center Point Large Print edition is published
in the year 2015 by arrangement with Bay Forest Books,
an imprint of Kingstone Media Group.

The text of this Large Print edition is unabridged.
In other aspects, this book may vary
from the original edition.
Printed in the United States of America
on permanent paper.
Set in 16-point Times New Roman type.

ISBN: 978-1-62899-412-4

Library of Congress Cataloging-in-Publication Data

Peterson, Doug.
The disappearing man / Doug Peterson. —
   Center point large print edition.
   pages ; cm
Summary: "Based on the true story of Henry 'Box' Brown's amazing
escape from slavery, a gripping tale about the lengths to which people
will go in seeking freedom brings to light one of the heroes of the
Underground Railroad"—Provided by publisher.
   ISBN 978-1-62899-412-4 (library binding : alk. paper)
   1. Brown, Henry Box, 1816– —Fiction. 2. Fugitive slaves—Fiction.
   3. Underground Railroad—Fiction. 4. Slavery—Virginia—Fiction.
   5. Large type books. I. Title.
PS3616.E842755D57 2015
813'.6—dc23
                                                      2014037686

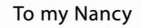

To my Nancy

ACKNOWLEDGMENTS

I would like to thank my wife Nancy and my two boys, Michael and Jason, for their ever-faithful support. I am eternally grateful that Nancy suggested we visit the National Underground Railroad Freedom Center on the day we had a free afternoon in Cincinnati; there, I first encountered the amazing tale of Henry Box Brown and had a chance to squeeze into a replica of his box. As my first reviewer, Nancy's input on the manuscript was insightful as always.

I am thankful to my agent, Jonathan Clements of Wheelhouse Literary Group, for his dedicated work, and to my friends at the Gideon Media Arts Conference, where I met the Kingstone Media Group's Art Ayris. The Gideon Conference was also where the talented writer Kathy Mackel first encouraged me to pursue this story.

I am also grateful for the fine editing work by Thom Lemmons, and for David Webb's insightful review of the original manuscript and his invaluable recommendations on restructuring the novel. Tom Hanlon's encouragement and feedback were vital as well, meeting with me on so many early mornings. I greatly appreciate his generosity and professionalism as he helped me work through the entire story, inspiring several new chapters.

Other readers who provided important feedback along the way were Heath Morber, Kathy Gullang, Ric Peterson, Bill and Jane Sutton, Leanne Lucas, and my mother Irene Bland. All made excellent sounding boards.

In addition, I am grateful for the prayer support from so many people, including Gary and Val Durack, Bill and Jane Sutton, Ric and Hilde Peterson, Carrie Peterson, and my wife and sons. Scott Irwin, my prayer partner, has been a source of constant support and counsel as I break out of my creative box and move in a new direction.

The Valentine Richmond History Center staff allowed me to go through their archive of photos, and I am thankful for their kindness. Finally, I am grateful for the vision, energy, and support of Art Ayris and all the folks at Kingstone. It's a joy and an honor to work for Kingstone—and the King.

1

Richmond, Virginia
March 23, 1849
4:00 a.m.

Henry Brown ran his eye down one edge of the small trick box. He turned the box over in his hands, admiring it with a woodworker's attention to detail.

The drawer slid in and out smoothly, as it did when he had first used the box to perform magic on the Hermitage Plantation so long ago. John Allen busted the box a couple of weeks earlier, but Henry had painstakingly pieced it back together. Seemed like he was always piecing one thing or another back together.

The trick box with the false bottom was for making things disappear. A coin. A hatpin. An apple. This one had been with Henry since he was twelve, when a traveling magician showed him how to construct it out of pieces of good, solid ash. His master at the time had supplied him with the wood to make the magic box. Those were kinder days.

Setting the box aside, Henry used a knife to pry up two loose floorboards in the corner of his home. It was a stark, one-room home in the

Shockoe Bottom neighborhood of Richmond, not far from the docks of the James River, where a large number of slaves and free blacks boarded. Henry's home was the lower level of a two-story tenement, adjacent to a row of decrepit shacks, all leaning in different directions as if in danger of imminent collapse. Henry's roof leaked, and the air whistled through the walls any time the wind kicked up. But this back-alley room gave him more privacy than he had ever known in his thirty-four years. Still, he wouldn't miss the place.

Henry set the trick box carefully under the floorboards and pounded them back down as best he could. He was ready to go.

As Henry looked out his window, lightning lit up the maze of tenements in Shockoe Bottom, followed by rolling thunder. He could smell the rain, feel it deep in his bones, cold air sneaking in over warm, stirring up the night like a witch's brew.

He pulled his straw hat down tight and eased out his back door, into the alley. Henry knew the wind would soon swing around to the north just before the clouds let loose, as it always did. His left hand, wrapped in a bloody bandage, ached with every movement. He prayed that infection wouldn't set in. He had seen people die from cuts not nearly as bad.

Henry made his way north through the dark alleys behind the buildings along Fourteenth

Street. The darkness was heavy like a tomb, giving Henry a dread sense of confinement. It was a closing in, a boxing in, an uneasy feeling that he might bump up against an impenetrable wall at any second.

He picked his way along the buildings until his night eyes came to him. The streets appeared desolate, but he knew this was deceiving. Richmond maintained a small army of patrollers who watched for slaves roaming at night. So Henry stayed to the shadows and the pitch-dark alleys. Briefly, he was illuminated by the lightning of the fast-approaching storm. Still no rain.

A sudden bang, and Henry flattened his back against the wooden wall of a small, lopsided building. He made out the ghostly image of a door slamming shut in the breeze, then slowly squeaking open on its hinges, only to be slammed again. He moved on.

Henry was in a hurry, but he made himself go good and slow, so he could avoid any obstacles or confrontations. Yet when Henry reached the end of an alley that spilled out onto Broad Street, someone grabbed his shirt and yanked him backwards.

"It's a colored!" the man shouted.

Henry didn't dare turn and show his face. Panic seized him just as fiercely as the hand on his shirt, and he tore loose, his shirt ripping as he took off. He was now flying, sprinting across

Broad Street. A flash of lightning gave him away, followed by deafening thunder.

"Shoot him!" hollered a second man. Then a gunshot.

Henry was moving so fast that he wondered if he might outrun the bullet at his back.

"That way!"

"I see him!"

Henry pulled off his hat to keep it from flying away and made his way toward Monumental Episcopal Church. It wasn't his church. The First African Baptist Church was just east on Broad Street. Monumental was a white church, but Henry knew the lay of the place. He ran for cover in the church's portico and slid quietly behind the dismal monument for which the church had been named. With his hat in one hand, he ran his other across the cold face of the stone marker. He couldn't read or write, but he knew there were seventy-two names carved into the marble, the names of whites and blacks, all killed when the old Richmond Theater burned to the ground. All were buried beneath the church, and Henry could feel their eyes looking up at him.

His heart was thumping so bad he was sure he'd wake the dead. He knew he'd have to get himself quieted down or he'd be found out for sure.

"You certain he went this way?" said one of the voices.

"I'm sure of it."

Henry recognized the first voice: Callahan, one of the overseers from the tobacco factory. Of all the people to stumble into . . .

They were near. Henry could hear their footsteps as they made their way into the covered entryway of the church. If they caught him, he would surely be subjected to "the thirty-nine"—the same number of lashes that Jesus received.

"Spooks me out here at night," Callahan said.

"Don't tell me you're thinkin' of the spirits of the dead."

Callahan didn't answer.

Henry pressed himself against the cold monument, wishing he could melt into the marble like a ghost. The two men had split up, and Henry could hear them working their way around the monument, coming at him from both sides. If he didn't do something soon, he'd be trapped for sure.

And so he bolted.

Callahan leaped backwards and let out a yelp, as though the sudden rush of movement was more ghost than flesh.

"Grab him!"

But Henry was flying again. He was past Callahan before the overseer had a chance to react.

"Did ya get a look at him?" the other man shouted.

"Shut up and run!" Callahan said.

A couple of blocks from Monumental Episcopal Church was Capitol Square, where Henry hoped his footsteps would be muffled by the lush grass. The lightning had let up, and his pursuers soon lost the trail without the flashes to guide them. Henry leaped into an old chestnut tree and crouched on a low branch thick enough not to sway under his weight. He saw two shadows stop not far from the capitol building, which loomed dark and hulking.

"Any idea where he went?" Callahan asked.

"It's like he just disappeared."

A lightning flash revealed Henry perched in the tree only a stone's throw away. But the two men had their backs to him, so they had no idea their quarry was nearly on top of them.

"Let's split up. He couldn't a gone far."

Callahan and his companion broke off in different directions, and Henry waited a safe spell before dropping down from the tree. Then he took off running, having lost all sense of caution. His feet hardly touched the ground, and he didn't slow down or look back until he was knocking on the back door of a narrow, one-story brick house a little east from the capitol on Fifteenth Street. Samuel Smith opened the door, and Henry slipped inside. Samuel was white, a gambler who made a meager living with a shoe shop. James Smith, Henry's closest friend and one of many free blacks living in Richmond, was there too, and he caught Henry as he stumbled into the room.

"What happened?" James asked. "Looks like you seen a ghost. And got chased by one."

"I was spotted," Henry rasped. "Two men. Callahan and another. Lost 'em, though. No way they followed me."

"Did they get a good look at you?" Samuel asked.

"I don't think they saw my face. But they knew I was a slave."

James looked from Henry to Samuel. "Should we go through with this?"

Henry held up his bandaged hand. "I ain't gonna stage this a second time."

"So it's either now or we come up with another plan?" James said.

"It's now!" Henry was unmovable. "I promised Nancy. I'm goin' through with this."

"All right, all right. If we learn that alarms have been raised, we still have time to back out." Samuel looked at his pocket watch. "The driver will be here to pick up the package in less than an hour."

Samuel reviewed the escape route in detail one last time—when and where the box would be carried by train, steamboat, and wagon.

Finally, James took a deep breath and said, "You ready for this?"

Henry didn't even pause. "I am."

He put his hat back on and glanced over at a

wooden box sitting in the middle of Samuel's home like a coffin in a funeral parlor. It was smaller than he remembered. The box carried a Philadelphia address, and on another side were the bold words *THIS SIDE UP WITH CARE*.

"Here." James handed Henry a beef bladder filled with water.

"And the biscuits?"

"They're in the box," said Samuel. He handed Henry a gimlet drill. "Just in case you need more air."

"You *sure* you want to go through with this?" James asked.

Henry's eyes drifted back to the box. "Yes."

Standing next to the box, Samuel grinned and held out his hand, like a coachman motioning to the open door of a carriage. "Then your coffin awaits."

With the gimlet and water in hand, Henry stepped carefully into the box and lowered himself. He rested his shoulder and head against one end and braced his feet against the other. The box was only three feet high and less than two and a half feet wide. Henry weighed two hundred pounds and stood five feet, eight inches tall. He put the drill and water down next to the biscuits where he could get to them and settled in.

"You comfortable?" Samuel asked.

"That's a fool question."

"We're sealing you in," said James.

Henry nodded. James and Samuel picked up the wooden cover and placed it over his head, plunging Henry into a tomb-like darkness. *This is it,* he thought. *Boxed in again.*

Henry was being mailed to Philadelphia. No more masters. No more boxes. No more being somebody else's property. Philadelphia was on the other end of the line. Philadelphia was freedom.

2

Louisa County, Virginia
1826: Twenty-three Years Earlier

Henry sprinted through the rain and lightning across an open field. Mamma had told him that lightning liked to pick out big targets. So at eleven years old he was counting on being too small for lightning to care enough to strike him dead.

Henry saw the horse disappear into the forest on the far side of the field, and he hoped it would come to a rest in the shelter of the trees. Though it was a summer afternoon, the sky was black as tar. The storm had hit with sudden ferocity, and Mr. William wasn't able to get back to the barn in time. A streak of lightning had spooked his horse, and he was thrown to the ground. The horse had bolted, and before Henry could even think, he heard himself shouting that he'd get it back. William Barret, the master's forty-year-old son, had taken a liking to Henry, and Henry leaped at the chance to retrieve his horse.

The sky lit up with white-hot rivers of electricity branching out in all directions. The rain was coming down in sheets, and Henry could barely see ten feet in front of him. His clothes clung to him heavily, as if he had fallen into the river. But when Henry plunged into the woods, the canopy provided a natural umbrella, increasing visibility. He kept his eyes peeled for any sign of the panicked horse. The woods lit up every few seconds, briefly changing the leaves from gray to green. Henry thought he caught a glimpse of Mr. William's buckskin-colored horse, but whatever he saw was soon gone, like a ghost. He listened for the crashing of underbrush, but it was difficult to hear with the hiss of rain and barrage of thunderclaps coming so quick in succession.

Strange, but Henry didn't feel much fear—more excitement than anything. He had always been drawn to the large thunderheads that swept across the Piedmont region of Virginia. When he was very young, he used to think Master Barret was the one calling down the storms. After all, the master had control over every other thing that happened on the plantation.

Henry moved quickly, dodging low-hanging branches and hurdling thick roots that snaked out of the ground. He followed what he thought was the most logical path for a large animal. When the rain let up and the noise of the storm subsided for a moment, he came to a sudden stop in the middle of the forest.

He had heard a human voice.

Henry spun around in a circle, listening, determining the direction from which the voice had come. Two human voices, actually. One angry and low, the other scared and high. It was a spooky sound, two voices carried on the wind through the trees. Some on the plantation said these woods were haunted. But Henry was more frightened by flesh-and-blood people. They could hurt you.

Almost instinctively, he found himself moving in the direction of the voices, forgetting momentarily about the horse. The voices became louder, clearer.

"Don't do it, Pappy! Don't!"

"You're a thief! Take your punishment like a man!"

"But—" The next words were swallowed up in thunder.

Then Henry heard whimpering, the crying of a child. A boy. It was a pitiful sound, like a spirit in torment. Then the sky exploded, and Henry saw a flash to his right and heard the sound of a tree, a large one, falling to the ground, cracking and crashing and taking down branches and leaves before hitting the dirt.

Still, he was drawn to the voices.

Henry reached a small clearing in the forest, an open patch where trees had been cleared just upslope from the creek. When the lightning flashed again, he spotted them: a man and a boy. The man was tying the boy to the base of a tree. Henry wanted to run then, but his legs wouldn't move. He was both repelled and riveted. The rain came down heavy again and washed over the two figures.

"I only borrowed your pipe! I didn't steal it! I won't do it again, Pappy!"

"You're right you won't!"

Henry knew the boy. It was John Allen, a white boy a few years older than him. John Allen lived alone with his father in a cabin in the woods, just off of plantation property.

"I'll be kilt!" the boy shouted.

"That's for God to decide. I'll let Him judge. If He wants to punish you with a lightning bolt, who am I to deny Him?"

From where Henry was hiding, the two figures were just shadows in the rain and gloom until a flash threw them into sharp relief. For a moment, they stood out as though caught in the glare of a burning barn. It was definitely Mr. Allen. Would he really leave his son out here in the storm? Henry wouldn't put it past him. Henry and John Allen played together when they were younger, and he had been in the presence of Mr.

Allen a time or two. That was enough for him.

Mr. Allen finished tying up his son. The rain let up again, and the man stood back and smiled.

"You have to admit. Your father knows how to tie a strong knot. You ain't goin' nowheres."

"Don't leave me, Pappy! I'm sorry, I'm sorry!"

"You'll be sorrier after you stayed here a spell."

Mr. Allen turned and began to march downhill, toward the creek.

"Don't leave me here! I'll be kilt!" John Allen was sobbing, choking on his words.

Mr. Allen didn't answer. He just kept walking.

Henry felt sorry for the boy. Henry's mamma could be stern, and she wouldn't hesitate to use a switch. But she would never leave him tied to a tree in a storm. But then, Mamma didn't drink. Mr. Allen did.

Henry watched the figure of Mr. Allen move off into the woods beyond the creek, heading in the direction of their cabin. Henry had been taught not to interfere in the ways of white folk, but he couldn't just leave John Allen to die. On the other hand, if Mr. Allen found out he'd untied his son, the man might shoot him dead in the field. Master Barret was always complaining about Mr. Allen hunting on their land. What would stop the man from shooting Henry and claiming it was an accident?

Another flash, another explosion.

The boy hollered, then whimpered like a beaten

dog. Henry moved a little closer. When two lightning strikes followed in close succession, the boy's frantic breathing became audible. John Allen struggled against the cords.

"Oh God, save me. Save me!"

A notion struck Henry like a bolt: Maybe God had picked him to be here at this very moment. Mamma said God had important chores for us all to do. We just had to open our eyes to know what they were.

Henry wasn't about to just walk into the clearing where he could be seen by Mr. Allen or the devil. So he swung around to reach John Allen from behind, staying within the protection of the woods. John Allen's tree was at the very edge of the clearing. Henry waited for the next lightning flash to know for sure that Mr. Allen was gone.

"Who's there? Oh God, oh God, oh God!"

The boy must have heard Henry moving amidst the bushes. Henry wanted to calm him, to tell him there was nothing to fear, that he wasn't a ghost or a bear. But he didn't dare speak. Not until he was closer.

In one final rush, he slipped behind the tree, behind John Allen. "Don't worry," he said. "Don't make a sound. It's me. Henry."

John Allen strained to see around the back of the tree but couldn't manage it. "Henry Brown?" He sniffed back tears.

"Don't be afraid. I'll get ya untied."

"I ain't—"

Lightning and thunder erupted, nearly simultaneously. The strike was close. John Allen let out a shout, which dissolved into a whimper. He began shaking uncontrollably. "Hurry. Can't ya hurry?"

"I'm tryin'. Your pappy's right. These knots is tough."

John Allen sniffed again. "Don't ya have a knife?"

A knife? In the hands of an eleven-year-old slave? Henry didn't even bother to answer such a fool question. He kept working the knots.

Henry suddenly felt the hair on his head stand on end, and less than a second later the air exploded just to his left. Lightning struck a massive tree with a burst of brightness, and then for a few seconds everything went black. Henry was blinded, and evidently, so was John Allen.

"I can't see! Henry, I can't see!"

Henry felt panic rising inside and almost started shouting himself, but it took only moments for his sight to slowly return, as though he were emerging from a dark cave. "You okay, Johnny? Can ya see?"

"Hurry!"

Henry finally pried the knot loose, and the rope began to unravel in his hands. John Allen thrashed and threw out his arms and kicked at the ropes as they fell limp around his body. The next moment he was on his feet and dashing into the woods. "Run! It's my pappy come back, and he got a gun!"

Henry didn't see any sign of the boy's father, but he wasn't taking any chances. He was soon crashing through the woods on the heels of John Allen. He didn't stop running until he reached the long, open field leading back to the plantation.

Chest heaving and legs burning, Henry stooped and put his hands on his knees. But John Allen kept running until he reached the safety of the plantation barn. When Henry raised himself up, he heard a thrashing, crashing sound and was surprised to see Mr. William's horse, its reins caught in the low branches of a thicket of smaller trees. The horse was close to the edge of the woods, just a few steps into the forest.

The peak of the storm had passed, but the lightning continued as it passed to the east, and the horse kicked and pulled at the reins with every flash. Henry managed to calm the horse enough to untangle the reins. Then he led the horse back to the barn, where he was met by William Barret. John Allen was there with him, completely transformed. He now strutted around with his hands in his suspenders, play-acting at bravery from what Henry could see.

Mr. William clapped a hand on Henry's shoulder. "Thank you for rescuing my horse, Henry. That was mighty courageous of the two of you."

The rain had stopped, and Master John Barret, William's elderly father, hobbled over from the house to the barn to size up the situation. From a distance, Master Barret was a distinguished man with silver hair and thick muttonchops. But up close the ravages of eighty or so years was evident: red splotches, deep wrinkles, and flakes of skin peeling from his forehead.

Master Barret stared down at John Allen. "You're Tom Allen's boy, aren't you?"

"Yes, sir."

"Bad storm to be outdoors. Your father will be worried about you."

John Allen wore an odd, uncomfortable smile. "Yes, sir. But I ain't bothered by a little storm, and my pappy knows it."

"Good boy," said Master Barret. "You hungry? C'mon in. Henry's mamma's got some biscuits and gravy already cooking. But first let's get you into some dry clothes."

"Thank ya, sir."

They all trooped across the yard to the Hermitage, a wide, two-story home set in the middle of rolling pasture, surrounded by fields of corn, cotton, and tobacco, and then trees as far as the eye could see. The storm was moving off now. The lightning fired some parting shots, but they were feeble and distant. The low, black clouds moved away quickly.

Once inside the house, the white folks headed to

the main dining room while Henry made for the kitchen. He took a seat near the stove to dry out.

"Whatcha doin' runnin' into the woods like that?" Mamma said under her breath as she worked on supper. "You gonna git yourself killed."

"But it was Mr. William's favorite horse."

"Well, you my favorite child—one of 'em, at least. You even think of that?"

"No, Mamma."

Henry watched his mother bustle in and out of the kitchen, serving up the meal to the Barrets and their unexpected guest. When everyone in the dining room had been taken care of, she served Henry his own portion, and it went down warm. He ate his meal in the kitchen, like any other servant. Master Barret was a true Virginia gentleman, and he always called his slaves "servants." More refined that way, he said.

As Henry helped Mamma clean up, he caught snatches of the Barrets' table talk coming from the other room. John Allen's laughter ricocheted off the walls.

In the days and months to come, John Allen would never once thank Henry or even acknowledge that the events of that afternoon had ever taken place.

3

Richmond
March 23, 1849
4:30 a.m.

When John Allen first heard the pounding on his door, he thought it was the pounding of his head. He had gone to bed with an excruciating headache, and it still felt like the devil was inside his skull, trying to crack his way out.

Bleary-eyed, he lit a candle and managed to see on the pocket watch by his bedside that it was just past four-thirty in the morning. Who would be banging on his door at this time—and in such a storm? When he had gone to bed, he knew rain was on the way, and now it was coming down heavy, pounding his roof. Opening the door, he found Callahan on his doorstep, soaked through from head to foot.

"This better be good, Callahan."

"Sorry for rousin' you out of bed, John, but I knew you'd wanna know this."

Callahan paused, as if waiting for an invitation to come in out of the storm. He didn't get one.

"Out with it, man!" Allen bellowed.

With rain streaming from the brim of his hat like a waterfall, Callahan explained what had happened. "I bumped into a slave on the streets. He wouldn't stop and tore away from us. From Davis and me."

John Allen groaned. "You're useless, Callahan. How long ago did this happen?"

"No more than a half hour ago. I know you've been specially vigilant about runaways since the Blevins affair. It mighta been one of the slaves from the factory."

As head overseer at William Barret's tobacco factory, this was the last thing John Allen wanted to hear from Callahan, his twenty-eight-year-old assistant. He stroked his stubble. "How do you know all this? You see the slave's face?"

"Not completely, but—"

"So how do you know it was one of ours?"

"Just a hunch, Mr. Allen."

John Allen growled. "Just a hunch!" He was being dragged out of bed at four-thirty on a hunch.

"But I think I recognized him from the factory. Should we get a slave patrol goin' on this?"

Callahan stood there, waiting for an answer, and John Allen didn't say anything for a few moments. John Allen took great pleasure in pulling together slave patrols, but not on nights like this, not when his head hurt so badly that it made him nauseous. Still, a slave on the streets at this time of the night could spell trouble. He scratched his dab of a moustache and thought this through. He had close-cropped hair, not much

28

of a chin, and his eyes were close-set, small, and intense. He was stronger than he looked, a narrow barrel of gun-powder that could go off at any moment.

Growling, John Allen turned to get his boots, which he had flung somewhere in the corner when he had crawled into bed, half drunk, not that many hours ago. A sudden flash of lightning illuminated everything in sight, followed by an explosive peal of thunder.

John Allen flinched. He tried to conceal his fear, but his startle reflex was difficult to hide. He paused and looked out the door. Callahan followed his gaze.

"Would you prefer not to go outside with the lightnin' and all, Mr. Allen? I can get the patrol together for ya."

If John Allen had been holding his boot, he would have smacked Callahan in the face with it.

"I don't care about any lightnin'!" he shouted. "I just think you're makin' a big to-do about nothin'!"

"But one of our slaves on the streets . . . It might be an escape."

"The slave was most likely seein' some whore and is probably back in bed by now. As I should be. Why didn't you hold on to him, anyways?"

"Sorry. His shirt tore."

John Allen shook his head and took a step

closer to Callahan, careful not to move into the rain. "Did ya snatch a piece of the shirt?"

"Um . . . Davis was the one who grabbed him. But come to think of it, a piece mighta come off in his hands. I suppose."

"You suppose? Then where's this piece of shirt?"

"Back on the ground. I suppose."

"Try thinkin', not supposin'!"

"Sorry, Mr. Allen."

"If you wanna do some good, get that piece of shirt and bring it to me at the factory . . . when I'm wide awake."

"Sure thing. Sorry for disturbin' ya." Callahan turned and strode off through the pouring rain, trying to sidestep a deep puddle. His foot went into the water past his ankles.

John Allen slammed the door with a bang, and the night sky responded in kind. Lightning ignited the air with an electrified boom, and he couldn't keep from flinching. At least this time no one was around to notice it.

Henry Brown knew darkness, but not like this. He sat in the box, his knees drawn up into his chest, arms hugging his legs, head slightly bent over, and back arching forward, beginning to ache. There was no room to maneuver, and he wondered if he had had the box made too small. Henry felt a coin-sized circle of tension in the middle of his back, just a little right of center. As long as the circle didn't expand, he could tolerate it. He was conscious of every little thing about his body. An itch just above his right ear. An itch just above his left eyebrow. As soon as he scratched one itch, another took its place somewhere else on his body, as if an army of ants was crawling all over him.

It was still dark outside, so no light showed in any of the small holes in the box. Everywhere was complete darkness. Henry closed his eyes. Darkness. He opened them. Still darkness. It was like he had gone blind. Henry turned to the right. He couldn't even see the sidewall of the box, inches from his head. The darkness seemed to be shifting and moving before his eyes, a trembling sheet of night. He looked straight ahead and tried to imagine that his box extended out in front of him for miles, like a tunnel, giving him a greater feeling of freedom, less a sense of confinement. For all he knew, the world did extend forever in front of him. He drifted in space.

The box sat in the back of a wagon, shifting and sliding ever so slightly as the wagon rattled over ruts in the road. The Adams Express driver had arrived a little before six o'clock, just before sunrise, and Henry's box had been loaded into the back. From inside his wooden cocoon, Henry tried to follow the path they were following. Down Broad Street, left turn on Fourteenth, a few blocks to the Adams Express office. It had stopped raining, and he savored the fresh, after-the-storm smell that seeped into his box.

Adams Express was located in the bottom floor of the Exchange Hotel, the most elegant hotel in all of Richmond. Henry could hear the sound of wheels, probably draymen hauling hogsheads of tobacco down to the line of factories near the river. It was too early for shops to open, but he thought he caught the distinctive, deep voice of George W. Ruff, a successful black businessman who did his barbering from a shop very close to the Exchange Hotel.

The wagon came to an abrupt stop when they arrived at the Adams Express office. There he sat for maybe fifteen minutes. The sun had risen and the clouds had broken up, so Henry could now see pencil-thin streams of light penetrating the holes in his box. Living in a world of sound only, he was amazed at all of the noises he took for granted—signs of the city coming to life all around him. Doors opening. Horses stomping and snorting. Wagons creaking. The snap of a rug being shaken out. The swish-swish of broom bristles on wood.

"Mornin' there," came a voice, so sudden and startling. It seemed as if the voice was inches away from his ears. The voice was so close that Henry almost wondered if the person was greeting *him*.

"Mornin' to you, Mr. Fowler," came another voice.

His box was moving again, and he seemed to be floating in air as the men transferred the box from one wagon to another. This wagon would take him to the train; and not until the locomotive began to roll out of the terminus could he breathe a little easier.

"This box must weigh a ton! Whatya suppose is in it?"

"Don't know and don't care."

"Let's shake the box, see if we can figger out what's in it."

Henry braced himself.

"Are you insane? I ain't shakin' a box this heavy just to satisfy your curiosity."

Henry smelled cigar smoke, drifting in through the tiny holes in his box. One of the men must have had a cigar clenched in his teeth as he lugged the box. Henry held his breath as long as he could, then gulped in a mouthful and nearly choked. His eyes burned as the acrid stench filled his box, and he struggled to keep from coughing. Putting his hands over his mouth, nose, and eyes, he filtered out the smoke by breathing into his palms.

The two men slid the box into the next wagon, and the smoke slowly dissipated. But as the box slid along the bottom of the wagon, it caught on something, and the men flipped it over. Henry put out his hands to catch himself, so he wouldn't collapse against the wall, making an awful racket. He found himself looking face down. That wouldn't be so bad, but they didn't just turn the box over once. They turned it over a second time.

Henry was now upside down.

Blood rushed to his head, and Henry's skull began to throb as pressure built up behind his eyes. *Don't panic,* he told himself. The trip from the Express office to the train was only seven blocks. Surely, the box would be set right side up when it was loaded onto the locomotive. Couldn't they read the words on the side of the box? *THIS SIDE UP WITH CARE!* Were they blind? Illiterate? Or just plain stupid?

Calm, calm. Just pray. Just hope. Don't make a sound.

The pressure was strong inside his head, as if his eardrums were about to burst. Already, the top of his head was beginning to get sore from its contact against the inside lid of the box. He tried to reach down and push up to lift his head from the wood just a fraction of an inch, for relief. Gravity had become his mortal enemy. If he remained in this position for the entire trip, he would die.

The wagon began to roll, and Henry attempted to gauge how close they were getting to the train terminus, but he gave up trying. The pressure was tremendous; he couldn't stand it. His skull was going to bust open. Seven blocks can be an eternity

34

when your head is pointing in the direction of hell.

Only a half hour into his escape and already Henry regretted that he ever came up with this insane plan. Samuel had been right in the first place: This wasn't a box. This was a coffin.

4

Louisa County, Virginia
1830: Nineteen Years Earlier

Henry had rarely seen a finer day. He enjoyed the gentle jostling of the wagon and the colors of the forest on both sides, the yellows of the beech and ash and the reds and russets of the oaks. His brother Edward shook the reins and shot a glance at him as the wagon rattled along a rough, barely discernable path through the woods.

"Watcha gawkin' at, Henry? Looks like you in a trance or somethin'. You act like you ain't never seen a tree before."

"Ain't never seen *these* trees before."

True enough. Henry had never been off of the Hermitage Plantation in all of his fifteen years, except for one visit to a neighboring plantation a few miles down the road. Now, Mr. Barret had sent his brother and him on a trip to the Ambler Mill, a full ten miles from the Hermitage Plantation, to get a load of corn ground up into flour.

"You was always one to gawk at amazements." Edward smiled and glanced over at Henry again. "Remember when you thought Master Barret was God?"

Henry grunted. His brother never tired of reminding him how he once thought his master was the Almighty Himself. Edward was being more playful than cruel, but Henry still didn't like being reminded of his ignorance—even though he wasn't yet six years old at the time.

"Y'all also thought William was Jesus."

"Ya don't say." Henry tried to think about something else, tried to identify the trees he was seeing. His mamma had taught him the names of most of them.

Edward laughed. "When Dicey said the Son of God died for our sins, you thought *Mr. William* had gone and died!"

Henry didn't respond, hoping Edward would get the message that he didn't want to hear any more. But Edward just smiled back and nudged his eyebrows up and down, his grin growing. Henry couldn't help himself. He responded with a smile, as he always did when his brother made those faces.

Edward shook the reins, threw back his head, and laughed again. "Lordy, Henry! You thought Mr. William died for our sins. If only he'd really died, and Master Barret with him, then maybe we'd a been free!"

Henry's smile vanished. Joking about the death of your master and his son was risky talk, even though they were already several miles from home and there were probably no white folks within a hundred yards. Henry would never dare such a jest. Sometimes, Edward didn't seem to have any sense at all.

"The Lord will set you free!" Edward exclaimed. "And Master Barret, he's gonna set us free, too. He's gittin' old, and when he passes, he's gonna set us free. He told me so right to my face, Henry."

The words settled uneasily with Henry. "But if he frees us, what a we gonna do? Where'll we go to?"

"Don't you worry none, brother boy. You and me, we'll be all right. Long as we together, we'll be all right."

They drove along in silence, taking in the full splendor of the day and the distance from the plantation. Afternoons like this always reminded Henry Brown of the autumn day when his mother took him to the edge of the woods on the Hermitage Plantation. That long-gone day had been serene and silent, except for the wind passing through the forest like rushing spirits. Henry had only been seven at the time.

Mamma crouched down beside Henry and wrapped an arm around his shoulder. The sights, the sounds, even the smell of someone burning wood nearby, were all so vivid. Sunlight flickered in the moving branches, and the wind stripped leaves from the trees, scattering them through the woods, spinning them in circles, and flinging them in every direction. A mad flurry of reds, oranges, and yellows.

Henry had no idea why his mother had taken him to the edge of the forest. He wasn't in trouble, and she didn't have a switch in her hand. When he had asked what they were doing, she didn't answer.

Mamma crouched down low and drew him closer. "Henry, the life of a slave, your life, is like the leaves," she said as the wind picked up slightly. "The wind scatters 'em, scatters 'em where it will."

A sudden gust broke the stems of a hundred leaves, ripping them from the branches.

"And there ain't no gettin' 'em back."

Henry watched the leaves skitter across the ground in a chaotic stampede and vanish into the forest. Then Henry's mother drew him even closer, as if she were trying to protect him from the wind, as if she were trying to keep him from being ripped out of her arms and blown away through the forest along with the leaves.

Henry noticed the tears on his mother's cheek, but he was too young to understand what she was trying to tell him. He could feel her fear, and he could feel the wind. It was blowing, tugging at his shirt, yanking at his hair, pulling at his pants. He held onto his mother tightly.

"Sing us a song," Edward said out of the blue, but Henry didn't answer. He kept looking at the trees, taking in the autumn smells. "C'mon, Henry. If you don't, I's gonna sing myself. And you wouldn't want that."

Edward had a point. His voice sounded like someone had put a badger inside a sack and was beating it with a stick. Henry gave him a playful push on the shoulder. Then Edward began croaking out words, making good on his threat.

> "Old Satan is a busy old man,
> He rolls stones in my way!
> Jesus is my bosom friend,
> He roll them out of my way!
> O come-e go with me,
> O come-e go with me
> O come-e go . . ."

"Enough, enough. You gonna scare every bird for miles."

"I warned ya, brother boy."

So Henry began to sing as their wagon wound its way along the river. His voice flowed as smooth as the stream.

> "I don't feel weary and noways tired,
> O glory hallelujah!
> Just let me in the kingdom

While the world is on fire!
O glory hallelujah!
Goin' to live with God forever
While the world is on fire!
O glory hallelujah!
And keep the ark a movin'
While the world is on fire.
O glory hallelujah!"

Edward was mercifully quiet as Henry sang them into the next county.

They soon came upon the Ambler Mill, a two-and-a-half story frame structure built on a limestone foundation. The mill was a hive of activity, the center for trading gossip and goods. People came from all over to have their grain ground into flour, as well as to pick up feed and medicine for their animals.

This was Henry's first trip to the mill, although Edward had made it several times before. Henry was astounded. Living water raced along the wooden sluice, powering the twenty-one-foot overshot waterwheel, which made the grist mill look like an enormous side-wheel paddleboat run aground in the middle of the woods. Inside, the mill was more like the interior of a giant's pocket watch, with oversized cogs turning the runner stone that spun around and around on top of a bedstone, pulverizing the corn funneled in between the two stones and grinding it into a fine, soft flour. The noise was deafening. Henry had never seen machinery so powerful before, and he couldn't comprehend that someone had concocted this process.

After delivering the grain, all Edward and Henry had to do was wait their turn for the grain to be pulverized into flour. On busy weeks, Edward said they might have to wait a couple of days before the miller got to their load—a long reprieve from field work back on the plantation. But today, they were out of luck. They would get to stay only one night.

"This is gonna be the best part," said Edward, retrieving two fishing poles from the wagon. He handed one to Henry.

"Perfect day for fishin'," said Henry, grabbing the can of worms. The sky was slightly overcast, the temperature moderate, and the breeze light.

"Wish I'd a thought of bringin' poles on my last trip. It's a mighty good day for fishin', brother boy."

"Sure is," Henry said, surveying the knot of white men up the slope at the mill.

"Don't you worry. We'll be out of sight of the Amblers right quick."

Henry nodded. Edward had warned him to steer clear of any Amblers, the family that ran the mill.

"Be especially watchful of Colonel Ambler," Edward had said. "He's a tough old man, as hard as the rocks that grind our grain. When he looks you over, ya get the feelin' he'd like nothin' better than grind *you* between two stones."

Before heading off to fish, Edward and Henry found a spot to sit on a log just outside one of the cabins. They unwrapped their provisions for the trip—some chicken and sweet potatoes.

"If we can catch us some fish, we can have ourselves a regular feast tonight," said Edward, handing a chicken leg to his brother. As Henry raised the chicken to his mouth, his eyes were drawn to a group of six forlorn slaves who shuffled in their direction like gray ghosts. Ambler's slaves. The colonel owned more slaves than anyone in the area, Henry knew that much. The slaves stared at Henry and Edward as if they were from another world.

In a way, they were.

Ambler's slaves wore no shoes and no hats. Their shirts looked as if they had been cut from coffee sacks, and their pants were so thin that it seemed as if the slightest wind would tear them to shreds. Henry and Edward both wore stiff brogans on their feet and straw hats. They also wore vests—hand-me-downs from the Barret sons. Edward's vest was yellow and Henry's charcoal.

Self-conscious under the stares of the other slaves, Henry looked away. He had an inkling that Master Barret provided for them better than most owners, but he had never seen slaves like this. These men, each of them, were as thin as the starving cats that hung around their slave cabins, hunting for scraps of food.

"Would ya like somethin' to eat?" Edward said, rising to his feet and approaching the men.

Henry's stomach growled at the thought of giving up his meal, but he knew his brother was right. These men needed the food more than he did. Even at age fifteen, Henry was developing the stocky build of his young manhood.

"Don't you worry, Henry. We got our fishin' poles. We'll still eat tonight," Edward whispered as they approached the six men. Henry and Edward tried to distribute their food as fairly as possible, but with twelve hands reaching out and the men devouring the food as quickly as it reached their fingers, it was hard to keep track of who had eaten what. The feeding frenzy lasted only minutes before every morsel was gone.

"I'm Edward. And this here's my little brother, Henry. Wish we had more grub to give ya."

"Brothers?" said one. "You mean you ain't been split up and sold off?"

"Our master wouldn't do nothin' like that," said Edward.

Several of the men stared at Henry and Edward's clothes as hungrily as they had eyed the food. One of the slaves, a man barely over five feet tall, kept fidgeting and looking every which way. "Thanks y'all for the food, but we gotta be movin' before we be caught dawdlin'."

Too late for that. Henry noticed one of the mill overseers charging in their direction. So he and Edward gathered up their fishing poles, while the slaves moved on. Looking over his shoulder as he hurried away, Henry saw the overseer shove one of the slaves into the dust.

"Let's get away from here," Henry said. "Let's get fishin'."

"I hear ya, brother boy." Edward lifted up the can of worms, as if he were raising a toast. "Let's hope we catch somethin' or we'll be eatin' nothin' but these worms tonight."

Edward began whistling, for although he couldn't hold a tune when singing, he was proficient at whistling. Henry slowed down to cast another glance over his shoulder, but the Ambler slaves were gone.

"This way's the river," Edward said, putting a hand on Henry's shoulder and turning him in the right direction.

As they walked on, Henry brushed away the dust from his vest. The vest was a little faded, but it showed no patches. He thought about the times he would stare at the fine clothes of his master's four sons, spruced up in their sleek, black tailcoats and top hats. He wondered if he had stared with the same intensity as the Ambler slaves.

Edward and Henry hadn't gone far down the

road before they spotted two white boys coming in their direction—both about their age, from the looks of it. One seemed vaguely familiar from a distance. Something about the way he walked. As the two sets of boys converged, Henry's eyes were opened.

One of them was John Allen.

After the incident in the storm four years ago, Henry had been terrified for months that John Allen's pappy would get his revenge on him for rescuing his son, but Mr. Allen never learned the truth. Turned out that John Allen told everyone he had used his own skills to escape his father's ropes, and Henry never contradicted this version of the truth. He didn't dare—although he did tell a few people the real story, including Edward.

Henry had crossed John Allen's path only a few times in the last four years. The last time they had seen each other, nearly two years ago, John acted as if Henry didn't even exist. He had come to the plantation with a horse that his father had sold to the Barrets. Henry said hello, but John Allen walked right past him.

John Allen's pappy had recently taken a job working at the mill, and Henry wondered if he might stumble across either the father or the son. John Allen was going to have a hard time ignoring him this time. They were heading on a collision course.

"The one on the left, he's one of the Ambler

boys," Edward whispered. "Best stay out of his way."

Edward tugged on Henry's shirt, pulling him to the other side of the road, but the Ambler boy matched their move. He led John Allen across the road, and Henry noticed that John had something in his left hand. A whip.

"Good evenin', sirs," said Edward, tipping his hat.

The Ambler boy was plump and pink and well fed, giving him the look of a pig in fine clothes. But the boy's attitude was more razorback, all gristle and tusks, and he gave Henry and Edward a challenging glare. Henry didn't know what to do or say. Even his brother was uncharacteristically at a loss for words. As for John Allen, he wouldn't even look at Henry. He kept his eyes on Edward, while the Ambler boy looked them up and down and did the talking.

"Who gave you these clothes?" Ambler demanded. Henry was terrified that he would make them remove the clothes right then and there in the middle of the road.

"Our master, Mr. John Barret, give us these clothes, sir," said Edward. It was always good to remind them who their master was; Mr. Barret's name carried authority in these parts.

The Ambler boy walked around them, still sizing them up. "What do you think of this, Johnny?" He spat into the dirt. "You think a slave

46

has any business wearing the same clothing that his master wears?"

Henry thought he caught John Allen looking in his direction for just a second. John paused before answering. "It ain't the way things are supposed to be."

"You're right, ain't natural," said Ambler. "Animals don't wear fancy clothes."

Henry and Edward didn't dare respond. John Allen stared off in the direction of the mill and fidgeted with his whip. Ambler continued to look at Henry and Edward from head to foot; and then, out of the blue, he smiled and asked, "Have either of you ever been whipped?"

Henry's eyes were immediately drawn to the whip in John Allen's hands. John shifted it from his left hand to his right, as if he were trying to hide it behind his right leg.

"No sir, we ain't never been whipped," Edward said. "Our master don't believe in it."

That was only partly true. Just recently, the overseer on their plantation started using a whip for the first time, with the master's approval, but Edward and Henry had never felt its touch.

Once again, the boy spit in the dirt. "Well, neither of you will be of any value then."

John Allen took a step backwards and looked at the ground.

"Johnny here . . . I've been giving him lessons with the whip," Ambler said. "He's pretty good with it, too. Someday, he'll be able to hit a can blindfolded."

Ambler smiled and let that sink in. Henry held his breath.

"Let's get back to the mill," Ambler finally said, tapping John Allen on the shoulder and motioning him forward. Henry thought he saw John let out a sigh of relief.

The two white boys started to turn to stalk off, but Edward couldn't leave well enough alone. Henry wished his brother had more sense around dangerous humans. He was like that around wild animals too, never understanding when to give some distance.

"We brung along our fishin' lines on this trip, sir," Edward said. "Would ya give us the privilege of fishin' in your stream?"

Ambler stared at Edward in disbelief. Henry knew what his answer would be even before he spoke it: "We do not allow nigras to fish. You hear that?"

"Yes, sir," said Edward.

Then the boys turned and marched off. Edward went stone silent as he watched them head toward the millhouse. Henry could tell that Edward's mind was beginning to move like the mill cogworks, and that could only spell trouble. Henry preferred to stay in the background, part of the scenery. But Edward: He pushed the limits. Always had.

"We goin' fishin'," Edward finally decided.

"But the fellow said . . ."

Henry didn't finish his sentence. He was too busy thinking about John Allen's whip.

"Don't you worry, brother boy, we ain't goin' to fish his stream," Edward said, reading Henry's thoughts. "There's other streams around here, and the Amblers don't own all of the Lord's creation."

Edward usually knew exactly how far he could push matters with white folks without ever crossing the line, but Henry wondered if this was going too far. If Edward were a soldier, he'd probably take great pleasure in getting as close to the enemy line as possible while still remaining just barely beyond the range of enemy muskets. But not Henry. He saw no need to tempt enemy fire. He could do without the fishing today.

But in their relationship, Edward's decisions were gospel, so they tramped their way to another stream, off of the mill property, and they dropped in their fishing lines. Henry wished he could say that he felt like a free man, enjoying the day at his favorite fishing hole. But he didn't. He was constantly looking over his shoulder, expecting trouble.

When they returned to the mill, they had a healthy supply of fish to more than make up for the food they had given away. Henry wanted to get back to the cabin where they'd be staying the night; he wanted to get out of sight, out of the path of any Ambler or Allen. But no such luck. As they came down the road, they were spotted. The door to a nearby building was thrown open and out rushed the Ambler boy—with John Allen a few steps behind. The two white boys cut them off. Henry was relieved that John Allen wasn't carrying his whip this time.

"Where did you get those fish?" Ambler demanded.

"Not at your stream, sir," Edward answered. Henry noticed the hint of a smile on Edward's face, a sign of delight in getting under the boy's pink skin; but on the surface, Edward remained polite and deferential. "We been to a different stream to fish. Not on your property, sir. We wouldn't do that, sir."

"And how am I supposed to know that?" Blood rushed to the Ambler boy's cheeks until they nearly radiated anger. "We don't brand our fish to show where they've come from!"

Edward didn't answer. Sometimes, he actually knew when to go quiet.

Ambler just stared at them. Henry knew that the boy would love to get his whip and thrash them, if he had his way. But even white boys had lines they couldn't cross, and whipping a powerful man's property was going well beyond the line.

Ambler tapped John Allen on the shoulder. "Take their fish."

John Allen looked at Ambler, eyes wide and mouth open. He didn't move.

"Whatcha waitin' for? Take their fish. We can feed it to the pigs."

John Allen shot a look at Henry. Was it an expression of shame? Hard to tell. Obeying Ambler's command, John Allen walked up to Edward, then paused.

"Say, you're John Allen, ain't you?" Edward said, grinning. "Henry rescued you in a storm a few years back, didn't he!"

Henry closed his eyes. That was exactly the wrong thing to say, but Edward probably knew that and said it anyway.

When Henry opened his eyes back up, he saw that John Allen's face had gone bright red. "No, he didn't, and if I hear you say so again, I'll whip you bloody, I don't care who your master be."

"Sorry, sir. I must be sorely mistaken."

John Allen yanked the string of fish out of Edward's hands and hurled them to the Ambler boy.

"Watch what you're doing!" Ambler tried to catch the slimy fish off to the side so they wouldn't stain his fine clothes. But the fish slipped through his hands and landed in the dirt. John Allen snatched them from the ground and stormed away without looking back. This time, Ambler did the following.

Henry and Edward didn't budge until the two

boys were a safe distance away. Henry's stomach growled.

"Don't worry, brother boy," said Edward, smiling big. "Tonight we still eat."

"Eat worms, you mean."

"Tonight we eat *fish*. Look at this: I can multiply the fish just like Jesus done."

Edward reached both hands into his pants and pulled out a couple of fish, one in each fist. He showed them to Henry for only a second before jamming them back into hiding.

"The secret is thinkin' ahead, brother boy." Edward was all grins. Even Henry couldn't help but let out a smile.

Henry and Edward had caught themselves a mess of fish this day. But in some ways Henry felt a little bit like a fish that had just barely escaped with his life. The young slaveholder would have delighted in skinning them alive. But he and Edward had wriggled off his hook and would live to see another day.

5

Richmond
March 23, 1849
7:10 a.m.

Henry remained head downward, dizzy and disoriented. The two tiny holes on each end of the box allowed in a small stream of light and air, but he fretted that it wasn't enough to sustain him. He felt like he was being slowly smothered.

The wagon came to a stop, and he heard the hiss of the nearby train. Richmond did not have a depot at this time, so trains were loaded directly from the streets—in this case, Broad Street. He also heard the sound of men talking and shouting and moving about, and suddenly his box was being lifted, and he heard the grunts and groans of two men who were unwittingly lifting two hundred pounds of human flesh and bone. The men loaded the box onto the train, but they must not have noticed the words THIS SIDE UP WITH CARE because they kept the box upside down when they slid it into the boxcar. Henry despaired. Ahead of him lay a long train ride, and he did not believe he could make it the entire way in this position. With the weight of his body pushing the top of his head down against the box, his scalp was feeling raw. The dime-sized pain in his back had expanded its circumference, and his wounded hand throbbed. He itched at the bandage wrapping his left palm.

More sounds swirled around him, and Henry was relieved to hear the voice of Samuel Smith, the white shoemaker who had helped him plot the escape. "Hold on! Watch what you're doing there."

Henry didn't expect Samuel to be here. He didn't think Samuel was going to take the chance of seeing the box off at the train, or being connected in any way to the package. But here he was. Would he notice Henry's predicament?

"Hold it!" Samuel said again.

"Whatya want?" said another man, one of the cargo handlers for the railroad company, Henry figured. "Who are you?"

"The owner of this here box."

Henry's heart jumped when he heard a sudden tapping on his box. Samuel's voice was close.

"Can you read?" Samuel asked.

"Not standing on my head I can't," said the cargo handler.

Then Henry heard a third voice, probably the wagon driver who had delivered his box to the railroad station—the Adams Express man. The fellow sounded out the upside-down words on the side of Henry's box: "This side up with care." A pause. "Oh."

"Would you please be so kind as to place my package right side up?" Samuel said.

"Yes, sir," said the Adams Express driver.

The cargo handler groaned, but that was the extent of his protest. Henry soon felt his box being slid forward. He braced himself against the wall on either side.

"What's in this box anyway—your mother?" said the cargo handler. "Weighs a ton."

"It's equipment," Samuel bit out. "And it needs to be upright. If you got a problem with that, I can talk to your boss."

No answer.

The box was turned over once, hurling Henry onto his back. A pain shot up his neck, briefly, but he didn't make a sound, not even when the gimlet was tossed around like a coin in a cup. The drill had been lying loose on the bottom of the box, and when Henry was thrown onto his back, the gimlet struck him in the face. Hit him right in the forehead, stinging something awful.

"Something shook loose inside there," he heard the Adams Express man say. "You think something's broke?"

"It's fine," said Samuel.

"We can open up the box if you need to check." The Adams Express man was being much too helpful.

"No. I said it's fine."

"Okay, okay, just asking."

But the cargo handlers weren't done yet. They turned the box over one more time, putting Henry right side up and bringing relief. The blood rushed down from Henry's head into his core, nearly causing him to pass out. Henry wiped the sweat from his forehead, and he felt a bump beginning to sprout where the gimlet had smacked him. It was tender to the touch. He took shallow breaths, afraid of consuming too much air. And that's when he noticed another change. The box had gone dark. No streams of light penetrated the interior. Henry ran his hand against the wall directly in front of him until his fingers found the indentations of the two small holes. No light was coming through, and no light meant no air. He turned around and looked at the wall behind him. Again, no light, no air. The holes were blocked on both sides! Henry leaned forward to put his mouth against one of the holes and tried to draw in air. He drew in nothing but sawdust. He was begin-ning to suffocate. This time for real.

John Allen marched through the tobacco factory, a bow-legged swagger. He came into a wide, open room with three long rows of tables. Women, children, and old men stood at the tables, removing tobacco leaves from the thick stem, the plant's backbone. The stemmers were careful not to make eye contact with John Allen as he passed by. Many years ago, under a different overseer,

56

the room would have resounded with slave songs by this time of day. But not under John Allen's watch.

John Allen jammed a wad of tobacco into the corner of his mouth and surveyed the tables, watching for any slouchers. He knew that some of the slaves hadn't shown up yet, and he planned to make their life miserable when they did. Never show weakness, never bend, never break, and they will respond. They will obey. His system never failed.

John Allen was a faithful overseer, always arriving at the factory well before work time, a habit that the factory owner, William Barret, admired. But Mr. Barret had no idea that he arrived early so he could load his wagon with coal, oil, and wood—supplies that just happened to wind up at his own residence without anyone the wiser. John Allen smiled just thinking about it. He was proud of his natural-born intelligence, and he expected that someday he would be running a factory of his own. *Mr. Barret is such a fool.*

If he were running the place, he would find a way to house slaves on the grounds, like at Tredegar Iron Works. He detested the system in which slaves boarded out, away from the master, and he had been scandalized by it when he first came to the city. There was far too much freedom for blacks in Richmond, nothing like what he had seen out on the plantation. Why, some free colored folks owned their own slaves—a ploy to prevent families from being split apart. Free black women even bought their husbands and then freed them! It made John Allen boil, just thinking about it.

As he continued to watch for the slightest drop in productivity, Callahan strode through the main factory door, and John Allen turned on him.

"You're late, Callahan!"

He was preparing to give him an earful when he noticed something in Callahan's hand. A piece of a shirt. Callahan held it out in front of him and didn't say a word. The soggy scrap of shirt spoke for itself.

He snatched the piece of clothing out of Callahan's hands and studied it. A look of recognition slowly crossed his face.

"This here's the piece a shirt we tore off that slave last night," Callahan said. John Allen didn't respond, so Callahan filled the silence. "I went back to the spot. There it was, right there in the mud. You know whose it is?"

John Allen looked back at Callahan. He didn't answer. He pushed past Callahan and headed for the door. "Keep an eye on things."

"But do you know whose shirt it is?"

Still no answer. John Allen stalked from the factory. Like a bloodhound, he had picked up the scent.

6

Louisa County, Virginia
1830: Nineteen Years Earlier

It was an autumn evening, a few weeks after the trip to the Ambler Mill, and the hard work under the sun had ended. Henry had spent the long, grueling day moving through the field, splitting tobacco stalks down the middle and cutting them at the ground. Then the tobacco plants were left out on the field for a spell so they could be wilted—killed by the sun, they called it. Henry knew the feeling, for some days he felt like he was the one wilting under a killing sun. After hanging the plants on scaffolds and curing them, the tobacco would be sold to Richmond, only forty-five miles from the Hermitage Plantation.

With the breathtaking Blue Ridge Mountains to the west, the Hermitage sat in the heart of the Piedmont region, a land of gentle hills and thick forests. Henry lived there with his mother, four sisters, and three brothers, working in the fields to grow corn, cotton, and tobacco. The plantation was home to forty slaves and one free black man.

"Now you see it," Henry said to Lewis and Robbinet, his two youngest siblings, who had gathered outside the cabin, with darkness settling in. Lewis was six years old and Robbinet only four.

Magic performances offered Henry a chance to step out of his shell, to shed his skin. He didn't feel like a slave when he was doing tricks for an audience, even if his audience was only two small children. He didn't feel like Henry Brown.

He held up a single coin for them to see. Then he slid open the drawer of his magic box and dropped in the coin. It hit the wood with a clunk. Henry closed the drawer and waved his hand over the box—much the way he had seen the traveling magician do.

"Now you don't."

With a flourish, Henry slid open the drawer and tilted it for Lewis and Robbinet to see. The coin was gone. Clean gone. Robbinet gave out a small gasp.

"How'd you do that?" Lewis demanded.

"I can't tell ya. Magicians don't give away their secrets." Henry paused just a moment before making his next move. "But what's this . . . ?"

He reached for Lewis's right ear, and the coin suddenly reappeared in his hand, plucked from the air like a piece of cotton. He displayed the coin for them to see.

"Give it!" Lewis shouted and lunged for the coin. Henry playfully drew his hand back, and Lewis tumbled into his arms, a squirming mass of moving legs and grasping hands. The coin, always out of reach. Robbinet leaped onto Henry as well, and they wrestled, all arms and legs and uncontrollable giggles. Then . . .

"Henry!"

His mother's voice. Something was wrong. Their wrestling stopped the moment her voice came snapping across the field. Mamma trudged up the slope, puffing and holding up the hem of her heavy dress. She fought against the autumn wind, which scattered leaves around her feet.

"Somethin' the matter, Mamma?" Henry asked.

Mamma stopped, caught her breath. She looked bone weary. "Master Barret would like to see us. Both of us."

The statement jolted Henry. He had been waiting for those words for some time; but now that he heard them, he wasn't so sure he was ready. His master, so close to death, must have made peace with the Lord. Henry always supposed that Master Barret would free his family upon his death, but things had been changing. Master Barret had changed. He had once been a kind man working in the unkindest of systems. But now he was withered and harsher in his old age, like a fruit that had been left on the vine for too long. At over eighty years of age, Master Barret could no longer supervise the slaves himself; and for the first time he had hired an overseer. For the first time, the whip was used on the Hermitage Plantation. For the first time, the word "escape" had been whispered at night amidst the slave cabins.

"Will he keep his word?" Henry asked Mamma as they made their way to the Big House. The house had an enormous front porch, like the deck of a large ship.

"Hard to tell. That was many years ago."

"But he said—"

"*Henry,* it was many years ago."

"He said he would free us after he passed on."

"He said many things."

Henry could always hope. Some slaves kept hope alive by working at a trade so they could earn money enough to buy their freedom. But for most, buying your way out of slavery was pretty much impossible, considering that it could cost anywhere from $500 to $1,000. And even if you saved up enough money, there were no guarantees. Henry heard tell of a slave who saved up enough money to buy his freedom *twice.* Both times, the master pocketed the money and did not let him go.

At the threshold of the house, they came to a stop, and Henry caught his breath and removed his hat before they entered. They were led upstairs where Master Barret lay in a darkened room that smelled of death. Buried under blankets, he looked so old and so small. His sideburns were long and scraggly, his voice ragged. Was this really the man who held such power over their lives for so long? He seemed so fragile—as if a puff of air could snuff him out like a candle and all that would remain would be a curl of smoke.

John Barret had fought in the Revolutionary War; he had known the great Patrick Henry, and he had even served as the mayor of Richmond at one time. But now he had been reduced to this. Henry almost felt sorry for him.

"Closer, Henry," said Master Barret.

Henry inched closer to his bedside, but Mamma kept her distance. She knew her place.

"You asked to see us, sir?" Henry said.

Henry started to feel dizzy. He didn't think he could wait a second longer to hear what Master Barret had to say.

"Henry," he said, turning his head slightly to look straight at him. Master Barret's eyes were watery and red, and his breathing struggled out in a rattling wheeze. "Henry, promise to be an honest boy."

"I will, sir."

"Never tell an untruth."

"I won't, sir."

"Do as I have taught, and you will make a good ploughboy . . . or a fine gardener."

Yes, but will I be a free ploughboy? Or a free gardener?

"Thank you, sir," Henry said.

With his gnarled finger, twisted by arthritis, Master Barret motioned toward a glass of water on the nearby table.

"Be a good boy."

"Yes, sir."

Henry took the glass and held the water to the master's lips. Then he used his handkerchief to wipe away a trickle that dribbled down the master's chin. He felt like a mother dabbing the face of a child. All the while, he felt like screaming. He had to know! Now!

Finally . . .

"Henry, I have decided what will become of you," the master said.

There they were. The words hung out in front of him, as tantalizing as the coin that he had held out in front of Lewis and Robbinet. His freedom was within reach. He wanted to snatch it, make it his own.

Mamma made a slight move forward. Henry could tell she wanted to take his hand, but she stopped. Master Barret poked one of his hands out from under the quilt, grasping for Henry, clawing the air. Henry took Master Barret's hand.

Then the master spoke the words: "I am giving you to my son, William."

Just like that, Henry's freedom was snatched away from him—like the coin that he had dangled in front of his brother and sister. Now you see it. Now you don't.

"Did you hear what I said, boy?"

"Yes, sir."

"You must obey William from now on."

"Yes, sir."

• • •

The family was scattered in all directions.

Henry's brother Edward was given to one of the four Barret sons, and just like that he was gone only a week after Master Barret passed away. Henry's sister Mary and her children were flung in a different direction: another brother, another town, another life. John, Lewis, and Robbinet went with Stronn Barret, and Henry never saw them again.

Henry stood by and watched while John and Lewis were loaded into the back of a wagon. He knew he should do something, anything. But what could he possibly do to keep them from disappearing into a cloud of dust on the road leading away from the plantation? All he'd get is a club across the back of the head, or worse. Still . . .

Mamma wouldn't let go of her youngest, Robbinet. She wrapped her arms around Robbinet to the point that she almost smothered her. The overseer tried to peel her away, but Mamma just held on tighter. Robbinet was crying while the large overseer tried to get in between them, shouting and cussing and trying to pry her mother loose. *Do something!* But Henry couldn't move.

"The life of a slave, your life, is like the leaves." The wind was constant, hissing in Henry's ears like a steady rain, picking up intensity and then pulling back at times, but

constant. The trees swayed and the leaves shook, straining to hold on.

The overseer, furious, stepped away from Mamma and kicked up dust with his boot. He spit out a few choice curses, put his hands on his hips, and just stared at Mamma. Then he picked up a stick, a sturdy one, and circled Mamma like he would a dangerous dog.

Henry had to act. He knew it now. It was awful enough just standing there watching his brothers and sisters thrown into the back of a wagon like sacks of grain. He wasn't going to stand by and watch his mother beaten like an animal. Edward would have taken action by now, but Edward was gone.

"The wind scatters 'em, scatters 'em where it will." A sudden gust. A breaking apart. A tunnel of wind, like an invisible train, roared through the trees, stripping away a thousand leaves.

The overseer moved behind Mamma and raised his club, targeting the back of her head. Mamma leaned forward, shielding Robbinet. The overseer paused just long enough for Henry to rush forward and step into the line of attack.

Shocked, the overseer held up. "Outta the way!"

Henry didn't respond, didn't budge.

"If you don't move, I'll clear you outta the way!"

Henry just stared back at him.

The overseer shrugged and then cocked his arm. "Suit yourself."

The back door of the Big House swung open, squeaking on its rusted hinges.

"Olson!" The voice was that of William Barret, Henry's new master.

Olson, his arm still cocked, held back once again. He glanced over at the house, where William Barret stood on the edge of the porch, looking down on the scene.

"Put down the club," Master Barret said.

Olson shook his head and slowly lowered his arm. Master Barret turned his eyes on Henry. "Talk to her."

Henry crouched down in the dust and put his hands on Mamma's shoulders. Gently. "C'mon, Mamma, c'mon," he said softly. "Ya still got me, Mamma. Ya still got Jane and Martha."

"But she's my baby."

"I know, Mamma. But ya still got me."

Mamma looked over her shoulder at Henry, her face powdered by the dust. He felt so helpless, so powerless. He was the only man of the family left on the plantation, but he didn't feel like a man. He *wasn't* a man. He was only fifteen.

"C'mon, Mamma."

He thought about wrapping his arms around Mamma and Robbinet, becoming their shield, and just letting the overseer do what he needed to do. But the thought was gone in an instant, another impulse not acted upon. Instead, he did Master Barret's bidding. He always did his bidding. He was a good boy. Problem was he didn't feel like a good *son*.

When Mamma finally let go of Robbinet, she latched onto Henry as if she were drowning. Seeing his opening, the overseer swooped in to yank Robbinet by the arm and drag her to the waiting wagon.

"And there ain't no getting' 'em back." The wind just wouldn't let up. It kept on coming, a train with a million cars, rolling, crushing, spinning leaves into oblivion.

"Ya still got me, Mamma, ya still got me."

But even that was not true. Henry didn't realize it at the time, but Mamma, Jane, and Martha would remain on the plantation, while he was going with William Barret to Richmond to work in his tobacco factory. Within a day, Henry was gone, seated beside a huge slave named Thomas and watching the Hermitage Plantation fade away behind him. This time, there was no scene, no screaming, no clubs. Mamma, Jane, and Martha just huddled together and watched his wagon roll away south to Richmond. Henry wished Edward were with him. Edward would know how to deal with the new world he was entering. Edward would know what to say and what to do. But Henry was on his own now.

"Ya don't talk much, do ya, boy?" said Thomas,

one of William Barret's slaves from the tobacco factory, given the job of bringing Henry in from the plantation. The wagon seemed on the verge of shaking apart as it bounced across a bumpy road and approached Richmond after a long day's trip.

Henry looked over at Thomas, a six-foot, four-inch giant with arms like oak. "I'm just thinkin', sir."

Thomas grinned. "Just don't think too hard. Your head'll bust if ya don't let out your thoughts sometime."

"Yes, sir."

Thomas was not the strong, silent type, for he loved to hear himself go on and on. However, Henry couldn't remember much of what he said during the ride to Richmond. He kept thinking about what lay ahead, and he didn't perk up until they rolled across a bridge that spanned a rapid-moving river at the city's edge.

"This here's the James River," Thomas said. "Now don't you try swimmin' across unless your mamma is part fish. The current will pull you under faster than you can holler help."

The James River was dotted with several forested islands, and a couple of bridges carried trains and other traffic across the wide span. Paralleling the river was a canal, which bristled with traffic: keelboats, dugout canoes, and flat-bottomed bateaux.

"And don't you think of sneakin' off in a boat neither," said Thomas. "Police are all over the docks, always checkin' for runaways."

Henry nodded. He was used to "don'ts."

The wagon moved into the heart of the city, and Henry was stunned. So much noise and dust and shouting. It was overwhelming to a country boy. He saw more faces than in all his life out on the plantation, and so many of the faces were black. Thomas told him that about half the population was black, either slave or free.

"Y'all will be boarding out with Wilson Gregory, the factory overseer," Thomas said.

"I'm boardin' with an overseer?" Henry didn't like the sound of that.

"Don't fret," said Thomas, laughing. "Mr. Wilson is blacker than me. He's a free black man, but of course that don't mean he goes easy on us. He works us hard and watches us like a hawk."

Henry's head was spinning, for everything in Richmond seemed upside down. The very idea of boarding out somewhere, separate from the master, was strange and disturbing. And he would be boarding with a free black man? They had one free black living on the Hermitage Plantation, but he had never heard of a free black serving as an overseer.

"Close your mouth and don't you look so surprised, Henry," said Thomas. "Richmond is crawlin' with free blacks. But they don't get no better treatment than us—'cept they's free to leave."

Henry looked up at the row of factories—iron and carriage foundries, flour and corn mills, but most of all, tobacco factories. Richmond was an industrial monster. The city was also hilly, and Thomas drove the wagon down one of the steepest roads, deep into Shockoe Bottom, a bustling, haphazard maze of hovels with all types of buildings, from tottering shanties to monstrous brick factories. The streets were packed with shopkeepers and shouting vendors. Some sold flowers. Others hawked fresh game: rabbits and chicken. Henry spotted a row of taverns, and a booze-blind man staggered out of one and fell onto the dirt road, nearly getting trampled by a passing horse.

Thomas took the wagon down a narrow street, flanked tightly on either side by factories and warehouses, where slaves unloaded and loaded boxes. He eventually brought the wagon to a stop before a huge, three-story building on Cary Street, not too far from Fourteenth. The side of the building displayed the gigantic words, "Anchor Brand Chewing Tobacco," which faded into the wood like a ghost.

"Here we be," said Thomas. "Home sweet home—'cept the only sweet thing here is the tobacco."

Henry didn't answer. He simply stared up at the imposing walls.

"Now get a move on and climb on down,"

nagged Thomas. "We'll get ya settled in no time. Y'all will probably start out as a stemmer."

A blank stare from Henry. He had no idea what he was talking about.

"You tellin' me ya don't know what a stemmer is? Boy, what'd they teach you on that plantation of yours? Y'all will be takin' the tobacco leaves, moistenin' them all up, and removin' the stem. The stem's like the leaf's rib. Just like ol' Adam lost his rib, y'all will be takin' ribs out of these leaves. But you won't be fashionin' any women from them, sorry to say. Just chewin' tobacco made outta the leaves."

Still unsure what Thomas was talking about, Henry climbed out of the wagon, carrying a sack of extra clothes and his small, wooden box for doing magic tricks.

Thomas started for the front door of the factory, where six strangers—all of them black—stood staring at Henry. So many strange faces, strange buildings, strange smells, strange sounds. Henry suddenly froze.

"C'mon, Henry!" Thomas waved him forward. "Get a move on. I can't be shepherdin' ya along all day, ya know."

Henry stumbled forward and kept his eyes fixed on Thomas's wide back as he followed him toward the front door. He ran a gauntlet of strange eyes but wouldn't turn to look at them. *Keep lookin' at Thomas.*

When Henry crossed the threshold of the factory, he plunged into darkness. It was like being devoured, swallowed whole by a whale. Now he knew something of what Jonah must have felt.

7

Richmond
March 23, 1849
7:20 a.m.

Henry wasn't sure how many breaths were left inside his box. He needed more air holes, so he fumbled for his gimlet in the dark.

The gimlet was more like an auger, a sharp, nail-like bore with a small wooden handle that fit into your palm. But which side of the box could he ventilate without drawing attention from the cargo handlers outside? The bottom? No, he would only strike the floor of the train. He could drill through the side facing out of the train, but that would be risky. The two men would surely see the drill bit poking through. So he really had only one choice. He had to drill through the top.

Henry wanted to wait until the boxcar door was shut before drilling, but he didn't have the luxury of biding his time. The cargo handler didn't seem to be in any hurry to close up the car. Henry's forehead was hurting, his back was hurting, his hand was hurting, and it was getting more difficult to breathe. Fighting the urge to kick his way out of the box, he put the sharp point of the gimlet against the top of the box and slowly, silently started to twist. The auger began to bite into the box and eat its way through the few inches of wood. Carefully, he kept twisting the handle and applying steady pressure—but not too much because he didn't want the drill to bust through with too much force, drawing the attention of the cargo handlers. He had to be patient, had to be calm. He wiped the perspiration from his eyes.

"So whatya standing there for?" came the voice of the cargo handler from just outside the boxcar.

"I'm planning to watch the train off," Samuel said. "You have a problem with that?"

"Don't care too much for people staring over my shoulder, that's all."

Finally, the drill bit broke through. But as it did, the wooden handle of the gimlet suddenly snapped, coming off in Henry's hands. To his horror, he dropped the handle, and it bounced against the bottom of the box. This left him with no way to retract the bit, which protruded from the top of his box, visible to the world. Breathing hard and using up valuable oxygen, he groped around, but for the life of him he could not put his hands on the wooden handle. So he tried yanking out the drill bit without the aid of a handle, but it was impossible to get a good grip. *Stay calm, stay calm.* Henry clutched the bit as tightly as he could and tugged, but his sweaty fingers couldn't hold on. *How could this be happening?* He attempted to wiggle the drill loose, twisting it around, pulling back, yanking harder, hands slipping, frustration rising. But nothing worked.

Samuel couldn't believe what he saw. John Allen, the overseer at Henry Brown's tobacco factory, was moving west down Broad Street and coming right toward him on horseback. The horse was cantering and kicking up mud, a reckless speed considering all of the foot traffic on Broad Street at this time of day. But John Allen seemed oblivious to the pedestrians darting in front of his path. He nearly ran over a well-dressed gentleman, who had to leap out of the way to keep from being trampled. The gentleman landed feet-first in a mud puddle, emitting language nearly as filthy as his splattered clothes.

John Allen slowed his horse to a trot when he got closer to the train terminus and fixed his eyes on the locomotive. Samuel Smith despised the man. John Allen was as savage as a meat ax, a penny-pinching miser, and the most cantankerous jackass in all of Richmond. He treated the workers in William Barret's tobacco factory monstrously and had recently beaten Obadiah Johnson so severely that the slave was laid up for a week. Samuel wondered why Barret hadn't done anything to stay his overseer's hand, but maybe he was kept in the dark about such matters.

Samuel and John Allen had exchanged punches on one occasion at a local rum-hole, and Samuel wondered if this would be another one of those days—especially if John Allen tried to apprehend him on the spot. John Allen wasn't a big man, but Samuel knew that when he came unhinged, he could whip his weight in wildcats.

Samuel tried to avoid eye contact with John Allen, but he could sense his approach in his peripheral vision. Did the overseer know what was happening here? It was possible that the men who spotted Henry on the street during the night had reported the incident to him. But even if that were true, how could John Allen possibly know that they were putting Henry on the train as freight? Samuel reached down and touched the revolver hidden beneath his jacket, taking cool comfort in its proximity.

"You're a shoemaker, ain't you?" asked the cargo handler.

Samuel pulled his jacket tighter. "That's right."

"Then whatya carryin' a weapon for? There ain't too many boot thieves in these parts that I know of." The cargo handler displayed a tobacco-stained grin.

"Never know when I'm gonna need firepower to quiet an ornery freight handler."

The man's grin vanished.

Samuel kicked himself for being too obvious with his gun. And when he glanced back into the open boxcar, his heart nearly stopped. Something was sticking out of the top of Henry's box! Samuel squinted. It was the gimlet poking through the wood. What was Henry thinking? Why drill fresh holes out in the open when he could wait until the train car was shut up?

Then he saw it: Henry's air holes were blocked by adjacent boxes packed in tightly when the freight had been rearranged. Henry needed air, he needed to drill fresh holes now. But why hadn't he retracted the drill back into the box? It was sticking out for the world to see.

"Only a few more boxes," said the wagon driver to the cargo handler.

"Someday I'll get me a cushy job," said the cargo handler. "Hammering on shoes all day sounds like a soft existence."

Samuel ignored the insult. He now faced trouble on two fronts. John Allen was almost upon him, and the cargo handler was about to spot the drill. The cargo handler had hold of a large sack and was preparing to load it on the train. Samuel had to act fast, so he stepped in front of the freight man, blocking any view of Henry's box.

The cargo handler glared. "You're in my way."

"Pardon me," said Samuel, "but I have to check something with the box."

"You what?"

"Hold on just a moment."

Keeping his body between the cargo handler and Henry's box, Samuel climbed into the train car and knelt down in front of the box—as if he were praying. Since he was already in this position, he tossed off a quick, silent plea to the heavens. Samuel surreptitiously grabbed the drill bit by its sides, carefully avoiding the pointed tip, and he tried to push it downwards, but the gimlet was stuck fast. When he glanced back over his shoulder, he saw that he had gained a wider audience—the cargo handler, the wagon driver, and now John Allen, who had stopped to stare. The cargo handler just stood there, his arms wrapped around the bulky sack, killing Samuel with his stare.

"C'mon, I can't hold this all day," the cargo handler said. "What're you up to?"

Samuel took off his bowler hat and slapped it down on top of Henry's box, covering the drill. Then he turned to face his audience.

"Well?" said the cargo handler.

"Well what?"

"Have you finished doin' what you're doin'? We got schedules to keep, you know."

"Yes, I believe I'm done." Samuel didn't budge.

"So get on down from there."

"Oh. Yes. Sorry." Taking his sweet time, Samuel climbed down from the train, conveniently leaving his hat on top of the box, covering the drill.

"And take your hat!"

The cargo handler tossed aside his sack, climbed into the train, and reached out for Samuel's hat. Samuel closed his eyes. Everything was about to fall to pieces—with John Allen looking on.

8

Richmond
1831: Eighteen Years Earlier

Henry puckered his lips, lodged his tongue against his bottom teeth, and blew out. All that came out was a sputtering stream of air. Not even a trace of melody.

"No, that ain't it, ya ain't got it at all." Wilson Gregory, the black overseer at the factory, clapped his hands to get Henry's attention. "Watch me. Just watch and do, watch and do."

Wilson began to whistle, letting out a melody that sounded for all the world like someone playing a flute. The whistling drifted into the night from the front porch where Wilson and Henry sat on overturned wooden boxes. All along the street, slaves were porch-sitting—talking, laughing, and finding a rare respite from their backbreaking work. The sun was setting in Richmond, transforming everything to grays and shades of black, except for the flare of orange in the west.

"You can sing up a storm, Henry, but you ain't worth nothin' whistlin'."

Wilson could be an unforgiving taskmaster on the factory floor, but Master Barret had told him to take special care of Henry. So he took Henry under his wing and gave him lessons on how to remove tobacco stems quickly and efficiently and how to recognize high-grade tobacco. Wilson Gregory also took Henry in with him to live in a ramshackle tenement in the Shockoe Bottom district of Richmond, just one block from the factory.

Henry had been working in William Barret's factory for about a year now. The factory specialized in making flavored tobacco, much of which was shipped across the Atlantic to England. It employed one hundred and fifty people, but not all were slaves. Thirty were free blacks. William Barret owned only a handful of the slaves in his factory, while the rest were hired out from other masters in the region.

Henry had not seen any of his family in the past year, although Master Barret assured him that his mother and sisters Jane and Martha were doing well back on the plantation in Louisa County. Henry had heard nothing about Edward, and Master Barret had nothing to report because the

Barret brother who had inherited Edward did not keep close contact with the rest of the family. Henry ached whenever he thought about Edward and Mamma, but he learned to master his tears. The two times Wilson caught him with tears in his eyes, the old man had threatened to go against the master's wishes and use the whip on him. Wilson couldn't abide crying.

But on this evening, with dark setting in, Wilson was in a good mood. "Did I ever tell ya 'bout the time I snatched me a pig?"

Wilson had, but Henry shook his head anyway. "No, sir."

Wilson had a hard time getting the story started because he kept laughing out loud at just the thought of what had happened. "Our overseer back on the plantation, we called him Look-e Here 'cause that's what he was always saying to us. 'Look-e here, you black rascal you stop doing that!' Or 'Look-e here, you work harder now!' Look-e Here was a mean old sinner, and the only one he would ever treat nice was this big old hog named Sam. Look-e Here treated Sam like he were a king, givin' him the best victuals you could imagine, and us goin' hungry all the time. So's one day, Look-e Here had to go off and visit his relations 'bout fifty miles from the plantation. He was goin' to be gone for most of a week, so we got to thinkin' this was our chance to be settlin' a score with old Sam."

Wilson leaned back and picked at his teeth with a sliver of wood. This had to be the fourth time Henry had heard about Wilson snatching that pig on the evening when it was so quiet "you could hear a rat pee on cotton," as he put it. Wilson told Henry how he spirited the pig back to their cabin, where his wife (long since deceased) slit the pig's throat and started chopping him up for a feast. What they didn't count on was Look-e Here's sidekick, Ben, who noticed that the pig had gone missing. Ben was in quite a state, for Look-e Here had put him in charge of making sure that his pig was well taken care of while he was gone.

"So Ben come straightaway to our cabin, and my wife and I is hauling bits and pieces of that pig off to the woods to get rid of the evidence. But when Ben is only a short distance from our cabin, we still had plenty of pig to hide. My wife, Molly, had a big pot of persimum cookin' away on the hearth—'cause the master was wantin' her to be cookin' up some beer for when he returns. So she takes all those remainin' pig parts, blood and all, and she dumps it in the big pot!"

This was the part of the story when Wilson became the most animated. He leaned forward, his hands flapping every which way like he was directing a band. He said that Ben, the overseer's young assistant, looked everywhere in their cabin, sure that they had done something terrible with Sam the pig. When Ben was finally satisfied that they didn't have the pig, he jerked his thumb at the big pot and said, "Now draw me some beer."

"My wife, she coulda fainted right there on the spot. So, with her hand a-tremblin' like she seen a ghost, Molly dishes up some beer, and Ben takes a big, smackin' gulp. I'm standin' there thinkin' that we're about to be whipped to death. If we got caught, the master would chop us in little bits like we done to Sam. But then God in heaven looked down on us and give us a miracle! That Ben licked his lips and said, 'Very good, this beer. Draw me another.' He musta drunk three or four cups, and he went away sayin' it was the best beer he ever done tasted."

Wilson broke out laughing—a loud, rollicking sound. Henry wasn't a big laugher, but he grinned wide, for he delighted in Wilson's stories. The overseer was most likely in his fifties, but he looked ancient; his skin was leathery and wrinkled, especially at the neck. His nose looked as if it had been broken a few times, and he had a deep furrow running across the bridge. His head, mostly bald, sloped backwards dramatically. He was usually seen wearing the same black, tattered vest.

Wilson was ruthlessly obedient in doing the master's bidding at the factory, but outside of the factory his rebel streak peeked out around the edges. In his younger days, his rebellion took the form of stunts like stealing a pig. These days, it was usually something subtler—like whistling.

Two men, clearly drunk and clearly white, came around the corner, weaving their way down the darkening street and occasionally bouncing off of each other in their stumbling, meandering way. Wilson started in whistling, a beautiful, simple tune. As the two men passed by, one of them cast an evil eye—and nearly tripped over his feet, which can happen when you're liquored up and you take your eyes off the path in front of you.

The two white men were still well within earshot when Wilson altered his tune. His whistling became more like that of a bird singing—like a bird *communicating*.

One of the two white men stopped and turned to peer at Wilson with narrowed eyes. Like most in Richmond these days, the man probably thought the whistling was a system of secret signals, passing messages up and down the street to other blacks who were lurking behind their doors with knives and tools, ready to come roaring into the streets, pouncing on any unsuspecting white folk. Black rebellion was white folks' worst nightmare.

"Jeet-jeet, jeet-jeet, jeet-jeet!" Wilson's whistle danced through the air, sometimes loud, sometimes soft.

Fear of a slave revolt had been strong lately, ever since Nat Turner's Rebellion set Richmond abuzz in August. In Southampton County, south of Richmond, Nat Turner had decided it was time for him to wreak the Lord's vengeance on slavery. In the night, he ascended a ladder that he had set against the side of his master's house. Carrying a hatchet in his mouth, he climbed the ladder like a pirate scrambling up the shrouds of a ship, and with four other slaves at his side, he killed the entire family. Then Nat Turner led his four rebels from house to house to house. Methodical. Merciless. After the Travis house, the Francis residence. Then the Reeses. His band had grown to fifteen men on horseback when they swept through the Whitehead estate, leaving destruction and death. Other homes followed, other families.

Nat Turner's band killed close to fifty slave-owning family members before they were caught and hung. In retaliation, white mobs brutalized blacks in and around Richmond. Henry heard how some blacks were "half hung"—strung up in such a way that they lived on, while mobs pelted them with fruit and rocks. White authorities in Richmond also reacted by passing all kinds of new laws, such as forbidding more than five blacks from congregating at a time, except at work and at church. This made it much more difficult for Wilson and his friends to conduct their whistling contests on street corners before curfew. People were on edge.

The first drunk stared at Wilson, who was still sending bird whistles into the air; and if you closed your eyes, you'd think you were hearing real birds, real communication. Henry was worried. This could be real trouble. It didn't take much to ratchet up tension among blacks and whites in Richmond. Just the wrong tone of voice or the wrong look. Or a whistle.

"What's that you whistling?" the drunk shouted, his words slurring.

"That a Baltimore Oriole, sir," said Wilson.

Stupefied, the drunk continued to stare, while his friend stopped and also looked back at Wilson. Henry could sense that the second man was a little afraid of any "Nat Turners" lurking in the area. Henry had to admit it: he savored the man's fear. It gave him a feeling of power. At the plantation, he had never seen the Barrets afraid of anything, except when Master Barret was on his deathbed.

"Here's a black-capped chickadee," called Wilson, as innocent as could be. "Fee-beee! Fee-beee! Fee-beee!"

Henry didn't know how Wilson produced such amazing sounds.

"C'mon, leave these scamps to do their warbling," said the second drunk, unable to keep the fear out of his voice. Other slaves on other porches had stopped their talking and stared at the two men.

The first drunk continued to scowl.

"Let's go, Jones. I got things to be doin'!" his

friend urged once again. The friend began to walk away, moving at a fast clip. But Jones didn't seem all that afraid—just irritated. Henry wondered if maybe the man was armed. Was Wilson playing with fire?

"Fee-beee! Fee-beee! Fee-beee!"

Finally, Jones shook his head in disgust and called "Hold on" to his friend, who had already turned the corner. As soon as they were out of sight, Wilson gave a wink to Henry and stopped whistling his bird songs. He went back to his lessons.

"C'mon, anyone can learn to whistle, Henry boy. Just curve the tongue, just do what I say, do what I do."

Henry puckered up and blew, but all he could muster was a stream of air, with a few hints of a whistle buried somewhere in the flow. This set Wilson off laughing again, laughing so hard that tears came to his eyes. That was the only kind of tears he tolerated.

Henry slung the sack of clothes over his shoulder, said his thank you to the shopkeeper, and plunged into the sunlight and heat. Wilson Gregory had sent him off on a simple chore, a welcome break from the monotony of stemming tobacco. Over his shoulder was a sack of mended work clothes—the coarse cotton clothes that slaves were issued in most factories up and down the river. Two sets for every slave: one for warm weather, the other for cold. Pantaloons and a shirt. Not much, but people made do.

Henry didn't often get the chance to leave the factory on errands. He figured that Wilson didn't want to be seen favoring him by sending him off on chores regularly, so it was a rare treat. This expedition to Seventeenth and Main took him only a few blocks from the factory, but venturing there in the middle of a workday was like a holiday.

Henry soaked up the light. The sun could be brutal back on the plantation doing fieldwork, but he had come to miss it, working all day in the dismal interior of the tobacco factory. He stopped, stood in the street, and let it warm his face. He even closed his eyes, until he felt something nuzzling his foot. Henry looked down and saw a small, black dog licking his shoes.

"Hello, boy, where'd y'all come from?" Henry said, crouching down. He ran his hand along the filthy, knotted fur of the dog's back. The dog took to licking the back of his hand before scampering off. "Come here, boy!"

With the sack banging against his back at every step, he took off after the mutt. But the dog was halfway down the street and had turned a corner before he could build up any speed, especially lugging a sack of clothes. He lost the dog, and it suddenly dawned on him that he was also losing something else. He was "losing time." That's what the Richmond slaves called it—losing time. With almost half of the population in Richmond being slave, spread out across a city and working in factories away from the master's home, it was nearly impossible to keep track of everybody's movements. So losing time became a game for slaves. They'd see if they could slip away for short stretches of time. Or see if they could dawdle during errands, to lose a little time on the way back.

Losing time: Edward would have become an expert at it, Henry was sure of that. It was just a small rebellion, but it gave him a good feeling, a feeling of power. For the next half hour, he would be the master of his own time. For the next half hour, nobody could tell him where to go and what to do. Not Master Barret, not Wilson Gregory . . . Henry stopped in his tracks. *Lord, what have I done?* He turned around and started back for the factory, but then he stopped again to think this through. Wilson had his own small rebellions: snatching pigs, whistling on the porch. Henry just wanted the same, that's all.

So he turned and kept on strolling down Seventeenth Street, looking into shops and keeping his eye out for the small, black dog. He wandered by Mr. Snyder's corner store, a small grocery store run by a free black, and he couldn't resist leaning through the open door and taking a gander. There was a commotion inside. Laughing. Whooping. Men, all of them black, huddled on the floor, with something going on in the midst of them.

Henry ventured in, losing time again. His fears began to slide away. The corner store was dark, but enough light came in through the front door for him to see that the men were throwing dice. They placed pennies on one of six numbers—one through six—scrawled on the wooden store floor. Then the dice, shaken up in a can, were cast down and sent skipping along the floor.

"Two fours! Double me. Double me!" Hoots. Hollers. Curses.

Bets were made again, the can was shaken, and the three dice went flying. Henry had heard of the game—chuck-a-luck—but he wasn't exactly sure how it went. With the sack still slung over his shoulder, he leaned forward and peeked over the backs of the hunched-up men, who knelt on the floor as if worshiping the numbers. Remembering the preacher's warning about gambling, he made a move to leave.

"Where ya goin', boy?"

Mr. Snyder, the store proprietor, suddenly appeared at Henry's side and put a hand on his shoulder. He was a large man, both vertically and horizontally, and his hand weighed a ton. Henry glanced over at Mr. Snyder's fingers, pressing into his shoulder blade. His fingers were huge.

"Whatcha got, there, boy?" Mr. Snyder's right

hand remained on Henry's shoulder, while his left went to work, rooting through the sack.

"Just work clothes."

"Ah. Care to wager? I can teach ya the game."

"No . . . No thanks, sir. Ain't got no money, sir."

"Then bet these clothes. You're rich in work clothes."

"No, thank ya, sir."

Henry tried to break away, but Mr. Snyder tightened his hold.

"One game. Just one try. I won't tell your boss you came in here if you just play one game."

Henry stopped struggling and surrendered to the inevitable. He was Mr. Snyder's slave now.

"All right, but I can't wager any of these here clothes. I got me a penny."

"A penny! You been holdin' out on us, boy! Let me tell ya how it's done. You bet on one of the six numbers. If one of the dice comes up with your number, it's even money. Don't lose, don't win. If two dice come up with your number, you double your money. Three dice, you triple it. If your number don't show at all, ya lose. Simple as that."

"Here, let me watch your sack while ya play," said one of the men crouching on the floor. But Henry just held on tighter as he dug out a penny. *Lord, get me outta here!* The man kept grinning and grabbing for the sack of clothes, and Henry was tempted to kick him in the teeth, what teeth the man had left.

Henry held out his coin. "Put it on three. Number three."

"Good Bible number, boy. You don't look like you gamble much. You rather sit in church, that right, boy?"

Henry didn't respond. The dice were shaken. The men, some crouching, some kneeling, all leaned forward as the dice were released and bounced crazily across the floor. Even Mr. Snyder eased his grip on him for a second to gaze at the results. Henry saw his chance. He tore away.

"Hey!"

One of the crouching men spun around, and his hand snapped out as quick as a whip, snagging Henry's pants leg, and for a second he thought he was going to fall flat on his face. But he kept his balance, yanked loose, and raced out the door, banging his shoulder on the doorjamb on the way out.

"Get back here!"

"You won double, you rascal!"

"Collect your money!"

Henry didn't care, didn't believe a word they said. He ran into the light, made a hard right turn, and sprinted back to the factory. He didn't stop until he was through the factory doors, puffing like a steam engine. But he wasn't in the clear yet. Another hand snagged him, and this time it was Wilson Gregory.

"Where you been, boy?" Wilson spun him

around, had him by the shoulders, and stuck his face inches from his. "You been losin' time, Henry? Is that it, boy?" He shoved Henry back two steps.

"Just gettin' the clothes, sir. Here they are."

Wilson swatted the sack from his hands. "No one loses time on my watch. Turn around!"

"What?"

"Turn around! Put your hands on that post!"

Every ounce of freedom had been kicked out of Henry, first by the gamblers and now by Wilson. He didn't understand. Wilson always treated him kindly, but at this moment the man's face was like the devil. Mr. Barret told Wilson never to whip him, and the overseer had obeyed . . . until now. Wilson stood over him with a whip in his hand, and Henry had his hands against a post. He tried to keep back the tears. He had never been whipped in all of his sixteen years, and it was going to happen at the hands of a black man. He looked over his shoulder and saw that the room of workers had paused in their labor. All eyes were on him. *Lord, make it not hurt.*

Crack!

The whip snapped, and he flinched and gasped. But he didn't feel a thing, and he wondered for a moment if God had worked a miracle. Wilson leaned in, put his mouth to his ear. "When I snap the whip, boy, it'd shore help if you shout out, ya hear me?" he said quietly.

Henry nodded. He didn't know why Wilson was telling him to shout, but right now he would do just about anything the man told him. Wilson stepped into the next strike, and the whip snapped the air. This time Henry shouted out, even though he didn't feel a thing, not a sting, not a cut.

"Next time I send ya on an errand, you come right back!"

Crack!

Henry hollered. But still, the whip didn't hurt.

"One more for good measure!" Wilson threw all of his weight into the next snap, and Henry gave out an extra loud shout. He collapsed forward onto the floor, pretty good acting on his part. Wilson hoisted him to his feet and dragged him into the corner. Keeping his back to the other workers, the overseer leaned in close to Henry. A slight grin broke through his stone-hard gaze.

"Pretty good, ain't I? That whip got within a inch of your back, but didn't touch. Now what I want you to do is tell everyone here you got whipped good. They can't be seein' anyone losing time and not gettin' punished for it. Not with me in charge. Ya hear?" Wilson shook him by the arm.

Henry, still in shock, nodded. Then Wilson winked at him and hardened his look, like slipping on a mask. "That's the last time you'll be losin' time, you scamp!" he shouted.

Wilson gave him a small shove and strode away, tossing aside his whip and yelling to the roomful of stunned workers: "Show's over! Back to work!"

9

Richmond
March 23, 1849
7:30 a.m.

Samuel glanced over at John Allen, who leaned forward on the horn of his saddle, staring directly at the hat that Samuel had left sitting on top of Henry's box. Samuel slipped his hand under his coat and put a hand on his revolver. Just in case.

But when the cargo handler reached into the boxcar and lifted the hat, the gimlet was gone. The drill had vanished, like a perfectly timed magic trick. The handler hurled the hat to Samuel who plucked it from the air with a one-handed grab.

"Thank you, sir," said Samuel with a grin. He plopped the bowler back on, but the railroad man did not return the smile. So Samuel shifted his gaze to John Allen, who was still leaning forward on his horse, taking everything in.

"Morning, Mr. Allen," Samuel said jauntily. He knew that John Allen hated that tone of voice.

Their eyes met, and they exchanged wordless

disdain for each other. Then, to Samuel's utter amazement, the overseer simply shook his head and spurred his horse forward. John Allen said nothing and did nothing to stop this shipment.

Feeling the tension release from his body, Samuel watched the horse walk away down Broad Street. John Allen had his back to him, so Samuel raised his hand like he would a pistol, looking down the barrel of his forefinger.

"Pow!" Samuel's imaginary bullet hit John Allen squarely in the back.

"Good shot," said the wagon driver.

"Don't encourage him," said the cargo handler.

Samuel kept his eye on John Allen for a few moments more, and that's when he noticed something sticking out of the overseer's back pocket. A piece of clothing. It had a plaid pattern like Henry's shirt. Henry's torn shirt.

Can't be, Samuel thought.

But it could.

A thin stream of light shot straight down through the freshly drilled air hole in Henry's box. It struck him in the face, illuminating a forehead slick with perspiration. Henry strained his neck upwards, tried to get his mouth as close to the hole as possible, and drew in what little air he could, like a thirsty man trying to suck up a few drops of dew.

Henry needed to drill a couple more air holes,

but one would have to do for now. He couldn't take another chance until the boxcar was closed up.

He had heard Samuel climbing into the boxcar and figured out that he was trying to push the drill bit back down. Henry also knew he had only seconds before being discovered, so he had clutched the drill in his right hand and jiggled it wildly from side to side, finally widening the hole and pulling the drill free. Just in time.

But tension was still running high. He had heard Samuel greet a "Mr. Allen," and there was only one Mr. Allen in Henry's world. John Allen. He couldn't imagine why John Allen would be here at the train terminus, other than looking for him.

Henry wiped away the perspiration from his forehead with the back of his right hand, then leaned back in his box and scratched at his wounded left palm, which itched terribly. With the finality of a tomb being sealed by stone, the boxcar door slammed shut, casting him into darkness.

John Allen had a hunch that Samuel Smith was up to something.

Samuel was a swindler who had cleaned him out in cards on several occasions over the years; that was why John Allen took great satisfaction two years ago when he learned that Smith had fled to Baltimore to avoid paying off a big debt.

When Samuel showed up back in Richmond last year, John Allen foolishly agreed to another card game. Never again.

But Smith was up to something. He was sure of it. Ever since John Blevins was caught helping slaves escape last summer, John Allen had kept his eye on Smith. Blevins was a shoemaker and so was Samuel Smith, and the two men had lived close to one another for a spell. They were also both thieving cheats in his book. They stole, whether it was by dealing from the bottom of the deck or by sneaking out of town with a wagon loaded with pilfered human property. John Allen prided himself on his vigilance, and he despised anyone he couldn't keep under his rein. He especially despised Samuel Smith.

When Callahan had brought the scrap of shirt to the factory, John Allen immediately headed home to retrieve his gun, taking him past the train terminus on Broad Street where he spotted Samuel Smith. He had no intention of rooting around in the Shockoe Bottom slave district without being armed with his Paterson Colt, a large, powerful black-powder revolver he had acquired from a veteran of the war with Mexico. With the gun strapped to his waist, he back-tracked in the direction of Low Town.

John Allen's mount trotted through the slave district, the mud making a sucking sound with every step. He wouldn't want to be walking through this swamp on foot. All of the water from Richmond's seven hills drained into Shockoe Bottom, and the previous night's downpour had left the streets especially sloppy. Huge ruts, filled with stagnant water, looked like small lakes. A stray dog, with its low-slung belly covered in mud, picked at a pile of trash. It looked up and snarled, and John Allen was tempted to put a bullet in its head. But this was not the time to be causing a scene. He passed by a cluster of shacks with walls partially caved in and patched with scrap wood. The houses looked like makeshift shelters assembled from the flotsam of a sunken ship. Two small boys slogged around barefoot in the mud, laughing and chasing a small dog. When he passed by an open sewer, thick with flies, the smell nearly knocked him from his horse.

John Allen steered the horse off the main street into an alleyway, where families crowded into two-story tenements. Laundry lines crisscrossed the air like ship rigging, and the drying clothes snapped in the wind like gray sails. Finally, he reached his destination and dismounted, his feet sinking several inches into the muck. He cursed the ground he stood on. An elderly woman watched him tramp through the slop, her expression calm and unchanging. She was a thin, black woman wearing a clean, white shawl and white apron over her heavy brown dress. Her face had more wrinkles than John Allen had ever seen on one person, deep wrinkles moving up her cheeks and converging on her eyes like so many channels and tributaries. She sat on the front porch of a nearby tenement house, just watching him.

John Allen tried to ignore her gaze as he stepped out of the mud and onto the wooden porch, stamping the wet earth from his boots. Then he stormed the house like a soldier. He didn't knock before entering, unless you count the sound of his mud-caked foot connecting with the door as he kicked it open. Gun drawn, John Allen rushed in and looked around for any sign of life. The home was a simple, one-room dwelling, so it didn't take long for him to deduce that no one was there. As suspected, the slave was gone. If he wasn't at home and he wasn't at the factory, there was only one conclusion. He was on the run.

John Allen kicked over a chair and cursed. He would pull together a slave hunt—and quickly. The question was where to focus his search. Slaves were always trying to slip onto boats, but the police had that route watched closely. Blevins had taken four slaves out by wagon last August, so the patrollers were also watching closely for any covered wagons.

If the runaway had escaped on foot, John Allen would need dogs. Boone Wilkins had several Cuban bloodhounds, the best for tracking. They were strong, they could pick up the smallest scent, and they were aggressive. Some owners didn't like them, though, because these dogs had a tendency to damage the property. Teeth will do that.

Whatever the escape route, John Allen knew Samuel Smith had to be involved in some way. John Allen had seen him at the train, and he was acting awfully suspicious.

The train . . .

It suddenly hit him: The train had to be the key.

John Allen barged out of the house and ran to his horse, slipping and sliding in the mud and nearly falling on his backside. He was never tentative in his actions. Without a bit of doubt in his mind, he knew exactly what he had to do next. He had to reach the train before it pulled out of Richmond.

10

Richmond
May 1836: Thirteen Years Earlier

Henry couldn't help but notice her. He hadn't seen the girl before in the church choir, but there she was, rocking and swaying and stepping with the music. Henry couldn't keep his eyes off of her.

Henry, with his powerful baritone voice, was one of the strongest singers in the choir of the

First Baptist Church. He had been attending the church for five years, ever since 1831, when the combination of an eclipse and Nat Turner's Rebellion got him thinking that the world was coming to an end. The church had separate services for whites and blacks, and it had been that way for years because the greatly outnumbered whites decided they couldn't put up any longer with black worshippers speaking out, jumping around, and making a Spirit-filled commotion. Although blacks had their own service, they were still required to have a white preacher run things and handle the preaching. Henry didn't like that at all. Reminded him too much of an overseer, and he couldn't stomach overseers, even if they dressed like preachers.

At age twenty-one, Henry had reached his adult height of five feet, eight inches, and his skin was a dark brown. His face was clean-shaven, and his black hair wrapped around his head like a halo. His physique was stocky and strong, and his eyes were soft and dark. While Henry sang out, he let his eyes drift to the left, down to the end of the row.

The new girl was striking, with a lustrous, light brown skin, and she wore her coal-black hair long beneath her peach-colored bonnet. Their eyes connected, but only for a moment. Embarrassed, Henry broke away and tried to refocus on his singing. Beside him, Henry's good friend James Smith leaned forward, ever so slightly, and glanced down the row of singers, looking for what or who had taken Henry's attention.

A few moments passed, and Henry stole another look down the row. The girl did not notice his attention, so he drew away and tried to refocus on his singing.

"Steal away, steal away, steal away to Jesus!
Steal away, steal away home, I ain't got long
  to stay here!
My Lord calls me, He calls me by the thunder;
The trumpet sounds within-a my soul, I ain't
  got long to stay here."

Minutes later, Henry ventured another look, this time letting his eyes linger. If she sensed his eyes on her, she didn't give it away. Her eyebrows arched above almond eyes. She was tall, perhaps five feet, seven inches, and her nose was broad to match her smile. By this time, Henry had almost forgotten what he was supposed to be singing, so he gazed back out at the congregation and attempted to focus once again.

"Steal away, steal away, steal away to Jesus!
Steal away, steal away home, I ain't got long
  to stay here!
Tombstones are bursting, poor sinner stands
  a-trembling;
The trumpet sounds within-a my soul, I ain't
  got long to stay here."

The fourth time that his eyes strayed in her direction, they connected with hers. They held the gaze, but for only a few moments. She smiled. Slightly. Henry was in heaven. Quickly, he drew his eyes away and threw himself back into his singing with gusto, suddenly singing louder than ever. James gazed down the row once again, then tried to read Henry's face. Henry ignored him and looked straight out at the congregation, belting out the words.

James Caesar Anthony Smith was Henry's closest friend in Richmond. James was a free black —or as some would say, a slave without a master. Only twenty-five years old, James operated a cake shop on Broad Street, between Third and Fourth Streets, a place where many blacks gathered to swap news. Some people still called him Dr. Smith because James once practiced dentistry in Richmond—which essentially meant that he had strong wrists and carried a pair of pliers with him at all times, ready to pull a rotten tooth when asked, even if the procedure had to take place in the middle of the street. A really good dentist could even pull a tooth while seated on the back of a horse. Like many dentists of the time, James also did some leeching work, drawing blood from customers. But he tired of extracting things and decided there was more reward in feeding people—with cake. James was literate, not unheard of among free blacks in Richmond, and he loved to read Shakespeare and the Bible. He was good-spirited and a bit of a dandy with his fine clothes and wisp of a moustache. He was also as thin as a rail. Henry felt like a slab of stone standing next to him.

"You sure seemed distracted today, Henry," said James. They exited the church side by side and stepped out into a bright, blazing day.

"Did I?" Henry glanced back at the front door of the First Baptist Church. Black churchgoers, over one thousand strong, poured out of the door and then promenaded up and down the pathway, showing off their Sunday-best clothes. Henry searched for the mystery girl amidst the parade of bonnets and hats.

"Looking for someone?" James asked.

"Hmmm?"

They strolled the path. Blacks didn't earn much money, free or slave. But with what little money they had, they bought the finest Sunday clothes they could afford. In fact, black churchgoers were usually more gussied up than whites. The men wore black coats, black trousers, and white pocket-handkerchiefs, as well as wide-brimmed hats or bowlers; many also carried walking sticks. The women wore silks and muslins of many colors and large and varied bonnets with ribbons and feathers. Workday clothes were plain, coarse, and cotton, but on Sundays the colors and styles bloomed in profusion. Henry wore a low topper hat and a double-breasted, light-blue vest—hand-me-downs from the Barrets, but still in good condition.

Henry's face lit up when he spotted the mystery girl coming straight toward them, with a friend flanking her on either side—all of them carrying white parasols and all wearing flowered and feathered bonnets. The girl's bonnet had a compact brim that arched above her forehead and displayed a colorful cluster of flowers in the front. Henry froze, unsure what to say or do. So he simply removed his hat and gave a shy nod of his head.

James bowed and swept the bowler from his head. "A blessed Sunday to you, ladies." Smoothly done.

The three women nodded, smiled in return, and continued on their way. Henry and James kept walking in the opposite direction, but Henry couldn't help glancing back a couple of times. The mystery girl threw a coy look over her shoulder.

"What if I told you my shop was burned to the ground last night and I lost everything I owned?" James suddenly blurted out.

"Uh-huh." Henry still had his neck craned around, gazing down the pathway.

"It didn't, by the way."

"Uh-huh."

Henry was lost to another world.

•••

Joe and Matilda Jones clasped hands and took a running jump over the broom, leaping over the stick to applause and laughter. Joe effortlessly cleared the broom by the greater distance, which meant he would be the head of the household. Matilda was a woman of great substance, both spiritually and physically, so she didn't get very far off the ground.

Henry clapped along with everyone else, but in his mind he was picturing himself leaping the broom with Nancy at his side. That was her name: Nancy. James had taken the initiative to discover her name; and even though Henry had only recently learned that she was called Nancy, wedding scenes such as this were already nudging him in the matrimonial direction. Already, he wondered if he would be able to out-jump Nancy and lay claim to the family headship. She was fairly tall for a woman and was much slimmer than his stocky one hundred and eighty-five pounds. She might just be able to out-jump him.

But marriage was all a pipe dream at this point because Henry had yet to jump one other important hurdle: He had yet to say even one word to Nancy.

A picnic followed the wedding for the new Mr. and Mrs. Jones, and it was held on the wide expanse of grass in front of the First Baptist Church, a gray brick structure with two wings flanking the main building. It was a hot Sunday in June, and the men cooked inside their suit coats and ties and long shirts. The women didn't fare much better in long dresses and high-collared blouses.

Sunday was the only day for slaves to let down, and today was no exception. It was the Lord's Day, while the other six days belonged to the masters—an unfair distribution in Henry's mind. During the summer, the slaves toiled for fourteen hours per day, six days a week in the tobacco factory; and during the winter their hours were boosted to sixteen per day, which included time for lunch and supper.

Henry, distracted by Nancy, kept to himself for much of the celebration. He wandered the grounds and wondered if he should dare talk to her. Food overflowed the small tables, threatening to buckle them with kale, pokeweed, ham-hock, chitterlings, chicken, rabbit, bread pudding, potlikker, and more. There was also music, and the Williams twins—two scrawny men in their sixties—entertained the crowd by patting juba. This rhythmic drumming was done without the benefit of actual drums. The Williams twins slapped their hands against their thighs, chest, arms, and shoulders, faster and faster and faster, building up wild momentum like two dueling drummers.

For Henry, the drumming just made him feel tense.

After listening to the juba patting and watching the new couple jump the broomstick, Henry moved through the crowd and contemplated his own jump of sorts, his leap of faith. He watched Nancy move among her friends, laughing so freely.

"Have you talked with her yet?" James said, sneaking up from behind. "I mean have you spoken *with words?*"

Henry shrugged. "Mebbe not."

"You do know that talking is usually required before courting and marrying, don't you?"

"I don't know what to say."

"Begin by telling her your name."

Henry shrugged and played with the cuffs of his coat, two inches too short.

"Well . . . ? You going to do it or not?"

"Sure, sure." Henry would say anything to get James off his back.

"Talk to her." James took Henry by the shoulders and turned him in the direction of Nancy. "Just talk."

Henry wasn't like James, who had numerous lady friends over the years, some at the same time. He was envious of James's ease, although he didn't desire a parade of women, as James did. He just wanted one.

Henry spun around to say something to James and found that his friend had vanished, probably off to chase a woman of his own. Then he looked across at Nancy, who was laughing with friends. Was she laughing at him? He took a few steps in her direction, but quickly veered off to the left when she looked right at him. He circled around and came back to the same spot near the Williams twins, who were still drumming, still beating a relentless rhythm. He tugged at his tight collar.

Henry also felt a tugging on his sleeve. He looked down to find Ella, James's little niece. Henry broke into a smile, for he knew what Ella was going to ask him. She was going to beg him to do another one of his magic tricks. She was always asking for a show, and he always obliged. He could be relaxed around females, as long as they were half his height and he had magic to perform.

"Hi, Uncle Henry!" Ella was a spark of light.

"Hi, Ella."

"I learned me a magic trick. Can I show you?"

This was a new one on Henry. "You can do magic, Ella?"

Ella nodded. "Uncle James taught me. Can I show you?"

Ella didn't wait for him to answer. She took Henry by the hand and led him through the crowd. She tugged at him like an impatient pet on a leash, and Henry followed, trying not to be dragged crashing into other people. He kept his eyes on Ella, delighted by her enthusiasm. In fact, he was so intent on looking at Ella that he wasn't paying attention to where she was leading him.

When Henry finally looked up, his smile turned to a look of horror. Ella had led him straight to Nancy, who appeared equally startled. Henry stared at Nancy, his tongue thick and his mind blank. He had spent many moments gazing at Nancy over the past few weeks, but never from such close proximity. From this distance, he could pick up the subtle scents of her skin. He could see the small birthmark just above her lip, on the left side. Henry looked away.

But Ella would have nothing of it. She was at the perfect height to take Henry's fingers in her right hand and Nancy's fingers in her left hand. Ella brought the two hands together.

"Magic," she said. With her sleight of hand accomplished, Ella went skipping off across the grass. It was obvious to Henry that Uncle James had been the mastermind behind this so-called magic trick.

Suddenly aware of their connection, Henry drew back his hand as if he were pulling it away from fire. Embarrassed, he stared down at his feet, still at a loss for what to say. Finally, he mustered the courage to look back up. Nancy smiled at his awkwardness. His mouth had gone bone dry. *Say something. Anything.*

"My name is Henry Brown."

"I know."

"You do?"

Nancy smiled again, nodded, and reached out. She took Henry's hand.

When the wedding celebration was over, Henry couldn't keep from whistling all the way back to his home, which he still shared with the black overseer, Wilson Gregory. Over the years, Henry had actually become quite good at whistling.

"So who's the lady?" Wilson asked not too long into the evening. He and Henry still spent many a Sunday night sitting out on the sagging porch. "Gotta be a lady to make you this kind a happy."

Henry smiled. "It's a lady in the choir."

"A good Christian woman, then. That mean she be marryin' material?"

"I sure hope it."

Wilson let out a hoot. "Well good for you. 'Bout time you got a woman. I ever tell ya the story of how Molly and me met?"

"No, sir," Henry said, although he had heard it at least three times before.

Wilson launched into the retelling. "I done met Molly at a corn-shuckin' when folks came from plantations all over, and we danced hack-back all night. I spotted her off in the distance, the prettiest, spunkiest girl in the place. And when we got to playin' 'please and displease,' I told Molly she could sure please me by givin' me a kiss. Well, that set the stage for a fierce squabble with some other fella claimin' Molly's favor, and before the night was over we were wrestling on the ground to see who be Molly's man. The fight went on for most of an hour or more."

Henry recalled that the last time Wilson told this story the fight had lasted closer to a half hour. Henry leaned back and half listened to the rest of the tale, admiring the large mountain range of clouds, purple and blue along the bottom, with a peak lit up like snow in the setting sun.

Wilson hadn't yet completed his story when three men came strolling down the street. In the dying light, it was obvious that the men were white, and Henry recognized two of them as police. His chest tightened. He hoped Wilson wasn't going to play one of his whistling games, not with two of them being authorities. *Let 'em pass, let 'em pass.*

But the three men didn't pass. They stopped directly in front of the tenement and turned to look at Henry and Wilson.

"Evenin', sirs," called out Wilson, and Henry added his own "Good evenin'."

Henry felt a pressure building inside.

"One of you Wilson Gregory?"

Wilson stood up, and Henry followed him to his feet. "That be me. Wilson *Noah* Gregory."

The two policemen were young and strong and carried an ironclad air of authority. But the third was an older man—paunchy in the waist. He also had the skinniest neck Henry ever did see, sunken eyes, and a weak little moustache that looked more like a leech had latched onto his upper lip.

One of the policemen, the taller of the two, stepped up onto the porch and motioned toward Wilson with his thumb. "That him?"

Wilson, whatya done now?

The skinny-necked man followed him onto the porch and walked within two feet of Wilson. He leaned forward, adjusted his spectacles, and carefully studied the black overseer's face, like a nearsighted gent trying to read the words of a broadside posted on a tree. "Yup. That's him."

"There a problem, sir?" Wilson said.

"Sure is. This man here claims you're a runaway."

Henry felt his heartbeat quicken. Wilson put his hands on the back of his chair to steady himself.

"You're dead wrong," Henry said, stepping beside Wilson.

"I ain't no runaway, sir," Wilson insisted. "I been a free man for seven years now."

The skinny-necked man got all excited at that statement. "My slave, we called him Burrell, and he up and run away about seven years ago."

"Can you show us your freedom papers?" asked the second policeman—the stockier, clean-shaven one.

Henry cast a look at Wilson. He was afraid that something like this would happen. Two months ago, Wilson had lent his freedom papers to his brother, a slave who bore a striking resemblance to him. Freedom papers listed name, age, color, height, body type, scars . . . as much detail as possible to identify a person. His brother had begged to borrow the papers and use them to flee north, promising to mail them back just as soon as he reached Philadelphia. No papers had returned.

Wilson responded as if the policeman's request was something he heard every day. "Sure thing, sir. Please come in." Wilson turned around and nearly tripped over his chair. Henry had to catch him to keep him from falling. Wilson was shaking.

Everyone crowded into the house, and Wilson started rifling through his clothes, pretending to look for his papers.

Being free and black in the South—anywhere, really—was like living your entire life on the edge of a cliff. One false step and you fall back into slavery. All it took were missing freedom papers, the commission of a crime, false accusations, or some mixture of the three. Henry wondered how this rogue had found out about Wilson's missing papers.

"Listen, he's got papers. I seen 'em," Henry said. "I'll vouch for him."

The skinny-necked man laughed, and Henry wanted to punch him in the face. "*You* vouch for him?" the man exclaimed. "Might as well ask the family dog to vouch for him."

Henry made a threatening move forward and the man shuffled back a step. One of the policemen reached for his club, hanging from his belt. Wilson put a gentle, restraining hand on Henry's chest and gave him a look that warned him not to do anything foolish. But Henry was sick and tired of not doing anything. Everyone told him to watch his mouth, watch his attitude, watch his behavior. He was tired of watching. He stood around and watched his brothers and sisters divvied up like furniture. He wasn't going to stand around and watch Wilson have his freedom stolen away.

"This don't make no sense," Wilson said, rummaging through his clothes for a third time. "I saw my papers just the other day."

"He's a black liar! A black liar!" said the skinny-necked man.

"You better come with us," said the taller policeman, grabbing Wilson by the right arm. Henry could see Wilson's entire body tense at the policeman's touch, but the overseer didn't fight back. He knew better.

"Where you takin' him?" Henry asked, moving into the doorway and blocking their way.

"Step aside, this ain't no business of yours," said the taller policeman.

Henry didn't budge.

"Do as the man asks, Henry," said Wilson. "We'll get this sorted. Don't you worry, we'll get this sorted."

Henry turned sideways, giving them barely enough room to pass. He stared daggers at the skinny-necked guy, who diverted his eyes. Henry could stir fear in men like him, but that was as far as his power went.

Wilson looked over his shoulder as he went down the steps. "Talk to Mr. Barret 'bout this. He'll sort this out."

That's right, Henry thought. That's right, Master Barret will help. All free blacks had to be careful, and one of the ways to be careful was to make sure you had white folk in power who could speak up for you. Master Barret would do that. Henry was sure of it.

"I'll talk to him for ya this very night!" Henry shouted. Then he leaned against a post and watched them lead Wilson away. That was really all he could do.

11

Richmond
March 23, 1849
8:15 a.m.

The horse wouldn't move fast enough. John Allen provided brutal encouragement with his horse quirt, a two-tongued whip, but his animal kept slogging. Head bobbing, legs straining, the horse struggled to pick up speed on the steep, muddy street. John Allen cursed the Richmond hills, he cursed his horse, and he cursed Samuel Smith.

John Allen's curses didn't work any better than his quirt, but that didn't prevent him from screaming in his horse's ears. He considered running to the train on foot, but he knew how unforgiving a muddy road could be for anyone, four legs or two.

The train was scheduled to leave Richmond at eight o'clock, and John Allen was well aware that the minute hand had already raced past that hour. The clock didn't have to contend with mud, so nothing slowed it down. But he also knew the train was notorious for being behind schedule. He was counting on it. He had a runaway to snag.

John Allen believed he was the true master at the factory, punishing slaves when they wandered off. Losing time, they called it! He recently caught Obadiah Johnson losing time, and he had made him pay with a good whipping. But if he had his way, slaves would lose more than time. Losing a finger would teach them not to wander. That's what his pappy would say. John Allen could control a man as easily as a horse. Slaves, horses, even slave owners, they were all animals to him, and they all felt pain. They feared it. Pappy taught him that if you are the master of pain and the master of fear, you are the master of men.

His right arm ached from the constant thrashing with the quirt. If he reached the train in time and caught the runaway, Samuel Smith would be next in line for a whipping.

The ground leveled off when John Allen reached Broad Street, and he forced his horse to the left, digging in his heels and flashing the quirt. The horse moved into a canter and then a gallop, with two dogs in hot pursuit and a couple of men off to the side of the street urging him to slow down.

Up ahead was the train, just beginning to chug forward. The whistle sounded, smoke poured out of its large, funnel-shaped smoke stack, and the mass of steel strained to move. The train inched forward, and it was going to take awhile for the locomotive to build up enough steam to outrun a horse. He figured he had plenty of time to race alongside the train's cab and flag the locomotive to a stop.

He was so focused on the train that he didn't see a man push a cart of coal out of a side street and directly into his path. But his horse saw the obstacle, panicked, and tried to stop. John Allen kept moving forward—in mid-air. He shot out of the saddle and reached out for the horse's neck with one hand, still gripping the reins with the other. The horse lost its footing in the mud, and a thousand pounds of flesh thudded sideways onto the road, shaking the ground. He felt the burn of leather as the reins slid out of his hand, noticed he was airborne for one tick, and landed on his left side in the man's cart. The side of his face crumpled against a clump of coal.

Bystanders rushed in from all sides.

"You coulda killed somebody!"

"You don't own the street!"

Ignoring their judgments, John Allen moved onto his aching back, the wind knocked out of him. He stared up at the blue sky and waited for his breath to return. By the time he sat up, the train had already moved far down the tracks, and his horse had gone in the opposite direction. Slowly, achingly, he climbed out of the cart, picked up his hat and hobbled to the side of the street. Taking a seat on a wooden crate, he fished a pouch of tobacco from his pocket, cursed his foul luck, and contemplated his next move.

While he sat there, who should walk out of the nearby telegraph office but Samuel Smith. John Allen stood up and stepped directly into his path. If Smith wanted a fight, he was ready for it. But Smith just gave him that smirk of his, tipped his hat, and strolled around him.

"I know what you done!" John Allen called out.

Samuel stopped, turned. He removed the cigar from the corner of his mouth and tapped off some ashes into the street. "I just sent a telegram to my dear mother. Is that what you're talking about?"

"You know what I mean. I know what you done."

Samuel just shrugged, jammed the cigar back in his mouth, and went on his merry way.

John Allen stared at the departing figure, wishing he could put a bullet in his back. He wasn't done with Samuel Smith.

The train rolled along with Henry in the freight car, alone in the dark. He nibbled on a biscuit and sipped his water sparingly. He also found the gimlet handle and drilled three more small holes in the top of the box to let in more air. But even with the additional breathing holes, it was like an oven in the box, with sweat drenching his entire shirt and dripping down his forehead. He fanned himself with his hat almost continuously and dabbed his face with a little water. He couldn't spare much, not with such a long trek ahead.

The train, part of the Richmond, Fredericksburg, and Potomac line, was the first link in his journey to Philadelphia. It headed north for the Potomac River, about a seventy-five-mile journey that would take roughly four hours. In total, Samuel had estimated that the trip to Philadelphia would be twenty-four hours. An entire day in a box at the mercy of outside forces.

Henry was exhausted, but he didn't want to doze. The train would be making many stops to add freight, and he didn't want to be caught making sounds in his sleep. So he forced himself to stay alert, running spirituals through his mind.

The tallest tree in Paradise, the Christians
   call the tree of life,
And I hope that trump might blow me home
   to the new Jerusalem.
Blow your trumpet, Gabriel, blow louder,
   louder,
And I hope that trumpet might blow me home
   to the new Jerusalem.

Paul and Silas bound in jail, sing God's
   praise both night and day,
And I hope that trump might blow me home
   to my new Jerusalem.
Blow your trumpet, Gabriel, blow louder,
   louder,
And I hope that trumpet might blow me home
   to the new Jerusalem.

*Henry and Nancy were running. They ran,
hand-in-hand, down a crowded street. Nancy,
lifting the hem of her long dress with her right
hand, was laughing—the finest sound in the
world. Her hand was soft, amazingly soft for a
woman who spent her days as a laundress.*

*Henry and Nancy didn't stop running until
they were around a corner. Henry drew Nancy
toward him, reeled her in until she was up
against him, his left hand settling on her lower
back. He leaned in toward her.*

"Henry!" she said, laughing. "We ain't alone."

"We will be."

Henry led Nancy into an alleyway running alongside an old, dilapidated brick building. Once again, he pulled Nancy in until her body was up against his. He could feel her contours through the thick clothing.

"This better?"

Nancy looked around. She stared back into Henry's eyes. She nodded.

Henry was leaning forward to kiss her when he heard the dog. He looked up, and a Cuban bloodhound bounded down the alleyway. Cuban bloodhounds were nothing like the peaceable bloodhounds with folds upon folds of loose skin. The Cubans were taut tigers with short, cropped ears, a powerful neck, and jaws that could bite through bone.

Henry grabbed Nancy's hands and they ran again, this time farther down the alleyway until they reached a dead end. He shielded Nancy with his body and turned, throwing up his arm for protection. All he saw was teeth and fur.

Henry was jolted awake by the sudden lurch of the train. He looked around at the darkness, ran his hand along one of the walls, and thanked God he wasn't in an alley with a Cuban blood-hound on his back. He wasn't sure how long he had slept, but it was long enough for him to wake up with a sore neck and a knee aching for relief.

Henry vowed to stay awake. He couldn't afford

to drift away again. So he fanned his face and sang softly to himself, the sound smothered by the rolling of steel on rails.

> "There's no rain to wet you—Oh yes, I want
>   to go home, want to go home.
> There's no sun to burn you—Oh yes, I want
>   to go home, want to go home.
> There's no whips a-crackin'—Oh yes, I want
>   to go home, want to go home.
> No more slavery in the kingdom—Oh yes, I
>   want to go home, want to go home.
> No evildoers in the kingdom—Oh yes, I want
>   to go home, want to go home."

12

Richmond
June 1836: Thirteen Years Earlier

Henry knew there would be trouble, but not this soon. It was only Wilson's first day back at the factory.

"You workin' too slow, old man!" chided one of the slaves passing through the stemmer's room. Henry was among the group moving through the room on the way to dinner, and he looked at Wilson Gregory to gauge his old friend's reaction. Wilson acted like he didn't even hear a word. He kept his head down and continued to work, plucking leaves off of tobacco stems.

Wilson Gregory was just another slave.

Free blacks like Wilson, caught without their freedom papers, sometimes lingered in jail for weeks, months, or even a full year. But with Master Barret's influence, Wilson was released from prison in only a week. There was a catch, however. Master Barret and the judge had worked out a compromise with the man from Georgia who claimed that Wilson was his escaped slave. Barret agreed to compensate the Georgian, and Wilson Gregory would become Barret's slave. Simple as all that. Wilson could remain at the tobacco factory, but only as a common worker, because a slave could not be an overseer, of course.

After six years as overseer, Wilson had made his share of enemies on the factory floor.

"You don't produce, and I'll reduce your wages," taunted another slave, this one named Pike. "You don't produce, you get reduced . . . don't produce, get reduced."

"Don't produce, get reduced" was one of Wilson's favorite threats, although he almost never enforced it. Pike was one of the few slaves who actually saw his wages cut by Wilson for insubordination.

Pike glared at Wilson, waiting for a response. He was young and strong, about twenty-four years old, so Wilson was wise not to react. But when

Pike saw that he didn't stir so much as a glance from Wilson, he slipped up behind him, put his hand on the back of his neck, and squeezed. Wilson wheeled around and struck out, clipping the guy in the ear; he still had some fight in him, and he moved faster than Henry thought possible. Pike staggered back a step, holding his stinging ear and staring in disbelief.

"You gonna answer for that, old man." Pike charged Wilson.

Henry was across the room in an instant, locking the younger man's arms from behind, and Pike became as mad as a bull, shaking him from side to side. Then Pike's friend jumped into the fracas and started pounding on Henry, thumping him on the back of the head, and Henry broke loose to take a swing at this new adversary, connecting to the side of his mouth. A sharp pain shot across his knuckles. Two other slaves, Henry couldn't even see who they were, started swinging wildly, while everyone in the room was on their feet, hooting and cheering. Henry hit someone in the gut, hoping it wasn't a friend, but it was hard to tell in the tangle of puffing, grunting men, locked together like wrestlers.

The fight was over in a matter of minutes, but Henry was totally spent, and he had bruises on the back of his head, a split lip, and stinging knuckles. He tasted blood.

He would always wonder if it was this fight that

led Master Barret to hire the hardest overseer yet seen in their factory. If Henry had known the future, maybe he would have stood back and let Wilson take his lumps. Anything would have been better than what they got.

Two days later, the entire factory was given the news. Wilson's replacement would be a young tough, only about three years older than Henry.

The next overseer would be a man named John Allen.

Nancy didn't know if she could wait forever for Henry Brown to come calling.

She didn't mind that Henry was quiet; that was part of his appeal: a strong, solid presence. After her previous ordeal working in the fields of South Carolina for a villain named Dr. Stephenson, she wanted a man with strength. Deep down, she knew that Henry would never be allowed to use his strength in her defense, but she still craved a protector, someone who could stand between her and the Dr. Stephensons of the world. She sensed that in Henry, even though most of their interactions had only taken place at a distance— every Sunday in the church choir, stealing glances. He had broad shoulders and a chest that looked like it could survive the strike of a sledgehammer. But more importantly, she sensed an internal solidity, and his quietness heightened the effect.

But Nancy was beginning to wonder . . .

After the Jones's wedding, she thought they had finally taken the first small step toward courtship. But here it was, three weeks to the day, and Henry had gone back to his old ways. Always hovering in the distance, his eyes constantly seeking her out. She was tired of this game.

It was another Sunday, and hundreds of black members of the First Baptist Church had packed the banks along the James River for baptism. A line of men and women stood in the water nearly waist-deep, all of them dressed in white and the women wearing bright white headwraps; several deacons stood nearby, all dressed in black. In the distance, a group of white families had collected on the side of the hill, curious onlookers drawn to the music and the African style. White fathers held their children in their arms, lifting them up so they could get a better look. The day was picnic perfect.

"The water is wide, brothers and sisters!" declared Deacon Will. He stood close to shore, about thigh-deep in the water, and spoke to the crowd on the bank. The white leadership of First Baptist had appointed him as one of the black deacons to shepherd the Negro segment of the congregation.

"Oh, call upon his mighty name!" came a shout.

"Grant it, Almighty God."

Raised hands swayed from side to side like wheat.

Deacon Will pressed forward. "But the Lord, He has a ship to carry us across to the far shore! He has a ship! And this ship is bound for Glory. Can I hear hallelujah?"

"Hallelujah!"

"Oh, help him, Jesus!"

"Call upon His holy name!"

The amen corner was roused.

"And this ship has a mast in the middle, and that mast, my brothers and sisters, is in the shape of a cross!"

Nancy closed her eyes and let herself be swept away, way out to sea, far from her troubles on land.

"And on that cross, there's a billowing sail! Can I hear an amen? The sail takes in all our sorrows; it captures our sorrows like it captures the wind. And it carries us across the water! It carries us to Glory, oh shout hallelujah!"

Brother John—with his eyes squeezed shut—started jumping up and down like he had springs in his shoes. Sister Melba wrung her hands and shook her head so hard that her hat nearly came flying off. Brother Jake fell on his knees and buried his face in his hands.

Deacon Will was just getting warmed up. So was the crowd, and so was Sister Nancy. She leaned back, extended her arms wide, and looked straight up in the sky, picturing herself on the ship, cutting across the ocean, free as a bird.

"The water is also *deep,* brothers and sisters! The water is deeper than the grave. And when we are buried beneath the waters, my brothers and sisters, when we are buried in the deep, when our ship sinks to the darkest depths, God reaches into the waters, He reaches in with His mighty hand, He reaches in and scoops us out of the watery grave, He raises us to safety and new life, glory hallelujah!" Deacon Will paused to wipe his brow with the handkerchief that he kept clutched in his right hand during the entire exhortation.

Brother Jasper moved through the crowd, shaking hands with everyone he could and exclaiming, "I'm so glad! I'm so glad!" Sister Sarah held both hands high in surrender. "There's a fire burnin'! A fire's a-burnin' in my heart!"

Under the open sky along the river, close to thirty people were being dunked in the James River, for the church had been attracting many new members from the steadily increasing slave and free black population in Richmond. Their numbers were beginning to make the white segment of the congregation feel mighty nervous.

When the baptism celebration was over, Nancy came back to earth. She moved through the crowd, her eyes still fishing for Henry Brown.

"Hello, Sister Nancy, praise God, praise God, *praise God!*"

Nancy whirled around to face the voice, but she already knew who it was.

"Glory hallelujah, Sister Nancy." Making his way through the crowd was Ned Cooper, a slave who certainly had no hesitation when it came to approaching Nancy or talking her ear off. He also had no fear of singing, even though his voice should have been a good reason to show humility. But Ned never seemed to hesitate about anything. He began to sing as he made his way to Nancy: "Marching up the heavenly road, marching up the heavenly road, I'm bound to fight until I die! Marching up the heavenly road!"

Ned extended an arm. "Sister Nancy, would you do me the pleasure of accompanyin' me to the cookshop?"

Nancy hesitated and cast a glance around the crowd once again. Henry was nowhere to be seen, so she turned back to Ned, who was pretty much Henry's complete opposite. Where Henry was powerfully built, Ned was thin as a stick. Where Henry was shy, Ned bordered on the cocky. Where Henry had the voice of an angel, Ned had the voice of a frog.

The only thing Ned and Henry shared in common was their work, for they both toiled at the same tobacco factory. But even that was different in nature, for Ned had a way of working the system. He was an aggressive, even ambitious slave, whose master allowed him to "hire out." He worked through one of the many professional slave brokers in Richmond, who made arrangements each year for labor between slaves and employers. His clothes also showed flair, and on this day he wore a green silk vest, a wide-brim hat, and shoes with buckles as large as doorknockers.

Ned was a rooster who strutted his feathers and made plenty of noise. His bluster seemed too much for Nancy, but perhaps Ned was the kind of man she really needed. Perhaps she needed a crafty man, not a stalwart man.

Ned grinned and continued to offer her his arm. "My arm's feelin' a might lonesome, Sister Nancy. I hear Sister Letty has outdone herself with the fixins' on her table today. So please, won't ya join me?"

Nancy looked around one more time. Still no sign of Henry. She smiled awkwardly at Ned, who continued to beam back, and finally she just gave in and latched onto his arm. They headed away from the river into the slave neighborhoods and wound up at Letty's back-alley cookshop, a small hole-in-the-wall joint where slaves and free blacks gathered and swapped stories. Living in her master's home across the river, Nancy had never had much chance to explore the cookshops and crannies of Richmond's slave districts, so she found it new and exciting.

Those who did overwork and made a little extra money could get a good meal at a cookshop for only a handful of pennies. Letty, a free black, served the best-tasting barbecued pig's feet in all of Richmond, but she was also known for her seafood gumbo. Letty's place consisted of four wobbly tables, and she could have packed in plenty more people every day if she had wanted to expand; she just didn't want to draw attention to her operation for fear of bringing the authorities down on her. As long as cookshop proprietors kept a low profile, whites would often turn a blind eye to the many black operations tucked away throughout the city. What usually got cookshops closed down was too much noise or too much liquor, although one popular joint was recently shut down when white riverboat men started showing up. Race mixing was not the kind of gumbo that Richmond elites could stomach.

Letty did all of the cooking, and it was obvious from her size that she enjoyed her food as much as the next person. Her husband Martin did the serving, a fast-moving, fast-talking man whose constant movement kept him thin, at least in his legs, chest, and neck. In between his bird legs and sunken chest, he had a potbelly that looked as if he had strapped on one of Letty's mixing bowls underneath his shirt. This was the only evidence that Martin stopped moving long enough to enjoy his wife's cooking. Even when he was sliding a plate in front of Ned and another in front of Nancy, he barely slowed down.

"I'm gonna buy my freedom, Sister Nancy, just as sure as you're sittin' there," said Ned. He wiped the grease from his mouth before snatching up another piece of chicken.

"If Ned says he's gonna do it, he'll do it," said Martin, sticking his head out of the kitchen door and adding his two cents' worth. Nancy and Ned were the only customers in the cookshop that afternoon, so Martin and Letty had only one conversation on which to eavesdrop.

"What'll ya do once you're free?" Nancy asked.

"I got big plans. Big plans. When I'm free, I'm gonna head on up New York way, start me one of my own cookshops. A real smart place, too."

"Just don't start one in Richmond, Neddy." That was Martin again, sticking his head from the kitchen. "We don't need no more competition."

"You don't worry about that. I'm goin' north where I can be free as a bird."

"Just watch yer step," said Martin. "Birds wind up in cages."

"And on plates. Could you bring me another chicken leg, Martin?"

"Sure thing, Neddy."

Ned proceeded to go into excruciating detail about the kind of food he'd serve in his cook-shop, the kind of customers he'd have, the kind of music he'd bring in, and so on. Nancy admired his dreams, but she wished he had asked her something about herself. If he had bothered, he might have discovered that she dreamed of being reunited with her parents, whom she hadn't seen since they were sold off the plantation before she was five years old. If Ned had any interest in courting, he should find out if she had parents around to ask their blessing.

Nancy wondered if she fit into his big plans and whether he was fixing to buy her freedom as well. Just the possibility of freedom made him seem much more tolerable, appealing even. Ned was certainly a cut above the boy who took a fancy to her several years back on the Stephenson plantation. That boy thought he could use conjuring to get her to fall for him, and he even tried putting a spell on her by wearing the bones of a dead frog around his neck.

"Mark my words, Nancy, I'm gonna buy my freedom," Ned said again. " 'Cause when Ned Cooper sets his mind to somethin', he gets what he wants."

Ned looked at Nancy pointedly as he said this.

"But some things can't be bought," Nancy said just as pointedly.

Ned grinned. "When you're right, you're right, Sister Nancy."

"She's right!" came Letty's voice from around the corner, from deep within the kitchen where she scrubbed away at plates.

"You watch yer step around this one, Miss Nancy," said Martin. He rushed by their table and snatched up an empty plate without even breaking stride. "He don't take no for an answer."

"Speaking of which, there's somethin' I been meanin' to ask ya, Sister Nancy."

Nancy nearly choked on her okra. Surely, Ned Cooper wasn't going to talk marriage. Not now. Not here. Ned wasn't one to beat around the bush, but this was too much, even for him.

"Can't it wait, Ned?"

"No, it can't."

Ned's statement was so surprising that even Letty set down her soapy plate and peeked her head around the kitchen door. Ned hadn't gotten down on one knee yet, so Nancy's heart hadn't completely stopped.

"Nancy, there's a fancy dinner party bein' held some weeks down the line. I was wonderin' if you'd do me the honor of accompanyin' me."

Nancy was so relieved that Ned wasn't talking marriage that she almost accepted the offer on the spot. But she hesitated just long enough to gather her wits.

"A fancy dinner party? The only way white folks'll let me into somethin' like that is if I'm wearin' an apron and holdin' a tray."

"That's where you're wrong, Sister Nancy. This dinner party, it's just for slaves and free black folk. I'm helpin' put it all together, and we got the whole basement of the Washington Hotel set aside."

"How in the world would white folks be allowin' such a thing?"

"This is Richmond, Sister Nancy. It ain't the plantation."

That much was true. Since Nancy had come to Richmond, she had been shocked by all of the ways for black men and women to mingle in addition to Sunday church. Besides the cook-shops and grog houses, slaves gathered at grocery stores or places of business like James's cake shop, where they whiled away what little free time they had, talking and playing checkers or throwing dice. There were even small dinner parties and dances, secret frolics held in tenement rooms, away from the prying eyes of the city's patrollers. But a formal dinner? That was daring even by Richmond standards.

"You mean ya'll gonna be dressed fancy for somethin' other than churchgoin'?" The very idea was beyond words, beyond belief.

"That's what I'm sayin'. We gonna get some fine music, too—our very own church choir'll be there singin', if I can make all the proper arrangements. So it's gonna be real respectable, Sister Nancy. No dancin' or drinkin' and carryin' on."

"Amen!" shouted Martin from the kitchen. "For you Baptists, dancin' is for devil legs."

"This is a once-in-a-life chance," Ned said.

"But if the choir'll be singin', I'll be there anyway, Brother Ned."

"That's right, that's right. But if I could escort ya there, it'd be doubly special."

"I don't know, Brother Ned. Let me think on this."

If the choir was going to be singing, that also meant Henry would be there. She didn't know if she could hurt Henry by being seen on the arm of another man right smack in front of him—especially if that man was Ned Cooper. But it was mighty tempting. If Ned could organize something like this, he had surprising qualities. Still, something held Nancy back from giving him a quick and easy answer. To his credit, Ned didn't push the question any further that day at the cookshop. Perhaps he didn't want to force a "no" out of her, right there in front of Letty and Martin.

Of course, that didn't stop him from asking her the same question every week after church. Sunday service always ended the same—with Ned Cooper walking her out the front door of the church, always flitting around, trying to impress her with his grand plans, and asking if she would accompany him to the fancy party. With the dinner party only one week away, she could not keep Ned at bay much longer.

"Henry, if you don't ask her, I'm gonna ask her for you," said James.

"Maybe you could send your niece to do one of your magic tricks," groused Henry. He was almost as disgusted with James as he was with himself.

"Listen, Ella's trick was the only thing that brought you and Nancy together so far."

Henry knew he was right. He and James were standing outside the First Baptist Church, a good distance from the prying ears of any church members. It was a hot afternoon, and perspiration beaded on Henry's forehead.

"I dunno, James. She seems fixed on Ned Cooper."

"I'm not so much sure she's fixed on him as *he's* fixed on her. Like a leech. And believe me, I know leeches. I spent the good part of a year slapping them on folks."

"So I should just stroll on up to her? Just like that?"

"That's the way it's done."

"But Ned's always around her after church."

"Then ask her to step aside to talk private."

"But why do I even need to be askin' her to this doings? We're both gonna be there to sing, so what's the purpose of askin' for me to escort her there?"

James let out a long, weary sigh. "Henry, don't you understand the situation? I heard tell that Ned Cooper has been trying to coax her into attending the affair with him as her escort. You need to stay a step ahead of him."

"Then he probably done asked her already."

"He probably has. But if he has, she hasn't accepted him yet, from what I've heard. That's a good sign for you."

Henry could never work up the nerve to walk up to Nancy when she was surrounded by her female friends, so how could James expect him to do it when Ned Cooper was standing right there? The situation was ripe for humiliation.

"You can't give way to Ned without even trying," said James. "It's in the nature of the He to pursue the She." That was one of James's favorite sayings.

Henry took out his white handkerchief and patted his forehead, which glistened.

"This may be your last chance, Henry."

Henry dabbed his upper lip, folded his handkerchief methodically, and stuffed it into his coat pocket. Perhaps James was right. If he didn't do something soon, Nancy would be forever out of his reach. *It's in the nature of the He to pursue the She.* Shading his eyes in the bright sun, Henry looked around for Nancy. He knew what she was wearing today—a yellow dress with a yellow bonnet. His eyes tracked the many multi-colored smocks, skipping across a couple of other ladies in yellow, like a bee looking for just the right landing place. His eyes finally landed on Nancy.

Henry drew out his handkerchief again, for his forehead had become a veritable waterfall of perspiration. Nancy was standing there with Ned

Cooper, just as he feared. This set the waterworks flowing even more. If he could harness the sweat flowing down his face, he could power a gristmill. Ned looked dapper with his red embroidered waistcoat, black jacket, and top hat. Henry noticed how worn the cuffs of his own coat were looking.

Henry took several steps in Nancy's direction before stopping. He glanced over his shoulder and saw James leaning up against a tree. James was watching. And waiting.

After adjusting his tight collar, he charged ahead; and when he suddenly appeared in front of Nancy, she gave a start. The last time that he and she had come this close, it was Ella's doing.

"Afternoon, Sister Nancy." He tipped his hat.

"Afternoon, Brother Henry. You know Mister Ned Cooper, I reckon."

"Surely do. Afternoon, Brother Ned."

"Hello, Henry." Ned didn't smile. Henry also noticed he made a point of not addressing him as "Brother Henry."

He tried to keep his eyes on Nancy, but he couldn't do it for very long before he found himself gazing down at his feet.

"Can I talk with ya, Miss Nancy?" he asked his shoes.

"Why of course, Brother Henry."

Ned butted in. "But Miss Nancy, I was thinkin' we could take a stroll on down Broad Street."

"It'll only be a moment."

Ned put his hand on Nancy's forearm. "But Miss Nancy, if I'm to be takin' ya to the dinner party next week, I thought a stroll would only be fittin'."

The words couldn't have hit Henry any harder than if Ned had pulled back and struck him in the jaw. Henry reached for his handkerchief again and mopped his forehead and upper lip.

"Ned Cooper, now you can just wait," Nancy said, flaring up a little. She slipped out of Ned's grip, took Henry by the arm, and led him aside—to the shade of an elm tree. Henry was dying inside. He blamed James for this.

"What's it you wanted to say to me, Henry?"

Henry looked over at Ned, who had sidled over a few feet closer, glaring at him, daring him.

"I don't reckon it makes any sense now," he said.

"Was ya gonna ask me about the party?"

Henry was shocked by Nancy's boldness. He nodded and stared back down at his shoes; he probably had every scuff on them memorized by now. "Yes, ma'am."

Nancy put a hand on Henry's arm, sending a swift, sweet sensation through his skin. "I wish ya coulda asked me sooner."

Henry didn't hear the meaning in her words. He was just trying to figure out a way to make his exit.

"Thank ya, Sister Nancy, but I best be off."

Before Nancy could say another word, Henry wheeled around and moved away at a quick clip. *It's in the nature of the He to be humiliated by the She* was all he could think. He didn't know why he ever listened to James.

13

Richmond
March 23, 1849
9:10 a.m.

John Allen's horse slogged up another steep incline, this one leading to the corner of Cary and Fifth, where William Barret's house looked down on Shockoe Bottom. After getting tossed on his head, John Allen had tracked down his runaway horse and decided he better report the slave escape to Master Barret. This time, Allen allowed his animal the luxury of moving slowly and methodically to maintain its footing on the steep, muddy road. John Allen was still in a hurry, but not enough to risk another tumble.

The Richmond landscape was a reflection of the city's social stratification. The city had seven hills, with the high ground claimed by the gentry, whose stately homes looked down on the valley below like masters of the world. The wealth and size of these hilltop homes made John Allen sick; he, more than anyone, deserved one of these mansions.

John Allen tied up his horse and marched around to the front of the house, then pushed open the black, wrought-iron gate that enclosed the small front yard. A short, steep flight of stairs took him up to the large front door, flanked on either side by a Grecian column. He pounded on the door, and a house slave, Fanny, answered.

"I'm needin' to talk to Mr. Barret. Now!" He barked his command and barged into the house, scattering the three dogs that greeted him at the door. Fanny went running for Mr. Barret, but she didn't need to run very far. Mr. Barret had already appeared in the foyer, a looming presence. Something was wrong.

Fanny disappeared into a back room, but John Allen knew she was probably still within earshot. Snooping. They all snooped.

"State your business," Mr. Barret said harshly. He crossed his arms and struck a wide stance, as if trying to block a doorway.

"We got reason to believe one of the slaves escaped, sir."

Mr. Barret's mouth became pinched. John Allen did not intimidate easily, but he instinctively shrank back. This wasn't going according to plan.

"You think a slave escaped?" Mr. Barret said.

"Well yes, I guess you could say he's escaped. In a manner of speaking."

"So you know about it, sir?" News traveled faster than he thought.

William Barret took another step closer, crowding John Allen, who slinked back. "Yes. He escaped in a box, Mr. Allen."

"A box, sir? Which way has he headed?"

"I suppose that will be decided by his Maker."

His Maker? What in the world is that supposed to mean?

"Sir, I don't understand. If Obadiah is on the run, what does God have to do with it?"

"Obadiah is in a coffin."

John Allen still didn't get it. "You mean he's dead, sir?"

"That's the most common reason people are placed in coffins."

John Allen went white as a ghost.

"Obadiah Johnson died last evening of the beating you dished out a couple of weeks ago," Mr. Barret explained.

John Allen shrank back another step. He recalled the beating that Mr. Barret spoke about, although he could remember it only in fragments, for he had been plenty drunk. He hoped Mr. Barret was unaware that he had repeated the beating just a couple of days ago. Obadiah had been exaggerating his injuries to miss work at the factory, he was sure of it, and Obadiah needed to be taught a lesson. Use pain and fear wisely, and you can control anyone.

"I don't understand, sir," John Allen said. "Obadiah seemed healthy enough when I checked on him the other day."

"Is that why you whipped him again?"

John Allen just stood there, speechless. Eventually, he managed a feeble defense. "Whoever told you that I did such a thing is lyin', sir, if you'll excuse me for sayin' so, sir."

William Barret upped the intensity of his glare. "Do you know how much a healthy male, age twenty-six, strong back, good teeth, costs me?"

"Don't rightly know, sir. Never bought a slave."

"You'll find out soon enough. You're paying for this one out of your wages."

"I'm truly sorry, sir. It ain't gonna happen again, sir."

"That's right. It won't."

Eager to be off the premises, John Allen hurried toward the front door before he could be completely humiliated.

"One other thing, Mr. Allen."

"Sir?"

"Do anything like this again, and you'll be the one on the other end of a whip. Understand?"

John Allen blanched. "Yes, sir. My apologies, sir."

Now his humiliation was complete.

• • •

James had a front row seat to the unfolding disaster. His cake shop was located on Broad Street, just down from where Henry Brown's box was loaded on the train. He had seen it all from a distance. He saw John Allen checking out the freight car and arguing with Samuel. But even worse, Samuel had stopped by to report what John Allen said. "I know what you done." Those were Allen's exact words.

Samuel suggested they continue with their days, same as normal, but James wondered if it would be wiser to take the next train out of town. He spent the morning working on a cake ordered by Mr. Brewer, a wealthy railroad man; but the thought of railroads pushed James's mind in the direction of Henry, whose train was partway to the Potomac by now. In fact, everywhere he looked were reminders of Henry. Along one table were several tin cake boxes, each with the large word "Cake" painted on the front. The boxes had small ventilating holes to keep mold from growing on the cakes, and that reminded James of Henry's box, with its own air holes.

James had vowed that he would never put the life of a slave in his hands again, not after what had happened when he tried to help three slaves escape a few years back. He wished he had remained faithful to that vow.

James went into the back kitchen and took the

cake out of the oven, setting it on a wooden trivet on the long counter. He grabbed a piece of straw, folded it in half, and poked it into the thickest part of the cake. When he pulled out the straw, it slid out cleanly. The cake was done. He had just started to clean up the mess when he heard the door of the shop open. Normally, the opening of the door meant either fresh customers or fresh gossip, but today he wondered whether it could be the police. He contemplated slipping out the back door.

"James! You here, James?"

It was a woman's voice — Fanny, a house slave who worked for William Barret. James had taken a cotton to her, and they had been seeing each other regularly now. Fanny had no idea that Henry Brown was on the run, and James didn't let her in on the secret. Better to keep it that way, because Fanny had a knack for spreading news faster than any newspaper hound or telegraph operator.

Wiping his hands with a towel, he emerged from the back room to find Fanny rushing into his arms, her smile as wide as the sky. She planted a kiss on his lips and then pulled away, giving him a quizzical look.

"Somethin' wrong, sweet thing?"

James didn't answer. He just stared down into Fanny's soft, dark eyes. She was a good head shorter than him—pretty and petite. Fanny moved to his side and massaged his right bicep.

"You're awful tense, sweet one."

"I know." James leaned over and planted a kiss on her forehead—almost a perfunctory move.

"Lordy, that was one passionate kiss, my man," Fanny said sarcastically as she broke into laughter. "Somethin's clearly botherin' you, but I got glad tidings to cheer ya."

"Oh?"

"John Allen's been made the fool. I heard it all with mine own ears."

This news struck a nerve. "John Allen's been made the fool?"

"That's what I said, honey. That blame fool John Allen came to Master Barret to report that Obadiah had gone and escaped. Can you believe all that? He thought a dead man was escapin'!"

"What are you talking about? Who died?"

"Obadiah! Didn't ya hear that Obadiah Johnson passed on last night?"

"Yes, but . . ." James was trying to piece it all together in his mind. "You mean John Allen thought *Obadiah* escaped?"

"That's what I'm sayin'!"

"And he didn't know that Obadiah had died?"

"John Allen found out about Obadiah's demise from Master Barret his self. It was a wonder to behold, glory be!"

Slowly, the words sank in, and James felt the tension drain away. John Allen had never really suspected Henry of escaping. The fugitive was

Obadiah Johnson. It was Obadiah all along!

"Can you believe that durned fool?" Fanny hooked arms with James.

"What did Mr. Barret say to Allen?"

"John Allen won't be so easy and free with the whip in the future. Mr. Barret give him an earful."

James laughed out loud and gave Fanny a powerful hug, lifting her from her feet and swinging her around the room.

"Now that's my man!" Fanny exclaimed. "Where you been till now?"

James took Fanny by the hand and drew her into the back room, where the Brewers' cake sat on the counter, fresh from the oven and smelling sweet.

"Time to celebrate," he said, sinking a knife into the sponge cake.

"But James, ain't that baked up for a customer? A white family?"

"I can bake another any old time. It isn't every day that John Allen gets his head served on a platter."

"I love your cakes, sweet thing, but I have to say that John Allen's head on a platter is even sweeter. Praise God, you shoulda been listenin' to Mr. Barret as he—"

Fanny got no further as James slipped a bite of cake into her mouth.

The trip to the Potomac wore Henry down. The train stopped several times to take on more freight; and during one of the stops, Henry's box was shifted around to make room for additional boxes. In the process, he was flipped upside down once again. Henry wondered if the freight handler had done it on purpose, just to spite Samuel. The only consolation was that the boxcar was closed back up in no time, giving him the freedom to shift his position without worrying about anyone hearing him make noise.

With the clatter of the train—a hundred different sounds—Henry's movements were well covered. However, flipping his body was no easy task. It meant jamming his knees into his face, pulling himself into a tight ball, pushing off the box wall with his hands and feet, squirming and rotating like he was doing an upside-down somersault in slow motion, all while jammed tight in the box, his head scraping against the wood. It took about a half hour to pull off this contortionist stunt, and his neck ached from the effort. But he was right side up again, thank God. The intense strain of small movements left him breathing hard and wondering if he was suffocating again. He spared a little water to splash his face.

Twenty minutes later, they made another stop, and Henry couldn't believe his bad fortune. While shifting freight around, the handler flipped the box over, putting him on his head *again*. It was almost as if the cargo man was taunting him. Another half hour's work and Henry was back in an upright position, but his shirt was drenched from the sweat of exertion, his neck a bundle of tension and stress. The wound on his left hand had reopened and Henry could smell fresh blood.

The train passed through Fredericksburg, and by about noon it arrived at the Aquia Creek landing, where the creek met the Potomac River in northern Virginia. Aquia Creek landing was the end of the line for the Richmond, Fredericksburg, and Potomac Railroad, so the boxcars were emptied and freight lugged on board the awaiting steamboat. Henry could smell the water and the fish and the sweet, strong smoke of cigars; and he could hear the splash of water, as well as rhythmic, hollow, thumping sounds and the voices of so many workers and passengers.

As one final insult, his box was tumbled onto the cargo deck of the steamboat, and it landed upside down, of course. Only this time, his predicament was the most serious yet. On the steamboat, Henry's box wasn't placed in a dark, secluded space as it had been on the train. It was dropped on the open cargo deck, with passengers milling all around, so he couldn't make a sound. He couldn't even let out a groan. Trying to shift his position for a third time was out of the question. It was dreadful.

The steamboat moved out into the wide river, with the roar of the paddlewheel sounding like a cascading waterfall. Henry also heard the bells and the steam whistle, but he was most conscious of the sounds of passengers so close to him. The random noises of the steamboat would not be enough to cover up his sounds if he tried moving around.

The time dragged on, and Henry felt his eyes swelling as the blood rushed to his head. The veins on his temples filled with pressure. Very close by, people chatted in a carefree manner, while he lay in agony, upside down and slowly dying inside the box.

14

Richmond
July 1836: Thirteen Years Earlier

Henry tied his cravat in the reflection from a glass bowl in James's cake shop on Broad Street. "Can't believe you talked me into this. I already done made a fool of myself once."

"If you want a woman, you got to be prepared to make a fool of yourself at least a dozen times," James said. "You're just getting started."

James picked up his black walking stick and twirled it a couple of times before heading out the door with Henry right behind. There were rumors that the city was going to pass a law banning blacks from carrying walking sticks. Could be they didn't want blacks posing as wealthy gentlemen; or maybe they just feared that walking sticks made dangerous weapons should the Negro population rise up in rebellion.

"What if Nancy's with Cooper all night?" Henry asked as they approached the entrance to the Washington Hotel in the heart of Richmond.

"Doesn't mean you can't talk to her. Look for your chance."

"I don't know, just don't know 'bout this."

Even though the church choir was singing at the big event, and Henry had one of the best voices, he had vowed to stay as far away as possible from Ned Cooper's dinner party. But James wore him down, and now here they were. The party was not much of a secret, being held in the basement of the Washington Hotel; and when Henry and James strolled into the large room, the place was filled with sound—laughter and shouting—and the air was hot, almost stifling. Henry was tempted to turn around and leave on the spot, and he might have done so if James hadn't been there beside him.

"You're not leaving here until you talk with her," said James, just seconds before he vanished into the crowd, in search of female companionship of his own. James had a sweet tooth for cake and an even sweeter tooth for women.

Henry surveyed the overheated room, which was packed with sprucely dressed black men and women. Some of the men wore coats borrowed from relatives so they wouldn't show up wearing their Sunday go-to-meeting clothes—as Henry had done. One man told Henry he was going to "borrow" his master's son's new suit coat—figuring the son wouldn't miss it for one night. That seemed like something his brother Edward would have done, which brought a smile to Henry's face.

"You sure look happy tonight, Henry Brown," came a voice from his right. It was Mary May, a woman his age whom he suspected had designs on him. She was a short, stout woman, with a commanding presence and a voice to match. At first glance, you might think that Mary May was wearing a hoop dress, but that was all Mary beneath the fabric.

"Hello, Miss Mary," Henry said with a bow.

Henry stared around the room, taking it all in. Round tables were scattered all about, each one covered in a fine white tablecloth with nice plates and tableware—just like at the white dinner parties Henry observed at the Hermitage Plantation growing up. If Ned Cooper had a hand in organizing such an event, Henry had to admit he was impressed. Ned had style, and Henry felt so much like a bumpkin, so out of place. He surveyed the place for any sign of Nancy.

"Lookin' for anyone in particular?" Mary May asked.

"Hmm? No, just lookin' 'round."

"Why you need be lookin' 'round when I'm down here?"

Henry felt his face warm. "Sorry."

Henry gazed down on Mary May; but when she beamed back up at him with gleaming, almost wild, possessive eyes, he shifted his focus to a spot just a few inches above her head. Henry could smell honeysuckle and rose, emanating from the petals that Mary had slipped down her bosom.

"You singin' tonight?" Mary May asked.

"Oh yes, ma'am. I'm singin'." Henry didn't elaborate. He didn't know what else to say.

"Eyes, eyes! Eyes down here, Henry," Mary May demanded with maternal insistence when his gaze wandered off again.

Mary May started in talking, something about how impressed she was with his singing voice. But he wasn't paying attention. His ears were alert for the sound of Nancy's distinctive laugh, but all he could pick up was the talk going around about Pete Lynch, a First Baptist member being punished for being seen gambling at the race-track—not an unusual activity for Richmond men, black or white, churchgoers or not.

"Eyes, eyes!" Mary May said once again, and Henry refocused.

"Sorry, Sister Mary."

"Fine weather we havin', ain't it?"

"Oh yes, ma'am. Real fine."

"Feel like rain comin', though. I can always sense it comin'."

"Ya don't say."

After the two of them explored everything that could possibly be said about precipitation, clouds, temperatures, and wind, Henry excused himself and worked his way to the far corner of the room, where he finally spotted Nancy—with Ned Cooper. Henry pulled back into the crowd. He was overwhelmed with a sense of missed opportunity. James was right. He should have made his move weeks ago. Nancy was stunning in her long, sweeping, ivory dress with lace at the neck; she also wore a necklace—the kind women made by painting chinaberries and stringing them together.

Ned was a scrawny man in Henry's estimation, at least seven years older than him, although it was always hard to know. Most slaves didn't have any knowledge of their birth date, as if their entrance into the world carried no more consequence than their departure.

Henry had always been envious of Ned's greater autonomy and confidence. And now this. Henry caught Nancy's eyes, and she looked away quickly. She was cutting him to the quick.

In Henry's mind, Nancy and Ned fit together. Even their names had a ring to it. So he decided it was time to call it a night; he didn't have a stomach for either the food or the singing. He hadn't felt this defeated since the day that the older Mr. Barret decided, on his deathbed, against freeing his family. Henry headed for the exit.

Suddenly: whistles. Police whistles.

The loud hum of voices came to a sudden stop. A couple of women screamed. The high spirits that had filled the room only moments before was gone. A team of police had appeared in the hotel basement with clubs and guns, and they rushed in like foxes in a hen house and began rounding up prisoners. Some men made a run for the door but ran into clubs in motion, knocking them flat. Others took their women by the hand and bolted for the back of the basement, hoping to find other exits. Some just kept on eating and talking, as if nothing out of the ordinary had happened. And a couple of men tried to reason with the police.

"We got permission to run this dance," said Ishmael Cubbins.

"Not according to the mayor."

"Look here," said Billy Timms. He waved a slip of paper at one of the policemen. "I got my master's pass, plain as day."

"It ain't plain and it ain't day," said a policeman, and he grabbed Billy by the collar.

Henry's immediate thought was Nancy. With police whistles ringing in his ears, he fought his way back through the crowd, elbows and arms hitting him from all sides, people shouting, faces jumping out at him in a frenzied blur.

"Nancy!" Henry found her toward the back of the room, by herself in a corner. "Where's Ned?"

"What?" Nancy shouted. The whistles and shouting made it hard to hear anything else.

Henry leaned in closer. "Where's Ned?"

Nancy bristled. "He ran!"

Ned, the ambitious one, had done what he did best—look out for himself. Henry took Nancy by the hand. All of the tentativeness and shyness that had plagued him for weeks was gone. Action was something Henry could relate to more than the restrained rules of courtship.

"This way!"

Henry took Nancy's hand and led her through the crowd and the storm of noise; he thought he heard someone shout his name, but he didn't turn to even look. He guided Nancy to a back hallway, but it simply led to a maze of dead-end basement rooms. Other couples were also looking for a way to escape, with no more success. In moments, the police would find their way into every corner of the basement and root them all out. The whistles were a constant reminder: They were boxed in from all sides.

Another room. Another set of four blank walls. No doors. No way out. But then, in the next room, Henry spotted a window.

"This-a way!"

Henry yanked on the frame. Stuck. The window, covered in dust and cobwebs, probably hadn't

159

been opened in years. Henry thought about breaking the window, but there was no way he would expect Nancy to slip through jagged glass. He tugged again. The window loosened. Again and again he pulled. Henry put all of his weight into the next yank, and the entire window frame suddenly pulled out and broke apart in his hands, glass shattering. That was one way of doing it.

Fortunately, Nancy wasn't trapped in one of those monstrous hoop skirts that the wealthy white women wear to balls or else she would have been surely trapped inside this basement. But with a less formidable dress—and a lift from Henry—Nancy made it through the open window, and Henry was right behind her. Nancy lifted the hem of her dress off the ground, and they ran down the alleyway, hand in hand. By this time, Nancy was laughing uncontrollably.

Henry smiled—probably the first time Nancy had seen him let down his guard. This was one way of sweeping her off her feet.

The dinner party brouhaha was big news the next day, as nearly ninety participants were hauled into court, and hundreds of slaves and free blacks came out to watch, clogging the streets around city hall. (James wasn't one of the ninety, for he had slipped through their net.) The mayor was hoping this catch would prove to the city his efficiency in keeping the slave population under control. But he was embarrassed to discover that every single one of the slaves who had spent the night in jail was able to produce passes from their masters—except for one man, who was given ten lashes.

Ned was among those who spent the night in jail, for when he deserted Nancy to save his skin, he ran right into the clutches of a waiting policeman, which was easy to do since they didn't wear uniforms. Ned wound up the loser in more ways than one. His party had been a disaster and he had lost face. He had also lost Nancy.

From that point on, Henry and Nancy saw each other at church every Sunday. They would promenade in front of First Baptist, arm in arm, attracting stares and setting tongues wagging. It embarrassed Henry at first, but he got used to it, and he discovered, at last, that he could talk to Nancy without speaking to his shoes. With Nancy on his arm, Henry figured he would finally be free of James's constant prodding about matters of the heart, but he should have known his friend better than that. James wasn't done with him yet.

"You need to be courting her *with style,*" James said one Sunday afternoon at the cake shop. "You don't want Ned slipping back in there, taking your place now, do you?"

"Course not."

"Then you need to do something dramatic. Sing

to Nancy. Serenade her after church. You've got the voice. So use it! Ladies love it."

Henry, sitting on a rough bench along the wall, leaned back and gave it some thought. "Serenadin' after church? But folks'll hear me."

It was one thing to walk arm and arm in front of First Baptist. It was quite another thing to be singing to your lady right outside in the glare of day.

"How 'bout I serenade her at night? Isn't that the way it's done anyways? By the light of the moon and all?"

James's grin—and his eager attitude—vanished instantly. "You don't want to do that."

"Why? I ain't afraid."

"You ought to be. You heard about Wilkins and Dover, didn't you?"

"Course I have. But them two were fools."

David Wilkins and Jack Dover, both free blacks, tried serenading their women at night, and they ended up with ten lashes apiece. Serenading was not uncommon in Richmond—but it was dangerous sport.

"Those two sang right under their lady's window in the Big House, of all things, and they woke all creation," Henry said. "That ain't gonna happen to me."

"But it seems a foolish risk when you can sing to her after church."

"It's not risky if you don't get caught."

James pulled up a stool. "You're telling me you're less afraid of getting caught out on the streets at night than being seen singing to your woman in broad daylight?"

Henry thought about it for a moment. "That's about it."

In fact, the more Henry mulled it over, the more he liked the idea of using his strong voice to express his even stronger feelings to Nancy. Singing was the only way he could imagine himself doing something like that.

"If you get caught, I'm going to blame myself for planting the thought of serenading in your mind." James was seriously concerned, Henry could tell.

"I wouldn't blame ya, not for a moment, James. Singin' by the light of the moon is my idea. And a good one too."

"I should have kept my mouth shut."

"You won't get no argument from me on that score." Henry grinned. "Just remember, it's in the nature of the He to pursue the She."

James didn't smile back. "Yeah, but it's in the nature of the patrollers to pursue *us*."

Normally, getting to Nancy at night would be a near impossibility. She lived with the Hancock Lee family in Chesterfield County across the river, which was reached by Mayo's Bridge. Getting across without being spotted by the patrollers would take a magician. But to Henry's good fortune, Mr. Lee had loaned out Nancy to a brother in Richmond whose most valued house slave had just died. It was the end of July, and Nancy would be in Richmond for one more week doing the washing and other work for the Albert Lee family.

Slaves were not allowed out on the streets of Richmond after the bells rang at nine o'clock, a law that was strictly enforced. But Henry decided to take his chances, making his way from Shockoe Bottom, where he still boarded with Wilson Gregory. It had been a steamy day, but the night breeze made the evening much more tolerable. He thanked God for this small mercy.

Henry made his way carefully in the dark to Church Hill, where Nancy would be working and living for another week. He knew the house she spoke of, so he slipped in and out of shadows, making his way carefully across the cityscape. For once, his very dark skin served him well. It would have taken keen watchmen eyes to pick him out of the darkness, and most of the patrollers were not that attentive. But it was still a big risk. If he were caught snooping around these stately homes, he could be charged with burglary. The white authorities were not always vigilant in enforcing certain slave laws, but something like burglary was another thing entirely. The law would land on him hard, and Henry knew it.

He made his way softly, like moonlight on

water. The home was a three-story brick structure; and when Henry came at it from the back, he saw that all of the lights were extinguished for the night. The neighborhood was dead quiet, but the pervasive sound of crickets gave him at least a meager blanket of noise. Behind the house were three small cabins, where most of the slaves lived. Henry crouched outside the window of the first building, praying it was the correct cabin. It was beginning to dawn on him that he hadn't thought this through very carefully.

The wooden shutters on the cabin window were open to let in the night breeze. So Henry began to sing, very softly, barely audible, afraid of rousing anyone in the Big House.

"When we do meet again. When we do meet
  again.
When we do meet again, 'twill be no more to
  part."

Henry chose this song because it gave him the chance to insert Nancy's name into the lyrics. He increased the volume—but not too much.

"Sister Nancy, fare you well, Sister Nancy,
  fare you well.
We'll sing hallelujah when we do meet again."

"Who go there?"
Henry nearly jumped out of his skin. The voice,

a harsh whisper, came from the nearest window. It wasn't Nancy's voice. And as he approached the window, he could see it wasn't Nancy's face. This woman's face was as round as the moon, with a broad nose and skin as dark as Henry's.

"It's Henry Brown," he whispered back, even though the name meant nothing to this stranger.

"You Henry Fool is who you are. Whatya doin' here this time a night? You lookin' for a whippin'?"

Henry didn't know how to answer. This was not turning out to be the romantic encounter he had been hoping for.

"Henry?" This time it was Nancy's voice, coming from inside the same cabin. The moon-faced woman pulled back from the window, tsk-tsking as she did, and Nancy's face appeared in her place. "Henry, what do ya think you're doin'? You gonna get yourself whipped skulkin' here at night."

Henry beamed. "I'm serenadin'."

"Don't be a fool, Henry Brown. You gonna get caught."

The word "fool" had already been used twice in the span of a few minutes, and Henry wasn't expecting that. He groped for a suitable answer. For a moment, all was quiet, except for the crickets that provided a constant background sound, while other insects interjected clicking noises of all kinds.

"You still there?" Nancy asked, for Henry had stepped back into deeper shadow so he could think what to do next.

"I'm here."

"I sure liked your song."

"I didn't really get very far into it."

"That's all right."

"I can sing some more if you like."

"No, no, I really don't want ya riskin' it."

"But I'd risk *anything* for ya."

"I know."

Henry moved in closer to the window until he was standing only inches from her face. He couldn't kiss Nancy, not with a cabin full of slaves just behind her out of sight. It wouldn't seem proper. But if he didn't kiss her, shouldn't he say something? He couldn't stand here like this all night. He was so close that he could feel Nancy's breath on his lips. His heart was galloping, and his mouth was as dry as a desert. Their eyes locked, and Henry could see that she wanted him to do something, say something. Anything.

Before he even knew what he was doing, the words came tumbling out.

"Nancy. Would you be my wife?"

Nancy pulled back, stunned. Even Henry was shocked by the words that had just spilled out without warning. He couldn't have been more surprised if a frog had hopped out of his mouth.

"You proposin' marriage, Henry?"

Henry realized he should get down on one knee; that was the way it was done. So he dropped to his knee, trying to act more sure of himself than he felt. "I'd like to be your husband, Nancy. I always wanted it."

Suddenly: squeaking hinges. The opening of a door. The back door to the Lee house had opened wide. Nancy stepped back from the window, and Henry threw himself into a nearby clump of bushes. He hoped the rustling sound didn't travel all of the way back to the Big House. A branch jabbed him in the rib under his left shoulder, but he didn't make a sound, didn't budge.

Next: light. Someone had lit a lantern, and the light was moving across the expanse of land, as if it were floating in air, carried by a ghost. Henry could not see the figure of a man until he was almost upon the slave cabins. The man held up the lantern in his left hand, and he carried a revolver in his right. He swung the light to his left. Henry was off to his right side, just beyond the edge of the light. The man was Gilbert Lee, the middle of three sons. Twenty-nine years old. Henry knew the face, but he didn't know the man.

Gilbert circled the cabins, stopped, turned, and seemed to be staring directly at Henry. But Henry was still beyond the light, just deep enough in darkness to be out of sight. Then Gilbert Lee took two steps in his direction. That was all it took. The light snared him like a net.

Gilbert aimed his pistol directly at Henry. "Who goes there?"

Before Henry could answer, Nancy spoke from the window. "Master Lee?"

Gilbert glanced over his shoulder. "Is that you, Nancy?"

The young man talked to her kindly—almost too familiarly, Henry thought. Nancy had been at this house for only a couple of weeks, yet Gilbert Lee seemed to have taken a fancy to her, and that was always a two-edged sword. Every slave wanted a friendly master with amicable sons and daughters. But an overly familiar one? That could create problems of a completely different nature.

Henry climbed out of the bushes, and Gilbert snapped his head back in his direction. "No further."

"I'm sorry, Master Lee," said Nancy. "He come to see me."

Gilbert glanced between the two slaves. Then he smiled. To Henry, the smile seemed sympathetic, certainly not malicious.

"Ah. I understand."

"He came askin' for my hand in marriage."

No, don't be tellin' him that! Some masters would take that as an invitation to demonstrate their power—an invitation to take a slave woman into their bed.

Gilbert laughed lightly. "You sure have a lot of nerve," he said to Henry. "What is your name?"

"Henry. Henry Brown."

"I like your audacity, Henry Brown." Gilbert lowered his pistol. "But perhaps you're a bit foolish coming out here at night. You could get yourself killed."

There was that word again—"fool."

"I'm sorry, Master Lee." Henry lowered his head and looked at the ground. He prayed that Master Lee was a gentleman, even to slaves.

"Well?" said Gilbert.

Henry looked up in puzzlement.

"Well?" he repeated. "What was your answer, Nancy?"

Nancy stared at Gilbert, looking a bit bemused at first. Then she smiled and stared Henry directly in the eyes. "I said yes, of course."

15

March 23, 1849
12:15 p.m.

Henry's box had become a torture chamber. Flipped on his head, his scalp felt raw and irritated from constant contact with the bottom of the box. He tried to adjust his head, so his weight would be placed on another part of his scalp, but there wasn't much surface area on the top of his skull to work with. Any large movements were out of the question. There were people standing only a few feet from his box, and he could hear their every word. They would hear any movement he made.

Henry's box was on the cargo deck of the steamboat, surrounded by other boxes, barrels, sacks, lumber, food, and coal—also a goat and a pig from the sound of it. For short trips, such as this one up the Potomac, people often bought standing-room tickets to ride on the cargo deck, along with the animals. Cheaper that way, much cheaper than booking a spot on the cabin deck. Henry heard several people shuffling around near his box, but two voices—two men—were especially close.

"Hello there . . . The name's Sebastian Rawlings," said one of the men. A jaunty tone.

"Reginald Abernathy," said the other, and Henry pictured them shaking hands.

From the sound of it, Rawlings was a garrulous man, while Abernathy had a wary tone; he probably didn't want to spend his trip making small talk with a perfect stranger.

"I couldn't help but notice the book you're reading," Rawlings said. "Good thing you're reading Poe by the light of day. Reading him at night gives me a fright."

"So you've read him?" asked Abernathy.

"Read him? I've *met* Edgar Allen Poe. He gave a reading in Fredericksburg."

"Really? What was he like?"

"Gloomy. No surprise there. I heard Poe's back in his hometown, Richmond, this exact week, giving regular readings in the Exchange Hotel. Wish I could hear him, but work calls me to Washington."

A silence descended. Perhaps Abernathy had started reading his book. Henry caught the fragrance of pipe tobacco and figured that one of the men had begun to puff away. No visible smoke penetrated the box—not like the cigar smoke earlier in the day—so he could breathe easy. But he hoped to hear more talk, something to get his mind off of his pain. A minute later, Rawlings obliged.

"I've read a lot of Poe, but I haven't read *The Premature Burial*. Is it good?"

"Uh-huh." That was all Abernathy had to say.

"I had an aunt who was mightily afraid of being buried alive. So she was buried in one of those safety coffins."

"You don't say?" Henry heard the first hint of mild interest in Abernathy's voice. But Henry wasn't sure if *he* wanted to hear about people being buried alive. Reminded him too much of his own predicament.

"If they buried her alive, she could pull a string to ring a little bell on the outside of the coffin to signal for help. There was even an air tube built into the coffin. She was taking no chances."

"Saved by the bell?"

"That's the idea. But after she was buried, the bell never did ring. She was as dead as dead can get."

"Precautions can't hurt, though."

"True enough. When they opened the vault of John Duns Scotus the philosopher, they found his body outside the coffin. He broke out of the coffin somehow, and he'd been trying to claw his way out of the concrete vault. I read that in a book once."

"Well if that don't beat all . . ."

The men were silent for a moment, and Henry wondered if the conversation had ended. But Rawlings wasn't about to let it die. "So the hero in your book gets buried alive? Couldn't think of a worse way to go. Much worse than being blown to bits by an exploding boiler."

Abernathy had no response for such an odd observation.

Rawlings explained himself. "I had a cousin once who had a room on the cabin deck directly above the steamboat's boiler. He was blown to kingdom come, along with the captain and three other passengers. No wonder they call steamboats 'floating coffins.' "

Rawlings sure seemed fixated on death in all its forms, Henry thought.

"But don't you worry," he told Abernathy. "On the cargo deck here, we're well out of range from any exploding boilers."

"Good to know." Henry could tell that Abernathy wanted the conversation to end. Rawlings didn't get the hint.

"I'm a bookbinder, and I'm heading to Washington to talk to a congressman about some books that need binding. That's why I pay close attention to books, like the one there you're reading. Pretty good job of binding, from what I can tell from where I stand."

The conversation became a monologue, as Rawlings talked on and on about bookbinding, even bringing in a little history of books. Somewhere along the line he brought up the Egyptian *Book of the Dead*, which took him full circle to his favorite topic: death. The conversation became exceedingly dull, and it didn't do much to take Henry's mind away from his own Poe-like horror.

Henry felt light-headed and started to shake. At one point, he tried to raise his hand to his face, but he couldn't. He couldn't move his arms! His heart began to race. Fear took complete control. He broke into a cold sweat and wondered if death was close. Being upside down, he felt as if his eyes were going to burst from their sockets. His head throbbed, and the veins on the side of his head pounded like hammers.

Henry didn't have a bell that he could ring, like the woman in the safety coffin. So he did what anyone would do in such a terrible place. He prayed. It was his way of ringing a bell—ringing a bell to catch the attention of God.

When John Allen strode through the door of the tobacco factory, he spotted Callahan ducking into a back room. The coward. It was Callahan's paranoia that had sent John Allen on the manhunt for Obadiah in the first place. The fool said he'd seen one of their slaves running out on the streets just before the storm hit. But now the real storm had hit; he was made to look ridiculous, and right in front of Barret. He needed to take out his frustration on someone.

"Callahan!" John Allen shouted for his underling, but Callahan didn't answer, didn't come running. John Allen put his hands on his hips. "Callahan!"

Still no answer.

John Allen regretted ever coming to Richmond. He had been a slave patroller back when he worked on a plantation so many years ago, and he should have stayed there. Slave patrollers in the countryside had the authority to enter any cabin or home without a warrant—even the master's home. *That* was real respect, real power. Some of the wealthy plantation owners accused him of abusing this privilege. They said he violated the Southern sanctity of a man's home, but in his book these masters were soft; some of them even thought they could get the fieldwork done without a whip. Fools, all of them. Without patrollers like him, there would have been insurrection. He had left the countryside because of mollycoddling slave owners, but the city turned out to be even worse.

When John Allen first arrived in Richmond, he had been part of an urban slave patrol—a paddy-roller as the slaves called them. But the patrol captain, a by-the-book sort of man, did not appreciate his techniques. The captain said punishment was only supposed to be issued when a majority of the patrol came to agreement first. But slave patrolling was not a democracy! Turned out, all of his hard work keeping the peace got him fired, and he wound up working in William Barret's factory. And now this. Why couldn't the fools see that pain and fear kept the peace — not rule books!

John Allen tried to muster as much dignity as possible as he entered the stemmer's room. Every single slave in the room avoided eye contact with him. Avoiding eye contact was nothing new. What was new was the undercurrent of pleasure that he detected among the slaves. The workforce knew that he had been rebuked by William Barret—that much was obvious. Word sure spread fast among these people. He could sense the subtle satisfaction in his slaves, and on most days he would have lashed out at somebody with his whip, making him pay for the collective pleasure in the room. But today was not most days.

"God sent old Jonah to the Nineveh land.
He didn't obey my God's command.
The wind blew the ship from sho' to sho'.
A whale swallowed Jonah and he wasn't no
    mo'."

Someone had suddenly started singing.

John Allen never allowed singing in his factory. The previous overseer, Wilson Gregory, had let them sing to their heart's delight, and it took all of John Allen's power to beat the music out of them. This was the first time in close to ten years that someone had had the nerve. Glowering, he looked across the room and saw that the singer was Rufus—a large slave with the mind of a child. The words just started coming out of Rufus, like a barrel that had suddenly sprung a leak. His voice grew stronger and louder, an expansive sound that filled the room. Some of the stemmers paused in their work, disbelieving what they were hearing. They cast quick looks at John Allen, afraid of what might happen next.

Almost instinctively, John Allen reached for the whip by his side. Rufus kept right on singing, kept right on plucking tobacco leaves off their stems, like pulling wings off a large butterfly.

"You'd better run, run, run-a-run!
You'd better run, run, run-a-run!
You'd better run to the city of refuge!
You'd better run, run, run!"

John Allen paused. For the first time, he was not sure what to do. He had just killed one of William Barret's slaves, and Rufus was one of Barret's as well. He didn't dare put a lash on Rufus's back. But he was singing about running! True, he was singing about Jonah running away from the city of Nineveh, not slaves running from their masters; but John Allen wasn't stupid. He knew the double meanings hidden within these spirituals.

A second voice joined Rufus, a woman's voice.

"Read about Samson from his birth.
He was the strongest man on earth.
He lived 'way back in ancient times.
He killed about a thousand Philistines."

John Allen's world was collapsing all around him. Oh, how much he wanted to use his whip. William Barret didn't have to find out. But the master would, he surely would.

Three voices. Four voices. Five voices strong. Other stemmers, most of them women and boys, were beginning to sing along.

"He had to run, run, run-a-run.
He had to run, run, run-a-run.
He had to run to the city of refuge.
He had to run, run, run!"

John Allen felt as if he had been lashed to that tree once again, tied up by his father and helpless to do anything. He was bound. His hands were tied, his tongue was tied. His father had beaten him, his employer had beaten him, and now he was being beaten into the ground by the music, driven into the floor by the pounding rhythm.

"God sent old Jonah to the Nineveh land.
He didn't obey my God's command.
The wind blew the ship from sho' to sho'.
A whale swallowed Jonah and he wasn't no
   mo'."

Once again, John Allen made a move for his whip, but as he did his headache came alive like a demon, pounding from the inside. He went weak at the knees and very nearly collapsed to the floor. The thunderstorm had moved into his skull.

By this time, close to ten slaves had picked up the song, and he couldn't lay a hand on a single one of them. So he marched out of the room, in search of Callahan. Someone had to pay for this day. Might as well be Callahan.

"You'd better run, run, run-a-run!
You'd better run, run, run-a-run!
You'd better run to the city of refuge!
You'd better run, run, run!"

16

Chesterfield County, Virginia
August 1836: Thirteen Years Earlier

When Henry got on bended knee and asked Nancy to marry him, it was only the first step. He also had to propose the match to her master—Mr. Hancock Lee. This wasn't the kind of proposal you make from bended knee, but if he had to get on *both knees* and beg, he would. Officially, the law didn't recognize slave marriages, but couples like Henry and Nancy wanted to be joined together just as much as any white pair.

Henry's master had given him a pass to leave the factory on a Saturday afternoon and cross the James River by way of Mayo's Bridge, traveling into Chesterfield County. Mr. Lee, a banker, owned the type of house befitting a man who sought people's trust. It was a two-story, square, brick home—no frills, just strong and solid like a bank vault.

As Henry climbed out of the wagon and made his way to the house, he wondered whether Mr. Lee guarded his human property as dearly as he guarded the money in his vault. Or would he allow his slaves to marry abroad? That's what they called it in the plantation system when you married a slave with a different master and living on a different plantation. Love was complicated enough without all of the added intricacies posed by having different masters.

Back when Henry lived in Louisa County, some slaves actively sought out women from other plantations. One fellow figured that if he could marry abroad, he would get to travel to see his wife and children every Sunday; it would be a rare opportunity to see the world, even if the "world" amounted to nothing more than another plantation two miles down the road.

Henry's old master, John Barret, had been known to purchase a spouse so a couple could be together, but not many masters would go that far. John Barret's son, William, certainly would not consider buying Nancy just to keep Henry and her together. Henry knew that for a fact. He had asked him.

Henry scooped the hat off of his head and knocked on the sturdy front door. An elderly slave named Elijah ushered him into the house. "Is Master Lee expectin' you, Henry?"

"I believe so. Nancy fixed it up for me to see him."

Elijah disappeared into a back room, and Henry sat down in the parlor. He looked around for any sign of Nancy. She handled the wash and sometimes worked in the kitchen, so perhaps she was there right now, for the smell of fresh bread filled the house. In contrast to the home's plain, brick exterior, the parlor revealed a woman's touch— lace curtains and chairs so dainty that Henry feared they would buckle under his weight. Mr. Lee's tastes ruled the home's exterior, while his wife clearly reigned inside.

"Good afternoon, Henry!" Mr. Lee came sweeping into the room dramatically, and Henry shot to his feet and gave a submissive nod of the head.

"Afternoon, Mr. Lee."

Mr. Hancock Lee was a plump man, well dressed with a round body balanced on ridiculously thin legs. His mouth was wide and his eyes large. Frog-like almost. It was an oppressively hot August day, and he wiped the sweat from his jowls with his handkerchief.

"Take a seat," he said before launching into a monologue on the heat. When the niceties were over, he asked Henry what was on his mind.

"I'd like to marry Miss Nancy."

After all of his rehearsal on the ride over, he decided to keep his request simple and straightforward. Mr. Lee loomed over him, and Henry glanced away. Outside, the summer locusts were broiling with noise.

"And would she like to marry *you?*" Mr. Lee leaned down as if he were speaking to a child. His tone of voice was polite, but for some reason Henry wished he could reach out and slap the man.

"Oh yes, sir." Henry looked up and stared Mr. Lee in the eyes.

"I do not like the idea of splitting up families," Mr. Lee said, turning away and pacing up and down the floor. "Breaking up a family is a terrible thing. Just terrible. Horrifying. So I would have to be assured, if you married, that you and Nancy would never be split apart by your master." He paused to dab his forehead with his handkerchief, as if just the thought of families being divided made him break out in a sweat.

Henry thought he caught movement in a back hallway, the flash of a person moving from one room to another. It was a slave, but he couldn't tell if it was Nancy or not. He wished he could see her, even for a moment. Then Henry realized that Mr. Lee was still talking, so he quickly brought his attention back to bear.

"It is difficult for a married couple to have different masters," Mr. Lee was saying, sounding more business-like, as if he were lecturing someone who had come seeking a bank loan. "If you and Nancy marry, your master might very well sell you to a different state. What then?"

"I been with the Barret family since the day I was born. I don't believe that'd happen, sir."

"But can you be certain? There is nothing more tragic than the sundering of a family, white or colored. Devastating."

"Yes, sir."

After more pacing back and forth, Mr. Lee planted himself directly in front of Henry. "If I permit my Nancy to marry you, rest assured that I would never sell her. *Never!*"

Henry chafed at the words "my Nancy" coming from this man. But he liked Mr. Lee's resolute promise. "Thank you, sir."

"I will discuss matters with your master, Henry. If he agrees to keep you and Nancy together, then you have my blessing." Mr. Lee motioned toward the door. "But if I permit you to marry my Nancy, I do expect children. You will be raising a large family, I presume."

Henry rose from his chair, running the brim of his hat through his fingers. "Oh yes, sir." Henry was well aware of what Mr. Lee was getting at. In these kinds of arrangements, the children were typically considered the property of the woman's master, and Mr. Lee wanted a return on his investment. Interest on the head.

Taking one last glance at the back hallway before exiting, Henry still saw no sign of Nancy. He went away with the fragrance of bread still spinning his senses.

"You make a beautiful bride," said Mrs. Lee, as she flitted around Nancy like a hummingbird, making last-second adjustments to the dress. Mrs. Lee had picked out a stunning white gown for her with a train, a tight waist, and ruffles along the bottom—although Nancy had added a splash of color of her own choosing. She wore a yellow sash, and her hair was adorned with yellow flowers, like the crown of a May queen. Mrs. Lee conceded that yellow was a nice touch, but she made it clear to Nancy that she should have been consulted.

The wedding day, in August of 1836, was hot and clear with no breeze. Nancy had assumed she and Henry would be married at the First Baptist Church, and then they would jump the broom afterwards. But Mrs. Lee had taken complete control, insisting that they marry in the parlor of Big House. She was a small, thin, fragile woman, but her emotions were oversized, hitting every extreme. Master Lee had little patience for his wife's volatility, so he usually gave her what she wanted. And what she wanted was a wedding.

"You're like a daughter to me," Mrs. Lee had told Nancy time and time again. The Lees were childless, so Nancy filled those shoes, but only when it suited Mrs. Lee. Real daughters were free.

Nancy's dearest friend, Emily, slipped into the room carrying Nancy's bouquet of yellow flowers, while Mrs. Lee continued to make final adjustments to Nancy's dress.

"The gown's the most beautiful I ever seen," Emily said.

"Thank you, Emmie," Mrs. Lee said. "And I

must say, my dear: You look handsome your-self."

Why shouldn't she? Mrs. Lee had picked out her gown as well.

"Thank you, ma'am."

"This morning, I finished putting the icing on the cake myself," Mrs. Lee said, the third time she had reminded Nancy of all the trouble she had gone through.

"That's sure kind of you," Nancy said.

"I don't suppose you have fancy cakes at most colored weddings. So I hope you appreciate all that I have done for you."

"Oh yes, ma'am."

Coming from the oppressive Stephenson plantation, Nancy really did appreciate what Mrs. Lee had done; but the expectations that came with all the fuss put Nancy on edge—made her afraid that if she didn't show adequate appreciation, Mrs. Lee might turn on her.

Over the years, Nancy had been visited by any number of disturbing dreams. Inevitably, she would be walking down a road and there lounging along the side of the path would be two cream-colored lions. They didn't attack, but they terrified her just the same. That was how it was with Mr. and Mrs. Lee. They were generous relative to other masters and mistresses—tame masters, you might say. But there was always the fear: When were they going to pounce?

"I'm sorry Mrs. Lee didn't have ya make the cake," Henry told James.

"The cake don't matter," James said, straightening Henry's tie. Mrs. Lee had borrowed a jacket with tails for Henry to wear, which was a good thing since Henry's coat was becoming thread-bare.

"You'll get to taste a *real* cake at the doings next Sunday," James added, and he began brushing the back of Henry's jacket.

Henry and James were in the library, just off of the parlor, where the wedding would take place, while the women occupied the Blue Room, directly across the hall from the parlor.

Mr. and Mrs. Lee did not want their house overcrowded with people of color, so they allowed Henry and Nancy to invite only James and Emily. The remaining wedding guests were the Lees' other staff—four slaves, two of them middle-aged and two elderly. Thankfully, James had set up a wedding party at his cake shop the next Sunday after church, so Henry's Baptist brothers and sisters could feel a part of the carryings-on, even if it was a week late.

James stepped back to size up Henry properly. "You're looking smart." Then he smiled and gently added, "You know, I believe I was wrong."

Henry smiled back. "You been wrong 'bout a lot of things. Which one you talkin' 'bout?"

"You remember how you once asked me why I hadn't ever considered settling down with one woman?"

Henry nodded. It was something they had talked about more than once.

"I told you I didn't want to be possessed by *anyone* now that I was free. But now that I look at you, Henry, I can see that I was wrong about marriage. Nancy has freed you. She has."

"So does that mean maybe y'all be takin' a wedding leap with a woman all your own?" Henry asked.

"I wouldn't go that far." James slapped Henry on the back. "Are you ready?"

"I been ready since the day I first laid eyes on her."

Henry and James strode into the parlor, and the wedding began. Mrs. Lee had selected the music, which was banged out on the parlor piano by her over-enthusiastic Aunt Susan. Mrs. Lee wept throughout the entire service, patting her eyes with a handkerchief. It was hard to tell if it was because she saw Nancy as the daughter she never had, or whether she was simply moved by the ceremony she had orchestrated. Most likely the latter.

At one point, the heat got to Henry, and he nearly thought he was going to keel over. But he remained upright, and the ceremony unfolded without a hitch. A white Episcopal minister did the honors, as Mrs. Lee had insisted, and he did a fine job.

There was only one thing missing in an otherwise ideal afternoon, Henry realized later. The minister never spoke the words: "What therefore God hath joined together, let not man put asunder."

17

March 23, 1849
2:45 p.m.

Lord, do somethin' to turn me upside right, I'm askin' with all I got. I know this world ain't my true world, but I don't wanna be shakin' St. Peter's hand any time soon. Don't make this box my coffin. Carry me, Jesus, carry me!

Henry was still in the box, still upside down, still praying. Blood still roared in his ears and pressure still built in his skull until it was about to crack open. He expected to pass out at any second—and he wondered if maybe he did black out momentarily a few times. It was hard to know; he was too disoriented.

Henry tried to sustain his sanity by praying. The words poured out.

You got me hooked in the heart, Lord, but don't be pullin' me to the other side just yet. Let me keep livin' 'cause I got things that still need doin', Lord. So don't bury me dead in this darkness. Gimme hope, gimme somethin' strong to hold on to, Lord.

Starved for light, he felt like he was in the bottom of a deep well. He had been in the box for so long that he wondered whether light even existed in its fullest form. All he had were meager streams of sunlight—rationed sunlight that cast his world into shades of gray. All he had were sounds from another world, the disembodied voices of men like Rawlings and Abernathy—the two passengers who had been discussing Edgar Allen Poe.

By this time, Rawlings had wandered back to his favorite subject, likely dragging Abernathy along, willing or not.

"I've also heard tell of graves with viewing windows built into them," Henry heard Rawlings say. "They allow grave workers to check the corpses each day. Make sure they're decomposing proper like."

"If a corpse waves back at them, they know they got a premature burial," said Abernathy. "That how it works?"

"Something like that."

"How long can someone survive inside a buried coffin do you think?"

"Don't rightly know. But it's long enough for the buried person to dwell on their predicament and be done in by fear and panic. That's the terror of it all. It don't happen fast. That's why George Washington asked that he not be buried until over a week after he died, just to make sure he's really gone. I read that in a book once."

"For me, it's not being able to move that would drive me mad."

Henry didn't want to hear any more. He plugged his ears and tried to block their words by filling his mind with prayer.

I'm at your mercy, Lord. Carry me in this box like you carried baby Moses down the river in a box. You made him safe, even with all the Egyptians lookin' to kill him, even with him bein' nothin' more than a child. Keep me safe, Lord, carry me, carry me, and keep me away from the ones who'd like nothin' better than to kill me. Turn me right side up, Lord, help me, help me, help me. Mercy, mercy, mercy . . .

Abernathy's next words broke through Henry's defenses. "All this talk of our final rest has got me needin' a rest right now. I've been standin' near two hours."

Two hours? Henry couldn't believe he had survived that long upside down. But it also meant he had another two hours of agony remaining before the steamboat reached Washington— maybe more if the box was not righted.

"I wish the cargo deck had seats," added Abernathy.

A pause, and then . . . "Why, we've had a resting

spot starin' us right in the face all the time," said Rawlings.

"Good idea."

Henry heard the shuffling of feet, and he started praying again. Then one of the men grabbed hold of his world and threw the box down on its side, and Henry found himself tumbling over and his body banging against the interior of the box. He nearly fainted as the blood drained back to his lower extremities, but the dizziness and the fresh bruise were well worth it, for his world had rearranged itself. He was now on his back, looking straight up. The two men sat down on opposite ends of the box, and he felt the groan of the wood all around him. The men groaned as well—in relief.

"Can't believe we didn't think of this sooner," said Rawlings.

Henry stared up at the roof of his wooden tabernacle. Their relief was his relief, seventy times over.

Henry Brown.

John Allen was trying his best to put the disaster with Mr. Barret out of his mind when Henry Brown invaded his thoughts. He suddenly remembered that Henry had gone home from the factory yesterday nursing an injury—just as Obadiah had done a week and a half before.

John Allen had never intended to kill Obadiah,

just get him working again. He couldn't help it if the slave didn't have a strong enough constitution to endure his discipline. But that's what worried him: Henry had come to him yesterday morning displaying a cut on his palm that looked like he'd stuck his hand in the jaws of a Cuban bloodhound. Cut to the bone, and John Allen had simply sent him home with the words, "Get a poultice of flaxseed to it."

For the first time, he felt concern about the health of a slave, for it was closely linked to his own well-being. He usually liked to let nature take its course with slaves. Some masters used their own personal physicians to treat slaves, and in one sense he couldn't blame them. Slaves were expensive property. John Allen worried that Henry needed treatment, something more than a poultice of flax-seed.

But Henry's injury wasn't my doing. No one can blame me if he drops dead.

But he could be blamed. And after what he had done to Obadiah, he *would* be blamed if anything happened to Henry. One dead slave was bad. Two in one week, even one month, would be a disaster. Obadiah and Henry were both owned by Mr. Barret, and the master would be furious.

So John Allen put Callahan in charge of the factory and paid another visit to the slave neighborhoods of Shockoe Bottom. Henry's place was just a few doors down from where Obadiah lived, a nasty reminder of the day's debacle. The sun had done a good job baking the ground, so the mud had solidified. However, one thing hadn't changed from the morning; the same old woman was still sitting on the porch—the woman with the face with a million creases. She stared right at him, expressionless.

John Allen didn't believe in knocking, at least not on a slave's door. He marched up the four wooden steps leading to Henry's tenement—the bottom floor of a two-story building—and threw open the door.

The room was empty. He spun around, but there wasn't any place to hide. It was happening all over again. First Obadiah, then Henry. A panic was rising.

He checked the privy outside, but all he found were more flies than an Egyptian plague and a smell that almost made him wish he could cut his nose off to spite his face. No sign of Henry.

"Henry! Henry Brown!"

John Allen circled the building and looked around for any traces of life. The same old woman was still there, her eyes following him everywhere he went.

"You know where Henry Brown might be?"

The silent woman shook her head.

John Allen folded his arms across his chest and took one more scan of the neighborhood. He had to face the fact. Henry Brown was gone. He was on the run.

18

Richmond
January 1837: Twelve Years Earlier

Nancy carried a basket of laundry up the curving, dark-wood staircase and paused at the landing. She set down her basket and put a hand over her mouth, afraid she was going to be sick. Normally, she was sick to her stomach first thing after waking up, and she would do it in the bushes just outside their cabin. But today the nausea was unrelenting.

It had only been five months since the wedding, and Nancy was already with child, well into her second month.

Mr. and Mrs. Lee had set up Henry and Nancy in a cabin behind the Big House—an extremely small cabin with barely enough room for a table, two chairs, and a pallet. But at least they didn't have to share it with another family, as was so common. Because the Lees were childless, they had plenty of room to lodge their other four slaves in the Big House. Henry remained the property of Mr. Barret, but he got to live with Nancy, and his master was freed from the expense of boarding out Henry somewhere else.

The wave of nausea passed, so Nancy picked up

her basket and made her way down the hall. She heard voices from the room at the end—the master bedroom. Raised voices.

Nancy had assumed Mrs. Lee would be ecstatic about the baby, seeing as it would be the closest to a grandchild that she would ever get. But it wasn't so. Instead, there was a growing tension in the house, and Nancy had her suspicions of what was behind it.

Thinking that she heard her own name being mentioned, Nancy slipped up to the closed door. She propped her basket on her hip and put her ear close to the wood.

"I think we should move Henry and Nancy into the house when the child comes," she heard the master say.

"But we don't have room in the house, and you know it," said an angry Mrs. Lee.

"Would you lower your voice?"

"I will not lower my voice in my own house." Mrs. Lee raised her volume even more.

"We can switch them with the Harrises. The Harrises are healthy enough to endure cabin life."

Then Mrs. Lee spoke the words that Nancy feared. "You just want that young girl under the same roof as you."

"Nonsense!" Now, Master Lee's voice had begun to rise.

Nancy edged away from the door, thinking she

should make herself scarce. But she couldn't resist hearing more.

"I have seen the way you look at her."

"I said nonsense! You're insane, woman."

Nancy knew that what Mrs. Lee said was true. The master had always let his eyes casually drift across her as she worked, but in the past few months she had caught him staring. Long, lingering looks, like a lion lazily sizing up its prey. Master Lee was not subtle in his attention.

It was a good thing that Henry was always at the factory whenever the master was around her because she didn't want Henry to know. If the master ever laid a hand on her and if Henry found out, he would kill the man. She was sure of it.

"The cabin is no place for a newborn," said Master Lee.

"And the house is no place for a mistress."

"You are imagining things."

"No. You're the one imagining things whenever you stare at her. What you're imagining I'm afraid to know."

Nancy thought she heard the thumping of footsteps charging toward the door. When the door handle began to move, she was already down the hall, her heart in her throat. She shot around the corner and down the staircase just in time.

Stopping to clutch her stomach, Nancy was nearly sick right there on the stairs.

● ● ●

Henry was almost bounced right out of his seat when the wagon hit the rut. The cake, which had been sitting in the back of James's wagon, was launched three feet into the air and came down on the dry dirt road. James didn't stop.

It was a Sunday afternoon, and Nancy had asked Henry to stay close to home, since she was so near to her time. But Henry ignored the request because he hated the idea of being around when the baby came. Birth was messy and terrifying, and the women could handle it. Lucy, the midwife, was only a shout away in the Big House.

Even when Abraham Fox came running into James's cake shop with news that Nancy's time had come, Henry was hesitant to head back to their cabin. But James insisted, and now they were flying at full chisel toward the Lee home with Abraham Fox bouncing around in the back, where the cake had been sitting just a few minutes earlier.

"I don't know why that witch wouldn't let me near Nancy," Abraham griped to Henry. "Your Nancy needs some strong protection from the spirits, but Lucy done swung a pan at me and drove me away."

James laughed. "What? Is your hoodoo not strong enough to handle a spirited midwife?"

Abraham didn't answer. He had been complaining about the midwife Lucy for most of the ride, and Henry was weary of it. Abraham called himself a conjurer, and he seemed to have hoodoo for every occasion. His most common conjuring involved concoctions to make a girl fall in love with you or to get the master to treat you right. He used to go around telling people that various ailments were caused by the "live things in them." He told folks that frogs, snakes, or scorpions could get inside your body just by drinking whiskey. Henry was almost tempted to believe this bunkum until the day he witnessed Abraham driving out a frog that he claimed had gotten into a man's leg. For a couple of coins, Abraham gave the man some medicine, ran his hands over the man's leg, said a few mysterious words, and sure enough a frog came hopping out. But Henry knew enough about sleight-of-hand tricks to realize that Abraham had pulled a fast one. He said so, and for almost six months Abraham would glare at Henry whenever they passed, acting like he was throwing a spell on him. It finally bothered Henry so much that he bought a potion to protect Nancy when she was with child. Henry didn't really believe the potion would work; he just wanted to make peace with Abraham so he'd stop giving him the evil eye. Ever since, Abraham had been coming to their cabin and nosing around Nancy.

"Henry, you gonna let me in there with Nancy, won't ya?" Abraham asked. "She needs some powerful conjurin' to make your child strong."

"Abe, Nancy's gonna have enough pain to handle without you being there creating more," said James.

Abraham glared at the back of James's head and said nothing. Henry wished Abraham had been bounced out of the wagon, rather than the cake.

They reached the small shack tucked behind the Lee home, out of sight from the Big House, and James brought the wagon to a rolling halt. They could hear Nancy shouting inside the cabin, and all three of them just sat there, taking it in. No one said a word, until Abraham finally spoke up.

"Sound like she need me. If that Lucy had a let me in there before, she wouldn't be screamin' like that, Henry."

James rolled his eyes. "Women do a lot of hollering, and you know it, Abe. It's as natural as rain."

They heard Nancy shouting out to Jesus.

"That sound natural to you?" Abraham asked Henry.

"I best go to her." Henry climbed out of the wagon and tentatively approached the cabin. With Abraham following close behind like a shadow, Henry slowly opened the door to their cabin. What he found was shocking. His wife lie on the pallet, sweat pouring down her face, her screams almost inhuman. The midwife, Lucy, stood by her bed-side and held Nancy's hand. She turned around with a speed that Henry wouldn't have expected from an elderly slip of a woman. Lucy let him have it with both barrels.

"What in heaven's name ya think you doin'?"

Henry didn't know how to respond, for the truth was that he didn't know what he was doing.

"This ain't no place for a man!"

James came up from behind and took Henry by the shoulders. "C'mon, Henry, let's leave them be."

Abraham peeked out from behind Henry; and when the midwife saw his face, she immediately reached for the nearby skillet. That sent Abraham scurrying. Henry and James retreated to a pair of tree stumps, a stone's throw from the cabin, but even from this distance, they could hear Nancy's screams. With several younger brothers and sisters, Henry had been around birth before; but his mother had kept her agony bottled. Not Nancy.

"It sound like she's dyin'."

"She'll be fine," James said. "She's in good hands."

Abraham, pacing a few feet away, snorted at that statement.

"I wish this could be easier for her," Henry said.

"Nothing that's worth anything is easy."

The only time Henry had heard such screams was when one of the plantation slaves, a boy, had his leg crushed under a wagon, and another slave had to cut off the leg to save his life. Henry had to help hold the boy down, and he still remembered him biting through the stick of wood that had been placed in his mouth; Henry would never forget the unholy screams.

For Nancy, this birth was like an amputation of sorts, a severing of two lives that had been joined together for nine months. And like all amputations, it involved plenty of blood and pain. As the time dragged on, Henry finally decided to get up and walk off to where the sound of Nancy's screams couldn't reach him. But before he could take two steps, a new sound reached his ears. The sound of crying. A baby's squalling.

Henry stared at the cabin.

"Go on," said James. "I think you're safe to go in now."

"I don't know," muttered Abraham. "Don't know if I'd trust that witch Lucy if I was you."

Henry went back to the cabin and eased open the door. He peeked in his head, afraid to cross the threshold. Lucy spotted him right away. "Now what you just standin' there for? Come meet your daughter."

Henry blinked in surprise. "A girl?"

"Most daughters are," said Lucy.

Henry slipped up to Nancy's bedside, where his wife held the bloodied child in her arms. Nancy was spent. Henry was overwhelmed. The baby girl glistened with moisture; her entire body was slick, as if she had entered the world by swimming up from the depths of the sea.

"You're a family now, Henry," said the midwife. "Ain't that somethin'?"

A family. It was surely something. But was it his family? Not in the law's eyes. Nancy extended a hand from under the bed cover, reaching out. It reminded Henry of the time that he sat at Mr. Barret's deathbed, and the old man clamped onto him. Only this time, Henry welcomed the hand. This time, he was witnessing a new life enter the world, rather than an old one depart.

"What's her name?" Lucy asked.

"Sarah," said Nancy.

After Sarah arrived in August of 1837, Nancy's worries returned, for the master's wandering eyes also returned, drifting across her figure as she moved about in the kitchen. Even worse, she was afraid that his hands would soon begin to wander as well.

Nancy did not have long to dwell on these concerns before the master threw her world completely upside down.

"I am selling you and your child," he told her one Sunday.

It was a hot afternoon, a year since the day Master Lee had promised Henry that he would never sell "his Nancy." Nancy began to cry silently, and the master made a move to comfort her with the touch of his hand. But he wisely retreated and handed her a handkerchief instead.

Nancy knew it was dangerous remaining in this house, but she was afraid of being sold away from Henry. That was her only explanation for the sudden tears.

"Don't you worry, though," Master Lee assured her brightly. "I am selling you to a Mr. Joseph Colquitt, a saddler in Richmond, so you and Henry will not be split up—just as I promised."

That wasn't exactly the promise that Nancy recalled him giving Henry, but no matter. She was relieved she would be staying in Richmond. Nancy wiped her eyes and took a deep breath.

"You did nothing wrong," Mr. Lee said. "That's not why we're selling you." He reached out and touched her shoulder. But when he heard a sound from a back room, he yanked his hand away and scurried halfway across the room. Nancy didn't think he could move that fast.

Master Lee became suddenly business-like. "You will also be gratified to know that I have made arrangements to keep you and Henry together in the same home. Mr. Colquitt says you and Henry will continue to live together in a cabin behind his house, so your living arrangements will not be any different; in fact, Henry will be closer to the tobacco factory, and that will work to his advantage."

"Yes, sir."

One week later, the Lees' oldest slave—Elijah—drove Henry and Nancy back across Mayo Bridge, on their way to a new home in the High Town part of Richmond. Nancy had their newborn, Sarah, cradled in her arms as she leaned against Henry in the back of the wagon. It was a cool morning in September, and the baby had kept Nancy awake much of the night. The rocking motion of the wagon had put Sarah to sleep and was about to do the same to Nancy.

"Maybe this is for the best," she said sleepily.

"I dunno," said Henry.

Nancy was fairly certain he had no idea of the real reason behind their departure. "The Lord will go with us," she said.

"He surely will," echoed Elijah, giving the reins a shake and speaking over his shoulder. "Old Moses bounced around all sorts of places all his life. Never could settle, but the Lord went with him everywheres he went, even traveling in a pillar of fire."

"I don't see no pillar of fire," Henry said.

"You gotta keep your eyes peeled. You too, Sister Nancy."

"I will, Brother Elijah." Nancy's eyes began to drift closed. She yawned. So did Sarah, almost in synch.

Elijah's words would prove to be truer than she could have ever imagined. It would take a few years, but it would happen. The dreams would begin. God would start sending visions to Henry, and they would burn in his mind like pillars of fire.

19

March 23, 1849
4:05 p.m.

Henry's back was sore, and his legs were cramping and crying to be stretched out. But Henry, lying flat on his back, couldn't act on his body's demands. He could only reach down and quietly massage his muscles because the two men remained perched on top of his box, with only a few inches of wood separating them from him. Occasionally, one of the men would stroll around the steamboat cargo deck and stretch his legs, but one of them remained on the box at all times—like two birds taking turns tending a nest. If they only knew that the box actually contained a human waiting to hatch out, they would be flabbergasted.

Henry's lower back was feeling especially sore, with the circle of stress continuing to expand, reaching to his upper back. He kept adjusting the weight of his body a little to the right, a little to the left, but it did little to relieve the pain. And what he wouldn't give for a pillow! Why didn't he think of putting some cushioning into this box? Straw. Blankets. Anything! The back of his head was sore from the constant contact with the box, and a headache was building. He kept lifting his head just a fraction to bring relief, but that required his stomach muscles, which were cramping. There had also been a few times when he felt an over-powering need to sneeze, and he smothered the urge several times before it finally dissipated.

By late afternoon, the steamboat leg of the journey came to an agonizing end. The boat docked, and a thousand different sounds came sweeping over him—bells, whistles, goats bleating, men shouting commands, and freight being moved about. Immersed in all of this noise, he adjusted his position without the fear of being heard. The steamboat had docked at the Washington wharf, where his box was transferred to yet another wagon. The wagon rattled along to yet another railroad station, this one at Second Street and Pennsylvania Avenue. Awaiting him there was yet another train—part of the Baltimore and Ohio Railroad line. His box remained upright for the brief, one-mile wagon roll.

When the wagon pulled into the Washington train depot, Henry heard boxes being unloaded, and he listened in on the conversations firing up all around him. One man regaled the others with a yarn about his favorite drinking hole, another bragged about a new horse, and a couple of men talked about the illness that had struck James Polk, who had just left office after one term as president. This being Washington, the talk was political, much of it having to do with the annexation of Texas and the war with Mexico. The war had been over for a year, but feelings still ran hot.

"I seen the Mexican land we got from the war. Ain't worth one drop of American blood."

"You're a fool then. We shoulda taken all of Mexico while we was at it, not just what we done. Make all Mexico part of the United States and we'd guarantee ourselves future peace."

"And bring in all those Mexicans, make them U.S. citizens? Who you callin' the fool?"

The two men carried their debate farther down the platform, and Henry wondered when his box was ever going to be moved. The train was about to pull out of the station without him, he was sure of it.

"Sir! Could you lend me a hand here?" a man asked. Was it the wagon driver? "This here box is too heavy for one person!" At last, something was happening.

But a second man, a cargo handler probably, couldn't be bothered. "Just shove it off the back of the wagon!"

Henry's heart thudded. Shove the box off the wagon? Was the man crazy?

The wagon driver paused before responding: "But the contents might be fragile."

Henry heard the cargo handler spit. "You worry too much."

"The contents . . . They might break if I push this box off the end," the wagon driver added. "Couldn't ya just give a hand for a second?"

"Don't worry about it! It don't matter if anything breaks."

"Whatya mean it don't matter? It'll matter to the owner of the contents here."

"If anything is broken, the railroad company will pay for it."

If anything was broken, it might be Henry's neck.

He heard the sound of someone climbing into the back of the wagon. Surely, the wagon driver wasn't going to act on such a ludicrous suggestion, was he? Henry braced himself, placing a hand against a wall on either side. *Lord, stop this fool from droppin' me.*

Henry's box was being moved, pushed along the bed of the dray wagon. The wagon driver grunted and was breathing heavily from the exertion, and the coffee on his breath carried into Henry's domain. The box stopped short of the tipping point.

"You sure you can't just give me a hand here?"

"Will you shove it off the end and be done with it! It'll be all right. Can't ya see I'm taking a break?"

Henry's box began to move again, scraping the bottom of the wagon as it slid closer to the edge. He pressed himself against the end of the box, opposite from the side that was going to fall first. The box teetered.

Henry wondered how far the drop would be, and he prayed he could keep from shouting when the box hit the ground. He was sure the box would splinter and break open like a walnut. Helpless, he sensed one end of the box sliding into mid-air, and in a split second he was falling fast. With a crash that rattled his entire body, the box smashed into the ground, and he couldn't help but let out a muffled grunt. He was thrown forward in the box, his head smacked against the wooden wall, and he heard something crack in his neck. Then he was swallowed up by sudden darkness, like blowing out a candle in a dark forest.

Samuel picked up a large piece of cake and bit into it. He closed his eyes and chewed slowly, savoring every morsel. The sponge cake was light as air and tasted of cinnamon.

"You've really outdone yourself," Samuel said to James.

"Thank you, Mr. Smith."

James had carried the cake to the shoe shop along with good news of John Allen's come-uppance. The cake shop was only three doors down from Fisher's shoe shop, so the news didn't have to travel far.

Samuel's ex-wife would have been furious to see him sharing cake with a free black man. She never liked it when he would get familiar with the two slaves they owned. But even Samuel had limits to his flaunting of social mores; that's why they were eating the cake in the back room of Fisher's shoe shop, rather than the front. If someone walked in to find him breaking bread with a black—breaking cake, actually—he could lose some good-paying customers.

"I would've loved to have seen John Allen's face when Mr. Barret told him he was hunting down a dead man," Samuel said. "Was Fanny sure of what she heard?"

"Fanny has a knack for collecting news, and I have found her to be extremely accurate."

Samuel nodded and grinned and cut off another piece of cake. He laughed and smiled easily; and when he did, his reddish face flushed an even brighter red, and his startling, light-blue eyes flashed.

"So you and Fanny . . . ," Samuel said. "Is there something permanent forming between you?"

James sat bolt upright.

Samuel took strange pleasure in making people uncomfortable with his blunt talk, and he knew perfectly well that asking James a personal question about his courtship habits would shock him. But Samuel also knew a free black would not let a white man's question go unanswered, no matter how intrusive.

"Yes, Fanny and I share company quite often."

Samuel laughed. "I never pegged you to settle down."

"Living with one woman does have its advantages."

"But one woman can be taken from you."

"It's a risk, I know." James lowered his head.

Samuel guessed that James spoke from experience; but as blunt as he could be, he didn't probe any further. He had pushed it far enough already. So he was surprised when James answered his unspoken question anyway.

"I wasn't always free, you know. When I was a slave, just a boy really, I had a girl sold away from me. We talked about marrying, but then a fellow from New Orleans bought her. Worst day of my life." James thought a moment more and added, "*Second* worst day of my life."

"The worst—what was that?"

James was long in answering. "An escape gone wrong."

Samuel stopped in mid-bite, catching the significance of that statement, in light of Henry's escape. He decided to change the subject. He didn't want to even think about the possibility of a disastrous escape. "I lost a good woman myself," he said.

James nodded. "I'm sorry."

"Mary Ann stayed in Richmond for a year after she left me. She's back on her family plantation, the last I heard."

Mary Ann was the reason Samuel even became a shoemaker. When he first arrived in Richmond, he knew that if he ever had hope of marrying a fine woman like her, he needed respectability and a decent income. So he became a shoemaker and eventually opened his own place—the Red Boot Shop, a fixture in the Low Town area of Richmond with its large red sign in the shape of a boot. The shop brought in a healthy flow of cash, enough for him and his new wife to purchase a respectable home and even a couple of slaves. Samuel's business also made it possible for Mary Ann to purchase all of the china and glassware and furniture that she craved, with enough left over to indulge his own passion for timepieces. Samuel's home at the time featured clocks wherever you turned, everything from small, intricate china clocks to the massive grandfather clock in the foyer. He once carried a different pocket watch each day of the week.

"She left me because of my gambling," Samuel said. "The shoe business was a plodding path to wealth, and I wanted to get rich quick. Didn't work out too well."

Samuel pulled his watch out of his pocket and dangled it in the air, like a mesmerist. "I lost everything—my home, even my clock collection, except for this one."

"Is that when you moved to Baltimore?"

"Ah. So you know my story?"

James did. He had heard that when the Red Boot shop closed in 1845, Samuel fled his creditors to Baltimore; and when he ran afoul of the law over swindling charges, he came running back to Richmond last year.

"When such a colorful man as yourself works on the same street, we hear things," James said as he wiped up some crumbs. "But you can never be sure what you hear is true."

"Unless the news comes from Fanny, right?"

James laughed. "That's right."

"Things didn't quite work out for me in Baltimore."

"But I'm glad you came back to Richmond. None of this could have happened without you."

That's more true than you think, Samuel thought.

"Another slice of cake?" James asked.

"No, thank you. But now I know why you do such good business. This cake is—"

The bell on Samuel's door jangled at the sudden arrival of a customer, and from the sound of it, the door had been thrown open harshly. Samuel motioned for James to stay put, stay quiet, and he got up to investigate. When he walked into the main room of the shoe shop, he was stunned to find John Allen standing just inside the door, hands on hips.

Allen didn't wait a beat before shooting off his mouth.

"Where's Henry Brown?"

20

Richmond
March 1844: Five Years Earlier

The train loomed large. With smoke belching from its stack, the train locked wheels, braking and bringing tons of black steel to a squealing stop. The train, at a standstill, hissed and vented steam. Then a box. Henry saw a box inside the train, a simple wooden box, barely more than three feet long or high. The lid was off of the box, and Henry felt himself hovering over it, as if he were suspended in air, like a bird that could maintain the same position in the sky. Looking down, he saw himself laid out in the box. His eyes were closed. Was he dead? Was this his coffin? How could he fit in a three-foot coffin? Then a hammer. And a hand. A hand was pounding nails into the box. Sealing it up. Sealing the coffin. Each strike of the hammer made an echo, and each echo started up before the previous one had ended, doubling, tripling the sound. Three nails. Four. Pounding, pounding.

Henry's eyes popped open. Just a dream. In the distance, a train whistle sounded, and he found himself breathing in and out so hard that he was afraid of waking Nancy.

"Bad dream?" asked Nancy. Too late. He had already awakened his wife.

"Don't really know," said Henry. It was true. The dream had nightmarish qualities, but it didn't really frighten him. Even the coffin didn't scare him.

Henry and Nancy lived in a one-room shack on the back of the property of Joseph E. Colquitt. Like their previous cabin, it was a compact box of a home, only twelve feet by twelve feet and barely seven feet from the dirt floor to the ceiling. The gaps between the logs were filled with clay, but they were peppered by cracks that let in a chill wind. Once again, Henry and Nancy didn't have to share their cabin with another family, and a good thing too. They now had three children.

"Go on back to sleep," Henry said, and Nancy murmured something unintelligible as she draped an arm over his side. Then the crying started. This time, it was no dream. Gideon, their newborn, was ready to feed—and he usually picked the darkest time of the night to suckle. The baby's squalling caused a stir from their two other children, Sarah and Adam. Groaning, Henry dragged himself from the straw-covered pallet and cupped his hands over his ears, which were numb with the cold. After rubbing his arms for warmth, he picked up the baby, who was wrapped in blankets in a box.

Without a word, he handed Gideon off to Nancy. She looked exhausted, but at least this was one time she didn't have to face the glares of Mrs. Colquitt, who hated to see slaves nursing their children during the workday.

Henry dropped back onto the pallet and quickly pulled the thin, coarse blanket up tight to his neck. Then he drew in his legs, so every part of his shivering body was beneath the blanket. His nose was cold, but there was nothing he could do about that.

Henry had just drifted back asleep when the thumping began, a pounding on the door. Sarah woke to the sound, and she rubbed the weariness out of her eyes. "What is it, Mamma?"

"I'll find out," Henry said, dragging himself out of bed again and stumbling to the door. Amos, one of the house slaves for the Colquitts, stood at the threshold, lantern in hand.

"Come quick, Henry! Master Colquitt wants ya!"

Although Mr. Colquitt was Nancy's master, his demands were Henry's commands. Henry looked back at Nancy, who was still nursing.

"Go," said Nancy. "I'll be fine."

"Pray for me," he said, slipping on his cold, stiff shoes before ducking out the low door and following Amos across the dark yard behind the

Big House. Amos's lantern cast dancing shadows on all sides.

"Is this about his illness?" Henry asked.

"Everything is about his illness."

Mr. Colquitt had recently taken to his sickbed; and according to stories making the rounds, he was getting worse. Abraham Fox, the conjurer, claimed credit for the illness, telling Henry that he had pointed a broom at Mr. Colquitt a few weeks back—a sure way to shorten someone's life, he said. Henry and Amos slipped past the gazebo overlooking a creek and garden, and a sense of death permeated the darkness. They followed a pathway to the Big House—an imposing house with ornate gables, a second-story balcony, and a cupola rising from the center. The cupola was lit up in the dark like a glowing eye, keeping careful watch on everything below—as if the house itself were as vigilant as Mrs. Colquitt, the mistress of the place. When Henry and Amos reached the Big House, Mrs. Colquitt stood at the door, a tall, thin, imperious woman who had perfected the art of intimidation, despite her relative youth at thirty-one years of age. She had a narrow, hatchet face, which was only fitting; Mrs. Colquitt used her hatchet-like tongue to regularly cut her husband down to size. She didn't believe in God or the devil, and some said she *was* the devil. No wonder she had been booted out of her church.

"Took you long enough," she snapped.

"Master Colquitt is askin' for me, ma'am?"

Mrs. Colquitt gave Henry a long look of disdain. "Yes, although I can't imagine why. He is becoming desperate, I suppose."

Mrs. Colquitt led Henry to the staircase.

"The doctors haven't helped," she said, "and the prayers of his church haven't helped. So now he's decided to try colored prayers. He'll do anything to keep breathing."

"Yes, ma'am."

"He thinks you're a magic man of some sort. In his book, you have got a direct connection to the Lord Almighty. But I'll tell you right now, I think it's all nonsense."

"Yes, ma'am."

Henry walked softly across the wood floor as he entered the room, lit up by a few candles and the glare of the fireplace, which wrapped him in its warmth. He found Mr. Colquitt in the large four-poster bed, buried in thick quilts, piled one on top of another.

Mr. Colquitt looked like a frightened animal, the kind Henry had seen caught in leg traps. He was thirty-eight years old, a heavy-set man, but not grossly obese, just plump. He had a round face and a slightly large nose, and his thick mutton-chops merged with his moustache, but his chin was whisker-free. He was always impeccably groomed, even on what he feared to be his death-bed.

Mr. Colquitt had been going through what seemed to be an interminable succession of chills and fevers. The doctor had bled him and doused him with calomel. And even though he was buried under a mountain of quilts, he couldn't stop shivering and shaking like a snake's rattle. The quilts were tucked tightly beneath his chin, so Henry couldn't see his body at all, even his arms. It almost looked as if his disembodied head was just sitting there on the pillow.

"Henry, pray for me. Ask the Lord to spare my life."

What could Henry say? Mr. Colquitt was his wife's master. "Yes, sir. I will, sir." Henry got down on his knees by the side of the bed and propped his folded hands on the bed. His right knee ached from a work injury, but he tried to ignore it. Mr. Colquitt turned his head in his direction, and Henry caught a whiff of his sickly breath. Henry squeezed his eyes shut.

"Almighty God, we ask that you reach on down from Eternity's Throne and heal Master Colquitt here." Henry paused, trying to picture the Lord reaching His hand down from heaven and into the room. The silence stretched on as he searched for just the right prayer.

"We ask that you pour eternity into him and wash this here sickness away. You promised that the desert will rejoice and sprout flowers. And Master Colquitt, he sure feels like there's a big ol' desert inside of him. His body's dry as a locust's shell, and it needs life, it needs your gentle rains, your living water. So pour down your healin' and make that desert sprout flowers. Pour your life into Master Colquitt!"

Henry paused. Sensing another presence in the room, his eyes drifted off toward the door, which was slightly ajar, and two cold eyes peered inside the room at him, glaring. It was Mrs. Colquitt, taking in every word. Henry quickly looked away from her stare, as if he feared that her gaze could turn him to stone. He found it difficult getting back into the flow of praying when he sensed the eyes of the devil boring holes in the side of his head.

Suddenly, he felt something cold—cadaver cold—take hold of him, shocking him back to reality. Mr. Colquitt had reached out and grabbed his folded hands.

"Keep praying. Don't stop now, boy."

So Henry prayed on. He really had no choice in the matter.

Nancy carried a basket of clothes toward the back door of the Colquitt house because she was planning to spend the morning washing laundry at the narrow creek that threaded its way across the land. She always seemed to be lugging baskets of clothes somewhere or other. Setting the basket on the kitchen counter to catch her breath, she gazed out the back window. A cluster of purple horse nettles grew wild not far from the house, and a large hare bounded by the door at top speed, changing direction with startling dexterity. It was one of the first warm days of spring, and all of the windows had been flung open. Flowered air filled the house.

The idyllic scene was suddenly spoiled by heated words coming from the room adjoining the kitchen. It was Mrs. Colquitt. Normally, Nancy didn't eavesdrop on Mrs. Colquitt, preferring to stay out of the woman's way as much as possible. But Mrs. Colquitt had been on the warpath ever since Henry and several other slaves prayed for her husband over a week ago, so Nancy was anxious to know what her mistress was plotting.

"You have become a laughing stock!" Mrs. Colquitt said for what seemed like the millionth time.

"Just because I had slaves pray for me?"

"And for letting them spread tales about how they healed you. Do you even realize how that looks?"

"I'm alive aren't I?" was Master Colquitt's defense, but it appeared to be a pretty feeble defense in his wife's eyes.

After Henry had prayed that first night, Master Colquitt felt somewhat restored come morning. Feeling hope for the first time since his illness struck, he had demanded that Henry return the next few evenings to pray at his bedside. He also commanded him to bring in reinforcements —several of Colquitt's own slaves, the holiest rollers. So Henry had gathered a group of slaves together, and they prayed for Master Colquitt three nights straight.

By the end of the three days, Master Colquitt was back on his feet.

Perhaps foolishly, Nancy made her way across the kitchen to the door of the interior room. She peeked through the door, which was slightly ajar, and saw Mrs. Colquitt standing over her husband. He was seated and still looked weary from his brush with death. He had lost weight, and his normally round, pink cheeks were grayish and hollow. Mrs. Colquitt's withering look shrank him even deeper into the folds of his stuffed chair.

"The prayers of coloreds and their mumbo-jumbo Jesus had nothing to do with your so-called healing, and you should not have let your slaves say otherwise. Isn't it time you showed some backbone?"

"I have already punished those who went telling people they healed me with their prayers. I whipped them good. They won't be spreading stories any more."

"But you haven't punished them all. You haven't punished the worst offender."

Nancy's hand flew up to her mouth. Mrs. Colquitt was speaking of Henry.

"Henry belongs to another man, and I will not touch another man's property."

Nancy backed away from the door in alarm and didn't notice that she brushed up against a ladle, which slid along the counter and hung on the edge, teetering.

"We don't have to be the ones to whip him," Mrs. Colquitt said, exasperated. "I know someone who *does* have the authority to put a hand on him."

It took a moment for Master Colquitt to respond. The words sunk in. "You mean John Allen?"

"I have already spoken to him. We have an agreement."

Startled, Nancy backed up another step, accidentally brushing against the ladle once again. That was all it took to tip the ladle over the edge and send it clattering against the floor. Quickly, Nancy picked up the ladle and put it back, and then she grabbed a hold of her basket on the kitchen counter and made for the back door. But Mrs. Colquitt was too swift for her.

"Why aren't you outside washing the clothes?"

Nancy stopped and turned to face her mistress. "Sorry, Mrs. Colquitt. I didn't mean no harm. I knocked the ladle down and I'm sorry."

Mrs. Colquitt put her hands on her hips and held her fierce gaze. The mistress knew she had been snooping. That much was clear. Mrs. Colquitt always complained about snooping slaves.

Nancy kept her eyes on the floor and made a slow move toward the door.

"Nancy!"

Turning back again, she raised her eyes to meet Mrs. Colquitt's gaze, afraid of what might be coming next, afraid of the whip.

"Yes, ma'am?"

"We have a mind to sell you. You know that, don't you?"

"Yes, ma'am."

"Now get on outside and start cleaning. Make your final days with us more productive."

"Yes, ma'am."

Nancy staggered out the door with the basket on her right hip, but the spring day had lost its appeal. She could think of only one thing, and it nagged at her all day. Would they sell her down South, as far as possible from Henry and the children?

Nancy would have preferred the whip.

21

March 23, 1849
4:35 p.m.

Henry exchanged one form of darkness for another. He emerged from the darkness of unconsciousness only to find himself still immersed in the blackness of the box. His vision had returned, but he wasn't sure if he had been unconscious for seconds or hours. The back of his neck was streaked with pain—as if somebody was sinking a knife into his neck every time he turned or tilted his head. When the box had crashed to the ground, his head struck the wall, and the box tumbled over several times down an incline, leaving him upright. Terrified that his neck might be broken, he checked to make sure he could still move his head, fingers, and toes. He still had feeling—too much feeling, too much pain. It was all he could do to keep from hollering.

Henry noticed that the little bit of light filtering through the holes seemed less intense than before. Something blocked the faint pinpoints of light that had been streaming in on the far side of the box. That "something" also seemed to be moving just outside the box, causing the light stream to flicker. He heard voices.

"Did you hear that?" asked the same cargo handler who had come up with the bright idea of shoving the box off the back of the wagon. His voice was close—just outside the box.

"Yeah, I heard somethin'!" shouted the wagon driver. "I heard the box nearly split apart—thanks to that ridiculous idea of yours!"

"I heard a cry, a sound inside this here box. Didn't you hear it? You was right there."

"Why you couldn't just lend me a hand I don't know," the wagon driver griped. "If you'd—"

"Shhhhhhhhh!"

Henry could sense the cargo handler close, and he pictured him putting his head up against the box, like a doctor listening for a heartbeat.

But the wagon driver wasn't letting go of his frustration. "We need to get this box on the train."

"Will you be quiet?"

The cargo handler shuffled from one side of the box to another. He tapped the side of the box. Then he shook it. Henry's neck screamed with pain, and his cut hand throbbed. Must've banged it during the fall.

"This is odd," said the cargo handler. "Do you see these holes here?"

"Boxes have holes. Knotholes, all kinds of holes. Just help me lift the box and be done with it."

"But these holes have been drilled. Why do you suppose?"

"Dunno. Maybe they're shipping an animal in there or something."

Henry heard the man scooting around to another side of the box. He noticed that the light flowing through the holes suddenly became completely blocked on one side, and he knew instinctively that the cargo handler was right there, inches away, peering through one of the holes. Henry wanted to become invisible, to merge with the darkness.

"C'mon," the driver pleaded. "I don't got all day. Let's get this box on the train."

"Will you shut your mouth! I told you . . . I thought I heard something inside this box. Something *living!*"

Henry held his breath. He didn't dare make a sound.

"You're insane, that's what you are. Help me get the box on the train and then you can spend all the time in the world putting your ear next to packages. You can listen to any box on the train. You can even *talk* to the freight if you'd like."

Henry thought he heard the two men scuffling, but no punches were thrown, from the sound of it. He also heard the wagon driver muttering under his breath. "We shoulda just kept the box on the wagon all along. Now it's gonna be twice as hard to lift from the ground."

It took him this long to figure that out?

"Will you quit your belly-aching?" The cargo handler's voice was more distant, but moving closer. "I gotta figure this out."

Had the man gone off to retrieve tools to open the box? Employees couldn't get away with that, could they?

All of a sudden, Henry gave a start and almost shouted out, more out of surprise than pain. Something had just poked him; something pointy had hit him in the lower back on the right side. Two quick jabs. He tried to look at what it was, but his neck hurt too badly to twist around. When it poked him again, he realized that the cargo handler was jabbing a stick through one of the holes.

"Whatya doing now?" complained the wagon driver.

"Just poking around, figuring this out."

Henry tried to squeeze himself into a corner, away from the probing stick. But there was no space to completely avoid it. He also couldn't make any sudden movements to dodge the stick. He could only move by inches. The stick shot through again, this time cracking when it jabbed him squarely in the back.

"Something's in there, and it seems soft. If it was an animal, I woulda thought it'd snarl, bark, do something," said the cargo handler.

Henry stifled an urge to shout. The cargo handler had a fresh stick, a sharper stick, and he was probing again, like an incompetent magician jamming swords into a box.

Samuel blocked the way into the back room, where James was hiding. John Allen had just barged into the shoe shop like he owned the place, with his ever-present whip at his side and a coil of rope slung over his shoulder.

"Where's Henry Brown?" the overseer repeated.

Samuel maintained a poker face, even though John Allen's words stunned him. How could Allen know anything about Henry's disappearance?

"Why are you asking *me?*" Samuel said.

"Don't act innocent. Where's Henry?"

"Now how am I supposed to know where you keep your own slaves?"

John Allen flung the coil of rope onto a nearby table. Then he picked up a man's shoe from the counter and rolled it around in his hands. "I've been watchin' you, Smith. I know you've taken a likin' to Henry Brown and his family."

"That isn't a crime. And don't touch the merchandise unless you're here to buy."

John Allen tossed the clunky shoe on the counter, and it skipped off the edge and clattered on the floor. "We believe that Henry has run."

Samuel maintained a tight-lipped expression. He folded his arms. "You sure he isn't just losing time somewhere?"

"He's not at the factory, not at his home, not anywhere."

"I'm sure he's somewhere, Mr. Allen. Everyone is somewhere."

John Allen put his hands on his hips. As he did, his thin black coat pulled back just enough to show a gun strapped to his waist. "Are you gonna help me or not? Or are you gonna be obstructin' this investigation?"

"Investigation? You make it sound like you're the law. And if you're the law, I'm the Pope."

John Allen took a step closer. He and Samuel were only an arm's length apart now. John Allen was a couple of inches shorter, but he rose up on his toes, putting them eye-to-eye. Samuel smiled.

He knew John Allen hated it when he smiled.

Reaching into his back pocket, John Allen pulled out a torn shirt. "I think this is Henry's. This was torn off a slave runnin' on the streets last night."

Samuel gave the shirt fragment a passing glance, concealing his rising alarm. "Looks like Obadiah's shirt to me," he said dismissively.

John Allen jammed the piece of shirt back in his pocket, and Samuel flinched, thinking he was going for his gun.

"You seem a little jumpy, Mr. Smith. I think this is from Henry's shirt, and I also think you know how he escaped."

Samuel turned towards his worktable and picked up a small hammer. "Well if that's all the questions you have for me, then I must excuse myself. I have work to do."

The moment he heard a click, Samuel realized he made a big mistake by turning his back to John Allen. Trying not to make any quick moves, he turned to confirm the sound. John Allen had a gun pointed at his gut.

Samuel raised his hands, palms outward. "Come on now, no need for this."

"I think there is. I ain't leavin' here until I know how you got Henry Brown out of Richmond."

"Then pull up a chair. You're going to be staying quite a spell because I don't know what you're talking about."

John Allen shoved a chair in Samuel's direction. "You take a seat. I'll stand, if you don't mind."

When Samuel didn't obey immediately, John Allen aimed at his kneecap.

"Just calm down now," Samuel said, easing into the chair and sizing up the weapon in John Allen's hand—a silver Colt revolver. He had heard that Allen was a poor shot, but the barrel was now pointed at his face, only two feet away. Even John Allen wouldn't miss from that close.

22

Richmond
April 1844: Five Years Earlier

The sky unleashed everything it had. All morning, storms had been rolling over Richmond, and a downpour had turned Cary Street, which passed in front of the tobacco factory, into a messy mix of mud and manure. Richmond's roads were all dirt, and when it rained they were all mud.

The factory was a large, plain, rectangular, brick building, divided into large rooms, each dedicated to a different job. In one room, women, boys, and older men did the stemming. After the leaves were stripped off the stems and dried, they were dunked in a sticky mixture of licorice and sugar; and after the leaves went through another drying, they were sprinkled with rum and other flavorings. The next room, the twisting room, was crowded with tall benches, where slaves twisted and trimmed the flavored tobacco into plugs and sent them on to be shaped into lumps. Then the lumps of tobacco went to the prizing room where Henry spent much of his day.

"I hear ya prayed Mr. Colquitt into health," said Thomas, the same giant of a man who drove Henry into Richmond so long ago. Thomas was now in his forties but still as powerful as ever. Henry was not nearly as tall as Thomas, but he was stocky and strong, an obvious choice to work in the prizing room. Thomas and Henry used a screw press to squeeze lumps of tobacco into compact shapes, ideal for boxing. A dozen screw presses were scattered around the prizing room, each manned by two strong men slick with sweat, even on this temperate day in early April.

"Who'd ya hear it from?" Henry asked.

"Can't rightly remember. But word of the healin' is goin' 'round, and I heard the Colquitts don't like it one bit."

"I told those fools who did the prayin' with me not to say a word. I knew the Colquitts would hate people knowin' that slaves healed him. They're afraid folks'll think we got closer relations with the Almighty than they got."

Thomas snorted. "If it hadn't a been for you, Mr. Colquitt mighta had *really* close relations with the Almighty. He mighta been staring God in the face, assumin' that's where he's headed. Don't make no sense to me. I'd a thought—"

Suddenly, Thomas let out a cry and lurched forward, as the snap of the whip cracked across his back, lightning fast. John Allen had snuck into the room unnoticed, and he had struck the highest tree: Thomas.

"Less talkin'! More workin'!"

Thomas gasped for air. "Yes, sir."

John Allen leaned over, simian-like, so he could snarl directly in the face of Thomas, who was still buckled over. "Mr. Barret put me in charge while he's gone. And you know what he says about me, don't ya?"

"He says Mr. Allen is always right," Thomas responded. Obediently.

Allen wheeled around on Henry and spit out the same question he had given Thomas: "What does Mr. Barret say about me? I wanna hear it outta your mouth too."

Henry didn't answer, *wouldn't* answer.

"I asked ya!" he screamed in Henry's face. "What does Mr. Barret always say?"

Mutely, Henry stared right back at him. So John Allen spun back toward Thomas and lashed out again at the large man. The whip didn't hit Thomas squarely, but the tip of the whip licked his cheek, leaving a small, diagonal slice.

Henry's stare turned to shock. He wasn't expecting Thomas to pay for his silent protest.

"Do ya hear me, boy? What does Mr. Barret always say?"

Henry averted his eyes but maintained the same furious expression. He bit out the words. "Mr. Allen is always right."

John Allen smiled and lowered his whip hand. "That's right. You remember that now."

Master Barret was well aware of John Allen's ways, but he never stepped in to halt it. The master often traveled for the sake of his sickly wife; and whenever he was gone, he always left John Allen in charge because, as he liked to tell his workers, "Mr. Allen is always right."

"With you squawkin' away like chickens, I'm gonna keep an eye on your day's output," John Allen told them. "At two cents a pound, you better not be short on your work, or I'll make you pay in flesh."

"Yes, sir," Thomas said, but Henry did not respond.

Thomas and Henry returned to work, turning the cold steel lever and squeezing the lumps of tobacco into molds that shaped them to fit snugly into boxes. Henry took out his frustration on the lumps, wishing he could squeeze them into oblivion.

John Allen sat down on a nearby barrel, dug a

pouch of tobacco from his hip pocket and took a whiff of it before jamming a wad into the corner of his mouth. He began to chew and calmly observe Henry and Thomas at work. No one said a word for the next few minutes.

Nancy had warned Henry that the Colquitts made a deal with John Allen, paying the overseer to whip him for the embarrassment caused by his prayers. But Henry almost wished he didn't know of the impending punishment; it was like being told you're going to die. The anticipation was almost worse than the actual event. He had never been whipped in all his life.

"You pleased with yourself, Henry?" John Allen suddenly asked matter-of-factly.

Still straining on the press, Henry squeezed out his answer. "Should I be?"

Thomas gave his friend a warning glance, and John Allen spit out a brown stream of juice. "Word's gone 'round that you and your colored friends healed Mr. Colquitt."

"God did the healin'."

"You sayin' I don't know what I heard?"

Henry didn't answer. In the distance, a low, long rumble of thunder passed through the atmosphere, and the rain beating on the roof increased in power. The downpour became a deluge. John Allen's eyes darted to the nearest window, and Henry could see the subtle signs of fear in his expression. Everyone in the factory was well aware that John Allen was terrified of thunderstorms.

"Nasty storm," Henry said, throwing a glance over his shoulder at the window. "I'd sure hate to be out in the woods on a day like this."

John Allen stopped in the middle of a chew, his mouth hanging open.

"What's that you say, boy?"

"Just sayin' it'd be awful bein' caught out in the woods with lightning standing your hair on end and blinding you with flashes."

Thomas kept glancing between Henry and John Allen, and he looked puzzled. Henry never told him how he had once rescued Allen in a thunderstorm. And in all of this time, John Allen and Henry had never once spoken a word about the incident, but it haunted their every interaction.

"You're real pleased with yourself. That true, Henry Brown?"

"No, sir."

"You sayin' I'm lyin' again?"

Henry didn't answer. Thomas's eyes went from Henry to the whip in John Allen's hands, back to Henry.

"You think you're a saint or somethin', don't you?"

"No, sir."

"You go 'round healin' people, helpin' people, that it?"

"I help—when people need helpin'."

John Allen stood up and circled Henry and Thomas as they continued to sweat and strain at the screw press. Henry wished he could insert John Allen's head between the press and do some real squeezing. He'd love to see that thick skull burst open like a watermelon.

"Maybe some people don't like your help. Ever think of that?"

"No, sir."

The sky suddenly lit up, and a thunderclap exploded. An extremely close strike. John Allen tried to conceal his fear, but Henry could see it in his eyes. Henry smiled, which made John Allen even angrier.

"You friends with God, Henry?" John Allen asked.

Henry had no idea where he was going with this question. "Yes, sir."

"You think you can pray this whip right out of my hand?"

"I can't perform magic, Mr. Allen."

"I didn't think so."

John Allen, his eyes a mixture of fear and fury, tightened his grip on the whip and advanced on Henry.

Henry straddled a chair in the middle of his cabin, his back on fire.

"I'm sorry," Nancy said.

"No reason to be. You didn't put these marks here."

Henry had his shirt off, revealing a bare back crisscrossed by lash marks, still raw and red. With a wet rag, Nancy gingerly cleaned the wounds, and Henry cringed under the touch.

Nancy dipped the rag in a bucket of water and wrung it out. "Maybe we should think about runnin'."

Henry spun around to look her in the eyes. "We can't run. Not with a family."

Trying to flee, just the two of them, would be difficult enough. But now they had three children, and one was an infant. What was she thinking?

"We also can't stay."

Henry reached out and took Nancy's hand. "Listen, I can take a few lashes from John Allen here and there. It's sure better than what they'd do to you and the children if we was all caught fleein'. It's a small price to pay to keep ya safe."

"But Henry . . ."

He swung away from Nancy. Matter settled. Nancy dabbed his wounds, then dipped the rag in the bucket and wrung it out. Reaching out again with the rag, she hesitated.

"Mrs. Colquitt's threatened to sell me," she said.

Henry cringed, even before Nancy touched his wounds.

• • •

"Mr. Colquitt is asking six hundred and fifty dollars for the purchase of your wife," Samuel Cottrell told Henry the next Sunday afternoon. "But I can afford only six hundred."

Samuel Cottrell was in the market for Nancy, but Henry still didn't understand why the man had asked to see him. Spouses had no say in sales, so he was suspicious. Henry sat at his sawbuck table, with its flimsy, X-shaped legs, and he kept his eyes on the man as he moved about their cabin. Cottrell was slim and tall with dark eyes and a dimpled chin. He was clean-shaven with wavy hair, a little unruly just above his left ear. He wore a dark jacket over a light tan vest, and his checkered cravat stood out beneath his starched collar. Quite the dandy.

From what Henry understood, Cottrell was a wealthy saddle and harness maker who numbered many customers among the Richmond gentry. Pretty good for a young man of only twenty-five. But evidently, it wasn't good enough.

Cottrell sent a sly smile in Henry's direction. "I don't have the money to purchase your dear wife, but there is something you can to do to help my situation."

Henry steeled himself for what was coming.

"If you could cover the additional fifty dollars, then I will be able to purchase Nancy. That way, you can be assured that she would not be sold away from you."

"Fifty? But that's pretty much everything I have."

"Your family is pretty much everything you have."

Henry paused to think. He could hear the voices of Sarah and Adam just outside the cabin, playing on this cloudy afternoon. When Cottrell arrived, he had asked to talk with Henry privately, and Nancy got the message. She took the children outside, but not until she exchanged nervous looks with Henry. She knew Cottrell's business concerned her.

"Mr. Colquitt has other buyers in mind, but I'm the only one in Richmond," he told Henry. "The others would take Nancy away from you. This works to your advantage."

Henry nodded. Sometimes, he wondered if Nancy would have been better off with Ned Cooper after all. Ned bought his freedom two years ago, just as he always said he would, and some believe he had even made it to New York. Right now, he was probably running that cook-shop he always envisioned.

"I'll set y'all up with a real nice, one-room place down in Shockoe Bottom," Cottrell added. "Y'all can keep living together as a family."

Henry had little more than fifty dollars to his name, money he had been saving up by doing overwork at the factory. Most slaves at the factories were not paid enough money to get by on, so they had no choice but to do overwork. For Henry, that extra money was about to disappear into the hands of Cottrell.

"Yes, sir, I agree to your generous terms, sir." Henry dropped his head. He was so weary of it all.

Cottrell broke into a great grin and slapped Henry on the shoulder. "I knew you'd be agreeable! I'll make arrangements with Mr. Colquitt. And once Nancy is in my service, I would not sell her away from you."

Henry looked up and carefully considered this promise. "Nancy's master, the one when we first got married, promised much the same thing, sir."

"But I'm not like other masters! I'm certainly not Mr. Colquitt, thank God, for that would make me married to Mrs. Colquitt, and that would be reason enough to put a gun in my mouth and pull the trigger!"

Cottrell laughed out loud. Henry was terrified to laugh at any joke at the Colquitts' expense, but he was also afraid *not* to laugh for fear of offending Cottrell. He compromised with an uncomfortable smile.

Slapping Henry on the shoulder once again, Cottrell made for the door. Then he paused and slowly turned.

"Henry, there's one other thing you can do to help yourself . . . and me."

Henry didn't like the sound of this. "Sir?"

"You must also pay for your family's lodging from your own pocket. And you must pay me an additional fifty dollars every year."

"But . . ."

This demand was highly irregular, for most owners provided something to cover the lodging fees for their slaves.

"If you don't, I will sell Nancy so fast it'd make your head spin. Good day, Henry."

Cottrell was out the door before Henry could even stammer another "Yes, sir."

Henry remained at the table, stunned. Outside, he heard the man give a hearty hello to Nancy and the children. Then Cottrell started whistling, and Henry listened to it fade away down the path.

"Well?"

Henry broke out of his daze and looked up. Nancy was at his side, with their infant Gideon resting on her right hip.

"You're staying in Richmond," Henry said. "Mr. Cottrell is your new master."

"That's a good thing, ain't it?"

Henry tried to shake loose from his nagging fears. He smiled back. "It is."

Nancy seemed convinced. Now he just needed to convince himself.

23

March 23, 1849
4:50 p.m.

"Into the back room," John Allen commanded. His gun was about a foot from Samuel's head.

The back room. Where James was hiding.

Samuel didn't respond instantly, buying time for James to slip into a hiding spot, if he hadn't found one already. John Allen stood directly in front of Samuel, and he waved his gun toward the back room. "On your feet."

Still no response from Samuel. When John Allen pointed the gun at his kneecap again, Samuel decided not to push his luck. He rose groaning from the chair, as creaky as an old man.

"And take the chair with ya," John Allen ordered.

Stretching his back, as if to work out the kinks, Samuel slowly, slowly picked up the chair and dragged it with him.

"Move it!"

Shuffling into the back room, Samuel scanned for any sign of James. Not a trace. There were really only two possible hiding spots—the wardrobe and a large shipping box. The back room didn't have any windows or doors, so James had to still be in here. Somewhere.

"Sit."

Samuel pulled up the chair, scraping it against the floor. He sat.

"Hands behind your back."

John Allen circled behind, keeping the gun pointed at Samuel. When Samuel tried to follow his movements, turning his head and peering over his shoulder, the overseer ordered him to keep his eyes straight ahead. Then John Allen tied his hands so fiercely that Samuel wondered if he had cut off blood flow. Once his hands were bound, Allen wrapped another piece of rope around his waist to secure him to the chair.

"This is awkward, but can you scratch my nose for me?" Samuel asked.

"Shut up."

"You know you don't have the authority to do this. You're not the law."

John Allen stepped back to admire his handiwork. "I'm quite good with knots. And I do have the authority, seein' as you stole William Barret's property, as I know you did."

"You also thought Obadiah escaped. How accurate was that?"

John Allen circled around to face Samuel from the front. He set his gun on the worktable and unhitched the whip from his belt. Samuel's heart began to gallop.

"I was thinkin' at first you snuck Henry on the train somehow by havin' him pretend to be someone else's slave, or pretend to be a freeman, or somethin' of that sort."

"Is that what you also thought I had done with Obadiah?"

John Allen lashed out, and the whip cracked the air. Samuel ducked to the right, but the dodge wasn't necessary. The strike of the whip was meant to frighten, not injure. It did its job.

"You mention Obadiah's name again, and I won't miss."

Samuel licked his lips, which had gone dry. His whole mouth was drought-stricken.

"I have to hand it to Henry," John Allen said. "He made himself a convincin' injury. Cut his self to the bone just to get a few days off from factory work. He must have a high threshold for pain." The overseer jostled the whip in his right hand. "How's your threshold for pain?"

Squirming in his bonds, Samuel discovered that John Allen was right about one thing. He knew how to tie strong knots.

"I'll give you another chance to answer, Smith. How'd you get Henry Brown out of Richmond?"

Samuel didn't respond. He stared at the whip, which coiled on the floor like a snake at John Allen's side. Allen stood directly in front of him and adjusted the whip so it stretched out behind him. Was he going to go for his face? Samuel's stomach muscles tensed. He had never been whipped, never been tied up. The combination of defenselessness and terror was a powerful drug. Samuel's body began to shake.

"You can do jail time for what you're doing," Samuel said. Fear was evident in his voice.

"And you will do jail time for aidin' a slave to escape."

Keep an eye on his right thumb, Samuel told himself. *Watch the thumb and you'll know where he's aiming, you'll know which way to duck.*

John Allen stepped into the strike, snapping back his hand. Samuel ducked to the left, and the popper, the thin strings on the end of the bull-whip, cracked just by his right ear. His dodge was pure luck, for he hadn't been able to track the aim of Allen's thumb.

"Good guess," Allen said, "but whatya think the odds are that you'll be able to guess which way to duck every time?"

John Allen struck again before Samuel even had time to think through the question. Samuel ducked to the left again, and the whip snapped right beside his ear. The crack set Samuel's ears to ringing. He blinked the perspiration out of his eyes.

"Two lucky guesses in a row. I'm impressed."

John Allen took his time, pacing around the room, playing with his grip. Anticipation was more than half the pain.

"You feel like talking yet, Mr. Smith?"

Samuel shook his head.

"You oughta know the odds on this, Smith. You can't keep dodgin' all day."

John Allen made a full circle around Samuel and then snapped the whip. Samuel ducked to the right—directly into the path of the fast-moving strap. The whip caught him just under the right eye, a stunning sting. Pain flared.

"You're insane!" Samuel shouted. His heart was pumping wildly.

"You better be careful, Mr. Smith. I ain't aimin' for your eyes. But you move wrong, you could lose one by accident."

Samuel struggled to catch his breath. This was madness.

"All right, all right." His head slumped forward to his chest.

"You'll talk?"

"I will."

Samuel leaned forward, watching two drops of perspiration fall between his legs and hit the wooden floor. "Henry Brown got out by wagon last night."

John Allen stared long and hard at Samuel.

"Liar!"

Samuel, with his eyes still focused on the floor, instinctively ducked to the left. Another wrong choice. The whip caught him under his right ear, and he shouted out in pain. His face was on fire. If he didn't think of something soon, his face was going to be picked apart, one small slice at a time.

Henry held in his groan. The stick, this one sharper than the last, hit him in the middle of the back. He ground his teeth and breathed in and out through his nose, absorbing the pain.

He heard a shuffling sound move around the box, and suddenly the stick came shooting inside the box through one of the holes directly in front of him. Caught him right in the stomach. It wasn't sharp enough to tear through his shirt, let alone break his skin. But it hurt, and the surprise of the jab made it difficult to keep from yelling. The stick retreated, but he knew it was coming back for another assault. *Should I grab the stick and break off its tip? Will the man think it broke apart naturally?* He couldn't take the chance.

Henry squeezed backwards into the corner of the box, trying to make himself smaller. He expected another attack from the front, but the stick came down from above through one of the holes he had drilled in the top. This time he caught a break. The stick came down inches in front of his face.

"Okay, enough of your games," he heard the wagon driver say. "We need to load the box, and we need to do it now. I gotta leave."

"Leave then," said the cargo handler.

Don't leave, Henry prayed. *Don't leave me at the mercy of this maniac.*

Another jab from above. This time the stick sliced a thin strip of skin from the very tip of Henry's nose as it slid past. The cargo handler had been probing methodically, but he suddenly went wild, jabbing the stick into one hole, then hurrying to another hole and plunging it through again and again, then doing it from the top, jabbing, jab-bing, jabbing. Henry curled himself into a ball, covering his face and head, taking the stabs, one after another.

The wagon driver shouted: "That's enough! You're gonna break whatever's in there!"

"So?"

"If it was an animal or something, it woulda made a noise. I'm partly responsible for this package, and I say that's enough!"

Henry heard scuffling.

"Get your hands off of me!" More sounds of shoving. Then: "I don't know what you're moaning about anyway," said the cargo handler. "There ain't room for this box on the train, anyway!"

He's lying.

"What are you playin' at?" said the wagon driver. "There's plenty of room on the train for this box, and you know it."

"No, there ain't. Not for this size box."

Don't believe him.

"You told me to push the box off the back of the wagon, and now you're tellin' me ya won't even put it on the train?"

Henry heard one of the men spit. "I never told you to push the box off the back of the wagon. Where'd you get that notion?"

"So you expect me to just leave the box here?"

"No, I expect you to take it away in your little cart and bring it back here tomorrow morning. It can go with tomorrow's shipment. Do you ever stop complaining?"

Tomorrow's shipment? Impossible. Henry would never make it that long. He would have started sobbing if he didn't know that two men stood only feet away.

24

Louisa County, Virginia
1847: Two Years Earlier

Henry's sisters, Jane and Martha, leaned on either side of him for support. It was a blustery autumn day—a bright, blue day, with leaves on the move by the thousands. Jane held the hand of Henry's first born, Sarah, and all four of them moved together as one body down the gentle, grassy slope. Sarah carried a cracked pitcher, which Henry had told her to bring along. Wind gusts pushed on their backs as they slowly approached the grave.

Mamma had died in her sleep; she just wore out and didn't wake up. Henry was thankful she had gone quietly and quickly. If her life wasn't easy, at least her death was.

Henry hadn't been back to the plantation since he was fifteen years old, the day his family was split apart, the day when all he could think to say to his Mamma was: "Ya still got me." This afternoon reminded him so much of that day seventeen years ago, except this time it was his sisters who leaned on him. Mamma didn't need his shoulder any more; she had broader shoulders to rest upon.

Henry, now thirty-two years old, wished Nancy could have been here with him so Martha and Jane could meet her at least once. Nancy's master, Mr. Cottrell, said he couldn't afford her being away for even a day, let alone a week. But at least Master Barret had given Henry permission to come to the plantation with Sarah. John Allen protested this kind of "pampering," but Master Barret said he wanted to give Mamma a good send-off. The master was not much younger than Mamma, and his memories of her went back a long way.

Sarah was now ten years old, thin as a reed and somewhat tall for her age. She took after her mother both in appearance and in voice, and she had just begun singing in the choir of First African Baptist. Henry couldn't be more proud. Sarah had never seen a plantation before, and her eyes took in all of the open space and quiet with the same amazement that he felt when he first experienced Richmond's congestion and noise. She had never met her aunts, and he could tell she didn't know what to make of these two sad women.

They shuffled through the leaves, moving down the slope to the patch of ground where all of the slaves were buried. A simple wooden cross with Mamma's name marked the spot where they had buried her. Two nights earlier, slaves from neighboring plantations—the ones who got permission—had come to the Hermitage to pay their respects and participate in a candlelight procession from the Big House to the slave cabins, where her coffin was set on trestles. Then everyone gathered around the coffin in the firelight to sing.

"Put the pitcher there on the grave," Henry told Sarah.

Mamma's grave was already covered with other pitchers, cups, jugs, vases, all of them cracked.

"Remember your Creator before the silver cord is loosed, or the golden bowl is broken, or the pitcher shattered at the fountain, or the wheel broken at the well," Jane recited. "Then the dust will return to the earth as it was, and the spirit will return to God who give it."

Mamma had been buried with her feet pointing east and her head in the west, so she wouldn't have to turn around when Gabriel blew his trumpet in the east. She could stand right up and march to Glory.

They all knelt on the ground, and Martha moaned as she rocked back and forth. Jane began sobbing, for Mamma had been her anchor. Henry put his arms around his sisters and wished Edward could be here with him; he would know what words of comfort to say. But Edward had gone west a year ago with his master, who had caught gold fever. Hunting for gold sounded like something Edward would relish.

While Jane and Martha trudged back to the cabins, Henry told them he and Sarah would follow shortly. He had a sudden idea, something he wished he had done with his oldest child a long time ago. They headed toward the forest— the very woods where Henry had once chased a horse in the middle of a thunderstorm.

"Is Grammy in Heaven?" Sarah asked, kicking up the leaves.

"Yes, she's with the Lord now."

"She happy?"

"I'm sure. Ain't no one a slave in heaven."

"Adam says that people turn into ghosts when they die and they hang around Earth just moaning."

"No, Grammy's with Jesus. Who ya gonna believe? Your brother or your papa?"

"My papa."

Sarah swung her father's arm back and forth like a bell rope. "Where we goin', Papa?"

"Just walkin'."

"Walkin' where?"

"Up ahead. To the trees."

The edge of the woods created a wide wall of color—autumn trees at their peak. The trees were beginning to shed, covering the ground with a quilt of color. Henry led Sarah underneath a massive tree that displayed leaves of three different bright colors, like the feathers of a tropical bird. It was brilliant yellow along the very bottom branches, with hints of bright green mixed in the foliage as you moved upwards; the top two-thirds was completely dominated by orange. Next to it, an all-yellow tree towered above them, a giant of a tree, and at its base was a burst of bright red bushes. Burning bushes. Holy ground.

Henry stopped and crouched down, putting an arm around Sarah. He felt the wind blowing, tugging at his shirt, pulling at his pants. He held onto his daughter more tightly.

"Mamma took me here when I was little, much younger than you," Henry said.

Sarah didn't answer. She threw her head back and stared straight up at the treetop, and her black, broad-brimmed hat fell off.

"Mamma taught me about bein' a slave."

Sarah picked up her hat and pulled it down tight

on her head, to keep the wind from yanking it off. Henry pointed at the leaves whipping and skipping along in invisible currents. "That's us," he said.

Sarah looked confused.

"The wind carries us wherever it wants to. Leaves don't get to choose where they go, Sarah. And we don't neither."

"That's us, Papa?"

Henry didn't expect Sarah to fully understand. His words were as much for him as for her. She scratched her head, poking her hand beneath her hat.

"The wind carries us, Sarah. We belong to the wind."

"I thought we belonged to Massa."

"It's the same thing."

"How's that?"

"Trees can't hold on to their leaves. Slave families can't hold on to their people."

Sarah picked up a single leaf, a large orange one, and brushed Henry's nose with it playfully. Henry wrapped her in a hug, and then they walked hand-in-hand back toward the Big House, putting their heads down and leaning into the gusts. Twice, the wind whipped Sarah's hat off of her head and she had to run to get it back.

Henry Brown whistled as he hiked along bustling Broad Street. The street was jammed with carts and wagons of all sorts, and an argument between two men was just getting heated on the corner of Broad and Sixth. It was summer of '48, a good nine months since Mamma passed on, and Henry was on his way to pick up a pair of shoes for Master Barret at Fisher's Shoe Shop, just a hop, skip, and a jump from James's cake shop between Third and Fourth. Henry scratched at his upper lip, for he had grown a moustache in the past month, and it still itched. The thin moustache was divided into two parts that didn't quite meet above his lip; but Nancy liked it and convinced him to keep it.

Henry and Nancy and their three children had been living in a tenement in Shockoe Bottom ever since Cottrell purchased Nancy from the Colquitts. The tenement could only be reached by walking down an alleyway, flanked on either side by shanties, crumbling stone walls, and rotted fences with so many missing pickets that it looked like a mouth of missing teeth. The tenement was falling to pieces all around them, it smelled of mold, and some of the rats looked to be the size of cats. The place cost six dollars per month, stretching Henry to the limit; but because it was tucked away in back alleys, the home gave Henry and Nancy a degree of privacy they had never before experienced. As a result, the last four years had actually been the happiest that Henry had known since coming to Richmond. He had learned how to stay out of trouble with John Allen, and he still had his singing at church, which was now called First African Baptist Church. The whites of First Baptist had finally formed a separate church back in 1841, and they sold their old building to the all-black First African Baptist.

Passing by the cake shop, Henry noticed that James still hadn't opened for business. Probably a late night for James and his latest lady friend. Up ahead, Henry was surprised to see Samuel Smith wrestling with a heavy box in the back of a wagon parked just in front of Stephen Fisher's shoe shop—the very place where Henry had business to do. He knew Samuel from his Red Boot shop in Low Town, because Master Barret used to get all of his footwear repaired there before it closed down. Samuel had always been a friend to him.

"Can I help with that, Mr. Smith?"

"Why thank you, Henry."

Henry got a good grip on the opposite side of the box and they slid it off the back of the wagon. "Where to with the box?" Henry asked.

"Into the shoe shop. These are my supplies and tools."

"The shoe shop? Ya mean y'all gonna be working for Mr. Fisher?"

"That's right, Henry. My Red Boot days are long gone, and I'm working for someone else now."

They maneuvered the box through the doorway and left it on a long, dusty worktable running against the back wall. Samuel wiped the dirt from his hands with his handkerchief.

"Mr. Fisher runs a good place, what I'm hearin'," Henry said. "Master Barret sent me here to pick up some shoes."

"True, Mr. Fisher is a fine man. But it's just not the same as being the one in charge."

"I'm afraid I wouldn't know, sir."

Samuel smiled kindly. "Perhaps I'll resurrect my lottery business—although I probably should know better. The lotteries already cost me everything; and as a consequence, all I own can fit into a box about the size of the one we just moved. I don't have much more to lose."

"We all have things to lose, Mr. Smith."

"I reckon you're right."

While Samuel emptied tools from the box they just brought in, Henry retrieved the final box from the wagon, a smaller one. And when that was done, Samuel held out a coin. "Thanks for the help."

"Oh no, sir. I couldn't be takin' that."

"Nonsense," he said, slipping the coin into Henry's shirt pocket. "You have a family to be thinking of. What is it now? How many children?"

"Three, sir. A fourth on the way."

"A fourth! Good man, Henry! Mr. Barret should be pleased with your fruitfulness. Mr. Barret, the tobacco man, I presume he's still your master and Nancy's?"

"He's mine, Mr. Smith, but he's never been Nancy's master. She's owned by a Mr. Cottrell."

Samuel gave a start at just the mention of the name. "*Samuel* Cottrell?"

"Yes, sir. That's him. You know him?"

Samuel stroked his chin distractedly. "In passing. He too likes to play poker and the lotteries. Maybe a little too much for his own good—like me."

Henry smiled awkwardly and looked away. It didn't seem right for a white man to criticize another white man in front of him.

"I guess playing the lotteries comes from being in bondage to gambling. And as you might say, Henry, we're all in bondage to something."

"Some by choice. Some not, Mr. Smith."

Samuel thought about those words for a second before breaking into a smile. "Very true, Henry. Now let me see if I can get you those shoes for Mr. Barret."

Samuel Cottrell wasn't really in any position to own four slaves. But four slaves put him among the Richmond elite, so he couldn't resist. He hadn't purchased a slave since he bought Nancy Brown several years earlier, and he was beginning to wonder if his latest purchase had stretched him past the breaking point.

Cottrell maintained a small house in High Town, which did not come cheaply, and he had turned to gambling as a quick and easy way to make money and clear his debts. He had the "quick" part down fine; it was the making money part that didn't come easily. He had always gotten by on his surface charm, which served him well with both customers and the ladies. But one of these days, he worried that his long string of debts was going to come back to haunt him, charm or not.

Today was one of those days.

Cottrell kept his saddler shop neat and presentable. One entire wall was covered with leather straps and saddlebags, all hung in a long, orderly row. His tools—the awls, steel needles, and knives—all had their proper place. And in the center of everything was a sturdy oak table, where he currently worked on a lavish saddle for a Mr. Worthington.

"Be right with you," he said without turning around to see who had entered his shop. But he could hear that a customer had just crossed the threshold. *Two* customers from the sound of it.

When he heard someone rummaging through the leather straps on his wall, Cottrell wheeled around to see who was toying with his materials.

"Can I help you . . . ?"

Cottrell dropped the piece of leather from his hands. Enoch and Caleb Benson came at him, and Enoch had a leather strap in his hands. These were massive men with disproportionately small minds. Cottrell fumbled for a tool to use as a weapon, but seconds after he picked up a bridle awl, Caleb had him by the wrist and squeezed and twisted until Cottrell thought his hand was going to be twisted completely out of its socket. He dropped the tool, and Enoch stepped around him from behind and wrapped the leather strap around his neck. Then squeezed. Cottrell's air was completely shut off.

"You're due, Cottrell," said Caleb, calmly running a hand across the Worthington saddle.

Cottrell wanted to explain himself, but right now he was more concerned about taking his next breath. Caleb picked up one of the bridle awls, a tool that came to a fine, sharp point—perfect for poking holes through leather. And eyeballs.

"You should be careful with these things," said Caleb, toying with the awl. "A guy could poke his eye out."

Taking Cottrell by the hair and yanking his head backwards, Caleb placed the sharp tip of the awl only inches away from Cottrell's fear-filled eye. Cottrell was terrified at the very idea of an implement plunging into the delicate workings of his eye. Since he owed them money, they were probably not inclined to strangle him just yet. But losing an eye? That was very real.

"Ya got our money?" Caleb asked.

Enoch tightened the leather strap, and Cottrell, desperate for oxygen, tried to speak, but all that came out were strangled sounds. He didn't dare thrash around to get free—not with a bridle awl so close to his eye. He couldn't look at the silver steel point hovering only inches away, so he closed his eyes, expecting the awl to penetrate his eyeball any moment.

Enoch took Cottrell close to the brink of darkness. Then he finally released the tension on the leather strap, while Caleb pulled back the awl. It was a good thing he pulled back the tool because Cottrell instinctively lurched forward when he was released; if the awl had still been in his path, he would have been minus an eye. Cottrell fell to his knees, grasping his throat and coughing, his body still struggling to draw in oxygen.

"So ya got our money?" Caleb repeated.

"I'll get it . . . get it soon."

"Ya'll been tellin' us that plenty. Ya know, our money supply is like our air, Mr. Cottrell. When ya won't give us our money, it's like you're chokin' off our oxygen. Ya know how that feels, or should my brother here demonstrate again?"

Cottrell shook his head, nearly in tears. "No, no, I'll get it, I will!"

"You do that. For now, we'll just be taking this fine saddle as your down payment. Okay?"

Cottrell had no choice but to nod.

"You know how to get in touch with us."

Cottrell kept nodding, still on his knees and still rubbing his neck.

"Oh—And here's your awl. Be careful with it, now."

Looking up, Cottrell saw it coming down swiftly, and he tried to dive out of the way, but it was too late. The steel point sank into his shoulder, as deep as Benson could drive it. Pain erupted, and before he fainted the last thing he saw was Caleb Benson hoisting the Worthington saddle over his shoulder.

The train loomed large as it roared into a station. Steam and sound, a jumble of faces. It was all so disorienting. People milled around the train, conductors and disembarking passengers, more faces, more colors, a dizzying, nauseating twirl of images and sounds. Then a large door. The door to one of the train's cars slid open with a bang. The inside of the car was nothing but blackness, like an open mouth. Then the box. Henry saw the simple wooden box inside the train again; he was hovering, looking down on the box, looking down on himself laid out inside the box. The next instant, he was still in the box, but now he was looking up and out of it. A bird, trapped inside the train car, fluttered above, trying to break through, but hitting walls on all sides. Henry couldn't see the bird, but he could hear its wings, hear its futility. Then a lid. Someone was lifting a lid—a coffin lid?—and it was being placed directly over him. Henry tried to call, "Stop!" But no word would come out. He tried to sit up, but he couldn't move, couldn't do a thing, couldn't make himself known, like being trapped in a trance. The box lid slammed down on him. Then darkness, complete darkness. A voice spoke in the darkness, a whisper, someone whispering in his ear. "Go . . . ," said the voice. That was it. "Go." Then the sound of hammers as someone pounded nails into the soft wood of the box. Three nails. Four. Pounding, pounding.

"The Lord give you another dream?" Nancy asked.

"Mmmm . . . He did," said Henry.

Henry, Nancy, and their three children were gathered around the table for breakfast—corn bread washed down with murky water. Food supplies had been running low, and Henry had cut down his own portions so the children would have more. Nancy could usually count on bringing back scraps of food from the Big House, where she did work in the kitchen in addition to clothes washing. But Cottrell wasn't letting any food leave the house of late, especially meat.

"Trains again?" asked Nancy.

"That's right. Makes no sense to me. But this time I heard a voice."

"The Lord's voice?"

"Don't know. It only said 'go'."

"Just 'go'?"

"Just 'go'."

Sarah set down her cup of water. "Do the Lord give us our dreams?"

"He give us everything, honey," said Nancy. "The whole world, dreams and everything. You thank Him ev'ry day, now."

Six months pregnant, Nancy was clearly showing. She was happy she could now catch the scent of food in the morning without needing to run out into the yard and be sick.

"I'm off to fetch some wood," Henry said after excusing himself from the table. But he hadn't even reached the door when he spotted a face darting by the window. Henry opened the door, and in swept Nancy's master, Samuel Cottrell, without so much as a greeting. Henry and Nancy exchanged looks. The day before, Nancy had reported that Mr. Cottrell came back from the shop with a deep puncture wound in his shoulder, and he had Nancy tend to it. Henry found the top of the shoulder an odd spot to accidentally puncture yourself while working, as Cottrell claimed.

"Good mornin'," said Henry, but Cottrell didn't respond. He was agitated. He walked over to the hearth and stared into the fire, not saying a word. Finally, he turned to face Henry squarely. "I need more money."

Henry was stunned. Hadn't he robbed him clean already?

"But I ain't got any more money to give, Mr. Cottrell. I already pay for my families' needs for meat and clothes, for my wife's hire, and for the rent for this house. I ain't got nothin' more to give."

Henry didn't know how much money Cottrell needed, but someone had obviously backed him into a corner, which is a dangerous thing to do to a snake.

"I will have money!" Cottrell slapped the table with an open hand. A cup tumbled sideways, spilling water, and their youngest child, Gideon, began to sob. Cottrell glared at Nancy and Henry, as if he expected them to suddenly pull a stash of cash out of a magic hat. But as he looked around the austere shack in silent frustration, he must have realized how foolish it was to think he could extract more money from them. He'd have better luck squeezing water from a rock.

"For your sake, I would try to get some money together right quick," Cottrell demanded. Then he stormed from the cabin as quickly as he had arrived, leaving Henry shocked and dumbfounded. Nancy slumped onto a seat, breaking down in tears. Sarah also began to cry, and Adam just looked furious.

Forces beyond their control were stirring. The winds were picking up again.

25

March 23, 1849
5:05 p.m.

John Allen was pleased. Pain and fear was doing its job on Samuel Smith, and the shoemaker had all but confessed to helping Henry Brown escape. But John Allen still needed to find out how.

"You have anything more to say, Smith?"

Samuel slumped back in his chair, his smirk gone. His left and right cheeks were slashed with thin lines of blood, and a trickle came down from his right ear. He didn't answer.

"I got lots of time, Smith. I can do this all day."

John Allen threw all his weight into the next lash. This time, Samuel's reflexes were not so quick, dulled by the pain. The whip hit him in the forehead, and Samuel cried out louder than ever.

Not wanting any passersby to hear Samuel's sounds of pain, John Allen scanned the room for any sign of rags—something to use as a gag. His eyes fell on the large shipping box stashed in the corner.

"If you're gonna wail away like an infant, you'll be needin' a gag. You got some rags in this here box?"

The shoemaker shot a glance at the box, and John Allen saw a flash of fear in his eyes. Just a split second of uneasiness. Samuel was troubled. But about a box?

No. It's not possible, John Allen thought. *Could it be that Henry Brown never left Richmond? Could he be hiding in this box in this very room, right under his nose?*

Setting his whip on a worktable, John Allen took out his gun and strode over to the box in the corner. It was a simple shipping box, big enough to hold a man. John Allen reached out slowly, carefully. He slipped his fingers under the edge of the lid, and in one swift move he hurled it backwards. Then he lunged forward and aimed his gun inside the box—an empty box. No sign of Henry Brown. No rags either.

But John Allen was sure he had seen something in Samuel's eyes. Something was going on here that he hadn't quite figured out. Leisurely, he walked back to Samuel, working this out in his mind. He pressed his gun against Samuel's knee. "What is it about that box? Tell me or I shatter your knee!"

Samuel's eyes bulged.

"Okay, okay, just pull your gun away!"

Samuel let out a breath as the barrel of the gun lifted from his knee.

"So what is about that box?"

Samuel took his time in answering. He wouldn't

look John Allen in the eyes. Finally: "We put Henry on a boat out of Richmond."

"And what does that have to do with a box?"

"Nothing! I'm just saying—"

"Tell me about the box!" John Allen put the gun up against Samuel's temple, pressing it into his skull.

"All right, I'll tell you!"

John Allen lowered the muzzle.

Sweat poured down Samuel's face, and Allen could see that the cuts had him in deep pain. He was primed to talk.

"We put Henry in a box. On the boat. That's what I'm saying."

John Allen considered himself an expert judge of liars. He knew the telltale facial signs, and Samuel was lying. Still, hiding Henry in a box on a steamboat did make sense. It all fit together, for he remembered seeing a large shipping box in Samuel's home a little over a week ago, and the shoemaker seemed obsessed about a box on the train just this morning.

The train.

The box was not on a boat. It was on a train.

John Allen's initial hunch about the train this morning had been on target after all. Wrong slave, but right hunch.

John Allen pulled up a chair and straddled it, facing Samuel from about five feet away. He shifted his aim back to Samuel's forehead. "I

270

think you're right about one thing: Henry Brown is in a box. But he's on the train to Philadelphia."

Samuel didn't answer, but John Allen had hit the mark. He could see it in Samuel's eyes.

For the first time, Henry thought about giving himself up. His lower back had begun to spasm so that the slightest move paralyzed him with pain. What he wouldn't give just to lay flat on his back and stretch out his legs. If he gave himself up, he could stand up, stretch out. He'd have to do it in a prison cell, but at least he'd be out of the box.

Henry never realized before how important it was for the human body to continually switch positions. It wasn't natural to stay folded up for this long. His bandaged hand was throbbing, and he feared that infection was setting in. What good would it do to arrive in Philadelphia with poisoned blood? He might step out of the box and directly into a grave.

Henry made up his mind. If the box wasn't put on this train, he would bide his time, try to wait until he wasn't surrounded by people, and kick his way out. He pushed on the ceiling of his box, testing its strength. It was solid. Was it even possible to kick his way out? He didn't have enough legroom to kick with power.

"I'm not puttin' this box back in my wagon," he heard the wagon driver say. The driver and cargo handler were still arguing about the fate of Henry's box.

"Fine. Leave it here on the platform all night for all I care. It's not going on this train. You leave it sitting here, and some hooligans will probably come by and bust it open for fun. I don't care a whit, but I'm sure your boss won't be too pleased."

Strange, but Henry was almost looking for an excuse to break out of the box. Giving up seemed so much easier.

"Sir!" the wagon driver called out. "Could you help me load this here box onto the train?"

It sounded like the driver was trying to flag down help from a third person. Another cargo handler?

"I already told the man there ain't no room on the train," said the first cargo handler. "The box'll have to wait till tomorrow."

"You heard him," said the new man on the scene. "If there ain't no room, then there ain't no room."

That settled it then. His box was marooned.

"But the box has been sent express," said the wagon driver.

Silence. Henry wished he could see what was happening.

Finally: "If it's express, then the box must be sent on." The new voice had declared final judgment.

"But there ain't no room, I tell you!"

"Then *make* room."

"*You* make room!"

The first cargo handler stomped away, from the sound of it. The remaining two men went to work, and Henry heard them positioning themselves on either side of the box. His box rose into the air to the sound of groans.

"Heavy stuff. What's in this thing?"

"Don't know. Just hope it ain't broke."

Henry couldn't agree more.

26

Richmond
July 1848: Eight Months Earlier

Thomas's bare back gleamed with sweat. He wrapped his thick arms around a hundred-pound box of tobacco and shoved it into place in the back of a wagon. The heat and humidity were brutal. The moisture was so thick that Thomas and Henry felt as if they were working on the bottom of the James River.

Moving ploddingly through the waterlogged atmosphere, Henry lugged another box to the wagon. He and Thomas were working alone just behind the factory, and Henry's white cotton shirt was sopping. Drops streamed down his forehead, stinging his eyes.

"Cottrell is actin' like he's aimin' to sell Nancy," Henry said. "I can't keep goin' on like this. I'm goin' outta my mind."

"Cottrell, he got himself into a gamblin' mess, that's what I hear," Thomas said.

"Just how bad is his money woes do ya think?"

"Really bad. He's got some big debts piling up, and the Benson brothers are after him."

"The Benson brothers? That don't sound good."

Henry paused to wipe away the sweat from his face with the back of his forearm. As he did, he left an ash-black smear across his forehead. He glanced around to make sure no one was within earshot. "Nancy's been talkin' 'bout runnin' again."

Thomas was about to pick up another box, but he stopped, straightened up, and stared at Henry. "With a family? You wanna try runnin' with young 'uns and her expectin' another? You'd never make it."

"That's why I told her no. But I'm startin' to wonder."

"Seems like a big risk to run. When she's been . . ."

Thomas paused as he suddenly noticed that Jeremiah, an elderly slave, had hobbled out of the back door of the factory and was just standing there fumbling with his hat. Jeremiah opened his mouth to speak, but the words wouldn't come. His jumble of black and white teeth looked like a bad ear of corn.

"Somethin' wrong, Jeremiah?" Thomas asked.

More fumbling with the hat. "It's Nancy, Henry."

The words hit Henry hard, like the kick of a mule.

"God, no."

"Cottrell took Nancy to the auction post this mornin'," Jeremiah said. "And the children. I'm sorry."

Without a word, Henry slid a box onto the wagon, fitting it neatly between two other boxes. He could barely breathe. These were the worst words he could have heard. When Nancy had been sold before—by Mr. Lee and Mr. Colquitt—the negotiations were made behind closed doors. But this time it was the auction block, and there was no telling who would buy her and where she'd wind up. People came to Richmond from all over the South to buy slaves—the busiest slave market this side of New Orleans.

Henry felt something building inside, a steamboat boiler about to blow. All at once, he threw all of his power behind his fist and punched a hole clean through the wooden box. When he pulled back his hand, his knuckles were torn and bloody and stained with tobacco.

Thomas put a hand on his shoulder, but Henry shook loose.

"I gotta go to her."

"But what can you do to stop Cottrell?"

"I aim to find out."

Henry wasn't going to stand around and watch her taken. Not this time. Not like he did with his brothers and sisters. He was going to make someone hurt. Henry stalked off of the factory grounds and began to run. Faster, faster, frantic and furious. He sprinted in the direction of the cluster of auction houses in Richmond's Low Town at Franklin and Fifteenth Streets, not too far from the tobacco factory. When slaves were put up for sale, they were kept locked in jails, like cattle waiting to be sold and slaughtered.

Henry's mouth went dry and his heart raced just contemplating what he was going to do. He picked up a sizable stick, a makeshift weapon lying by the road, and his mind played out fantasies of rescue and revenge. He saw himself breaking his wife and children out of the jail and then fleeing north. He saw himself taking a machete in his hand and cutting down anyone who stood in his path: Nat Turner come back to life.

"Ooompf!"

Wrapped in his fantasies, Henry didn't even see the white man jump out in front of him, and they collided. Panicking, Henry made a move to charge on by, for running into a white man could bring consequences. But the man grabbed hold of him. "Henry! Stop!"

It was Samuel Smith, the shoemaker. Samuel put two hands firmly on Henry's shoulders.

"Don't go to the jail," he said.

"But Cottrell's sellin' Nancy down south! My children!"

"I know! But they've also got orders to put you in jail if you interfere."

"I gotta try."

"You can't stop it with a club." Samuel eyed the thick, knobby stick in Henry's right hand. "You'll make it worse. They want to jail you."

"But I have to—"

"Talk to Mr. Barret. He can do something, surely!"

Henry wanted to break loose, break heads. But Samuel continued to keep his hands firmly on his shoulders. "You can't stop this with a club."

"Yes, I can."

Samuel put a hand on the club. Gently.

"Talk to Mr. Barret," he added. "You've got to try."

Samuel slid the club out of Henry's hands. The moment the weapon was out of his grip, Henry's shoulders slumped and he felt an overwhelming sense of desolation. He wanted to cry, but Wilson Gregory had broken him of that habit a long time ago.

"If you talk to Mr. Barret, you'll stand more of a chance. So will Nancy and the children."

Henry looked off down the sloping path toward the slave trading district, in the direction of Nancy. Maybe Samuel was right.

"Tell her I wanna come to her, but they'll jail me if I do," Henry said. "Tell her I'll find a way to see her. I will."

"I'll do that, Henry, I promise. I'll also tell her you're talking to Mr. Barret. He's got to help."

Henry pinched his eyes, to keep back the tears. "But I can't just . . ." His voice began to crack, so he went quiet.

"Go to Mr. Barret. It's the best thing you could do. Ask Mr. Barret to purchase Nancy. You've been loyal to him. He'll help."

"Just tell Nancy I'll find a way."

Samuel nodded, and Henry tore off. He had to keep moving, had to take action. He ran in the direction of Gamble's Hill and Mr. Barret's mansion. It was all uphill.

Samuel headed for the nightmare slice of Richmond. Birch Alley. Locust Alley. Exchange Alley. Wall Street. Crammed together in this back-alley wasteland were over fifty slave-dealing facilities. Richmond's version of Wall Street traded in souls rather than stocks and bonds.

Samuel kept his eye out for the red flag, which announced that a slave auction was in progress, drawing people like flies. If he found the red flag, he might find Nancy Brown and her children. Samuel made his way down a steep embankment and hopped over a gully to reach this part of

Richmond, the most squalid section of the city. He marched past several small prisons, where slaves—many of them from the countryside—were locked up, awaiting auction. Large fences blocked the view, but fences could not keep back the terrible smells, especially in this heat. Still looking for the red flag, Samuel came upon the most notorious slave-trading facility of them all in Richmond—perhaps the most notorious one in the country. It was Lumpkin's Jail, better known as "The Devil's Half Acre," and it was fittingly located where Grace Street came to an end. There was little grace to be found inside Lumpkin's Jail.

Robert Lumpkin established the slave trading post in 1840 and had placed it at the center of the whirlwind that was the slave-trading industry in Richmond. Lumpkin's Jail was actually a compound of several buildings. There was the Lumpkin home, as well as a guesthouse, complete with a barroom for wealthy slave traders visiting Richmond. For the most peaceful slaves awaiting auction, there were plain brick buildings; but for the troublesome slaves, there was the infamous Lumpkin Jail. This two-story, forty-one-foot-long monstrosity was what earned the place its name: "The Devil's Half Acre."

Just past the Devil's Half Acre, Samuel finally spotted what he had been looking for—the blood-red flag flapping in the wind. A slave auction in full swing. A cloud of tobacco smoke hung like a canopy over the outdoor spectacle, where black families were brought up onto a wooden platform and given a thorough going-over by prospective buyers. Some buyers had the slaves walk a short stretch, like horses, to make sure they were not hobbled in any way. Some examined muscles, pinching skin and squeezing arms. Others examined teeth. If a slave liked the look of a buyer, some were not shy about talking up their own attributes—or those of their family.

"Ya won't find a better man than me," said one tall slave, a man well over six feet. "My wife, Sally, she's a first-rate field hand. Almost as good as me. Stand out here, Sally, and let the gentleman see."

Like selling rope by the foot, height often determined price. Boys four feet high: five hundred to six hundred dollars. Boys four feet, three inches: six hundred to seven hundred dollars. Boys four feet, six inches: eight hundred to nine hundred dollars.

Samuel looked for any sign of Nancy and her children. She had come to his shoe shop on many occasions, running errands for her master, so he knew her well. He had taken a liking to her.

Cottrell, Samuel thought bitterly. Samuel had always despised the man, but he could have never guessed that his disgust for him would have unforeseen consequences for someone like Henry. How could he have forgotten that Henry's wife was owned by Cottrell? Samuel was furious at himself. He had cleaned out Cottrell in late-night poker twice. *Twice!*

Samuel had owned slaves of his own once, but he never felt comfortable with it. His wife Mary Ann had insisted. She cared about status, so he had played to the hilt the part of a gentleman. But now that his status—and his wife—had gone, his dislike of slavery had grown, although he wouldn't dare admit such thoughts out loud.

There was no sign of Nancy, which was probably a good thing. Perhaps she hadn't yet been put on the auction block. But as Samuel squeezed through the crowd, he felt a sudden shove from behind, and he went stumbling forward, nearly tumbling face-first into the dirt. Before he could regain his balance, he was given a second shove and went crashing into the arms of a very surprised and very overweight farmer. Samuel shook himself loose and turned to face his attacker.

It was Cottrell.

"Well if it isn't the card shark," said Cottrell.

Samuel was in his forties, so Cottrell had almost twenty years of youth on him. But Samuel also knew that Cottrell was soft, so he had no fear of the man. Cottrell could only put up a good fight if he was attacking unseen from behind.

Rushing forward like a bull, Samuel grabbed him by the lapels and forced him backwards, slamming him into the side of a shack.

"Where is she?" he demanded.

Cottrell didn't seem phased. "Where's who?"

"Where's Nancy Brown and her children?"

Cottrell grinned. "Why Samuel, you surprise me. Didn't know you had a taste for dark meat."

Samuel drew back his fist, aiming for Cottrell's nose; but even that didn't wipe the smirk from Cottrell's face. A split second later, Samuel found out why. A strong hand latched onto Samuel's forearm, holding back his punch and spinning him around.

He found himself face to face with Enoch and Caleb Benson. Unlike Cottrell, these two men were anything but soft.

"I paid back my debt to you today," Cottrell said to the two brotherly bruisers as he came around to get a better view of Samuel's startled face. "Doesn't that deserve a little reward? Would you be so kind as to break his nose?"

"No worry," said Caleb. "This fella did us in at the card table two weeks back. This fist is on the house."

Samuel didn't even have time to duck. He felt the startling smash of bare knuckles against his face, flattening his nose, and he heard the sound of snapping cartilage and breaking bones. His bones.

The nine blocks to Master Barret's house were all uphill, so Henry's run soon became a trudge.

The day felt so heavy, and the heat weighed down on him, making every step difficult.

The house servant Fanny escorted Henry down the main hallway to the office on the right. Master Barret owned several large dogs, and two of them followed Henry into the office, sniffing at his heels. The office was a well-lit room with a large window, a fireplace, and an expansive, polished, walnut desk, behind which Master Barret stood shuffling through papers. He didn't look up to greet Henry. Master Barret was in his early sixties, but he looked ten years younger, with a full head of hair and only traces of gray. He had a business-like air. Most masters kept a wall of formality between themselves and their slaves, but today this wall was like ice.

"Take a seat," he finally said, and Henry obeyed. He always obeyed. Master Barret continued to shuffle through papers as Henry just sat there, ready to burst. Henry was still drenched in sweat, streaked and smudged with dirt, smelling of slavery.

William Barret had always been a puzzle. Although he was often aloof, he went out of his way to make sure that Henry was taken care of, as his father had instructed. Barret was also a member of the American Colonization Society, which had a strange mix of members. Some were against slavery and some were for it, but they all had a common cause—shipping blacks back to

Africa. Like the Society, William Barret was an odd combination of contradictory beliefs.

"I know why you have come," he finally said after dispensing of his paperwork.

"And you know I been faithful all these years, Master Barret."

"And it's not your place to remind me."

Henry looked away and tried to control himself, but he couldn't hold back.

"But couldn't ya buy my family, Master Barret? Help me, I'm beggin'! Couldn't ya buy them? They're my life!"

Master Barret's response came without emotion. "Your family has already been sold. They have been sold to a man from North Carolina."

Henry absorbed this statement in stunned silence. He breathed in the words, felt their pressure, felt himself reaching breakpoint.

"But you can stop this sale, can't you, Master Barret? You can stop it if ya buy my family! Remember how your father raised me."

"The sale has been made. It's out of my hands. It never was in my hands."

"But couldn't ya buy them from the man? Please, I beg you. I been good to ya!"

"What's done is done."

Master Barret led him to the door, and Henry departed in a daze, not sure what to do or where to go next. He couldn't just return to work, as if nothing had happened. So he ventured close to the slave-trading center, hoping to catch a glimpse of his family. But all of the activity had wrapped up for the day. He felt cowardly, ashamed that he hadn't done more. He had to do *something,* had to keep moving, had to take action. He wasn't going to stand and watch his life fall apart. Not again. So he found himself trudging back up the long hill to Master Barret's house.

"I'm sorry what happened," Fanny said under her breath, as she let him into the house.

"Thank ya." Henry took off his hat and stopped to pet the two large dogs that greeted him at the door.

Fanny leaned in close to his ear. "The master ain't in too good a spirits just now," she whispered. "Bad business news, I think."

"Uh-huh."

Fanny led him down the hall, and the two dogs followed, like escorts. He found Master Barret sitting at his desk, poring over papers, so Henry just stood there, shifting weight from leg to leg, for a good five minutes. Finally, the master looked up from his work. He didn't appear pleased.

"Why aren't you at the factory?"

"Please Master Barret, I gotta find out where they're keepin' Nancy and my family. I gotta see them before it's too late!"

One of the dogs—the master's favorite, Cyclone—began licking Henry's hand, which dangled within reach. Master Barret rubbed the weariness from his eyes and then stood.

"You can see Nancy tomorrow morning when they take her away."

"But she's my wife, Master Barret. God brung us together! I gotta go to her tonight."

The master sighed. "You can always find yourself another wife," he said with a flick of his hand. "Don't trouble yourself about this one."

Henry was stunned. Master Barret's father would never have spoken such words. With restrained fury, Henry looked him straight in the eyes. "What God has brought together, let not man put asunder."

Master Barret's face flushed and his voice shook. "Leave my house."

Henry knew he should keep quiet. He knew that if he kept pushing, he too might wind up on the auction block. But he couldn't stop.

"Master Barret, I only want my family back. God gave 'em to me."

"Then talk to God about it, not me." William Barret exited the room and disappeared through another door, slamming it behind him. The door banged like a gunshot.

The next morning, Henry made his way through a crowd, white and black, who lined the street as if they were watching a parade. Young boys sat in trees for a better view. Men came out on the balconies of houses and leaned lazily on the railing, enjoying a cigar as they stared below. At least three hundred and fifty slaves paraded by in a slave coffle on their way further south, some of them in wagons and some on foot. Henry ran up and down the street, looking into every wagon, examining every face.

"Papa!"

The voice was that of his oldest child, Sarah, twelve years old. She had been packed into a wagon filled with other children, and she squeezed to the edge, reaching out for him. Henry ran into her arms.

"Can't you go with us, Papa?" she asked. The tears in Sarah's eyes brought tears to Henry's.

"I can't . . ."

It was happening again. The wind was whipping.

"Please, Papa, please."

As Henry ran a hand across her cheek, he also spotted his two boys in the packed wagon, trying to work their way closer to him. They were caught in the crush of bodies.

"Papa!" It was Adam's voice.

Henry leaned into the wagon, reaching out, straining to touch his boys' hands just one more time. His fingers found Adam's, but it was difficult to hold on as the wagon moved along, and he lost his grip. Then his youngest, five-year-old Gideon, suddenly emerged from the midst of the children, high above all the others, and he realized that Adam had hoisted his brother on his shoulders. Gideon wiped an eye with the back of his fist, while gripping Adam's head with his other hand.

"We'll see each other again, Gideon!" Henry called, still keeping up with the wagon.

"Promise?" Gideon shouted.

"Promise!"

Sarah leaned out of the wagon and hugged Henry's neck, and a strange boy clutched his shirt collar, trying to hold on to something, anything. Even a stranger's shirt would do.

Snap! A man walking alongside the wagon lashed out at Henry, and the whip tore through his shirt, slicing skin. He ignored it, as well as the second lash. But the third lash sent him reeling backwards, and he lost his footing, stumbling sideways into the dirt.

Henry climbed to his feet, and he watched the wagon roll out of reach. Then he spotted her—Nancy. She shuffled along in a group of women and had a heavy chain connected to an iron staple around one arm, linking her to another slave. A rope around her neck tied her to the other women, so that it looked as if they were all snared in one large spider web. Henry squeezed through the crowd, working his way up beside her, and they hugged—but only briefly because the coffle didn't stop for affection. Drawing apart, Henry walked alongside and took her one free hand.

"I'm sorry, Nancy. This is my fault."

"It's not."

"If I coulda paid Cottrell. Given him something. If I coulda broken you outta jail. If I coulda . . ."

Henry didn't finish his sentence. They walked hand-in-hand in silence. Then Henry said: "I will come for you."

Nancy stared at him in alarm. "Henry, don't do nothin' foolish."

"Is it foolish to get your family back?"

"Yes. It could be."

Before Henry could say anything more, a man on horseback appeared beside them.

"That's enough," the man said. "You must part ways."

"Please. She's my wife. Please."

The man stared at Henry without a word, his expression softening.

"Please."

The man looked around before conceding. "You can walk a ways with her. But not far."

"Thank you, sir."

Henry and Nancy continued to walk hand-in-hand—the last time Henry would feel her skin against his. In a year, would he even remember her face? He stared at her, trying to memorize every feature. Eyes, cheekbones, hair, nose, lips, everything that was Nancy. He looked down at her belly, which was showing new life within. Tears appeared in Henry's eyes, and he strained to keep them contained. He leaned over and kissed Nancy, and they walked together for a short distance more before someone finally told him it was time to let her go. Nancy broke down crying, and Henry wrapped her in his arms one last time and breathed in the scent of her hair. In their embrace, he felt the cold iron staple clamped on her one arm.

"I will come for you."

"Don't you do anything foolish."

They kissed again, and then their hands broke apart, a single leaf letting go of a branch, and she disappeared around the bend. Nancy was gone.

27

March 23, 1849
5:40 p.m.

James heard everything. He heard John Allen whipping Samuel, heard Samuel's shouts, and heard Allen figuring out their plan—the box, the train, everything. James was hidden in the mahogany wardrobe in the back of Samuel's shoe shop, standing behind a row of coats with a piece of firewood in his hand. He had grabbed the wood on impulse before leaping into hiding. It was the only weapon at hand.

"Stop aiming that thing at my head, I'm not

going anywhere," he heard Samuel say to John Allen. "You're going to discharge it accidentally if you aren't careful, and then you'll be up on murder charges."

"It ain't murder if I kill a slave thief."

"It is, actually. You aren't allowed to take the law into your own hands."

James wondered why John Allen hadn't left the shoe shop, now that he had extracted the information he needed from Samuel. James didn't think Allen would actually kill Samuel, a white man; he figured he was simply going to leave Samuel here, bound to the chair.

But John Allen wasn't going anywhere, and that was puzzling. James heard the sound of drawers opening and tools rustling.

"Don't ya got paper and pencils or anythin' of that sort around here?" he heard John Allen say.

"If you're going to write your suicide note, I can help you compose it," Samuel said.

James inched forward, hoping that the floor of the wardrobe didn't creak. It didn't. He leaned forward slowly, reached out, and nudged the door of the wardrobe open, just a crack, to get a peek. Through the crack, he could see John Allen leaning over the worktable, scribbling something. He had found a paper and pencil.

Clutching the piece of wood tightly in his hand, James realized this was as good a time as any to act. John Allen was about twelve feet away, with his back to him. So vulnerable. John Allen looked up in space, biting the end of his pencil and pondering every word he was writing.

James put his hand on the door, ready to throw it open. Any second now.

Suddenly, John Allen swung around to face the wardrobe. With eyes fixed on the paper in his hands, he didn't spot James, who pulled back into the darkness. But James had missed his chance. He had to attack John Allen from behind, and that meant waiting for another opportunity.

"Sorry, Mr. Smith, but you leave me no choice. I gotta do this," he heard John Allen say with obvious insincerity.

"I'm sure it tears you up."

James leaned forward again and peeked. John Allen was standing directly behind Samuel, and he had his gun in his right hand. Surely, he wouldn't dare shoot him in the back of the head. He raised his gun, and it appeared that he was going to strike Samuel with the butt of the weapon. John Allen had his back to James. It was now or never.

He bulled his way out of the wardrobe, and before John Allen could spin around, James was smashing the lumber into the back of his head. The cracking sound was the wood, but it was also Allen's skull. The overseer crumpled, bounced off of Samuel's back, and hit the floor.

"Lord, I hope I didn't kill him," James said,

staring at the cracked piece of wood in his hands.

"I hope you did. It took you long enough to finally do something. Quick. My ropes!"

When Samuel craned his neck around, James stopped in mid-motion and stared in shock. The shoemaker's face had at least a half dozen bleeding slashes.

"You can admire my face tomorrow. Untie my ropes."

Jolted back in motion, James began working on the knots and discovered that John Allen was right. He really knew how to tie them tight.

"It's not working."

"There's a knife in the drawer!"

James yanked open the drawer in Samuel's worktable and found a wide assortment of knives for shoemaking. He rummaged through them recklessly and nicked his finger—a good way to discover which one is sharp enough for the job. Using this blade, James sliced the rope as quickly as possible without taking one of Samuel's body parts with it.

"We need to treat your wounds," James said when Samuel was free and on his feet.

"Not yet. We need to drag this monster out into the alley. But first . . ."

Samuel dug into John Allen's pockets, first one side and then the other before plucking out a slip of paper.

"Only be a second." Samuel rushed over to the

worktable, made a couple of quick marks on the paper, and stashed it back into the overseer's pocket. Then they went to work dragging John Allen feet first out of the shop.

The train carrying Henry's box pulled out of the Washington station, heading northeast to Baltimore. Henry nursed his many wounds: his throbbing hand, his aching back and neck, the tender spot on his forehead, the multiple irritations from the jabbing stick, and his right knee, which screamed for relief after being in a folded position for so long. He dribbled a little water on his face and sipped some of it sparingly. He was beginning to feel an urge to relieve himself and didn't want to intensify the feeling.

Henry had prepared a hymn to sing in Philadelphia when he finally escaped from this coffin, and he began to run the verses through his mind —to keep his mind busy, to keep from going completely insane.

> I waited patiently, I waited patiently for the
>   Lord, for the Lord,
> And He inclined unto me, and heard my
>   calling;
> I waited patiently, I waited patiently for the
>   Lord,
> And He inclined unto me, and heard my
>   calling;

And He hath put a new song in my mouth,
  Ev'n a thanksgiving, ev'n a thanksgiving,
  ev'n a thanksgiving unto our God.

The pain in Henry's neck was still sharp and concentrated, and he worked at getting into a position to ease the stabs. By this time, his shirt was soggy with sweat. He nodded asleep a couple of times, despite his vow to stay alert; and it was hard to separate his dreams from his waking moments. At one point, he was hit by claustrophobic panic, a siren inside that told him he had to bust out of this box or he would lose his mind. He resisted the urge to kick out the sides of the box, and his breathing became rapid. Henry put his mouth close to one of the holes, trying to draw in more oxygen, to feel even a pinprick of cool air against his face. As he positioned himself by the hole, his neck muscles went into spasm, and he nearly cried out. Then darkness, as he fainted away. Then shadows and light and stifling heat, as his eyes opened again. He had no idea how much time had passed.

Henry drifted into dreams—images of trains roaring through his mind, steel and smoke, images of his mamma staring at him, helpless, from one of the windows of the passenger car, images of Nancy waving goodbye from the window, images of his children, their faces pressed up against the glass, images of the train curling around a bend like a black snake, then plunging off the edge of the world.

The pain in Henry's neck pulled him out of these brief, disjointed dreams; and without thinking about what he was doing he used his injured hand to rub his neck, triggering a burst of pain in his bloody palm. All he could do to keep going was to keep dreaming of his family and keep running music through his mind.

> Withdraw not thou mercy from me,
> Withdraw not thou mercy from me, O Lord;
> Let thy loving kindness and thy truth always
>   preserve me,
> Let all those that seek thee be joyful and glad,
> Let all those that seek thee, be joyful and
>   glad, be joyful, be glad, be joyful and glad,
>   be joyful, be joyful, be joyful, be joyful, be
>   joyful and glad, be glad in thee.

28

The Outskirts of Richmond
August 1848: Seven Months Earlier

It was almost midnight, and Reginald Black was dead tired. This hot, humid August night had drained every bit of strength from him. His shoes were riddled with holes, and a sharp rock had slipped inside about a mile back, leaving a nasty gash on the ball of his right foot. Each step triggered such pain that he tried his best to keep from putting his full weight down.

Reginald had been in Richmond for three days looking for work, but not a soul would hire him for a bartending job. Most owners were probably afraid he'd drink away their stock, which shouldn't have surprised him since he showed up everywhere stinking of liquor. So Reginald was hobbling back to his brother's farm just east of Richmond. The Prodigal Brother was returning, although he seriously doubted whether his older brother would kill a fatted calf to celebrate his return. His brother was more likely to kill *him* with hard work. Reginald was tired of his brother. He was tired of the farm. He was tired of everything.

It was almost midnight, and Reginald was still a long way from the farm when he first heard the sound off in the distance behind him in the dark. Wagon wheels. Horses. The jangling of bridles. That could mean only one thing: a ride home.

Wheeling around, he spotted lantern light a far ways off, but definitely heading in his direction. As the wagon moved within shouting distance, Reginald cupped his hands around his mouth and called out.

"Halt!"

The wagon continued, as if the driver was stone

deaf. So Reginald stepped into the road, directly in the path of the oncoming wagon. It was a foolish thing to do when he was just a shadow in the moonlight. But he was beyond caring.

"Halt!" Reginald shouted again, holding up both hands like he was surrendering.

The wagon finally came to a stop, only about five feet from Reginald Black. Two horses, one white, one black, stomped and snorted in the dark. A lone man was driving the covered wagon, and he held out a lantern to get a good look at what kind of fellow would leap in front of two horses.

With the driver hidden in darkness behind the glare of the lantern, Reginald couldn't make out his features, only his silhouette. But he could tell that the man was thin and wearing a tall hat—a stovepipe hat, like an undertaker.

"Who goes there?" the undertaker spoke into the night.

"The name's Reginald Black. Could you drop me off just a coupla miles up the road?"

For a moment: no answer. Then, "Sorry. Can't oblige."

Reginald was puzzled and perturbed. As a white man, he was accustomed to generosity among Southern strangers.

"I won't make no fuss. You're goin' that way anyways."

"Sorry, but you don't wanna get into the back of *this* wagon." The man cast a glance over his shoulder, and for a moment Reginald wondered if he really was an undertaker. Perhaps the man was transporting a dead body in the covered wagon. But Reginald could not smell the stench of death, and in this heat bodies would be especially pungent.

"In a two-mile trip, you might not make it there alive," said the man. "I won't be responsible for your demise."

Reginald walked around to the back of the wagon, where the entrance was blocked by a canvas covering. "Whatya got in there? Dead men?"

"Wish they were. I'm carryin' a cargo of troublemakers. I been hired to bring these criminals to Williamsburg."

Reginald was tempted to take a peek. But he didn't want to act brashly; he was still holding out hope that he could talk his way into a ride. He strolled to the front of the wagon. "Kinda quiet in there for criminals."

"They's sleepin', so I suggest you keep your voice down. They's also chained, but if you climb in with them and they wake up, they could strangle a feller like you in a minute. Sorry, I can't let you put your life on the line just for a ride. The walkin' will do ya good."

Any more walking and Reginald was afraid that his cut would get so bad that he'd wake up with his foot stinking black with gangrene. Getting strangled by criminals in the back of a wagon would be a faster way to go.

"Sorry I can't help ya, mister," the driver said, "but I'm lookin' out for your well being."

"But you got room up front." Reginald eyed an open spot on the seat.

"Sorry, official business. Can't take ya on." Before Reginald could utter a word in protest, the driver shook the reins, and the wagon lurched into motion. Reginald hopped aside, almost getting clipped; and as he watched the wagon roll away into the dark, he was mightily tempted to suddenly leap into the back and take his chances with sleeping criminals. But common sense and survival instinct held him back.

"Haven't ya heard of the Good Samaritan?" Reginald shouted. But the driver didn't answer. His wagon faded like an apparition in the night.

Reginald sighed and started walking once again. He was so sick and tired he could just spit.

James had expected romance, not rumors.

"You sure you don't want to go somewhere for a stroll?" he asked his latest lady friend—William Barret's house slave, Fanny. They sat across a table at Letty's cookhouse, but the place was jumping and Fanny was distracted. All of the tables were filled, and at least a dozen other people stood around, devouring the latest rumors more heartily than Letty's food. The noise was deafening, and the cigar smoke thick.

Fanny didn't even hear James's question. She had turned away from him and was embroiled in talk with Letty. "Any word on who the runaways might be?" she asked.

"Not yet, sister. But I heard there was five of them," Letty said.

Swinging back around to face James, Fanny leaned across the table and repeated the news: "You hear that, James? Five runaways!"

"I heard."

"They're sayin' John Blevins got 'em away in his wagon."

James had heard that too. According to the rumor mill, a fellow by the name of Reginald Black reported seeing a white man on the road at midnight on the day the five slaves disappeared, and this mystery man steered a covered wagon loaded with "troublemakers." Reginald Black said the man wore a black top hat, and he dressed like an undertaker. Blevins, a former shoemaker, was known for his undertaker apparel and stovepipe hat.

Fanny twisted around again and lost herself in conversation with Letty, and James gave up on salvaging this evening. He leaned back and absorbed the words winging from one end of the cookshop to the other.

"But that don't make no sense. Why would he

help 'em escape? Blevins owned a slave of his own awhile back."

"And he's been known to turn in escaped slaves for money."

"He's playin' both sides I tell ya, and some white folks are just itchin' to string him up."

"If they can even find him. They ain't found head or tail of Blevins anywhere in Richmond."

James decided he might as well join the speculation, so he leaned to his left and started talking to a man who thought he knew the identity of some of the runaways. The fellow threw out the names of at least ten people who might be on the run with Blevins, and James politely pointed out that one of those men was in the cookshop at this very moment.

Suddenly, James felt a soft hand settle on top of his hand, and he swung back around to find that Fanny had reached across the table. She had taken his hand, but she still wasn't looking at him. Fanny was still deep in conversation with Letty, and James found himself staring at the back of her head, rather than at her large, brown eyes. When her conversation with Letty became especially intense, she squeezed his hand, and James realized that the evening wasn't entirely lost.

With all of the excitement, the night turned out to be a long one, and James slept in on Sunday morning. He found himself running late for Sunday service, although "strolling late" was more like it because he was never one to hurry anywhere. There wasn't anything carefree about his stroll, however. He had woken up worrying about Henry, and he hadn't shaken the feeling. Before the previous night had ended, he and Fanny talked about Henry Brown's misfortunes, for she had been there on the day he showed up to Mr. Barret's, begging the master to buy his family. It was a somber ending to their night, and it stayed with him in the morning.

Lately, Henry had made himself scarce, missing church and not even showing up at James's shop. Henry became withdrawn. That wasn't a surprise, but James worried that his friend was going to do something drastic. Maybe make a reckless escape, maybe hurt somebody. He wondered whether his friend had it in him to kill a man. A month ago, he would have said no. But when Henry talked lately, he spoke of God's justice, God's righteous judgment, and James just wasn't so sure his friend would leave judgment completely in God's hands.

James sauntered east down Broad Street and adjusted the clean, white handkerchief that peeked from his jacket pocket. The sky was slate grey, but he didn't expect rain. He took his time. James was still in the choir, but even that was not motivation enough to arrive on time. It never was.

James strolled on by Monumental Episcopal Church, located on the site of the famous theater fire of 1811. Whenever James or Henry passed by this church, they inevitably thought about how Henry's master, in his younger days, very nearly perished in the theater blaze on the site. William Barret, just twenty-five at the time, had left the theater early—right before the fire broke out, killing over seventy.

Finally, James wound up at First African Baptist. And as he strode into the foyer and swept the top hat from his head, he was struck by the power of the singing coming from inside the sanctuary, loud and spirited. First African Baptist was known for having one of the finest choirs, black or white, in all of Richmond.

"Hold the wind!
Hold the wind!
Hold the wind!
Don't let it blow!"

When James reached for the door leading into the sanctuary, somebody darted out of the corner and grabbed him by the arm. James nearly jumped out of his jacket.

"James, I gotta talk to ya." It was Henry.

"Henry, you gave me quite a fright. Why aren't you in there singing?"

"I got my Jesus, going to hold him fast.
Hold the wind!

Don't let it blow!
I got my Jesus, going to hold him fast.
Hold the wind!
Don't let it blow!"

Henry motioned James away from the door of the sanctuary. With worship in full swing, no one could have possibly overheard them speaking, but Henry clearly wasn't taking any chances. So James followed him to the far corner of the foyer.

"What is it? You got me worried."

Henry glanced around to make sure no one was within earshot.

"I made up my mind. I'm escapin'."

"I'm going to stand on a sea of glass.
Hold the wind!
Don't let it blow!
I'm going to stand on a sea of glass.
Hold the wind!
Don't let it blow!"

James fumbled his cane and just barely snagged it before it clattered to the floor. "You're what?"

"I'm escapin'."

Now it was James's turn to glance around and make sure no one was within earshot. "But this is a dangerous time to be thinking of escape. Blevins is suspected of helping those five slaves run away."

"I know. Wilson Gregory was one of 'em."

"Wilson Gregory? Your old overseer escaped?"

James had always found Wilson's story sobering—one week he was a free black, the next week he was hurled back into slavery. Without even thinking, James reached into his coat pocket, just to touch his freedom papers.

"I can't stay here. I gotta find Nancy and my children. I promised her."

"But the authorities are on edge," James said. "They're watching for slave escapes."

"They's *always* lookin' for slave escapes."

"Talk about Jesus as much as you please.
Hold the wind!
Don't let it blow!
The more you talk I'm going to bend my knees.
Hold the wind!
Don't let it blow!"

Henry leaned in closer, face to face with James. "I need help from a free man like you, James. Will ya help me?"

James reacted from his gut. "Henry, I have my shop to think about."

"I'm askin' a lot, I know. But I can't just flee or the dogs'll run me down in a day. I need more. I need help."

"And I need to think on it, Henry."

"You ask me why I kin shout-a so bold.
Hold the wind!
Don't let it blow!
The love of Jesus sure is in my soul.
Hold the wind!
Don't let it blow!"

Henry's eyes darkened. "There's more to life than chasin' ladies."

James fired back. "I know. I know that as much as you do, Henry."

"Not as much as me."

James wanted to defend himself, wanted to tell Henry the things he had never told him before— the things that had happened to him. But James wisely held back. He put a hand on Henry's shoulder.

"I'm just worried about you. Have you even thought through how you're going to pull off something like this?"

Henry paused before answering. "I dunno. Thought I'd make contact with Blevins."

James shook his head. It all sounded much too dangerous.

"Henry, if I agree to help, promise you won't do anything rash? We have to think this through carefully."

"But I promised Nancy."

"And you can keep that promise. Just don't move too fast. Do I have your word?"

Henry nodded slowly.

"You ask me why I am always so glad.
Hold the wind!
Don't let it blow!
The devil missed the soul he thought he had.
Hold the wind!
Don't let it blow!"

"The Lord wants me to be free—like you, James."
"You're wrong there, Henry. The Lord wants us to be *more free* than I am."

Wilson Gregory didn't think they were going to make it. The wagon raced along a narrow pathway through the forest, speeding for the shore of the York River, where a schooner awaited. Over the past two days, they had had a couple of close calls, but nothing like this. First, there was the man on the road at midnight demanding a ride; Blevins had brushed him aside easily. The next day they found shelter in a remote home in New Kent County, and an unexpected visit from a neighbor nearly became their undoing.

Today, they were approaching the York River in the late morning hours when they had encountered a slave patroller making his rounds on foot. The patroller blocked their way and insisted on seeing the inside of the covered wagon. He wasn't going to be put off by any of Blevins' fictions, so Blevins responded by nearly running the man over.

They could hear the sound of pursuing horse

hooves. Their wagon, loaded down with five slaves, raced at full speed, nearly cracking an axle when it hit a hole on the path. But even at this speed, a loaded wagon was not going to outrun a man on horseback. They had two guns among them and four knives, which could be enough for a fight, depending on the size of force closing in on them. Wilson thought it sounded like only one pursuing horse, which gave them good odds.

"What a we gonna do?" asked one of the slaves.

Wilson had already been giving it serious thought. The other four slaves were all young. Wilson was well over sixty, and he was easily the best shot among them.

"Give me a gun. You keep runnin', and I'll hold him off, then catch up with ya."

"Whatya plannin'?"

"A little ambush."

Blevins slowed the wagon just enough for Wilson to launch himself out the back and into the brush. When he landed, his right foot bent sideways, and he heard a sickening crack. It wasn't the sound of a branch snapping. His ankle snapped, and a pain shot up his leg like someone had taken an axe to it. The gun flew out of his hand and into the bushes, and he collapsed onto his right shoulder, his head bouncing off of the ground. He had a hard time catching a breath, for the air was crushed out of him. But worse still, his ankle was broken. He knew it the moment he heard the crack. *I'm too old for throwin' myself outta wagons! Who do you think you is, Wilson Gregory?*

Wilson dragged himself along, like a half-squashed bug, toward the bushes where he thought his gun had landed. He hoped the weapon still functioned. The horse hooves coming down the path sounded louder. He scrabbled for something to grab onto, pushing off with his one good leg. He latched onto a tree root and dragged his body behind. His right ankle went wild with pain, and he thought he was going to faint.

The thought occurred to Wilson that his best chance for survival would be to do nothing. Let the horse go running by. It didn't sound like the patroller had any tracking dogs, and he wouldn't suspect for a moment that a slave lay hidden in the bushes by the side of the road. Wilson could crawl deeper into the woods, wait for nightfall, and create a splint and a crutch. He was resourceful. He could do this.

But he also knew that if he let the horse go by, the other four would never make it to the boat before the patroller caught up with them. They would be trapped at the river.

Of course, Wilson wasn't going to be any help to anyone if he couldn't find his gun. But there it was: The gun had come to rest against a small stone jutting out of the ground. The revolver looked to be in one piece. Grunting, sweating, biting back pain, Wilson inched his way to the weapon. The rider was almost upon him.

With one last surge, Wilson reached out, wrapped his hand around the handle, twisted his body to get onto his back, and swung the gun around. He raised himself just enough to see a blur of black came thundering by on the path. He fired, the horse screamed, and Wilson was thrown back by the recoil. The smell of gunpowder was strong. Flat on his back, he couldn't see what happened, but he heard the snapping of branches and could feel the vibrations of horseflesh slamming into the ground. The man on the horse shouted out as his animal folded beneath him, but his cry was cut off by a dull thud—a human body hitting a tree trunk, most likely.

Wilson went quiet and listened. He heard the horse snorting and trying to get back on its legs, and he knew it was the sound of a dying animal. But there was no sound of human movement. He couldn't believe his good fortune. If the rider was knocked cold, he still had a chance to get away.

Wilson tried not to look at his ankle as he fought his way onto his stomach and pushed himself up onto all fours; if he dared to look, he might see a white bone poking out of his skin and faint. The pain drained him of strength, and he thought he was going to vomit. He paused, waiting for the wave of nausea to subside. Then he reached out, using a tree trunk for support, and raised himself

311

up onto his one good leg. His broken ankle dangled loosely to the side, raging with pain.

It would do no good to head for the river. By the time he got there, Blevins and the others would be long gone, and he would be trapped with the river at his back. He needed to move into the woods, keep moving deeper and deeper. This could work. Things always had a way of coming out in the end for Wilson Noah Gregory. He had been in fixes before, just like the time with that old pig, Sam, which he and his wife had hidden in the persimum. That was a good story, but this one was going to be even better. Being free in the North, he wouldn't have Henry Brown around any more to tell his stories to, but he'd find someone new. He always did.

Wilson began to hop, but every hop felt like the bone was breaking all over again. He needed to make a splint, but first he had to put some distance between himself and the slave patroller. He took three hops, stopped to catch his breath, three hops, breath, three hops . . . He got a rhythm going—a rhythm to his pain.

Wilson figured that if he whistled, he could distract himself from the agony. He was afraid to make any sound, but he also knew that no one would be able to distinguish his bird whistles from the real thing anyway. He would blend in with the forest harmony, so he put his lips together.

"Jeet-jeet, jeet-jeet, jeet-jeet!"

That's a Baltimore Oriole, sir. Prettiest bird in the East. Wilson smiled. He was flying away to freedom. *Wouldn't that be the way to escape! Just fly away free.*

"Jeet-jeet, jeet-jeet, jeet-jeet!"

Wilson heard the crack of a branch. He stopped whistling. Time stood still. *Maybe just an animal or something.*

Slowly, Wilson turned to face the sound. The slave patroller stood fifteen feet away, and he had a gun in his hand, pointed at Wilson.

Distract him, Wilson. You can do it. These things always work out for you in the end.

"Here's a black-capped chickadee," called Wilson to the patroller, as innocent as could be. "Fee-beee! Fee-beee! Fee-beee!"

The man look confused and lowered his gun, giving Wilson just the opening he needed. Wilson went for his weapon.

29

March 23, 1849
7:00 p.m.

John Allen's head was splitting when he came to, and at first he figured it was just another one of his savage headaches. But when he put his hand to the back of his head, he felt a lump the size of a plum. He pulled his hand back from the tender spot and saw blood on his fingers. He remembered whipping Samuel, but he had no idea how he had wound up lying in a pile of wood in an alley running behind Broad Street, although it was obvious from the head wound that someone had whacked him in the skull. But who?

Groaning, he turned on his side. The alley odor was overpowering, and he wondered if men had been using this particular spot as a privy. That was before he realized that *he* was the source of the odor.

Dragging himself to his feet, John Allen discovered that his memory hadn't been knocked out of him. Henry Brown . . . the train . . . the box. Each of the memories was still rooted in his mind, and he remembered what had to be done: nab Henry Brown. But there was only one way to do it. By telegraph.

It had been almost two years since the telegraph connection was made between Richmond and Washington. John Allen could send a message to Washington and have it forwarded to Philadelphia, and it would arrive as fast as lightning. No train can outrun electricity, so he had plenty of time to get a message to Tommy McCarthy and Jeb Pleck—two slave catchers in Philadelphia. They were friends of his, and he had sent business their way many times. They would welcome news of an easy catch—a helpless slave trapped in a box.

Drawing out his pocket watch, John Allen saw that he had a good two hours to get home and dig out their address, then get back to the office of the Washington and Petersburg Telegraph Line before it closed for the night.

While he was at it, he'd get out of these stinking clothes.

Henry's stomach rumbled. He had one biscuit left and had hoped to save it. But the train made frequent stops, and he didn't want the cargo handlers to hear his box growling when they added new freight. So Henry nibbled away at the edges of the biscuit, like a mouse. The urge to relieve himself was also becoming stronger, but he tried to push it out of his mind.

Henry attempted to stretch his sore knee, at least what little he could stretch in cramped quarters; but nothing could relieve its steady ache. He closed his eyes and willed himself not to dwell on the pains that sprouted up all over his body like wildfires, but that just made it worse. He got to worrying about what would happen if he never saw Nancy again, never saw his children grown, never grew old alongside them.

"Henry, what do you think we gonna be like when we're old?" Nancy asked.

Henry shrugged. It was hard ever imagining Nancy old. "I dunno. Gray, I suppose. Slow movin'."

"No, I don't mean what-a we gonna look like on the outside. I mean what-a you think me and you are gonna be like together? Do you think we'll be weary of each other?"

Henry smiled. This was a much easier question. "Nah. I can't never tire of huggin' you and doin' what comes naturally, you know." He drew her into her arms, but she squirmed out.

"Don't you be foolin' with me, Henry Brown. That ain't what I mean. I'm not askin' if you're gonna still like gettin' under the covers with me. I don't suppose you'll ever tire of that. I mean are ya still gonna like just bein' with me?"

"Just bein' with you? You mean like sittin' on the porch together? Old and everything?"

"Yeah, that kind of bein' together."

Henry gave the question some extra thought. "Sure, I think I'm gonna like that too. Not as much as gettin' under the covers. But I think I'm gonna like it. I do."

"That there is an answer I like. So now you can be givin' me a kiss."

Henry thought about all of the friends at First African Baptist who had never grown old with their wives and children. They were split apart by slave sales, putting both them and the church in a delicate situation. Should those split apart by slavery be allowed to remarry? The black deacons at First African Baptist grappled with this question and decided they would approve of remarriage only if a husband or wife could prove that the marriage had failed. But Henry's marriage hadn't failed! It had been ripped apart, like when you tie a man between two horses and send the animals running in opposite directions.

He looked down and saw that he had unconsciously clenched his right fist. He wanted to put his fist through this wooden wall. He wanted to see God's judgment so badly; he wanted to see every white slaveholder dragged before the Throne and forced to look at God's holiness until it burned out their eyes.

Nancy had always rebuked him whenever he aired these kinds of thoughts.

Henry was weary, a dead man rolling down the rails. He leaned his head against the back of his box, closed his eyes, and wondered what it would be like to just slip away into death, to just suddenly not exist in this body any longer. Instead, he fell into sleep, and in his dream he was being trampled beneath a stampede of wild horses and trying to crawl for safety while the hooves pounded every part of his body. He could feel the pains all over his body, could feel the blood trickling down his forehead. And when he came awake, he noticed that he continued to feel the same sensation of trickling blood.

But it wasn't blood. Something was moving across his face, and it was alive.

30

Richmond
September 1848: Six Months Earlier

Wilson Gregory was dead.

There were all kinds of rumors about what had happened, but one thing was certain. Five slaves had run away, and one had come back in a box. Wilson had been shot down by a slave patroller, who claimed it was self-defense.

Henry watched the plain pine coffin being lowered into the ground. A large group of slaves and free blacks had gathered around the grave to say their farewells. Even Pike, the man who tangled with Wilson and Henry at the factory, was in the crowd, for strangely enough he and Wilson had become friends over the past few years. Wilson had a way of doing that—turning enemies to friends. The box vanished into the moist soil, as one of the deacons recited a passage from Scripture: "Being born again, not of corruptible seed, but of incorruptible, by the word of God, which liveth and abideth forever. For all flesh is as grass, and all the glory of man as the flower of grass. The grass withereth, and the flower thereof falleth away: But the word of the Lord endureth forever."

The prayer was accompanied by moans and shouts; then Sister Betty started in singing, and the others joined the flow.

"You may bury me in the East,
You may bury me in the West,
But I'll hear the trumpet sound in-a that morning,
In-a that morning, my Lord.
How I long to go, for to hear the trumpet sound in-a that morning."

When the service was over, Henry and James left the gravesite together, side-by-side. It was a cool day with heavy cloud cover, and they were silent for a while. The only sound between them was James's walking stick tapping against the hard ground.

"I think you should wait," James suddenly said.

Henry came alive. "But I can't. I'm tired of waitin'. I need to do somethin'. I need to get away."

"But escaping is too dangerous just now. The whole city is on high alert, and I don't want you ending up . . ."

James didn't finish his sentence, but Henry knew what he meant to say: ". . . like Wilson."

Henry and James parted company at Broad Street.

Things only got worse in the days to come.

When Blevins returned to Richmond, no evidence linked him to the escape of the four slaves, but that soon changed. Police staked out his home and caught him handing off forged passes. Blevins tried to swallow the evidence, but the policemen knocked him senseless before he could manage it. He insisted he wasn't involved in any slave escapes, saying he knew of people in power—"men who stood on high"—who were really behind the plots. No one was buying it.

The season turned to fall, and every time Henry looked at the leaves being scattered, he couldn't help but think about Nancy and the children and wondered if they were being treated well. Were they even alive? Before Nancy had been taken, Henry used to practice his whistling at night, but no more. No music. He dropped out of the choir, and pretty soon he stopped attending church entirely. The deacons came by several times to ask him to return. They were worried for his soul, and Henry began to wonder about it as well. He had once been baptized in the James River, immersed beneath the cold, dark water. But now it felt as if the devil had reached his long arm out of the baptismal water and yanked him back under.

Henry was drowning, and the devil was holding him at the bottom of the river. He went through each day barely feeling, barely seeing, barely moving, like a body suspended beneath the water. Whenever John Allen asked him, "What does Mr. Barret say?" Henry didn't resist. He obediently, unconsciously mumbled the words, "Mr. Allen is always right." *Just let me drown and die. Let the water fill my lungs, fill my body, and carry me away.*

James begged Henry to come back to church with him. But Henry couldn't get himself to do much of anything beyond dragging himself to the factory six days a week. Autumn slipped by and winter set in. Come Christmas, 1848, several members of the choir joined the chorus of people pleading for him to come back to church and at least make an appearance for a special concert. Henry had one of the strongest voices. They needed his voice, and deep down he knew that he needed them or his spiritual asphyxiation would be complete.

So Henry relented, and on Christmas Day he found himself back in the choir, side-by-side with James. Out of habit, he leaned forward and peered down the row of singers. But Nancy was gone.

First African Baptist Church was as alive as ever—feet stomping the rhythm, arms raised, voices soaring. By this time, it was one of the largest, strongest black churches in the country, with a little more than two thousand congregants. In so many ways, slaves found their greatest degree of freedom in the church. Although Negroes weren't allowed to preach, the deacons would give long, spirited prayers that were essentially veiled sermons. The "real" sermons were given by a white pastor, Robert Ryland, who owned slaves but was willing to dole out morsels of freedom. Ryland allowed Negroes to lead funeral services, and black deacons were able to settle disputes among members so they wouldn't have to go through the Richmond court system.

When Henry looked out on the filled-to-capacity church, he saw clusters of white faces, because the annual concert was so popular that it drew all kinds of people. Wanting to blot them out of his vision, he closed his eyes and lost himself in his singing.

"Dark midnight was my cry, dark midnight
    was my cry,
Dark midnight was my cry, 'Give me Jesus.'
Give me Jesus, give me Jesus;
You may have all this world, give me Jesus.
In the morning when I rise, in the morning
    when I rise,
In the morning when I rise, 'Give me Jesus.'
Give me Jesus, give me Jesus;
You may have all this world, give me Jesus."

It was close to the end of the program, right in the middle of a song, that a remarkable thing happened. James suddenly sat down. Was he feeling faint? Casting a glance to his right, Henry saw that James had his face in his hands. Perhaps he was simply overcome with emotion; but whatever it was, James kept on sitting through the last three songs. He didn't budge, didn't sing a word. Choir members on all sides shot looks at him, and when Henry glanced at James during the final song, he thought he saw tears in his friend's eyes.

"What happened?" Henry asked after the concert when they walked out of the church together just as dusk was setting in. It was a typical December night with a brisk, biting north wind.

"The Lord hit me. He spoke to me."

Henry came to a sudden stop and whirled around to face his friend. He stared at James, trying to figure out if he was serious or not. "Whatya mean God talked to you? Out loud?"

James shook his head. "No, no, he talked to me from the inside. Told me it was wrong being in this church—a church with a slaveholder preacher."

Henry and James had stopped on Broad Street, where the two of them normally split off—Henry walking toward the river and James walking west toward his cake shop.

"You sure 'bout this?"

"As sure as anything."

"How'd you know it was God talkin'?"

James shrugged. "I just know."

Henry cupped his hands around his mouth,

blowing out warm air as he took in James's words. "So you really think the Lord spoke to you?" He couldn't get the notion out of his mind.

"As clearly as you're talking to me, only in my thoughts."

They continued on in the direction of Henry's tenement, passing by a large row house, where—from the sound of it—a kitchen party was taking place. The white masters must have been gone, and a small group of slaves had gathered in the kitchen to dance and laugh.

"That mean you gonna be leavin' the church?" Henry asked.

"God's my only master. I'll not go to a church where the preacher is a slaveholder."

"But you'll have to go on north to find somethin' like that."

"I don't know what I'll do. I didn't care for living up north before."

Henry hated the idea of James slipping away north because he had already had enough loss in his life. His family went south, Wilson and his mamma had been buried facing east, and if his closest friend went north, he'd be left in limbo.

They continued down the street, neither of them saying anything until James said, out of the blue, "Did you know when I was in the North I helped with the Underground Railroad? I was a shepherd."

For the second time in ten minutes, James

stopped Henry dead in his tracks. "When was this?"

"A couple of years before I knew you. The Quaker family that purchased my freedom asked me to help with escapes."

"But you been the one tellin' me to be cautious when it come to escapin'. As an Underground Railroader, shouldn't you be encouragin' me?"

"I'm sorry, it's just that I've seen what can happen when a person isn't cautious. A family I helped didn't make it, and they paid a steep price. I couldn't take the constant fear."

"But we all are living in fear."

"I know. And that's why I sat down in there. I had enough of the fear."

There was a long silence before Henry spoke. "That mean you'll help me escape?"

"I will. But you'll need more than me, Henry."

"Then who?"

"Samuel Smith."

"The Red Boot man?"

"He's sympathetic."

"But he once owned slaves," Henry pointed out.

"So did Blevins."

"Will he be reliable? Smith's a gambler."

"Gamblers live on risk. We need someone like that."

Henry nodded, and for the first time in months, he felt his spirit returning.

"It's getting dark. I best be heading home,"

James said. But before he turned back toward Broad Street, he put a hand on Henry's shoulder. "Talk to Samuel Smith."

"Thank you, James." Then Henry hurried on his way, for he didn't want to be caught on the streets after hours. There was no sauntering when night was closing in.

Two days later, Henry maneuvered through a knot of well-dressed slaves, slave agents, slave owners, and factory owners. White men huddled in serious business discussions, while some slaves waved notes of recommendation from their masters. It was Hiring Week in Richmond, one of the most astounding displays of bartering and bargaining in the South. It was the week between Christmas and New Year's, and the streets were crowded as businessmen made arrangements for the next year's slave labor in a feeding frenzy of deal making. Some masters sent their slaves off to find new jobs on their own, carrying notes that said such things as, "If any person may be inclinable to hire Bob to drive a wagon, I can recommend him to be as good a wagoner as any in Richmond, he is an honest & cherfull fellow."

Under the cover of the noise and the bustle, Henry decided this would be the best time to approach Samuel Smith, assuming he found him alone in the shoe shop. He fought his way down Broad Street, a wide, dirt road clogged with wagons, horses, and people. Along the way, he was stopped several times by slaves he knew, informing him of their new arrangements.

"I'm gonna be residin' in the Wickham barns and workin' tobacco—like you, Henry!" announced Jasper Johnson, who had previously worked in a flour mill. "A barn give me a little more space to stretch out for sure, but maybe a little cold this time a year, do ya think?"

"I think ya'll be needin' to keep yourself well-buried in straw if you wanna stay warm," said Henry.

"Say, what you doin' out on the streets this day? Master Barret is still keepin' ya on at the factory, ain't he?"

"Oh yes. Just runnin' some errands for him."

One thing Henry never had to think about was Hiring Week, because he remained a fixture at Mr. Barret's tobacco factory year after year after year; it was the only thing of permanence in his life.

Henry continued to pick his way down Broad Street, as two barefoot boys—both black and both probably no more than six years old—came dodging through the crowd. With the temperature barely over freezing, their feet had to be frosty. Up ahead was Fisher's Shoe Shop, and Henry paused to catch his breath before opening the door. The bell on the door announced his arrival.

He was in luck. The shop was empty, except for

Samuel, who stood in the corner at a bench, fixing the heel of a boot. The logs in the fireplace glowed red-hot, and Henry felt the heat wrap around him like a warm coat. All sorts of footwear, shoes and boots for men and women, some sturdy, some delicate, hung along the ceiling and in front of the main window.

Samuel looked up, brightening at the sight of Henry. "Good morning, Henry!"

"Mornin', Mr. Smith."

"Hope you didn't get trampled by all the bosses out on the streets today."

"No, sir." Henry hadn't talked to Samuel since the day his wife was sold south, and he didn't know how to begin. "Busy day today" was all he could think to say.

Samuel glanced up, flashed a smile, and then looked back down at the boot. "What brings you out on Hiring Day? I assume you'll be remaining in your same place of work."

"Yes, sir. Same old factory, same old tobacco."

"And the same old shoes for me," said Samuel, tapping a nail into the bottom of the boot.

Henry glanced around the shop, envious of the high styles dangling in front of the window. He looked down at his own shoes—stiff, coarse brogans, ankle-high working shoes. Henry was thankful that the Barrets had always put shoes on his feet, even when he was small; but what he wouldn't give for a gentleman's shoes.

"You know," Henry said, "I could work in a business such as you're doin' . . . *if I was free.*"

Samuel looked up from the boot he was fixing. He eyed Henry carefully. "If you were free, you could also continue in your current business. Stay with tobacco and you could make good money . . . if you were free." Samuel grinned knowingly. The provocative words hung in the air: *If you were free.*

"You here to pick up shoes?" Samuel asked.

Henry had almost forgotten the pretense for his visit. "Oh yes, Master Barret has two pair for me to be pickin' up."

"I know exactly where they are." Samuel disappeared into a back room, leaving Henry alone with his worries. Henry was beginning to think this was all a mistake. He should just take the shoes and go. James said Samuel was sympathetic to slaves, but how did he know for sure? John Blevins was sympathetic, but he also turned in slaves for profit. Like Blevins, perhaps Samuel worked both sides. What if Samuel turned him in to the police for a reward?

Samuel emerged from the back room, two pairs of women's shoes in hand. Both were dainty, thin as silk, slipper-style shoes—a couple sizes too small for Mrs. Barret. But the small size was by design. The shoes kept the wives contained, restrained, and in some degree of pain. Discomfort was a small price to pay for the illusion of small feet—a sure sign of refinement.

Holding up one of the slippers, Samuel laughed. "Mrs. Barret might as well be as barefoot as a slave, thin as these are."

Henry smiled awkwardly. Then, out of the blue, he blurted out, "You know, Mr. Barret never assisted me to save my wife from bein' sold."

Samuel carefully set down the two pairs of shoes on the worktable, as if they were made of glass. "I know. I'm very sorry, Henry."

Henry glanced around the shop, just to make sure no one had slipped inside from the street. "You know, Mr. Smith . . ."

Henry paused, standing on the precipice. One more sentence would change his life. Henry took the plunge.

"You know, Mr. Smith, I been meditatin' on an escape plan ever since." A pause. Then: "Would you help me?"

Samuel didn't show any shock, seemingly absorbed by Mrs. Barret's shoes.

"So this is turning out to be Hiring Week for you after all, eh Henry? It appears you want to hire *me*." Samuel paused. "Aren't you afraid to talk about escaping so openly like this?"

Henry's heart began to race. This wasn't the answer he expected. "Some, maybe. But you believe ev'ry man's got a right to liberty. So I heard."

Samuel sighed.

"You also know what it's like to be worn down . . . like the leather on a shoe," Henry added.

"So I do, Henry. In this world, shoes carry all the load—like you and me." Samuel set aside the boot and added, "But escape plans take money. Are you prepared to pay?"

"Everything I have."

"Does that include your life?"

"I'll risk everything."

Samuel held out his hand to shake. "Then I think I might be able to do something for you."

31

March 23, 1849
8:40 p.m.

Jacob Thompson had never seen a message quite like it. Had he made a mistake in translating the dots and dashes into text? But Jacob didn't make mistakes. He had been with the telegraph office in Philadelphia since it first opened, and he was the finest operator in the city. Just for show in front of crowds, he would sometimes copy out a message in English and French simultaneously, using his right and left hands. Jacob didn't make mistakes.

He had seen all sorts of messages go across his desk over the past few years. Marriage proposals.

Birth and death notices. Jokes. Advertisements. He even remembered one rich young man who sat in the office and paid to have messages sent back and forth to a lady friend sitting at a telegraph office on the other end of the line— almost as if they were talking face to face. Jacob thought he had seen it all . . . until today.

The message he had just copied said that an escaped slave was going to arrive at a Philadelphia train station mailed inside a box. *Inside a box?*

The message was for a man named Jeb Pleck, and Jacob would bet money that the fellow was a slave catcher. Jacob had abolitionist sympathies, although he wasn't a radical like his Quaker cousins. He stared at the message and thought about the implications of this note. For a moment, he even considered ripping it up. But he was a professional, and he would lose his job if he were caught destroying a telegram. Besides, it was also entirely possible that the telegram was going to an abolitionist; but Jacob's gut told him this message was aimed at one of the slave catchers who infested the city, looking to score rewards for snagging runaways.

"Boy!"

One of the messenger boys, the next in line, leaped out of his chair, darted over to Jacob, and held out his hand for the telegram. Messengers were resourceful and quick; they had even been known to drop a telegram from a bridge onto a moving ship, just so it arrived in the right hands. So Jacob knew that as he sealed the telegram, he was sealing the doom of this poor slave. He paused for just a second, drawing back the envelope, and the messenger boy stared at him in confusion, hand still outstretched.

Finally, Jacob dropped the envelope in the messenger boy's hand and watched him run through the door. He had done his duty, and a slave would pay the price. Sighing, Jacob turned back to his telegraph key and lost himself in the clicking rhythms of Mr. Morse invention.

James closed up shop and sat in his room in the back in the dark, wondering if he should slip out of Richmond. He had helped a slave escape, and he had just knocked out a white man. If those weren't reasons to flee, what were? But he had run before, and he vowed he wouldn't do it again. Besides, being a free black out on the road or traveling by rail posed its own set of risks. Freedom papers weren't a guarantee of safety.

Samuel had assured him that John Allen didn't see his face and didn't connect him to the escape in any way. Still, he felt as if it was happening all over again.

When James opened his eyes, he found himself on his back staring up at the rafters of a barn, where midday light poured in through the wide spaces between planks in the wall. Set off in silhouette, the planks stood side by side in a stiff row, like prison bars.

James couldn't remember where he was. Then he saw the straw. Everywhere was straw, and it all came back to him. James was leading three slaves north through Loudon County, Virginia. He glanced around at the three fugitive figures, buried in the hay and sound asleep—Brister, his wife Eliza, and his younger brother Willie.

The day before, they had scrambled along the lower eastern slope of Catoctin Mountains. The oak and poplar forest was easy going, without the snare of brambles, and the thick, green summer foliage hid them from sight when they passed farms. But they became hopelessly lost, and James blamed only himself. He was a shepherd for the Under-ground Railroad, and whoever heard of the Lost Shepherd? Lost sheep maybe, but not lost shepherds.

Then there were the dogs. This very morning, they had been chased down and treed by hound dogs; but to James's astonishment, the man who caught them turned out to be a middle-aged farmer, a gentle man—a sympathetic soul. The farmer agreed to hide them in the mow of his barn so they could catch some sleep by day to rest for the next night's travel. The man spoke like a Quaker and he didn't carry a gun, so James trusted him.

Trying not to wake the three slaves, James silently climbed down the ladder leading from the mow. He was not going to be able to get back to sleep with a full bladder, so he decided to relieve himself in the woods just beyond the barn. It was an overcast spring day, although no rain had fallen. Keeping his eye out for poison ivy, he found a secluded spot; but it wasn't until James had finished his business that he heard the voices. Many voices.

James crept to the edge of the woods and crouched in the foliage. Six men, including the farmer, approached the barn. The farmer was leading them there.

"There's four of 'em, and they're sleepin' away in the hay, I tell ya. The dogs sniffed them out just this mornin'," the farmer said, no longer speaking with the distinctive "thees" and "thous" of a Quaker. It had all been a trap, and James was a fool to fall for it. The three slaves were about to be nabbed.

James probably should have started running the moment he saw the men. But he couldn't desert Brister, Eliza, and Willie. The men dragged the three of them out of their sleep and out of the hay. Eliza was crying and Brister was trying to console her. Willie looked plain angry. All three of them had to be wondering where James had gone. Did they think he had betrayed them? Did they think that he had led them into this trap and fled to safety, just to collect the reward? It made James sick thinking of that possibility.

"Where y'all headin'?" asked one of the men.

"Toward Gettysburg," Brister said. "We got aunts and uncles there we visitin'."

"Then where's your passes?" demanded the farmer. "And where's the fourth one? There were four of ya here this mornin'!"

"Don't know what you're talking about," said Brister, covering for James. "There ain't but the three of us."

"Then show us your passes!" shouted the farmer, his anger mounting.

James noticed that a couple of the men had ropes, and they were making a move to use them—either to tie up the slaves and take them to the magistrate . . . or worse. That's when Willie snapped. He drew his weapon from the pocket of his tattered jacket and fired the gun point-blank into the farmer's face, blasting the side of it apart in a spray of red. Eliza screamed, while two of the white men ran for cover. The other white men carried weapons, and they drew their revolvers, two firing at Willie and one taking aim at Brister. The last thing James saw was Willie's body hurled backwards by the force and hitting the ground like a scarecrow blown away in a windstorm.

James didn't see any more. He was running for his life.

Even today, James couldn't believe that he had made it North alive. He didn't stop running for hours that day, disappearing into the woods without a trace. It was the last time he had ever tried to help slaves escape, and he said never again. He spent the next year living in New York, but he never took a shine to the North. No one but the farmer had seen his face—and that farmer was dead—so the incident in Virginia was buried in the graves of Willie, Eliza, and Brister. James judged it safe to move back south to Richmond, and he set up shop as a barber, then a baker.

And now this: Against his better judgment, he had chosen to help another slave escape, and it was about to become the biggest mistake in his life.

Something crawled down Henry's face, moving along his forehead and heading for his nose. His reflex reaction was to swipe it away. Wrong move. When he brushed his face, his box suddenly filled with the droning of an angry wasp. Henry remained motionless and waited for the sting. He never forgot the time he accidentally dug up a yellow jacket nest in a field, and a cloud of wasps came out of the earth in force, as if the very dirt had come alive. He took a half dozen stings before reaching the Big House.

The buzzing stopped. The wasp wasn't any-where on his body—he didn't think. If it were on the outside of his clothes, he wasn't sure if he would be able to feel its small steps. He felt a slight sensation on his back but wasn't sure if it was an itch or the wasp. With the beginning of spring, bees and wasps had begun to emerge, and some liked the dark confines of wooden structures, like the eaves of houses. Henry's box, with its pre-made holes, must have appeared quite enticing, and this wasp had squeezed inside.

A buzzing again, this time in mid-air, directly in front of his face. Should he swat the wasp? In the dark, he'd probably miss, and the wasp would look for revenge. A fresh pain was the last thing he needed to deal with now. The wasp seemed to be only inches from his face, and he thought he saw the faint shadow of a wasp hovering at eye level. The droning filled the box, and then the wasp landed right on the top of his head. He felt it walking across his scalp, and he realized this was his best chance to squash the wasp because he knew precisely where it was in the dark. Carefully, he reached for his hat, which lay in the corner next to the gimlet. If he could catch the wasp in the fabric of his hat, he could slowly squeeze it to death.

The train came to a stop, and any minute they would be opening up the car and loading on more freight. He had to act now. Henry slapped his hat over his head and scrunched it together, trying to press the wasp into the folds, but the invader was faster than him. It launched itself off of his head, and now it was angry.

"Ahhh!"

The sting came at the back of his left arm. It felt like a hot needle had been jabbed into his flesh, and Henry clutched his arm but tried not to make any other movement. The wasp was still buzzing, bouncing off of the walls of the box in a flying frenzy, trying to get out. It dawned on him that the invader might be a yellow jacket because they can sting you again and again, without killing themselves in the process.

The boxcar door slid open, bringing in a meager amount of lantern light, and his arm began to throb. He gently massaged the sting site, but that was all the movement he would allow himself. The buzzing stopped for about twenty seconds before picking up again. This wasp had no intention of dying without a fight.

32

Richmond
February 1849: One Month Earlier

The train emerged from clouds of steam, like a large ship coming out of the fog. The train loomed large—roaring, rattling, the squeal of steel on steel. In the steam and the sound, people poured from the train, face after face flashing by, white faces, black faces, a pandemonium of noise and movement. Then a large door. The door to one of the train's boxcars slid open with a bang, and inside was the wooden box. The same box that Henry had seen in his mind before. Only this time, there were words on the box, a blur of words, but one stood out: "Philadelphia." Then Henry found himself floating over the box, staring down at himself in the box, laid out in the box, sleeping or dead — he couldn't tell. Then he was in the box, looking up and out, hearing the same unseen bird trying to fly out of the boxcar but hitting walls, still unable to find the open door, the futility of wings. Then a lid. Someone placed the wooden lid over him, sealing him in. Henry shouted, "Stop!" He tried to sit up, tried to rise, but his body wouldn't obey. The lid came down, blotting out all light. In the darkness, he heard the hammer. Someone was pounding the lid in place. Nails slid into soft wood like nails into flesh. Then the voice, the whisper in the ear. "Go . . . ," said the voice. "Go and get a box . . . Go and get a box, and put yourself in it." Five nails. Six nails. Seven. The pounding stopped. No sound. No light. Only coldness and darkness remained. "Go and get a box, and put yourself in it."

Henry rose up from his pallet, shivering in the cold. He looked around the sparse room, his eyes slowly adjusting to the dark. The fire had gone out, and his feet were nearly numb. He went to the window and looked out, stamping his feet alive. Richmond was quiet and cold. But at long last, he knew what had to be done.

"A box?" Samuel gasped. "You want to be put in a box?"

Henry knew that Samuel and James would react this way. Flabbergasted, both of them. The three of them had gathered around Samuel's table to throw around ideas. Over the past month, Samuel had devised at least a half dozen escape plans, but none suited Henry.

"A box?" Samuel repeated.

"Yes, a box."

Samuel made a steeple with his fingers and lost himself in thought.

"You're not seriously considering this idea?" James asked Samuel.

"I have to be fair, have to consider all options."

"But a box?" James threw up his arms.

"A box would offer some added concealment," Samuel conceded. "Blevins used a covered wagon to get the five slaves out of Virginia. Putting you in a box in the back of my wagon would be better. But still very dangerous. They're looking at every wagon heading out of—"

"But I'm *not* thinkin' you would carry the box

in your wagon, Mr. Smith. That's not the way the Lord would have it."

Samuel and James exchanged looks. "The Lord?" Samuel said. "What does God have to do with this?"

"He give me a vision."

"A vision of a box?" James asked.

"He said, 'Go, put yourself in a box.' "

"Are you serious?" Samuel asked.

"Yes. I am."

"You're *sure* God spoke to you?" James asked.

"As sure as you was when the Lord spoke to you in church on Christmas."

James stroked his thin moustache. He couldn't very well argue with that.

"So this box . . . ," Samuel said. "If it's not being carried in my wagon, how is it being moved? Is God going to wave His wand and whisk it through the air like a magic carpet?"

"No. The Lord wants me to be sent through the mail—on a train."

Samuel and James said not a word. Complete silence, except for the soft sound of a moth banging into the oil lamp.

"That's madness!" James suddenly burst out. "I've never heard such an idea."

"You ain't never heard of it 'cause it ain't been done. And if it ain't been done, they won't be watchin' for it."

Samuel tapped his teeth, lost in thought again.

"That is a good point. If we take you out by wagon, like Blevins did, we won't get far. They're watching every wagon closely, but they aren't checking the mail. Who would ever guess that a box might contain a living parcel?"

James leaned forward, scooting to the edge of his chair. "But it'd take a day at least to get from Richmond to Philadelphia in the mail. You'd suffocate!"

"I could drill holes. Very small holes."

James tried another tack. "But they'll hear you moving about in there. What if you sneeze? Cry out in pain?"

"Slaves know how to conceal pain. You should know that."

"What if you're upside down?" Samuel put in. "For an entire day."

Henry hadn't thought of that. "You can mark the side of the box. Show 'em which side is up."

"As if anyone will pay attention to that," James said.

"The Lord will make it work," Henry said.

"But the box could be your death," Samuel pointed out.

"It could also be my resurrection."

Samuel and James stared at each other. Then James looked away, incredulous. But Samuel broke into a grin.

"I like your audacity, Henry!" he suddenly burst, leaning back in his chair. "But we're gonna need

343

help from someone other than the Almighty to pull off something like this."

"Who?" Henry asked.

J. Miller McKim stood before a packed auditorium in Philadelphia. Standing room only. The crowd, mostly men, jostled for position like bees in a hive. The air was electric. With tousled hair and fierce gaze, McKim looked more authoritative than his thirty-eight years. He had no moustache, but a moderately long, precisely trimmed beard protruded straight down from his strong chin, giving him an Old Testament air.

McKim, a Presbyterian minister working for the Pennsylvania Anti-Slavery Society, was telling his audience about his experience in Washington, where he visited a "slave factory"—a prison for slaves waiting to be sold. If anything was going to reach the doubters in the crowd, this had to be it.

"I surveyed an area of about forty feet square, enclosed partly by high jail walls built for the purpose," McKim said. His voice rose with every word because the murmuring of the auditorium audience was louder than usual, and he had to speak above the hum.

"As it was very cold, the 'pen' was empty. The slaves were all down in the cellar, so I asked to go down and see them. The agent took out of his pocket a key, and he opened the lock of a huge, iron, cross-barred gate, which admitted us into the cellar. Here, in an apartment of about twenty-five feet square, were about thirty slaves of all ages, sizes, and colors. The wistful, inquiring, anxious looks they cast at me—presuming I came as a purchaser—were hard to endure. I discovered that there were three such rooms, and together they had held as many as one hundred and thirty-nine slaves at a time. I could hardly see how this was possible without them lying on each other!"

McKim paused, surveying his audience, which had suddenly begun to simmer down. He had caught their attention. Good, very good. He had them where he wanted, and he needed to answer the silence with Sinai thunder. But he had to time it right. He paused, letting the drama build. Then: "The blood of these slaves is on our hands, and make no bones about it, these men *are* our brothers! Their blood cries out to us like the blood of Abel when he was laid low by his own brother! Their blood cries out, and we are Cain!"

These words became the trigger. Taunts erupted from the pro-slavery forces in the audience who were roused by the accusation that they were sons of Cain. Retaliatory shouts from anti-slavery crusaders followed. It was a combustible mix, and McKim wondered if he had pushed too hard. So many angry faces. He could see shoving, and people toward the back passed around a bag of something. That couldn't be good.

"But the Most High God has made of *one blood*

all nations of men to dwell on the face of the earth! Our national existence is based upon this principle, that we are endowed by our Creator with certain inalienable rights, among which are life, liberty, and the pursuit of happiness!"

A piece of fruit shot out from the audience, and he caught sight of the red missile in his peripheral vision. He didn't have time to duck, but it wasn't necessary. The tomato sailed over his shoulder and exploded against the back wall like a bomb. He glanced over his shoulder and saw that it had left a bright red stain.

"Over seventy years since the American people made this pledge before Almighty God and the world, nearly one-sixth part of the nation are held in bondage by their fellow citizens!"

More hoots and hollers. And more fruit. Three more missiles shot out of the crowd, as if launched by cannon. One cannonball was white, probably a stale egg. The two others were tomatoes, and one of them caught him in the shoulder, splattering juice and bits of red tomato on his coat. He forged ahead.

"Slavery is contrary to the principles of natural justice, of our republican form of government, of the Christian religion, and of—!"

This time, someone flung a rock, and it struck McKim directly in the forehead, and a burst of white lightning exploded behind his eyes. He went wobbly and felt himself staggering backwards, but he stayed on his feet. Barely. His vision blurred, then came back into focus, and he could see that the crowd was boiling over. Two fights had broken out in the back. Fists were flying, and he knew he should quit the stage. Instead, he found himself looking around the stage for the rock. He picked it up and jostled it in his palm; it was a good-sized stone, about three inches in diameter, and he realized it could have killed him. He felt blood trickling down his forehead.

"Mr. McKim, Mr. McKim."

The voice came from his left. Dizzy, he looked over and spotted his clerk with the Anti-Slavery Society, a black man named William Still. William put a hand on his shoulder, to guide him to safety. But McKim shook loose. He raised his arm and shook the rock at the crowd.

"You can try to silence me, but if you do these very rocks will speak out! The object of the Anti-Slavery Society is the entire abolition of slavery in the United States!"

Head wounds bleed heavily, and McKim imagined that he must have made quite a sight, a bloodied prophet shaking a rock. But even through the fog of the pain and blood, he could see that no one in the crowd was listening any longer. Fists were flying. People were on the floor, getting stomped upon by heavy boots. More blood was flowing.

"Mr. McKim!" William had him by the shoulders now and was whisking him off the stage. He felt two more pieces of fruit hit him in the shoulder and leg. William handed him a white handkerchief, and he pressed it to his head as they made for the back door. Lewis Thompson, a white man who printed publications for the Anti-Slavery Society, met them in the alley behind the auditorium. He had a carriage waiting.

As McKim climbed inside, Lewis eyed the blood and food stains on his clothes. "You know, Mr. McKim, your laundry bills are becoming our Society's greatest expense."

McKim did not appreciate the jest. Lewis was a valuable aide, but he lived life in a state of constant amusement. Once inside the carriage, McKim continued to press the bloody handkerchief to his forehead, and he leaned back against the seat. He had failed to reach the crowd, and that hurt more than his forehead.

"Let me see how bad the wound is," said William.

"I'm all right, I'm all right," McKim insisted, keeping the handkerchief pressed to his wound. "If you want to help, just tell me the schedule for the remainder of the week."

"Does it offer any more opportunities to sample local produce?" Lewis asked.

McKim let that comment soar past.

"But Mr. McKim . . . ," said William.

"Don't worry about my head! I'm fine. Just tell me. What is next?"

William surrendered to the inevitable. He opened a large, leather-bound book and scanned the pages.

"Tomorrow night you address the issue of suffrage rights, so I'd say it's ripe for more trouble."

"If people would be as enthusiastic about Negro suffrage as they are for making Negroes suffer, we might get somewhere," Lewis interjected.

McKim ignored him. "What else is there?" he asked William.

As clerk for the Anti-Slavery Society, William Still kept meticulous records and organized McKim's itinerary. He reviewed McKim's schedule for the remainder of the week and other business, eventually coming to a letter they had just received from a shoemaker in Richmond, Virginia.

"The shoemaker wants to meet. He said it's an urgent matter concerning the delivery of an important package."

"And who is this Richmond shoemaker?"

"A Mr. Samuel Smith. Shall I reply favorably?"

McKim gave it some thought. He closed his eyes, but when he did the world inside the carriage began to spin. He opened them again, and tried to regain his stability.

"What was that again?"

"A shoemaker from Richmond wants to meet. Shall I reply favorably?"

"As long as he promises to keep his fruit and masonry at home, then yes I'll meet with him."

McKim followed this up with the hint of a smile. Only a hint.

Three weeks later, in early March, Samuel Smith came face to face with Miller McKim in the office of the Pennsylvania Anti-Slavery Society, located in a modest brick building with white shutters at 31 North Fifth Street in Philadelphia.

McKim responded predictably. "A box? In the mail? You can't be serious."

"I know it sounds preposterous," said Samuel. "I had much the same reaction when Henry Brown first offered up the idea."

"So you are entirely serious?"

"Would I travel this far just to pull your leg? I have better ways to spend my time and money."

McKim stroked his beard. Samuel saw the irony that he was trying to convince the minister by relying on the same arguments that Henry had used on him.

"The more you think about the idea, the more it makes sense," Samuel added.

"It makes sense if you are suicidal. He will die in that hot box. What is his name again?"

"Henry Brown. And he will be carrying a

bladder filled with water. To splash on his face. He'll also have a hat as a fan."

"And how do you plan to ship this . . . *package?*"

"The Adams Express Company in Richmond sends freight every morning at eight o'clock. It runs through Washington, reaches Baltimore by evening, and Philadelphia in the middle of the night."

Samuel, James, and Henry had worked out every detail, and the shoemaker had written out the entire plan on the sheet of paper sitting on McKim's desk. McKim read it over for a second time before pushing it aside.

"I cannot agree to be a part of this." He ticked off all of the same reasons that James and Samuel had already come up with for why the plan was doomed. But Samuel had an answer waiting in the wings for every objection.

"The plan puts no risk on the shoulders of the Anti-Slavery Society," he said. "All we ask is that you pick up the box when it arrives in Philadelphia. Just pick it up and bring it here to your office. Nothing more."

McKim didn't respond, but Samuel sensed him beginning to soften. He decided to exploit McKim's Presbyterian pedigree.

"God gave Henry this vision," Samuel reminded him. "Now I'm not a God-fearing man, but that's strong evidence, even for me."

"So that is all you ask? That we pick up the box at the station?"

"That's right." Samuel had the salesman's sixth sense that he was about to close the deal. "You have to admit. It's a novel idea."

"Baking yourself into a pie is a novel idea, but that does not mean it is a prudent idea." McKim stroked his narrow, billy-goat beard. "You say God spoke to him? Do you really believe this to be true, Mr. Smith?"

There was silence as Samuel's distant gaze gave the impression of deep thought. In truth, he was simply counting to ten before answering, "I do. Who else but God could come up with such a plan?"

"Very well then." McKim extended his hand and Samuel shook it vigorously.

The date for the escape was set: March 13, 1849. About a week and a half away.

33

March 23, 1849
9:10 p.m.

The buzzing filled the box so completely that it was almost impossible to figure out the location of the wasp—especially since the source of the sound kept moving in search of an escape route.

Henry's sting had gone from a sharp pain to a dull ache. It had also begun to itch, but he knew better than to scratch it. Scratching would drive him mad.

The freight handlers were still at work, loading more boxes into the train and occasionally jostling Henry's box. The wasp landed on top of Henry's face again, this time on his right cheek, and then it wandered in small circles before climbing on top of his nose. He closed his eyes, and to his horror the wasp crawled directly on top of his right eyelid. He thought about swatting at the wasp, anything to get it off of his eyelid, but it was better to play it safe. Become a statue.

The wasp shifted positions on his eyelid but remained perched on the curvature of his eyeball, with only a paper-thin slice of skin separating its stinger from the most sensitive organ in his body. He knew what it felt like to get a fleck of dirt in his eye. He couldn't imagine a stinger jabbing through his eyelid and penetrating the moist lens. If he were stung in the eye, he would have no choice but to break out of the box. His escape would be over. Of all of the dangers he expected on this trip, he never imagined that the worst would come from a creature the size of his fingernail.

The wasp moved into the corner of his closed eye, and he could feel every step of its hair-thin legs pressing down on his eyelid. Suddenly, one of the cargo handlers shoved his box, and Henry lurched forward. The wasp didn't like this, judging by the burst of buzzing, and Henry expected a sudden stab to the eyeball. But the wasp didn't sting—or even budge. Henry was sweating heavily, and he wanted to scratch his nose, but he didn't dare. He also needed to clear his throat, and he resisted the urge as long as he could, eventually clearing it softly. The wasp moved to the very center of his eye, tapping his eyelid with its two feelers before finally, mercifully lifting off.

Henry opened his eyes and saw the wasp—it was definitely a yellow jacket—moving along the wall directly opposite from him. The glow from the freight workers' lanterns streamed through the holes and put a spotlight directly on the wasp. He knew he shouldn't make a noise while the cargo handlers were near, but he couldn't pass up this chance. If the workers closed the boxcar back up, his box would be plunged back into darkness, and he would have no way to locate his enemy. Henry still had his hat in his right hand. He could do this swiftly and quietly, just slap the hat over the wasp and squeeze until he felt the soft crunch of the wasp's body.

Too late. The boxcar door was being closed. Henry made his move before the light was snuffed completely, and he slapped his hat against the box wall—and missed. The wasp was furious. The box plunged back into darkness and filled with the sound of buzzing again, and he felt a sting to his thigh. Henry became as angry as the wasp and started slapping everywhere, using both his hat and his free hand—his wounded hand—smacking his leg, his shoulder, the sides of the box, the ceiling of the box, his arms. The wasp was driven by the need to attack, and so was Henry. He took a third sting to his left forearm and swatted at the site of the jab—but the buzzing didn't stop. The wasp was still alive, and it seemed to be right by his left ear; the buzzing was so loud that the sound seemed lodged inside his head, driving him mad. He swatted his ear, but the wasp escaped, and he felt the stinger entering the flesh of his right wrist. Then he slapped down with his wounded hand, and he felt something moving inside his clenched fist. He had the wasp in his hand. He was being stung in the palm, but he was also squeezing the life out of the creature, feeling its feeble, final stabs, feeling its soft body flatten out.

The buzzing stopped.

Henry continued to squeeze just to make sure there wasn't a trace of life remaining in the wasp. Panting, he carefully uncurled his fingers. With his right hand, he scraped away the jelly-like mass that had once been the wasp. Then, in frustration, he pounded the wall of the box with his good hand. He had taken four stings and didn't think he could stand another moment of this life.

• • •

Jeb Pleck found Tommy McCarthy at his usual haunt—the saloon operated by Dominick McCaffrey on Eighth Street in Philadelphia. The place was crowded, dark, and smoky, filled with the usual pugs—the city's toughest scrappers. Most of them were Irish, and almost every one displayed a twisted nose that had been broken during an illegal bare-knuckle bout or an impromptu fight that erupted in the tavern on a regular basis. Tommy was a fighter of little renown, although he liked to tell the story about how he was once pinned on his back on hot coals during a brawl. He kept punching and thrashing, even as his skin cooked; and he eventually fought his way back to his feet, with his back smoking, and he pounded his opponent into the ground. Jeb didn't know if he believed the story, but he did know that it wasn't wise to cross Tommy McCarthy.

Jeb and Tommy had met each other in Richmond four years ago and both were looking for excitement, so they decided to team up as slave catchers. They had worked the James River, looking for runaways by water; but they also handled some hunts by land and had even pursued one slave for an entire week. At five dollars per day, plus expenses, they made a decent living. But Tommy decided to move north to pursue his love of bare-knuckle boxing, so they took their slave-catching expertise to Philadelphia a year ago. With so many runaways making a beeline for the City of Brotherly Love, they figured they could still cash in on lucrative rewards.

"You ain't gonna believe this one," Jeb said, slapping the telegram down on the sticky table.

"Another runaway?" Tommy's drunken eyes lit up.

"Not just any old runaway. Read."

Tommy plucked the cigar from the corner of his mouth and crushed it out on the corner of the table. Then he peeled the telegram off the sticky surface and held it in a patch of dull light and read to himself, moving his lips with every word. When he finished, he looked up at Jeb in astonishment and read the telegram a second time. Tossing the paper back down on the table, he laughed. "Is this serious?"

"I couldn't believe it either. A slave coming in by train—in a box!"

"You don't think John Allen is having a little fun with us, do ya?"

"He wouldn't dare. Besides, he's been good to us, giving us business over these years. He's never led us wrong before."

"A slave in a box. Now I've heard all!"

"It'll be easy pickings, that's for sure. No need for dogs or horses. Just stroll on down to the station and pick us up a special delivery."

"John Allen must want this one awful bad, offering a forty dollar reward."

"Pretty good for one night's work."

Jeb pulled up a chair and ordered a beer. In the corner, two pugs were beginning a shoving match, and before the night was over, a fight was sure to break out between them. Jeb didn't like to throw punches as much as Tommy, but he was an enthusiastic spectator. He took a deep gulp of ale and smacked his lips.

Life was good.

34

Richmond
March 14, 1849: Nine Days Earlier

John Allen leaned back and exhaled a cloud of smoke, watching it drift over the poker table.

"Have things settled down at Tredegar?" he asked Oliver Krauss, a puddler at the massive iron works factory. Things had been tense at Tredegar Iron Works almost continuously since the strike two years earlier, when white workers demanded that slave laborers be removed from skilled jobs at the furnaces.

"Things are as good as they ever get," Krauss grumbled, a man of few words. It didn't help that Krauss was having a poor night of poker.

"I'd a-love to get a look at that ironclad you built there," said Brandon Larkin, a good-natured fellow who had won big at the table. "How thick you suppose those iron plates are? And what keeps the whole thing from sinkin' like a boulder?"

"What I'm wonderin' is what kept your *game* from sinkin' tonight?" Krauss said. He could usually count on Larkin to fork over a stash of money in reckless card play.

John Allen tossed in his cards and drained the last dregs of his watery beer. "I'm callin' it a night," he said, scooping his coins from the table—a modest profit.

"Goin' already?" asked Callahan. "The night's young."

"I'd like to stay and take some more of your money, but I got business to tend to." He pushed away from the table and put on his floppy, wide-brimmed hat.

"Then I'll stay here and keep the horns of whiskey comin'." Callahan raised his glass and grinned widely, advertising a dire need for dental work.

"Just be sober when mornin' comes."

"G'night John," said Larkin, but Allen said nothing in return. He slipped out of the grog house and into the night, making his way along the river, past dingy docks. He even passed up all the usual temptations—burlesque halls and brothels—where busty women advertised their wares from garishly lit second-floor windows. He didn't even glance up at them. When he had business, he could be focused. John Allen trudged uphill toward Samuel Smith's residence because he was beginning to get his suspicions about the shoemaker.

An unrepentant snoop, John Allen saw the light flickering in Samuel's place and decided to do a little eavesdropping. Making his way around the side of the house, he slipped up to a window and put his ear to the dirt-smeared glass. He could hear voices, but everything was muffled, so he was going to have to settle for a more conventional appearance at Samuel's front door. But he didn't plan on waiting to be invited inside. He liked surprises, as long he was the one doing the surprising.

Samuel hated being the bearer of bad news.

"So—The escape is off?" James asked him.

Henry slapped the edge of the table. "No! We're goin' through with this."

Henry and James were gathered again in Samuel's small, brick home on Fifteenth Street, almost directly across from the city jail—an ironic location for a man like Samuel who had a habit of skirting the law. The three of them sat around the kitchen table, one of the few things he could salvage from the sinking ship that had been his marriage. Several feet from the table sat Henry's wooden box, specially made for the escape by a mulatto man.

Two obstacles had suddenly risen from out of nowhere. The first: Samuel had announced that the escape plan would have to be delayed. He had learned that ice on the Susquehanna River was preventing barges from crossing over. Since there was no bridge on the river, train cars had to be ferried; but the ice was making this impossible. Therefore, on March 10, just three days before Henry was set to escape, Samuel had written to Miller McKim and told him they would have to postpone a week or so until the March thaw took care of the ice . . . which led to the second, more imposing obstacle.

McKim decided to back out.

"I regret to say that I must withdraw our endorsement," McKim had written.

Samuel had read the letter aloud in its entirety, but Henry wasn't going to let the plan die easily. "There's gotta be someone else we can contact in Philadelphia."

"But if the Anti-Slavery Society will not accept the delivery, who else would?" asked James.

Henry and James both turned toward Samuel, awaiting his answer. Samuel had an idea, but it was risky.

"Samuel?" James said.

Samuel broke out of his daze. "What's that?"

"Who else can we go to in Philadelphia?

Who—" James's words were cut off by a sudden knock on the front door, and Samuel motioned for them to duck out the back.

No time for that. Whoever knocked was already turning the door handle.

Thinking quickly and moving even faster, Henry hopped inside the big box in the middle of the floor. Samuel slammed the lid on top and sat on the box, while James just stood there, frozen in place.

John Allen stepped inside the room, and Samuel stared at him stonily.

"Does a man's door afford him no privacy? Do you always just walk into people's homes, Mr. Allen?"

John Allen conjured up a mischievous grin. "I thought I heard you say, 'Come in.' "

Samuel did not think that such an obvious lie deserved an answer.

For Samuel to be sharing company with James, a free black, at this time of night would appear irregular. But it would have looked much worse if John Allen had found all three of them—a white, a free black, and a slave—gathered around the table. Over the years, Richmond authorities had passed ordinances to discourage interaction among the three groups; and even though many of the laws went ignored, John Allen would have been highly suspicious.

"A friend of yours?" he asked, sizing up James.

"We do business together," said Samuel.

"Ah. I have some business to be askin' you about myself."

John Allen glared at James, as if willing him to leave the house. James got the message. He was only too happy to be getting out of there.

"We can discuss that cake you have on order tomorrow, Mr. Smith. I must be on my way."

"Thank you, James."

James said good night to Samuel and John Allen, each in turn, although John Allen was not about to exchange pleasantries with a Negro. With James gone, the overseer was quick to make his displeasure known. "Can't understand why you want to be doin' business with free nigras."

"He bakes excellent cakes."

John Allen blinked. He didn't have a comeback for that.

"So what can I do for you, Mr. Allen? Some shoes that need repairing?"

"No, no, not that kind of business." John Allen couldn't take his eyes off of the box on which Samuel was sitting. "Nice craftsmanship."

"Yes, it is."

"Can I see it?"

Samuel paused, baffled why John Allen would be so interested in an ordinary shipping box. He couldn't possibly know what lay inside. Samuel understood that any resistance might heighten suspicion, so he hopped off of the box.

"Be my guest."

John Allen crouched down and ran his hand across the grain of the wood. "Nice workmanship . . . Who done it?"

"John Mettauer. The mulatto. So what kind of business do you have in mind, Mr. Allen?"

"I've been asked to check into the Blevins case some more." John Allen ran a finger over the air holes drilled into the side.

"But Blevins is in jail. I thought the case was closed."

Finally, John Allen rose to his feet and took a seat at Samuel's table—even though he hadn't been invited to stay. Samuel wandered over to a chair on the opposite side of the table and sat down, drawing attention away from the box.

"There's been talk that Blevins had help in aidin' those slaves to escape," said John Allen. "We think he took the slaves to a schooner on the York River."

"I heard much the same. What's that to do with me?"

"You're a shoemaker."

"So I've heard."

"Blevins was a shoemaker too. And you knew him."

"In passing. Blevins hasn't worked in shoes for some time, though. From what I understand, he worked in poultry."

"Worked freein' slaves was more like it."

"He also turned in slaves for money. He was working both sides, from what I heard."

John Allen leaned back in the chair and laced his fingers behind his head. "You seem to hear a lot, Mr. Smith. You sure you ain't heard somethin' 'bout an accomplice?" John Allen studied his face, and Samuel knew he was looking for some subtle sign of guilt.

"Haven't heard a thing. Sorry I cannot be of more help." Samuel rose from his seat and motioned toward the door. "I'll keep my ear to the ground. If I hear anything about an accomplice, you'll be the first to know."

"Appreciate that, Mr. Smith."

John Allen did not budge from his chair, so Samuel walked over and opened the front door, wondering if he was going to have to throw him out. Finally, John Allen slowly rose and sauntered toward the door, pausing to look back at the box. "What's that box for anyways, if you don't mind me askin'?"

Samuel did mind him asking. "Shoes. That okay with you?"

"No, no, makes sense. I'm just wonderin' why you went to a mulatto for a box like this when there's any number of white box-makers you coulda gone to."

"My business is mine alone, Mr. Allen."

John Allen shrugged. "I always take special note when white men take an unusual interest in coloreds and such. I heard you went lookin' for Henry Brown's wife the day she was sold off south."

"I promised Henry that I would. Now good night, Mr. Allen."

John Allen moved a few steps closer to the door before pausing again. He wasn't done yet. "Still seems a might odd, you tryin' to help out Henry and his woman. I mean, if you hadn't a cleaned out Cottrell in a card game, Nancy's master wouldn't even been in the fix he found himself in, and he probably wouldn't a had to sell Nancy Brown. But if y'all feelin' guilty about what ya did to Henry and his family, I say don't be. They's just slaves."

There it was: the deadly truth that Samuel had concealed from Henry.

"Goodnight, Mr. Allen," said Samuel. He was determined to get rid of the pest even if he had to hurl him out the door. But at long last John Allen departed on his own steam.

Samuel waited a long time after John Allen left to make sure the overseer was truly gone. The last thing he wanted was John Allen barging back in unannounced and finding Henry in his home. He also wanted to put off the inevitable—facing Henry Brown.

Finally . . .

Samuel rapped on the top of the box. "You can come out now."

Henry did so slowly, drenched in sweat. He stared Samuel directly in the eyes, but Samuel didn't look back at him.

"Is it true?"

Samuel set the lid of the box back in place, buying himself some time to think. But he saw no way to finesse his way out of this one.

"It's true, I'm afraid. But I didn't foresee the consequences. I wouldn't have set up a card game with someone like Cottrell if I knew it would've led to this. I didn't even know Cottrell was Nancy's master at the time. I'm sorry. I truly am."

Grimly, Henry made a move for the door.

"Henry, wait. We can still do this."

Samuel had one last idea. It was a slim hope, but it was something.

"You don't have to feel you gotta do this for me, Mr. Smith. You done enough already."

Samuel shook off the insinuation. "I know who can pick up the package in Philadelphia."

Henry sighed. "I'm listenin'."

"I say we still send the box to Miller McKim."

Henry rolled his eyes. "Why would we do somethin' like that? McKim's done backed out."

"*He* backed out. But *we* haven't. I say we take the John Allen approach."

"And what's that?"

"When John Allen wants something, he barges in. I say we 'barge in,' so to speak. We do this anyway."

Henry still looked puzzled.

"I'll write to Mr. McKim. I'll tell him that I'm mailing you to the Anti-Slavery Society whether he likes it or not. He'll have no choice. He'll *have* to pick up the box. The box will have his name and his address, so he'll be responsible for it. He'll be implicated if you get caught, so he'll do whatever he can to prevent that. Mark my word. He'll agree to pick it up."

Henry stared back into Samuel's eyes. Then he tossed up his arms, as if he didn't care one way or another any more. "All right, we go through with this. Whatever happens happens."

As Henry made a move for the door, Samuel repeated his feelings. "I'm sorry, Henry."

"So am I." Then Henry disappeared into the night.

Miller McKim stared at the telegram, disbelieving what he had just read.

"Bad news, Mr. McKim?" asked his clerk, William Still.

Setting the telegram down carefully, McKim tried to compose himself. He kneaded his forehead with both hands, processing what he had just read. William stood by, clearly curious about the telegram but too polite to ask anything about its contents. Without even looking up, McKim picked up the telegram and waved it in the air. "Read."

After a moment of hesitation, William plucked the telegram out of McKim's hand, and his eyes widened with every word. "Samuel Smith . . . He's sending the box against your wishes?"

"I thought you would be pleased. Isn't this what you wanted?" McKim said, running a hand through his hair. He was well aware that William was of a different mind when it came to Henry Brown. William wanted to accept delivery of the package, but McKim had decided that it was much too dangerous for the Anti-Slavery Society.

The smooth-talking shoemaker was wrong when he said that by collecting the box at the station, the Society carried no risk. There was a good chance Brown was going to arrive at the station dead on delivery, and if that happened, questions would be asked. The coroner would nose around and uncover the cause of death. McKim could face legal action, and who knew what might happen to the Anti-Slavery Society.

Handing the telegram back to McKim, William said, "It's true I wanted the escape to go through, but not against your wishes."

"I know, I know. I am sorry for being contentious, but this is so very upsetting." McKim studied the telegram once again. "Do you think Samuel Smith is bluffing?"

"Can we take that chance? We have to think about Henry Brown's fate."

McKim didn't answer. He silently stewed.

"The package will arrive next week—the morning of March 24. Shall I make arrangements to have it picked up?" William spoke hopefully.

McKim kept shifting in his chair, as if he were sitting on nettles. He had made his decision, and he wasn't going to be bullied. Not by Samuel Smith, not by anyone. Henry Brown's box could sit in the train depot until the Second Coming, as far as he was concerned.

"Mr. McKim? Should I have a porter pick up the box?"

"No."

"Sir?"

"I said no."

And that was final.

"As you can see, nothin' inside," Henry told the small boy, Louis, no more than eight years old. Henry pulled out the drawer of the magic box and let Louis peer inside. The boy stuck in his hand and felt around until he was completely convinced it was whistle clean.

"Nothin' there," he confirmed.

It was night, and Henry was sitting on the porch of his Shockoe Bottom tenement. The house faced the alleyway, which was pitch black, although Henry had a lantern to illuminate the setting, along with the meager light from nearby tenements and shanties. On his head sat a wide-brimmed hat, and in his hands was his old trick box, the same one he had made back on the plantation—the same one he had used to do tricks for his brothers and sisters. To keep his mind occupied by something other than his fears, Henry usually turned to magic, even if he only had an audience of one.

With only two days to go before the escape, the fears were piling up.

"This here box is empty, but so is my stomach," Henry said, pulling an apple out of his coat pocket and holding it before the boy. "I'm awful hungry, and I'd sure love to gobble up this juicy apple. But you're probably hungry too, and I don't really feel like sharin', so what should I do?"

"Share anyway?" Louis shivered with the wind, which had little trouble slipping in through the numerous tears in his thin jacket.

"I can sure do that. But you know what'd be better? What if I magically create a *second* apple inside this here box? Then we'd both have ourselves apples!"

Henry tossed the apple into the air; and as he caught it, he deftly guided it into the open drawer of the box. Henry slid the drawer back in. "Now I say the magic word. Can you say apple-cadabra?"

They spoke the word together as Henry waved his hand over the box. Then Henry tapped the box twice and pulled out the drawer with great drama. The drawer was empty.

"Whoa now, that's not what I wanted! Now I got *no* apples! Where'd the apple go?"

Louis shrugged.

"Ah, but wait a moment. I think . . . I see . . ."

Henry's hand darted inside the boy's coat, and he pulled out the apple. Louis laughed. "How'd you do that?"

"Bravo! Bravo!" came another voice.

Henry's grin vanished, and he snapped to high alert at the sudden sound of someone clapping in the alleyway darkness. He stared out into the night, and Louis edged closer to his side, eyes wide.

"Who's there?"

Henry's heart sank when John Allen staggered into the lantern light, obviously drunk and zigzagging like a Virginia fence. Henry motioned for the little boy to scram, but he wouldn't budge. Probably too afraid of the spirits in the dark.

"Fine trick, Henry, fine trick," slurred John Allen, moving further into the light. His breath reached Henry well before he did.

"Thank you, sir."

To Henry's dismay, the overseer stepped up onto the porch and sat down on the railing. But at least John Allen was smiling. He waved his hand and slurred, "Go on, go on, Henry, don't let me stop ya. I'm just on my way to check in on Obadiah Johnson down the alley a ways, but I like a good magic trick as much as the next person."

Henry paused. It was one thing to do a show for an eight-year-old boy. Quite another thing to perform for John Allen.

"Go on, I said."

John Allen did not appear threatening; alcohol occasionally had a way of softening the man, so Henry decided he'd better jump back into the magic while the overseer was still acting cordial. He slipped the apple into the magic box.

"Okay now, I got my one apple back, but I'm still needin' *two* apples. So let me try it again." Henry cast a glance at John Allen, and the overseer was still smiling and leaning forward with eager eyes on the box.

"Apple-cadabra! Say it with me!" Henry told Louis, and to his amazement John Allen joined in by shouting, "Apple-cadabra!"

For a moment, Henry saw John Allen as the boy he knew so long ago. The one he fished in streams with. The one who could be mischievous, even playful.

With a theatrical flourish, Henry pulled open the drawer to reveal . . . Ah-ha! Two apples! Only one problem. These were apple *cores*. The two apples had been eaten down to the quick. The boy grinned and sputtered laughter. Henry shot another look at John Allen and saw him grinning and shaking his head in amazement.

"This is gettin' maddenin'," Henry groused, tossing aside the apple cores and pretending to be at the end of his rope. "But don't you worry . . ."

He swept the hat from his head, passed his hand across it, and said, "Apple-cadabra!" Then, plunging his hand into the hat, he extracted an apple. A single, red apple.

Resigned to the fate of only one apple, he said, "I guess I'm just gonna have to learn to share. One-third for you. One-third for me. And one-third for you, Mr. Allen."

As he said the words, Henry's eyes met John Allen's, and he saw something he didn't often find in the man—an unguarded attitude.

"You was always a clever one, Henry," said John Allen, leaning back so far that Henry was afraid he'd tumble over the railing. "Always clever. You remember the time we caught that raccoon with the trap you devised?"

Henry remembered it well. It was the first day he had ever met John Allen's pappy. It was not a good day, as far as he could remember.

"When we told Pappy what we done, he was pleased as punch—until he found out you was the one who made the trap." John Allen's demeanor took a dark turn. "You know, he beat the tar outta me that day. He said I was lettin' a colored get the best of me."

Henry tensed. "I'm sorry."

"So was I."

"But you was always the better fisherman,"

Henry said. "I never seen someone catch so many in one day."

John Allen's smile returned. "You're right, Henry, you're right there. Not many can fish like me. But when I'd come home with a string of fish . . ." John Allen stood up and almost lost his balance. "When I'd come home with a string a fish, Pappy didn't believe I'd caught 'em. He thought my friends did the catchin'. One time he said he was sure you'd caught 'em for me."

"That weren't right. You caught 'em, and I know it, and you know it."

Shrugging, John Allen motioned for Henry to hand him the box. "Here, let me take a look at that thing of yours."

After a moment's hesitation, Henry placed the small trick box in his hands.

"How'd you do this?" he asked, turning the box over in his hands.

"I can show you if you like, Mr. Allen."

John Allen frowned. "Ya think I'm not clever enough to figure it out myself?"

"Oh no, sir, it's just that . . ."

Henry decided he should just be quiet before he got himself into even deeper trouble. John Allen kept turning the box over and over, studying it from every angle and sliding the drawer in and out, his frustration clearly mounting.

"Must be a trick bottom here somewheres."

John Allen yanked out the drawer so roughly that

Henry thought he was going to pull it apart. If Allen had been sober, he could probably figure out the trick. But in his drunken condition, he would have trouble figuring out how to open a door properly.

Growling, John Allen yanked the drawer completely out and started pulling at its sides. The wood suddenly snapped with a crack, and Henry made a move to grab the box—but wisely held back.

"Just hold on there, I can figure this out." John Allen kept glancing over at Louis, as if feeling the pressure to look clever in the eyes of a young black boy.

The irony was that John Allen actually was a clever and resourceful man in his own twisted way. The way he bamboozled Mr. Barret, pilfering supplies, and the way he made money on the side was a wonder to behold. Henry wouldn't put it past him to own his own factory some day.

But today, he couldn't figure out how a toy trick box worked.

More splitting wood. Henry winced at every snap and crack. John Allen picked the box apart, piece by piece. Finally, he just slammed the magic box down and stomped his boot heel onto the splintered wood, grinding it into the floor. The wood snapped like bones.

"This is what I think of trickery!"

"Yes, sir," Henry said quietly. He stared down on the busted bits of wood. He had had that magic box since he was a boy.

Putting his hands on his hips, John Allen breathed heavily. Then he rubbed his eyes roughly, wheeled around, and jabbed a finger at Henry.

"I don't like trickery in no one, but especially in someone like Obadiah Johnson. That nigra is fakin' his wounds, mark my words. Went home from the factory sayin' he's too injured to work, but I ain't gonna let him pull a fast one on me!"

Henry didn't respond. Better to just wait out the storm.

Taking off his hat, John Allen slapped it against one of the porch's posts and cursed. Henry put his arm around the small boy and pulled him in closer.

Still staggering slightly, John Allen navigated his way off of the porch, muttering to himself and striding off, further down the alleyway—in the direction of Obadiah Johnson's place.

Henry waited until the man was completely swallowed up in darkness before making any movements. Groaning, he leaned over and picked up the remains of his box. Louis helped him.

"Can you fix it?" Louis asked.

Henry stared at him, not realizing at first that he meant the box.

Henry sighed. "Yes, I think I can. I can fix it good."

"Just a little bit," Henry said, as James prepared to pour oil of vitriol on his trembling hand. Henry needed a nasty cut, and what better way to do that than with oil of vitriol, also known as sulfuric acid? Even a dilute acid would burn through his skin like fire.

"This is dangerous stuff, Henry. You sure?" James asked, holding the small glass vial above Henry's left palm.

"Do it."

James started to tip the vial. A drop of sweat chose that moment to slide onto his eyelid, so he drew back to wipe his eye.

"Sorry, Henry. I'm trying to do this one drop at a time."

"Don't hold back. My injury's gotta be real bad. It's the only way."

James took a deep breath and started to tip the bottle once again. His hand shook so hard that he was afraid he was going to splash the acid haphazardly across Henry's hand. The acid flowed to the very edge of the bottle. James tried to tilt it ever so slightly, just enough to allow one, maybe two, drops of acid to fall like fire-filled raindrops. James bit his lip, concentrating, concentrating . . .

At the last second, James drew back from the brink.

"I'm sorry, I'm sorry."

"Give it to me!"

Henry took the vial roughly. Enough tentativeness! He was going to do this himself. James stared in disbelief.

"Henry, what . . . ?"

Recklessly, Henry tipped the bottle over—Too much! When the searing liquid hit his skin, it felt as if somebody had driven a burning spike into the palm of his hand. The pain shot up his arm like wildfire. He dropped the vial and roared.

"My God!" James shouted.

Henry staggered across the room in agony, reaching for the nearby bucket of water but knocking it off the table by accident. The idea was to plunge his hand in the water for relief, but now all of that water was spread thinly across the wooden floor of James's cake shop. Henry grabbed a nearby rag and wrapped his finger with it, clutching, squeezing with all his might and stifling another scream. He crashed across the room blindly, knocking over a chair, stumbling into a wall, out of control and out of his mind with pain.

"What can I do?" James said, following by his side, eyes wide.

Henry buckled over and crumpled to the floor, cradling his wounded hand. Slowly, steadily, the initial flare of pain subsided, and he took deep breaths to calm himself. He let go of the rag, still wrapped around his palm. It was blood-soaked.

"Let me find a clean bandage," said James.

He frantically dug out another rag from a shelf, while Henry just moaned. It was the only sound he allowed himself.

"I'm sorry, Henry. I shoulda done it for you."

As he unwrapped the bandage, James recoiled

in horror. The acid had bit deeply into Henry's skin, exposing bone. Henry writhed with a new wave of pain as James wrapped a fresh bandage around his hand.

Slowly, Henry calmed down, blinking the tears from his eyes. He was still lying on the floor, staring up at a horrified James. For James's sake, he managed a slight smile.

"I think that'll do the trick."

With his bandaged hand throbbing, Henry passed through an oven-hot factory room where shirtless men stood at gigantic cauldrons, stirring a scorching mixture of licorice and sugar with large wooden paddles, while dippers baptized the tobacco leaves in the sticky, black liquid. Henry didn't find any sign of John Allen, but that was to be expected; the head overseer usually assigned an underling like Callahan to the hot task of keeping an eye on the workers in this room.

Henry finally tracked John Allen down in the lumpmakers' room, where slaves were just arriving, taking seats at long tables, and fashioning the twists of flavored tobacco into lumps of just the right size and weight.

"My hand's doin' poorly," Henry said, holding out his bloody, bandaged hand.

Allen gave him a long, hard look. "Whatya got? A splinter?"

"My hand's cut bad."

"If you're trying to get out of a day's work . . ." John Allen grabbed Henry by the left wrist and yanked back the bandage carelessly, ripping skin with it. Henry groaned, stifling a scream and blinking back the pain. John Allen couldn't hide his shock when he laid eyes on the slave's mutilated hand, and he burst out with an obscenity. "How'd you do this?"

"Cuttin' wood. Makin' a new magic box."

"I was thinkin' ya cut yourself on purpose to get a coupla days off. But no fool would cut his self to the bone like this. Get on home, you're no good to me today."

"Could I have a few days to mend, sir?"

"Get a poultice of flax-seed to it, and then let me be the judge of how long you're gone."

So Henry wandered back home, relieved and terrified all at once, for now he knew the escape was actually going to happen. For the rest of the day, he would try to sleep some, and he hoped to finish repairing his small, trick box and hide it beneath the floorboards for safekeeping. Then, at about four in the morning, the plan was to slip out of his house and make his way down the alley-ways to Samuel's where he would be sealed in a box for an entire day.

Looking down at his bandaged hand, which still throbbed, he hoped the most painful part of the plan was behind him. But he had a hunch that it wasn't.

35

March 24, 1849

Henry thought he was losing his mind. He tried to sleep, anything to escape reality, but he couldn't slip away. Too many parts of his body were on fire.

In Baltimore, freight was transferred to another line—the Philadelphia, Wilmington, and Baltimore, which shared the same depot. Two hours north of Baltimore, at about 1 a.m. on Saturday, March 24, the train reached the Susquehanna River, where barges ferried railroad cars across. Another ninety-five long miles still lay ahead before Philadelphia.

Mercifully, this stretch of the trip was without drama—no flipping the box upside down, no blocking of air holes, no wasps, just the constant, rocking rhythm of the train and so many stops along the way. Henry hugged his knees and curled into a ball and prayed for it all to end. But the train went on and on and on, jolting to a stop at so many stations—Stanton, Newport, Bellevue, Claymont, Marcus Hook, Chester, Lazaretto . . . If Henry could imagine hell, it would be an endless train ride in a box like this. He was sick to his stomach, and at last, deep into the pit of the night, he felt himself beginning to drift away. He wasn't sure if it was sleep or death. Either would be a mercy.

The wind, an invisible train, roars through the trees. "The life of a slave, your life, is like the leaves . . ." A train whistle sounds, and a hand pounds nails into soft wood. Then a voice, a whisper in the ear. "Go. . . . Go and get a box."

He reaches out. Nancy's hand is so soft—too soft for a washerwoman. "My name is Henry Brown."

"I know."

> Steal away, steal away to Jesus!
> Steal away, steal away home, I ain't got long
>   to stay here!
> My Lord calls me, He calls me by the thunder;
> The trumpet sounds within-a my soul. I ain't
>   got long to stay here.

Henry stands facing Nancy, and the preacher is speaking. "What God has brought together, let not man put asunder." Henry leans forward. Nancy's face rises to meet his, and they kiss in front of all creation.

> Steal away, steal away, steal away to Jesus!
> Steal away, steal away home, I ain't got long
>   to stay here!
> Tombstones are bursting, poor sinner stands
>   a-trembling;
> The trumpet sounds within-a my soul, I ain't
>   got long to stay here.

Henry has Nancy by the hand, and they are running for their lives, running down Cary Street, running along the Richmond docks, running past the edge of town, running by the old Hermitage Plantation in Louisa County, running past the Ambler Mill, running through the forest, deeper into the woods, finally coming to a breathless stop. Henry looks around, and Nancy is gone.

Henry drifted in and out of consciousness for hours until the train came to a stop—and remained motionless for what seemed to be an eternity. Henry perked up a little and tried to straighten his back. His wounded hand constantly ached, and it exploded with pain when he accidentally knocked it against the box's wall. Closing his eyes and taking a deep breath, he waited for the burning pain to subside back to a simmer. He listened. There was a little more activity than he had noticed at the sleepy depots along the way—although with it being very early in the morning, the platform wasn't bustling.

"Philadelphia!"

Henry heard the word, but he couldn't believe it. He rubbed his eyes with his good hand and felt all of his various wounds begin to throb, a synchronized orchestra of pain. He tried not to feel too much hope, for he had learned to expect the worst. Henry knew what it was like to have freedom dangled right in front of him and snatched away at the last second.

Now you see it. Now you don't.

The large door to the boxcar slid open, and faint light washed in.

Don't mess up. Not now. The finish line was close.

Henry had been inside the box for an entire day. But he had to be patient, had to be strong, so he willed himself to remain motionless because his box was surrounded by several cargo handlers, and he wasn't about to let himself be discovered at this stage. The handlers were all talking politics, something about the recent election of Zachary Taylor as president.

"I admire Taylor 'cause he wasn't about to be sworn in on the Sabbath. He ain't about to break a Commandment, even if it means puttin' off bein' president for a day."

"Yeah, but how did that make David Atchison president for one day?"

"Listen, Taylor didn't become the new president until March 5, instead of March 4, and that left one day without a president. That woulda made Atchison president. For a day."

"No it wouldn't. Next in line is vice president."

"The vice president and speaker also finished their terms on March 4, so Atchison was our acting president. For one day. Can you imagine? One day."

"The fellow oughta put it on his gravestone."

This Atchison fellow had nothing on him,

Henry decided. Atchison may have been president for a day, but he had been a dead man for one day. Being president was nothing compared to being Lazarus, buried in a graveyard of boxes.

Henry felt his box being lifted out of the darkness of the boxcar and onto the platform. The sun was still down, so there was no natural light, but the station's lamps allowed a feeble glow to seep into Henry's box. Thirsty for light, he lapped it up.

His box was shoved off to the side. Fifteen minutes passed. Twenty. Thirty. He didn't understand. Where was McKim? He should have been here long ago, waiting for the train, waiting for the box. The time stretched on and the worries mounted. Henry worked himself into a position so he could peer through one of the air holes. All he could see of the world was the far end of the platform—a small portion of the bricks of the station wall. It was like looking through the keyhole of a door. Had McKim forgotten? Or maybe the abolitionist had run into trouble with authorities and had to back off. If no one claimed the box, would they send him back on the train? What then? If they tried shipping him back, he would be better off breaking out of the box. People would be shocked to see him hatching out of this box, but at least they wouldn't send him back—would they?

Henry put his eye up to the hole once again and

saw a flash of blue. He thought nothing of it until a figure stepped directly in line with his small circle of vision. The blue was that of a uniform. A soldier's uniform. There were two of them, two soldiers talking at the far end of the platform. They looked like miniature men, perfectly framed by his peephole. Then all at once, one of them looked directly at Henry. From that distance, there was no way the soldier could have seen Henry's eyeball, pressed up against the hole. But it sure felt as if the soldier could see him as clear as day.

Henry pulled back from the hole. He wanted to scream. This couldn't be happening. Not when he was so close! Not after being nearly shot, not after nearly suffocating, not after nearly roasting, not after being placed upside down for hours and nearly dying, not after nearly breaking his neck! It can't happen!

Henry heard footsteps coming closer, as well as muffled voices, and he strained to hear what the soldiers were saying. Nothing. The words were indiscernible. Then he sensed two men very close, unseen threats just inches away, separated only by this thin skin of wood. He ventured another peek through one of the air holes and caught a glimpse of a soldier's sky-blue pants. Then he felt the box being raised up into the air. He was being moved. Grunts. Gasps. But he heard no words. Someone must have alerted the authorities in Philadelphia. They had sent soldiers to claim the box, he was sure, and they were transporting him to the city jail. He felt the box being loaded into another wagon, and he heard the wheels creaking as they began to roll along the Philadelphia streets. It had to be the soldiers, Henry thought. It had to be. If the driver had been Miller McKim, he would have said something to him by now!

The sun had risen and pinpricks of light penetrated the box from holes on two different sides and from directly above. Henry put his eye back up to the holes on both sides, but none of them afforded him a view of the soldier driving the wagon. But it did give him his first glimpses of a northern city.

The wagon made a racket, wooden wheels on cobblestone. But Henry heard another sound—the cooing of a bird. He put his eye back to the air hole, and he thought he caught the flash of a bird's wing, as if the bird was hovering right outside his box. Then he heard little scratching sounds on the box's lid, and he guessed that the bird was walking back and forth on top of his tabernacle and pecking at the wood.

The wagon couldn't have gone more than six blocks before it made a turn onto another street. Then a minute later, another turn. Henry was back to the air hole with his eye pressed up against the wood. He could see that they were moving down an alleyway to the back of a building before the wagon finally came to a rest. Henry heard a door open, then whispering. He had no idea what was being said. Peering through the hole, he saw the flash of a man's face. A young face. But it all happened too quickly to tell if it was one of the soldiers he had seen at the station. Just a flash of pink skin, and he was gone. The young man had climbed into the wagon and was shoving Henry's box, sliding it to the edge of the wagon. More whispering. There was a second man, but Henry couldn't see him. Suddenly, his box was in the air with a man on either side, lugging it clear of the wagon and getting the box perfectly positioned, adjusting their grips on the heavy container. The two men carried the box toward the open door of the building, one on each side like pallbearers. Still more whispering. Footsteps on cobblestones. The squeak of the door. Grunts. A curse. He heard a single profane word loud and clear. One of the men stumbled, and Henry nearly gave out a cry as his box tilted at a crazy angle.

The light suddenly dimmed, and Henry could tell they were now indoors. Then his box was set down, and all went quiet.

And then . . .

A slight rap on the side of the box.

36

So much can happen in twenty-four hours. One day ago, on Friday, John Allen had barged into William Barret's house bristling with authority. On Saturday morning, he was summoned to the Barret mansion, and this time he was afraid to go. But he had no choice.

John Allen was on horseback, and he took his sweet time getting to the mansion on Cary Street. Dismounting, he trudged to the door of the Barret house with his hat in his hand and paused before knocking. When the house slave, Fanny, opened the door, he didn't barge in.

"Mr. Barret asked to see me," he said, with just a hint of fire left to his voice.

"He's waitin' for ya in his study." Fanny led him down the short hallway to the office on the right, and John Allen shuffled into the room, coming to a stop directly in front of William Barret's large desk.

"Good mornin', sir," John Allen said. He played with his hat and stared at a nearby open chair.

Mr. Barret did not speak a word, did not even look up from his paperwork. He did not tell John

Allen to take a seat, so the overseer was left standing there, unsure what to say or do. John Allen glanced over at the fireplace against the wall. Hanging above the mantle was the painting of a dog—Mr. Barret's black Labrador, Cyclone. Mr. Barret had several dogs, but Cyclone was his oldest and favorite.

For the life of him, John Allen had no idea why Mr. Barret had called him to his office. Mr. Barret was probably planning to tell him the specifics of how he was going to dock his wages to get back what he lost with the death of Obadiah. What else could it be? It couldn't have anything to do with Henry Brown. He was the only one who knew about Henry's escape, and he didn't plan to say anything until the two slave catchers in Philadel-phia confirmed his capture.

Finally, Mr. Barret set aside his ink pen. He stared at John Allen for a few moments—until the overseer finally averted his gaze. John Allen was tempted to stare him down, like a mean dog would, but a sense of self-preservation took hold. This was not the time to show defiance.

"I have learned that Henry Brown went home with an injury on Thursday morning," Mr. Barret said. "Is that correct, Mr. Allen?"

John Allen shifted uneasily from one foot to another. "Yes, sir. He had a terrible injury to his hand. Cut his self to the bone doin' wood work."

"Are you sure about that?"

"Yes, sir. He was cut something bad. Told me his self that he cut it workin' on a box."

Mr. Barret didn't say a word in response, just kept staring at John Allen. Cyclone hobbled into the office and sniffed at John Allen's pants leg.

"Sit, Cyclone," Mr. Barret said, as if to underscore the fact that he hadn't invited John Allen to sit. Obediently, Cyclone sat just to John Allen's right, his pink tongue hanging out as he panted.

"You know, Mr. Allen, I once promised my father that I would never use the whip on Henry Brown."

"I didn't know that, sir," John Allen lied.

"But I was willing to overlook the times you whipped Henry Brown."

"But sir, I ain't never laid a whip on him. I'd never—"

"Don't lie to me. I know the Colquitts paid you to lash Henry, but I overlooked your indiscretion at the time."

"But sir, that was many years ago."

John Allen massaged his temples; he felt a headache coming on. Was Henry Brown dead? But if Henry had died from his wound, he would have found the body when he barged into his home. No, Henry had escaped in a box; and just as soon as he received word from the slave catchers, he would redeem himself.

"I didn't lay a hand on Henry Brown. I swear it, Mr. Barret. This time I'm tellin' the truth."

Cyclone looked up at John Allen, as if the dog was passing judgment on every word.

"We believe that Henry has escaped."

John Allen's eyebrows shot up. "That's just what I been thinkin', sir, but I didn't want to say so until I knew for sure."

"Samuel Smith informed me that you beat Henry so badly that he couldn't come to work. He said the beating drove Henry to run."

John Allen felt the rug pulled out from under him. "He's a liar. I didn't beat Henry! I swear it!"

"So Henry hurt himself without any assistance from you?"

"That's right, sir. Cuttin' wood, he told me." John Allen was going to strangle Smith the next time he saw him. His head pulsed with pain, as his headache hit full force. "The truth is that *Samuel Smith* helped Henry escape."

"You're telling me that Smith helped him escape and then reported the escape to me? Why would he do that?"

John Allen didn't know how to answer. And that big, dumb dog kept staring at him, just panting away.

"Don't worry, sir, I got men on the hunt. Two slave catchers in Philadelphia."

Mr. Barret stood up and leaned over his desk. "You hired slave catchers, but you didn't think to say anything about the escape to me? Seems to me you're hiding something."

"Sorry, sir . . . I just . . . I didn't want . . ."

"You didn't want to look like a fool again?"

John Allen didn't see a need to answer the question.

"A little late for that," said Mr. Barret.

John Allen looked down at Cyclone, who was still staring up at him, as if waiting for an answer. This dog was beginning to drive him crazy.

"If Henry Brown has escaped, I am holding you responsible, Mr. Allen. You injured him, you drove him to escape, you failed to keep him loyal."

"But I'm tellin' the truth, Mr. Barret. I ain't never laid a hand on Henry for the longest time." The storm inside his head gained strength, and he felt dizzy and nauseous.

Cyclone sniffed the air, picking up the smell of baking bread from the kitchen. John Allen wished he could smack that dog.

"Don't worry, sir, my men will catch him, and I'll make sure he don't ever run again," John Allen said, rubbing his forehead, trying to push away the pain.

"How? By whipping him again? Do you know any other way to keep my workers in line? You've cost me two strong workers in one week."

"I'll keep them in line, you can be sure of that, Mr. Barret."

"You will not have to worry about that any

longer, Mr. Allen. You are relieved of your duties."

The words struck John Allen like a slap. "What's that, sir?"

"You heard me. You no longer work for me. If you cannot control my workers, you are of no use to me."

"But sir—"

"That is all. You may go now."

John Allen wanted to call down curses, but he thought there might be a chance that Mr. Barret would change his mind. So he held his fire. Mr. Barret came around the desk, and John Allen wondered for a moment if his boss was going to physically remove him from the premises. But Mr. Barret had come around the desk to scratch his dog's head.

"Good boy," he said.

John Allen stared down at Cyclone in disbelief and fury.

"You can pick up your whip and other belongings today," Mr. Barret said. "I want you off of my factory premises by evening."

There was no way that John Allen was stepping back inside that tobacco factory to retrieve his whip or anything else. He wasn't going to let the slaves or Callahan have the pleasure of seeing him defeated.

"Could we discuss this further some other time, Mr. Barret? When Henry Brown has been brought back, he can tell ya his self that I didn't injure him."

"There is nothing more to discuss. Leave."

"But—"

"I said leave."

John Allen looked down at Cyclone, and the dog stared back at him.

"Do I need to get one of my servants to help you find the door?"

All John Allen could muster were a few feeble curses under his breath before wheeling around and staggering down the hallway, still tormented by his headache and harassed by that hound. Cyclone followed at his heels until he was out the door.

"Are you all right?" came a disembodied voice, just outside the box, only inches away.

Would a slave catcher or policeman ask Henry if he was all right? Should he answer? Should he dare? If they were the authorities, there was no escaping them now. He had nothing to lose by speaking, so he used his voice for the first time in a day.

"I'm all right, sir."

Henry could hear murmuring. Then someone went to work on the box, cutting the hickory bands that were wrapped around it tightly, like burial bandages.

And then . . .

"Almost there, Henry." Someone started prying off the lid of the box with a crowbar, and the wood splintered and snapped.

The lid was removed, and light poured into Henry's world, washing over him like a river. Henry felt the cool air settle down around him, and he stared up at the ceiling and blinked away the brightness. Faces appeared over him and beamed down on him. Three faces, two white and one black. All smiling. Henry had never laid eyes on these men before, but one thing was obvious: The faces were not those of slave catchers or policemen or soldiers.

As Henry discovered in due course, his box had been picked up by a porter, Dan O'Reilly, and one of the soldiers had simply helped Dan load the box into the wagon. Miller McKim, in all conscience, could not desert Henry, and he had ultimately given in and had the box picked up. Now, the box was sitting in the main room of the Anti-Slavery Society office at 31 North Fifth Street.

With stiff joints and sore muscles, Henry raised himself up, unfolding his body and standing up in the box. The looks on the faces of the three men around him could not have been more amazed if he had risen from the dead. He was a sight, drenched from all of the sweat and all of the water that he had poured out on himself to stay cool. He looked as if he had swum up from the bottom of the ocean, surfacing through a portal in the bottom of the box. Henry felt a slight breeze moving across the room, and that too was a sensation to savor.

Henry extended his hand—the uninjured one—to the nearest man and tried to speak as matter-of-factly as can be. "Good mornin', gentlemen!"

"You are the greatest man in America!" exclaimed one of the men wildly. Henry later learned that it was Miller McKim who made this extravagant claim, and that the other two men were William Still and Lewis Thompson.

"Steady now," said William.

Before Henry had much of a chance to take in this new world, he felt the room spinning around and he stumbled forward, only to be caught. William had him on one side and Lewis had him on the other, and they helped him step out of the box and led him to a chair. It was all hazy to Henry, but he remembered someone putting a mug of water in his hands and telling him to drink.

The next thing Henry remembered was the room reemerging from the darkness and the men asking him how he felt.

"Do you need a physician?" McKim asked.

"I'm fine." Henry tried to work up a smile. He was so exhausted and so hungry and so thirsty . . . and so happy. Happy it was over, happy to drink in his freedom, happy to taste liberty.

"Can you stand?"

Henry nodded; and with assistance from William

and Lewis, he rose to his feet. The room was no longer spinning.

"Are you all right?"

Henry nodded again and he took in the room, his first glimpse of freedom. The room was imprinted in his mind. The chairs, the desk, the hat rack, the fireplace . . .

The three men stared at him, as if waiting for him to say something profound. So Henry did what he had been planning from the very beginning. He began to sing. His voice was weak from exhaustion, but he began anyway.

"I waited patiently, I waited patiently for the Lord, for the Lord . . ."

Samuel handed the telegram to James, who read it hungrily. A smile broke across James's face, and he dropped back into a chair. Samuel wished he too could smile, but smiling stretched his skin and caused the cuts on his face to flare. He was feeling better, but it had been an excruciating twenty-four hours.

The telegram was from Miller McKim, and it announced Henry's safe arrival in Philadelphia.

"So I guess this means the slave catchers didn't show up at the train station this morning," James said. "Do you think?"

"I do think. But why would they show up after my little trick? I should become a magician like Henry."

James smiled. "That was quick thinking."

"Sometimes the best plans are the simplest."

Samuel's plan couldn't have been any simpler. After John Allen had been knocked unconscious, Samuel searched the overseer's pockets and found the telegram alerting the slave catchers. All it took was a few flicks of the pencil and Samuel changed Henry's arrival date in Philadelphia from March 24 to March 25. He switched the 4 to a 5 and stuffed the telegram back into John Allen's pockets.

"But John Allen could've noticed the change," James said.

"Could've, but didn't." Samuel never liked to think about what could've been. He took a seat and eyed the fresh cake that James had just taken out of the oven. It was another sponge cake, a replacement for the cake that James had shared with Fanny and Samuel the day before. The Brewers' cake.

"You still don't think Mr. Barret suspects us?" James said.

"Certainly not you. And I don't think he suspects me either. Why would he take John Allen's word over mine? John Allen beat Obadiah to death, and Mr. Barret thinks he also beat Henry."

"So he bought the story?"

"Seemed to."

"But it could've blown up in your face."

"Could've, but didn't. Mr. Barret was going to

find out about Henry's escape soon—from John Allen or Callahan or someone. So it was better to come from me first."

James rubbed the weariness from his eyes, stretched out his arms, and yawned. Samuel got up and wandered over to the counter, where the warm cake still roosted. He took a whiff.

"Don't you think this calls for another celebration?"

"The last time we celebrated with cake, John Allen interrupted the festivities with a gun," James said.

"I don't think we need to worry about Mr. Allen. He's been given the boot at the tobacco factory."

"I heard," James said.

"From your favorite news source?"

"Fanny came by earlier this afternoon."

Samuel leaned over and took another whiff. He grinned, but then just as quickly grimaced at the pain it caused. "Whatya say?"

Smiling, James slapped his knees and stood up. "I suppose I can make yet another cake for the Brewers. Here, let me serve ya."

No need for that. Samuel had already picked up the knife and was slicing a large piece.

37

Philadelphia
March 25, 1849
4:45 a.m.

Jeb Pleck was exhausted. It was still dark when he dragged himself out of bed and headed for the station of the Philadelphia, Wilmington, and Baltimore Railroad, on the southeast corner of Eleventh and Market streets in Philadelphia. In a cold drizzle, he and Tommy McCarthy approached a train that had just pulled into the station at a time when anyone with good sense was sound asleep. Tommy looked even more exhausted than Jeb, and he trailed two steps behind, as dazed as a sleepwalker. A large, round, ornate clock hung over the platform, taunting them with the time.

"This better pay off is all I'm sayin'," said Tommy, the first words he had spoken since they arrived at the station, other than a couple of grunts.

"Allen ain't steered us wrong before."

"You keep saying that, but he also ain't never told us to look for a slave mailed in a box."

Tommy had a point. They came to a stop on the station platform and surveyed the scene before them. All kinds of bags and boxes were being hauled out of the boxcars. The platform was mostly devoid of people, except for the men unloading the train and a few other railroad workers, who moved about slowly, like in a dream.

"Look for a box big enough to hold a man," said Jeb.

"Shouldn't be hard. I see only one."

Tommy was a large Irishman with cauliflower ears, a misshapen nose, a tangle of curly hair, a thick, untamed moustache, and lumberjack arms. Carrying a hammer in one hand and a crowbar in the other, it was no wonder that the two cargo handlers gave him a wide berth as he approached.

"Can we help you gentlemen?" asked one of freight men.

Jeb did the talking. "We have reason to believe that an escaped slave has arrived on this train."

The two cargo handlers exchanged looks. "There ain't no escaped slaves here. We'd a noticed something like that."

"Not if he arrived in a box."

"A box?"

Tommy strode over to the only sizable box in the bunch and rocked it back and forth to get a sense of what might be inside. "Feels like it could be a body. It's big. And it's heavy."

Tommy jammed the crowbar beneath the lid and started banging on it with his hammer, getting some leverage.

"Please sir, you don't have the right to bust that open."

Tommy looked up from his work and glowered, and that was all it took for the cargo handler to shut up and watch. The Irishman made quick work of the package, popping off the lid with the crowbar and splitting the wood in the process. Jeb was by his side, eager for a peek. Tommy hurled aside the box's lid, and they found themselves staring at a tangle of blankets—packing material.

The Irishman reached in and started digging.

All of a sudden, Tommy drew back his hands and backed away from the box, his eyes wide. "I felt an arm," he said. Jeb didn't often seen fear in Tommy's face.

"Just an arm?"

"I think he's dead. As stiff as a board." Tommy wiped his hands on his pants legs, as if trying to wipe the death from his fingers. By this time, the two cargo handlers had inched their ways closer. All they could see were the blankets on top.

"I don't smell death," said one.

He was right about that. So Jeb carefully reached in and pulled aside the layers of blankets. An arm appeared, sticking out of folds. A white arm, an abnormally thin, white arm.

And it was made of stone.

"What in the world . . . ?" Tommy yanked away the blankets and cursed himself red in the face. Nestled in the box was a four-foot-high statue of what appeared to be some sort of Greek goddess.

"Is this some kinda joke?" Jeb growled.

"So that's your slave?" one of the cargo handlers said, smirking. The other one turned away, trying to conceal his laughter.

"John Allen has some answering to do," growled Tommy.

"Next time you see him, enlist him as your sparring partner and knock the living daylights out of him."

Tommy let out another grunt and swung his hammer at the poor, defenseless goddess, knocking her head clean off. Then he marched out of the station, dreaming of the day he could do the same thing to John Allen.

38

Boston
June 3, 1849

It was the greatest day in Henry Brown's life, but he couldn't stop worrying.

"Will my family think of me the same?" Henry asked William Still. They sat side by side in a two-wheeled Boston chaise, rolling over cobblestone roads.

"Your children are very proud of what you

have done," William said. "Two *entire cities* are proud of you."

It was true. Philadelphia had embraced the strange story of a man who mailed himself in a box. Word of the escape had leaked out in the *Burlington Courier*, a Vermont newspaper, in April, and the story had people talking across the country. The story even filtered down to Richmond, but Henry's identity was not revealed. That did not happen until the New England Anti-Slavery Convention held in Boston in May, when Henry was brought out on stage before thunderous applause. He told his story, sang his song of Thanksgiving, and was quickly dubbed Henry "Box" Brown, a name that seems to have stuck.

After the convention, Henry decided to take up residence in Boston, and that city also embraced him. Now, he and William were heading for the Boston train station on an overcast summer day for the most important event of his thirty-four years. Henry's family was returning to him; Nancy and the children were coming North.

Henry stared down at his left palm, which had healed over but still displayed a nasty scar from where the acid bit. He had a habit of running his finger across the tender scar—a three-inch slash of discolored skin.

His mind also had a habit of running across his mental scars. He couldn't keep from worrying that Nancy would be upset that he didn't come down to North Carolina personally to get her. He wanted to go south, but the abolitionists wouldn't allow it; they said it was much too dangerous, so Lewis Thompson was escorting her north. Still, it made him feel helpless, and he hated the feeling.

Even more troubling, would Nancy and the children blame him for not stopping their sale? He had asked himself this question every day since they had disappeared down south. The truth was: He *didn't* protect them. He didn't protect Nancy or Sarah or Adam or Gideon . . . Every day, he was tormented by thoughts of what he could have done differently.

"Have you found a church here in Boston?" William asked.

"Yes, sir. Twelfth Baptist."

"Excellent. And you're singing in the choir?"

"Yes, sir, and I'm hopin' Nancy'll sing with me. That's how we met. In the choir."

Henry's stomach ached. He had been too nervous to eat anything, and he was beginning to regret it. It was starting to sprinkle, and the drops tapped out a Morse code on the wagon's leather top. Henry leaned out to look up at the clouds, and a drop caught him directly in the eye. He drew his head back under the leather top of the chaise.

"And you're certain everything went through with the sale?" he asked.

"We received confirmation by telegram." William had already assured him of this several times, but Henry had a hard time believing it. The abolitionists had tracked down Nancy and the children in North Carolina and raised money to purchase their freedom. But something was bound to go wrong, Henry thought. It always did.

"Will you and your family continue to live in Boston?" William asked.

"I hope to."

Henry lived at 41 Southac Street in an area where many black Bostonians resided. It was a thriving neighborhood on the western side of Beacon Hill, not far from Boston Common. Henry lived in a rambling, two-story house, but it was going to be a tight fit for Nancy and the children, because the house was packed with lodgers.

Henry leaned back in the coach, exhausted. It had been a whirlwind ever since the Anti-Slavery Convention. Seemed like everybody wanted to shake his hand. Rich people, famous people, influential abolitionists. Since May, he had been giving talks throughout Boston and was surprised to find that he was drawn to the stage. The stage was the opposite of a box—so open, so exposed. Was that the appeal? A publisher was interested in distributing his song of Thanksgiving, and he was even working on a book with a Boston printer, Charles Stearns. Things were moving fast, too fast.

Henry's hand went back to the scar on his palm.

"Do you think Mr. Douglass is right?" he asked. Another worry had surfaced.

"Yes and no," said William. A politician's answer.

The great black abolitionist, Frederick Douglass, had questioned the wisdom of publicizing so many sensational slave escapes, such as Henry's. He said it gave away too much information to slave catchers and others in the pro-slavery army.

"How can it be yes and no?"

"I think we need to keep as much information as possible close to the vest. But your case—it's unique. I don't think we're going to see a rash of slaves shipped in boxes any time soon. Telling your story inspires."

Henry grunted.

"Besides, it wasn't your fault that the *Burlington Courier* revealed your escape. And once the story was out, you might as well tell your tale far and wide."

"Mmm."

Henry held on to his hat when the chaise hit a bump. The wagon raced along a cobblestone road flanking a row of five-story, brick buildings, all in a perfect line, topped by rows of chimneys in a straight, soldierly formation. To their right ran two perfectly parallel rows of trees. Everything seemed so controlled, so orderly, so different than the hodgepodge of structures in Richmond's Shockoe Bottom.

When they wheeled around the corner, making a left turn, the Park Square station came into view and Henry heard the sound of a train whistle. He rose up in his seat and spotted the locomotive pulling into the station, smoke streaming backwards like a long, black feather.

"Is that the one?"

William nodded and grinned. "We timed it just right."

Before the chaise had even rolled to a complete stop, Henry leaped out and began running. The rain had let up, but the cobblestones were slick, and he nearly slipped racing toward an elevated platform, where people were already flowing out of the train. The platform was crowded, white faces, black faces, even some Asian faces. One wealthy gentleman asked if Henry could carry his bags, and Henry was tempted to knock the top hat off the man's head. No sign of Nancy or the children. But people continued to stream from the train. The door of one of the cars was clogged by a man who had to be close to four hundred pounds. He was having trouble getting through the doorway, and train conductors were pushing him from behind, as if he were a big, lumpy bag of potatoes. Henry tried to peek over the large man's shoulders to see if Nancy was standing behind him. She wasn't.

Henry hurried to the next car, where an elegant woman with a small, perfumed dog in her arms was being helped down. Nancy wasn't there either. People shouted and smiled and waved to relations; reunions were sprouting up all across the platform, but there was nothing for Henry. He backtracked down the line of passenger cars, but his view was blocked by the four-hundred-pound man, who came toward him like a large ship.

Henry stepped aside to let him pass; and when the man had gone by, Henry saw her. Nancy was standing at the far end of the platform, searching the crowd. Sarah, his oldest, spotted him first.

"Papa!" Sarah sprinted across the platform and Henry crouched down, ready to catch her. She hurled herself into his arms with such force that she nearly knocked him backwards. Hugging Sarah with one arm, Henry wiped away tears with his other hand. Even Wilson Gregory probably would have excused tears on this day. Sarah was twelve years old now, and she had shot up several inches in the past year. Her face was rounder; she looked like Nancy. Adam barreled into him next, and Gideon, five years old, climbed onto his back. Henry was covered in children, like a tree.

Nancy wore a long, heavy, brown dress, and she carried a child in her arms—a girl less than one year old. Henry stood to his feet, his children still clinging to him. He walked toward Nancy with a stiff right leg, for Gideon clutched his leg and sat on his foot, getting a free ride. Sarah held his right hand, and Adam trailed close behind.

Henry came to a stop about two feet from his wife, his eyes locked on the child.

What do I say?

"What's her name?"

"Henrietta."

Henry nodded.

When his eyes shifted from Henrietta to Nancy's face, he saw that she was crying. She walked into his arms and put her head on his shoulder. Henry breathed in the scent of her hair.

"Nancy, I'm so sorry," he said.

Nancy pulled away and wiped away the tears on her cheek. She looked perplexed.

"You're sorry?"

Henry choked on his words. "I shoulda done more."

"More? But you put yourself in a box."

"I shouldn't have let them take ya."

"You did everything you could."

"If I coulda broken you free . . . If I . . ."

"Henry, you did *everything*." Nancy shook him by the shoulders and smiled. "Henry, you fool, *you put yourself in a box!*"

There was that word again. Henry smiled through his tears. "That was pretty foolish, wasn't it?"

"It was."

When Henry reached out and put a hand on her cheek, Nancy noticed the three-inch scar. She took his hand in hers and studied the jagged wound. "What's this? What happened?"

"Just another foolish thing I did."

Nancy kissed the wound, and then she kissed her husband. They held each other and savored the moment, watching Adam and Gideon laugh and chase each other around the platform. Henry felt Sarah hugging him from behind, her arms around his waist and her head against his back. It began to drizzle again, and the family moved together down the emptying platform, clinging to each other for dear life.

39

Richmond
1885: Thirty-Six Years Later

"This where he hid, Mamma?"

"Yes, that's where he hid," said Sarah.

Sarah and her youngest son, Ezekiel, stood in the portico of Monumental Episcopal Church along Broad Street—her first time back to Richmond since the day she was sold south in 1848. Another autumn had arrived, and the trees lined the streets with color. Sarah ran her hand over the names etched in the stone monument and tried to picture her father crouched behind it in the dark, while two men came at him from both sides.

"He run over this way," Sarah said, leading Ezekiel down the street towards the Capitol grounds. She had heard the story so many times over the years that it was almost as if the memory was her own; she had also told her five children the story again and again, for she didn't want them to ever forget. Ezekiel, eleven years old, had shown the most interest in his grandfather's story, and he had begged his mother to let him join her on this trip to fulfill one of her father's final requests.

"James Smith's cake shop was down a ways there," Sarah said, pointing west along Broad Street. "And Samuel Smith's shoe shop was only a few doors down from it."

"Were they brothers?" Ezekiel asked.

"The Smiths? No, they weren't blood brothers, but they were brothers."

Sarah knew their stories almost as well as her father's. After the two Smiths helped her father escape, Samuel decided to roll the dice once more by helping *two* slaves run away in the same outrageous fashion—in boxes. James was hesitant to try it again, but Samuel convinced him, telling him that one of the slaves was in jeopardy of being sold down south if they didn't act fast. Miller McKim also tried to convince him to give up the plan; but Samuel, ever the gambler, wasn't about to heed cautious advice. So he and James went ahead with their plan and put two slaves— Sawney and Alfred—into two separate boxes.

The packages never made it past the Adams

Express office. A suspicious worker broke open the boxes with a hatchet and discovered the two terrified men. Samuel tried to make a run for it, hopping onto the train out of Richmond, but he was nabbed in Fredericksburg and hauled back to face his accusers. There was talk about stringing Samuel up, but he was spared the noose and sent to the penitentiary for six and a half years. He was a model prisoner, working as a prison shoemaker, but he was nearly killed when another inmate assaulted him with a shoe knife. He was stabbed up to six times, with one of the wounds coming close to the heart. After the attack, the penitentiary superintendent petitioned to have Smith pardoned, but the governor flatly refused to release such a notorious villain as "Red Boot" Smith. When Samuel's sentence was up and he was finally freed, blacks welcomed him to Philadelphia as a hero, and he survived to gamble another day.

For a short time, James avoided suspicion in the foiled escape of Alfred and Sawney. But he had to close down his cake shop because he couldn't keep it running with all that happened. In September of 1849, suspicions were rising, and James was arrested and sent to trial before eight justices. When one of the justices decided James was innocent, that was all it took to set him free. He fled north.

"This a-ways," said Sarah, and they started

moving downhill toward the river—backtracking along the path that her papa had taken on the night he escaped. They entered what folks in Richmond now called the Burnt District, a large section of the city that had been gutted by fire when Richmond fell at the end of the War Between the States. Out of the ashes, new buildings had sprouted—five-story, brick giants. One of the new buildings was a theater, painted lavishly in gold and red.

"Did Grandpappy put on shows in there?" Ezekiel said.

"No, Grandpappy never put on shows in Richmond. Just in the North—and England, of course."

Ezekiel had always known his grandfather to be a showman. In the first year after his escape, Henry created a spectacular production, *The Mirror of Slavery*, and he displayed it throughout the North with his good friend, James Smith. The show was called a "panorama" because they used large paintings, eight to ten feet high, and moved them across the stage, telling the terrible tale of slavery while Henry recounted his own story and sang.

But even in the North, things started getting increasingly dangerous after the Fugitive Slave Act was passed in 1850. This law made it easier to capture escaped slaves and drag them back to the South, and it nearly caught Henry in its net.

Several men attempted to kidnap him on the streets of Providence, Rhode Island, trying to pull him into a carriage—another box, another coffin just waiting to bury him in the Deep South. But he fought them off like a man on fire and decided to take his family to safety across the ocean to England. Sarah still remembers their arrival in Liverpool, where James and Henry showed their panorama at the Concert Hall on Lord Nelson Street. In addition to the panorama, Henry displayed his famous wooden box, and he and James sang together. From Liverpool, they took their show all across Great Britain, crossing paths with other famous escaped slaves, such as William and Ellen Craft.

"You think it'll still be there?" Ezekiel asked, picking up a stone and hurling it at a half-collapsed picket fence.

"It'd be a miracle."

Sarah and Ezekiel turned east on Cary Street and made their way just beyond the Burnt District. Sarah couldn't remember much about their old home, but she knew where to find it. The tenement was in an area that had escaped the great fire, but whether the place was still standing was any-body's guess. Shockoe Bottom no longer housed slaves, of course, but it was still as dilapidated as ever. All of the filth still drained down from on high, winding up in the James River and Shockoe Valley. Flies were still a nuisance—although not so bad this time of year.

Slipping down an old, familiar alley, Sarah was glad there hadn't been any rain recently. She could deal with dust easier than mud. Then up ahead, she saw it, and she almost couldn't believe it. The old building still stood—barely. It was a shambles—broken windows, paint peeling like snakeskin, and a gaping hole to the right of the door. She stood in front, taking in the sight and wondering what kind of history had gone on there over the past three and a half decades.

"This it, Mamma?"

"Land sakes . . . I do believe it is."

An old man, with a nose so large that it took up most of the real estate on his face, came out of a house across the street and stared at the two of them.

"Ain't nobody livin' there no more," the old man said.

"Then nobody would care if we go in and take a peek, would they?"

"Go on, go on in. Ain't no business of mine. Just don't blame me if the place collapses in on you."

Sarah smiled nervously and climbed the few stairs of the porch, unsure whether the rotted wood would hold. It did. Then she stepped into her old home, with Ezekiel right behind.

Sarah turned around in a full circle, sizing up the old place. The tenement had survived the war and the fire, but it had been eaten away by age, which does its destruction just as thoroughly as fire, only more slowly. Vegetation swarmed over the rotting wood. The only occupants now were weeds and mice.

She was shocked by how small the room was. It was just another one of the many boxes that her father had been cooped up inside of all of his life. She stared around the room—the few pieces of broken furniture, the cobwebs, the dust. It smelled of age and decay.

"Over here, Mamma! Is this where Grandpappy said to look?"

Ezekiel was off in the corner, tapping his foot on the floor to check for any loose boards. Sarah leaned her weight on the floor, checking for rot and sensing softness in the wood.

"Grandpappy said it were about a foot from the wall," Sarah pointed out.

"Let me try, Mamma!"

"Sure. Go on now."

Beaming, Ezekiel pulled out his pocketknife, stuck it under a floorboard, and pried it loose. Then he peeled back the wood, revealing the earth below. Sticking his head at floor level, he snuck a peek beneath the floor.

"Not here."

"Try another then."

So Ezekiel pried two more floorboards loose, with the same result.

"You think we're in the wrong corner?"

"I'm sure this is right. Try a few more."

After removing three more floorboards, Ezekiel struck gold.

"Got it, Mamma!" Ezekiel reached into the hole and pulled out a small box—the same magic box that Henry had used as a boy, the same one that John Allen had torn apart, the same one that Henry had repaired and hidden under the floor on the night he escaped. Ezekiel picked away cobwebs and brushed as much of the dust and dirt from the box as he could before handing it to his mother.

Henry had asked Sarah to come to Richmond to retrieve the magic box. At seventy years old, his health was deteriorating, so Sarah agreed, even though she was nervous about returning to a city haunted by so many slave memories.

"Maybe Grandpappy could use it in his show," Ezekiel said.

"You know he don't go on stage no more."

"But he still does shows for us."

Sarah smiled. "That's true, you're right."

After fleeing to England, Henry and his family remained overseas until well after the War Between the States and the abolition of slavery. They returned to America in 1875, and Henry continued to live life on the stage, only this time as a magician. He wasn't the finest magician in the world, but he knew how to put on a good show. He did tricks with cards, hats, and handkerchiefs, and he even had a stunt in which he made one of his granddaughters magically disappear from center stage.

Henry also did tricks with boxes, but his finest trick was the one that he pulled off with a box nearly forty years ago. He made a man disappear in Richmond and miraculously reappear in Philadelphia.

Sarah tucked the trick box under her arm and walked around the room, stopping to run her hand against the wall, as if she could feel the memories that had seeped into the wood.

"Everyone lived in this one room?" Ezekiel asked.

"We sure did, honey, and we thought ourselves lucky. So many slaves had to share rooms with other families."

Ezekiel shook his head in wonderment. They felt crowded in their Boston house with two bedrooms for five children, a room for two grand-parents, and a converted sitting room for Sarah and her husband.

Sarah and Ezekiel stepped back outside, into the light.

"You got what you're lookin' for, ma'am?" asked the old man with the oversized nose, who had taken a seat on the porch across the way.

"We got it." Sarah smiled and held up the box for him to see.

"Where y'all from?"

"From Boston."

"You come a long way just for a box."

"Yes, we came a long way."

Sarah and Ezekiel told the old man goodbye and headed for the riverfront, and along the way Sarah gazed at the streets and alleys where she had once played. A group of children played fetch with a small, black dog, and they stopped to watch Ezekiel and his mother stroll by.

"Grandpappy will be proud when I tell how you found the box," Sarah said.

Henry had been fighting a severe cough for half a year now, and lately he had been talking about his death. He kept talking about being fitted for a new box—the kind of box that's put in the ground, not thrown onto the back of a wagon or into a train car.

"I ain't afraid of dyin' 'cause I know what it's like to be in a box," he told Sarah just a week ago. "But I'm planning on givin' myself a little more leg room this time. That was a mistake the first time around.

"I also got me a little sleight of hand planned," he added with a wink. "I'm gonna trick the devil and turn a dead man into a living man."

Sarah and Ezekiel came to a stop at a wooden fence—gray with age, with just enough missing slats that Ezekiel could slip through. Sarah leaned on the fence and looked up at a massive tree, about twenty feet away. Wind whipped through the upper branches, stripping away orange and red and yellow leaves and sending them whirling. Ezekiel picked up a handful and tossed them in the air, watching them fly away in a sudden gust like a covey of birds lifting off.

Sarah pointed to the leaves. "Ezekiel, that's what the life of a slave was once like."

Ezekiel put his hands on his hips and followed her pointed finger. "Whatya talking about, Mamma?"

"The wind took 'em and scattered 'em. Slaves had no say where they could go. The wind was their master."

The wind picked up slightly and stripped a hundred more leaves from the upper branches, and they went spinning away in currents of air. Ezekiel leaned back as far as he could and watched them soar.

"You're right, Mamma. The wind tears them away."

Sarah smiled, for Ezekiel understood. He knew what she was trying to say. All at once she began to choke up, and she fanned her right hand in front of her face, as if she could wave away the tears.

Noticing, Ezekiel slipped back through the fence and gave his mamma a hug. By this time, she couldn't keep back the tears; they were flowing hard and swift, like the James River itself.

"Don't worry, Mamma. Don't worry, don't be sad."

Sarah wiped her eyes with the back of her sleeve. She wasn't sure what it was that hit her: the thought of her father dying, the thought of her children someday leaving to get married, or the memory of that day when she saw her father being whipped for trying to say goodbye to her.

"Don't be afraid, Mamma. I ain't gonna leave ya. I'll never leave ya."

Sarah kissed the top of his head. "Thank you, Ezekiel."

They watched the scattering leaves for another few minutes. Then Sarah adjusted the small box beneath her left arm, put her other arm around her youngest son, and they headed back into town. There was a late afternoon train for Boston, and she didn't want to miss it.

AUTHOR NOTES

The tale of Henry "Box" Brown is true. This book was built upon a framework of facts, many of them drawn from Henry's two first-person narratives—one written in 1849 and the second one in 1851. You can find them at a website run by the University of North Carolina at Chapel Hill: http://docsouth.unc.edu/neh/boxbrown/boxbrown .html.

All of the major characters and most of the supporting cast in *The Disappearing Man* are historical figures. But as with any work of historical fiction, I had to fill in the blanks and create scenes based on a blend of history, speculation, and imagination.

For example, the planning and execution of Henry's escape unfolded much as depicted, following the pathway through Fredericksburg, Washington, and Baltimore on the way to Philadelphia by train, steamboat, and wagon. He was flipped on his head numerous times along the way, with the longest ordeal occurring on the steamboat. Also, his box was pushed off a wagon, nearly breaking his neck. However, the air holes of the box were never blocked, the cargo handler did not poke him with sticks, and he did not have to share company with an angry yellow jacket.

The section in which I had the least amount of history to build upon was the courtship. There is no information about Henry's courtship with Nancy, so I created those scenes from my imagination. Nevertheless, I based key incidents in their relationship on actual historical events. For instance, blacks in Richmond organized a fancy ball in the Washington Hotel, and it was raided by police; in reality, though, the ball took place several years *after* Henry had escaped from Richmond. Also, I changed the ball to a dinner party because members of the Baptist church, such as Henry and Nancy, would have been risking trouble with the deacons if they had been seen dancing; they probably would not have attended a ball.

Every so often, I slipped in expressions spoken by real-life slaves and recorded in various first-person accounts, such as "hooked by the heart" and "It's in the nature of the He to pursue the She." In addition, Miller McKim's speech before the unruly audience was based, at least in part, on his own writings.

I walked the streets of Richmond and visited many of the sites in this story, but only a few of them remain. The beautiful Capitol building is there, of course, as is Monumental Episcopal Church (now known simply as Monumental Church). Henry's congregation, First African Baptist, still exists, although not in the same building. Also the home of Henry's master, William Barret, still stands on the northeast corner of Fifth and Cary Streets. It is now offices for financial advisers, who were kind enough to let me see the interior. Lumpkin's jail is now a parking lot, where archaeologists did excavation in 2008.

In addition to the first-person narratives, I relied on a stack of resources, with the most important one being Jeffrey Ruggles' excellent book, *The Unboxing of Henry Brown*, published by the Library of Virginia (2003). More than half of Ruggles' book is devoted to explaining what happened to Henry after his escape, as he went about the United States and England putting on his show, *The Mirror of Slavery*.

For background on the slavery system in Richmond, I turned to *Rearing Wolves to Our Own Destruction: Slavery in Richmond, Virginia, 1782–1865*, by Midori Takagi and published by the University Press of Virginia (1999). Takagi provides fascinating detail on the urban slavery system in Richmond, which is so much different than the plantation image that most people have in their minds. As the *Mississippi Quarterly* put it, industrial employment in Richmond "allowed blacks to carve out a degree of autonomy that sowed the seeds for slavery's potential demise."

Othere important sourse include:

American City, Southern Place: A Cultural History of Antebellum Richmond, by Gregg D. Kimball, the University of Georgia Press (2000).

American Negro Songs, by John W. Work, Dover Publications (1998, originally published in 1940 by Crown Publishers, Inc.).

Chains of Love: Slave Couples in Antebellum South Carolina, by Emily West, the University of Illinois Press (2004).

God Struck Me Dead: Voices of Ex-Slaves, edited by Clifton H. Johnson, Pilgrim Press (1969).

In Bondage and Freedom: Antebellum Black Life in Richmond, Virginia, by Marie Tyler-McGraw and Gregg D. Kimball, University of North Carolina Press for the Valentine Museum (2007).

A Richmond Reader, 1733–1983, edited by Maurice Duke and Daniel P. Jordan, the University of North Carolina Press (1983).

Runaway Slaves: Rebels on the Plantation, by John Hope Franklin and Loren Schweninger, Oxford University Press (1999).

Slave Songs of the United States, compiled by William Francis Allen, Charles Pickard Ware, and Lucy McKim Garrison (the daughter of James Miller McKim and daughter-in-law of abolitionist William Lloyd Garrison), Applewood Books (1867).

Slave Patrols: Law and Violence in Virginia and the Carolinas, by Sally E. Hadden, Harvard University Press (2001).

The Sounds of Slavery, by Shane White and Graham White, Beacon Press (2005).

The Tobacco Kingdom: Plantation, Market, and Factory in Virginia and North Carolina, 1800–1860, by Joseph Clarke Robert, the Duke University Press (1965, originally published in 1938).

The Underground Railroad, by William Still, Porter & Coates (1872).

ABOUT THE AUTHOR

The Disappearing Man is Doug Peterson's first novel after years of writing about talking vegetables. Doug is the author of 42 books for the poplular VeggieTales series and was co-storywriter for the best-selling video, *Larry-Boy and the Rumor Weed*. His book, *The Slobfather*, won the 2004 Gold Medallion Award for preschool books. Doug and his wife have two grown sons and live in Champaign, Illinois, where Doug also writes science stories for the University of Illinois.

Center Point Large Print
600 Brooks Road / PO Box 1
Thorndike, ME 04986-0001 USA

(207) 568-3717

US & Canada:
1 800 929-9108
www.centerpointlargeprint.com